THE CASE OF THE UNFORTUNATE FORTUNE TELLER

by

Cathy Ace

FOUR TAILS PUBLISHING LTD.

PRAISE FOR THE WISE ENQUIRIES AGENCY MYSTERIES

'…a gratifying contemporary series in the traditional British manner with hilarious repercussions (dead bodies notwithstanding). Cozy fans will anticipate learning more about these WISE ladies.'
Library Journal, starred review

'If you haven't read any of Cathy Ace's WISE cozies, I suggest you begin at the beginning and giggle your way through in sequence.'
Ottawa Review of Books

'…a modern-day British whodunit that's as charming as it is entertaining…Good fun, with memorable characters, an imaginative plot, and a satisfying ending.'
Booklist

'Ace spiffs up the standard village cozy with a set of sleuths worth a second look.'
Kirkus Reviews

'…a perfect cozy with a setting and wit reminiscent of Wodehouse's Blandings Castle. But its strongest feature is the heart and sensitivity with which Ace imbues her characters.'
The Jury Box, Ellery Queen Mystery Magazine

'Sharp writing highlights the humor of the characters even while tackling serious topics, making this yet another very enjoyable, fun, and not-always-proper British Mystery.'
Cynthia Chow, Librarian, Hawaii State Public Library in Kings River Life Magazine

'A brilliant addition to Classic Crime Fiction. The ladies (if they'll forgive me calling them that) of the WISE Enquiries Agency will have you pacing the floor awaiting their next entanglement…
A fresh and wonderful concept well executed'
Alan Bradley, New York Times Bestselling Author of the Flavia de Luce books

Other works by the same author

(Information for all works here: **www.cathyace.com**)

The WISE Enquiries Agency Mysteries
The Case of the Dotty Dowager
The Case of the Missing Morris Dancer
The Case of the Curious Cook
The Case of the Unsuitable Suitor
The Case of the Disgraced Duke
The Case of the Absent Heirs
The Case of the Cursed Cottage
The Case of the Uninvited Undertaker
The Case of the Bereaved Butler
The Case of the Secretive Secretary

The Cait Morgan Mysteries
The Corpse with the Silver Tongue
The Corpse with the Golden Nose
The Corpse with the Emerald Thumb
The Corpse with the Platinum Hair
The Corpse with the Sapphire Eyes
The Corpse with the Diamond Hand
The Corpse with the Garnet Face
The Corpse with the Ruby Lips
The Corpse with the Crystal Skull
The Corpse with the Iron Will
The Corpse with the Granite Heart
The Corpse with the Turquoise Toes
The Corpse with the Opal Fingers
The Corpse with the Pearly Smile

Standalone novels
The Wrong Boy

Short Stories/Novellas
Murder Keeps No Calendar: a collection of 12 short
stories/novellas
Murder Knows No Season: a collection of four novellas
Steve's Story in "The Whole She-Bang 3"
The Trouble with the Turkey in "Cooked to Death Vol. 3:
Hell for the Holidays"

PRAISE FOR THE CAIT MORGAN MYSTERIES

'…Ace is, well, an ace when it comes to plot and description.'
The Globe and Mail

'Her writing is stellar. Details, references, allusions, expertly crafted phrasing, and serious subjects punctuated by wit and humour.'
Ottawa Review of Books

'If all of this suggests the school of Agatha Christie, it's no doubt what Cathy Ace intended. She is, as it fortunately happens, more than adept at the Christie thing.'
Toronto Star

'…a mystery involving pirates' treasure, lust, and greed. Cait unravels the locked-tower mystery using her eidetic memory and her powers of deduction, which are worthy of Hercule Poirot.'
The Jury Box, Ellery Queen Mystery Magazine

'…a testament to an author who knows how to tell a story and deliver it with great aplomb.'
Dru's Musings

'Cathy Ace makes plotting a complex mystery look easy. As the threads here intertwine in unexpected ways, readers will be amazed that she manages to pull off a clever solution rather than a true Gordian Knot of confusion.
Cathy Ace's books always owe a debt of homage to Grand Dame Agatha Christie…the blend of "cozy" mystery, tragic family dynamics…
pure catnip for crime fiction aficionados.'
Kristopher Zgorski, BOLO Books

Dedicated to Mum
1934-2025
RIP
Thank you, for everything.

13th DECEMBER

CHAPTER ONE

Henry Devereaux Twyst, eighteenth Duke of Chellingworth, was terribly worried about his brother-in-law. He hadn't seen much of Julian Treforest since his sister had dragged him off to Egypt so their nuptials could be celebrated at sunrise on Midsummer's Day at the temple of Karnak in Luxor, so had to admit he hardly knew the fellow – but he was still concerned about recent developments.

Following the wedding, his always headstrong sister Clementine had decided to decamp completely from the family's London house, so that the couple could begin their married life at the Twyst pile in Scotland. This had necessitated a flurry of activity to 'get the old place in order'. Of course, Clemmie's idea of 'order' had meant that a great deal of effort had to be put in by the staff at both the London house and the Scottish one, which had led to some…tensions.

Fortunately, Henry's own beloved wife Stephanie had smoothed everything over, and now his sister and her husband were finally ensconced in northern climes. Henry had thought this to be an extraordinary decision; the place in Scotland was impossible to keep warm, there being draughts in every room, and he knew there was no money to be able to attend to them all. He wondered how his pampered sister would cope.

However, despite such challenges, Clemmie and Julian – Henry couldn't bring himself to think of the man as 'Jools' – had settled in well, so his mother kept telling him, and were only just now planning an extended stay at Chellingworth Hall, the Twyst family's Seat in the rolling countryside of Powys. Despite its 268 rooms, he shuddered at the thought of having to share his home with his sister for almost a month: she was to stay until Boxing Day, then return to Scotland to prepare to welcome the New Year in traditional local style.

He shuddered again: Clemmie's plans for that would lead to more 'tensions', no doubt.

It was their imminent arrival that had led to Henry's current discombobulation: Julian had telephoned him to ask if the two men might find an opportunity to have a little 'one-to-one' time, as soon after his arrival at Chellingworth Hall as possible. Henry couldn't work out why Julian hadn't simply asked for a chat; the 'one-to-one' term had unsettled him, though he wasn't entirely sure why. His sister and her husband were due to arrive in a few days, so he still had a little time to give some thought to why Julian might be seeking out Henry's…advice? Or…help? Well, anything, really.

He couldn't imagine it would be a conversation concerned with finances: Clemmie had a good allowance from the Chellingworth Estate, and still received income from her business interests and investments in various artistic enterprises around the entire United Kingdom. And Julian's family was blessed with not only a heritage that went all the way back to the Domesday Book, but also – if what Henry's wife had told him was true – an almost indecent amount of money at their disposal due to the fact they'd built a massive conglomerate of manufacturing organizations around the world, having begun their enterprises at the dawn of the industrial revolution. No, there was no way that Clemmie and Julian could be short of cash – which was a relief, because Henry was only too well aware that the Twyst family's coffers were under considerable strain, as always.

Might his sister have tired, already, of the hoped-for idyll of Scottish life? Was she already missing the flighty, party-going crowd with which she'd invariably mixed during what she was apparently now referring to as 'her London years'? Henry suspected that might be it; Clemmie had never been known for sticking to anything for very long. Was marriage was going to join the list of things she'd tried, but didn't fancy much after a few months? She'd been engaged sufficiently often before she'd made her vows for her groom to have spotted the warning signs.

And there he was…back to worrying about poor Julian. If Clemmie were to remain true to form – and decided to treat her husband the way she'd treated boyfriends, fiancés, artists she'd sponsored, and even female friends in the past – then a four- or five-month marriage might be all she were capable of; she'd dump Julian and simply move on. At least, that was probably what she'd be expecting she'd be able to do, because it was what she'd always managed to get away with until now. Yes, Lady Clementine Twyst had a reputation – a well-earned one, at that – for being passionate, and fun-loving, and adventurous…but never for being constant.

Henry sighed heavily, and poked at the Aubusson rug with his toe. The fire in the hearth would soon be replenished by Edward – whom Henry suspected was, indeed, the world's most reliable butler – and then there'd be lunch, before a, hopefully, calm afternoon where he could spend some wonderful moments with his wife, and their son Hugo, upstairs in their cozy apartment of private rooms.

Though…even Hugo was acting rather unusually at the moment. It wouldn't be long before the family celebrated the little chap's first birthday, a fact which Henry found to be almost unfathomable. How had almost a year passed, already, since his life had been changed forever by the arrival of the child who would, one day, become the nineteenth son of the family to carry its title?

Henry warmed himself as best he could beside the dying embers. It was a chilly day, and Edward had cleverly lit the fire earlier than usual. But now it wasn't throwing out quite as much heat as he'd like. Yes, he was sure that Edward would be along at any moment; he'd give it five minutes before he rang.

Almost a year…and, in that time, not only had he had to become accustomed to being a father, but his sister had gone and got herself married, and his mother had…well, what hadn't she done? Henry was keenly aware of the fact he was fast approaching the age of sixty, and he'd have thought that his mother – who was now over eighty herself – might have…grown up a bit. But ever since the women of the WISE Enquiries Agency had set up their private investigations business in the converted barn on the Estate, his mother had…well, 'changed' wasn't the right word, because she'd always been somewhat unpredictable, but, sometimes, she seemed to be acting more and more like a child, and less and less like an adult.

Henry paused…might his mother be reaching the age when some form of loss of capacity might affect her? He picked up the poker and decided to make the best he could of the remains of the fire, reminding himself that it had been he who'd originally summoned the WISE women to investigate similar suspicions on his part, just a few years ago. Then they'd moved in, and they were now firmly entrenched in the life of the locale, and his own, and – more to the point – his mother's.

It was true that the quartet of women had come to the aid of his family in many ways since their arrival. And, of course, his wife had become quite pally with one of their number – Christine Wilson-Smythe, who, as the daughter of a viscount, had been known to Henry, and his original point of contact with the investigators.

As Henry found himself, yet again, contemplating the passing of time, he wondered why that might be; it wasn't the sort of thing that usually concerned him. Indeed, if there were anything that Henry was proud of – in terms of having any pride in himself at all – it was his ability to live in the moment. Being the one responsible for the entirety of the Twyst family holdings meant he had to plan ahead, of course, but he was fortunate enough to be able to call upon a variety of professionals to help him do that, and Stephanie was proving to be so terribly good at all that sort of thing that Henry found himself having to worry about a shrinking list of matters that needed his immediate input these days. Which was wonderful, because it meant he had more time to paint…though the folly where his studio was set up was pretty chilly at this time of year, despite the installation of some natty little heaters, which – sadly – put no more than a dent in the bone-chilling wintery weather.

A knock at the door announced Edward's anticipated arrival.

'If it suits Your Grace, I thought I might attend to the fire?'

Henry rolled on his toes beside the hearth. 'Indeed, Edward. I did my best to keep the thing ticking over, as you can see.'

'Indeed, Your Grace.'

'Thank you, Edward.' Henry relished the praise. 'I'll just make sure that all's right in the world with Her Grace, and my son.'

'I believe you'll find them in the kitchen, with Cook Davies, Your Grace,' offered Edward. 'They were doing something that appeared to involve the use of a great deal of flour when I last saw them.'

Henry couldn't imagine what they might be up to. 'Very well, Edward, I'll toddle down to the kitchen. We'll take luncheon in our rooms today, I think.'

'Indeed, Your Grace.'

Henry ambled out of the library, crossed the Great Hall, and headed toward the door that allowed access to the stairs that led down to the kitchens. Before he'd even descended a few steps the sound of his son's anguished bawling reached his ears.

Oh dear, Hugo was performing again. Henry decided it might be a good time to pop along to have a chat with Bob Fernley, his Estates Manager, about progress with the renovations at the old school in Anwen-by-Wye; they hadn't spoken of that for some time.

Anything to keep his mind off his wailing son, or his soon-to-be-arriving sister…and brother-in-law.

CHAPTER TWO

Carol Hill flopped onto the sofa in the office of the WISE Enquiries Agency. 'I'm sorry I'm late, but Mam and Dad are arriving in a few days, and I haven't even unpacked all our boxes of stuff since we moved into Tŷ Mawr, let alone sorted the guest bedroom and bathroom for incoming relatives. Did you start without me?'

Mavis MacDonald couldn't help but smile at her colleague; Carol's always curly blonde hair was still a little damp, her full face was glowing with sweat, her long dress – worn with thick tights and boots, to accommodate the wintry conditions – had three stains on it that Mavis could see, and the huge bag that accompanied her wherever she went almost lost some of its contents when she dumped it on the floor beside the coffee table.

'We waited,' replied Mavis calmly, 'because Annie was more concerned with getting one of us to confess to having "stolen" all the custard creams from the biscuit stocks than in beginning our briefing ahead of meeting a potential new client.'

Mavis made sure she bestowed a steely glance upon Annie Parker as she spoke, and was completely unsurprised when Annie retaliated with a wounded: 'Oi…I bought them custard creams out of my own money, I did, and I had my mouth in shape for them this morning. We've got more ginger nuts in that cupboard than you could shake a stick at, but I just fancied a custard cream, and I know there was three packets in there yesterday.'

Mavis did her best to hide a smirk when Christine Wilson-Smythe threw up her hands in mock surrender.

'I confess – I stole your blessed custard creams. Sorry, Annie. At four this morning I was desperate for something sweet, so I ate the lot. Though there were only two packets, not three. And they've all gone now. I'll get some at Sharon's shop in the village when I go there, and replace what I guzzled. Sure you're in a grump this morning, Annie.'

Mavis was about to say something, but Annie cut across her. 'You been talking to your mum on the phone this morning, Chrissy? Gone back to your Irish-talk…so you have, begorragh.'

'Mammy doesn't talk like that,' snapped Christine. 'No one does…except on TV. But, yes, I have been chatting with her, actually. We have a lot to discuss.'

Mavis knew they did, because Christine seemed to spend a great deal of time with her phone clamped to her ear these days, much more so than before she'd been pregnant.

Carol asked, 'How's Lumpy, Christine?'

Mavis didn't care for the way that Christine and her fiancé, Alexander Bright, had decided to refer to their unborn child; when Carol had referred to her pregnancy bump as 'Bump', Mavis had thought that appropriate. But 'Lumpy'? It wouldn't have been her choice. In fact, she vividly recalled that she and her late husband had never felt the need to 'name' either of her pregnancies, until each of her sons had been born. Then, of course, the battles had ensued…but she was pleased, now, that they'd settled on James and Duncan; their names suited them.

'Thanks for asking, Carol,' replied Christine. 'This one's more concerned with her missing custard creams than anything else. Lumpy and I are both just fine…though there was that terrible craving I had – which passed, thanks to our biscuit cupboard.'

'You could have eaten one packet of custard creams and one of ginger nuts,' grumbled Annie. 'Instead of eating all of—'

Mavis knew it was time to put a stop to all this nonsense. 'Aye, well, she didnae, so let's get on, shall we?'

Carol, Annie, and Christine all sat up straight, which pleased Mavis a great deal.

Carol raised a hand. 'Sorry, Mavis, but I have to pop to the loo before we start. I forgot to go before I left the house. Sorry, I'll be quick.'

As Carol scuttled across the yawning office, which was housed in what had once been a yawning barn, Annie whispered, 'Don't have a go at Car, Mave…she's on pins. With her mum and dad having sold their sheep farm, and now being basically homeless – until they can find somewhere to buy that they can afford, and that they like – she's having to let them come and stay with her. David's a lovely bloke – couldn't be a better husband to Car, nor a better dad to Bertie – but it's got to be a lot for him, too. They've only been in that big new house for two minutes, and now Car's having to get everything ready for her parents to arrive, on top of what we all know is a heavy workload for her at the moment…and having Bertie to look after, of course.'

Mavis sighed. 'I'm well aware of all that, though thank you for being so supportive of your chum. And I was no' planning to "have a go at" Carol, whatever you might think. We're all only too well aware that without her amazing computing skills, and good contacts in the commercial world, we'd no' have the business we do. At least, we'd no' have the level of success we're currently enjoying.'

Christine asked, 'The books are looking good? Coffers full, Mavis?'

Mavis knew very well that Christine had no real need of an income from the agency's efforts, but was equally aware that Annie did, as did Carol and she, herself. 'Aye, pretty healthy, if I'm honest. We might even be able to have a bit of a Christmas bonus this year.'

Mavis noticed Annie perk up. 'Really, Mave? Oh, that would be brilliant…I've got Eustelle and Rodney coming for Christmas, and I know that the Chellingworth Estate has paid for all the renovations and decorating at the Coach and Horses, but it would be lovely to have the chance to add a few personal touches to their room.'

'Your parents are coming to stay with you and Tudor at the pub for Christmas?' This was the first Mavis was hearing of the plan.

Annie beamed. 'Yeah. They're looking forward to it so much. Now that Tude's got the bigger pub to manage, with the guest rooms that come with it, I've finally got enough space for them to stay. They'd never have fitted into my old cottage…well, not for more than one night. Eustelle was fine with that second bedroom – but both of them? Nah. And they want to see what Christmas is like in the Welsh countryside…as a change from Plaistow.'

Christine chuckled. 'How does Tudor feel about that? I know he likes your mum and dad, but the pub will be open all through Christmas, won't it? He'll be busy, but I suppose if there's any tension, he can escape to the bar.'

Annie laughed loudly. 'Not a real escape, if Rodney's around. They get along great. Tude's even getting in some bottles of Piton beer for my father, so he'll have a proper taste of St. Lucia in a pub in deepest, darkest Wales.'

Christine asked, 'Have you ever experienced a Christmas in St. Lucia yourself, Annie?'

Mavis thought Annie looked a little disappointed when she replied, 'Nah…you know I'm a real Cockney – born within the sound of Bow Bells, and all that – so it's not as if St. Lucia was ever my home, and we rarely had enough money for all of us to go over there, together. Both Mum and Dad have been a few times, but usually alone, and usually for a funeral. But me? Went when I was little, that's it. London was home for me…and now Anwen-by-Wye is, of course.'

'And the Coach and Horses, with Tudor,' whispered Christine, with a grin.

Mavis spotted Carol emerging from the loo. 'Now that Carol's back, maybe we can begin?' She checked the watch that was always pinned to her chest – a hangover from her pre-retirement days as a nurse with the armed forces, then as matron of a barracks for aging servicemen. 'Our potential client will be here in approximately half an hour, so let's begin the briefing. Annie – you were the person's first point of contact…and thank you for bringing this potential business to our door. The floor is yours.'

Annie never preened – Mavis liked that about the woman – and she could be businesslike, which she was now, thank heavens.

'Before I start,' said Annie, 'is Althea not joining us?'

Ah…Althea. Mavis replied, 'No, she announced to me, over breakfast at the Dower House, that she's expecting a guest today. No idea who it is; she says I'll meet them at tea, and that "all will be revealed" at that time.'

Annie giggled. 'No change there, then, Mave. Althea's always up to something, in't she?'

Mavis sighed. 'Aye, she is that. I just hope that she's no' planning something…big. Nothing that'll impact Paul Baker or Ian Cottesloe, in any case.'

Annie grinned. 'How's it going with Paul Baker at the Dower House? Is he managing to keep you two well fed?'

Mavis rolled her shoulders. 'He's a decent cook, as well as an excellent baker. And Althea and I have few expectations for fancy food; he's good at the basics, and that's what we both prefer.'

Carol appeared to be choking on a ginger nut, then managed to say, 'I wish I had a flock of servants to call upon when I needed it.'

'They're staff, not servants these days, Carol,' said Christine, with a wink.

Carol chuckled again. 'Of course, your lot's got them, too…I keep forgetting.'

'Mammy and Daddy have only the bare minimum when it comes to staff,' replied Christine. 'And I don't have any.'

Annie said, 'No need to sound so hurt, doll. Now – as you said, Mave – shall we get on? I've written a load of notes.'

Everyone nodded, so Annie tapped her phone's screen, and read aloud from it, stopping to make asides as she did so.

'I met Pauline Thomas when I was in Brecon doing a bit of legwork on The Case of the Irritating Irrigator…which is what I decided to call the case where that horrible man was spraying his allotment with foul-smelling fertilizer. Oh, by the way, Car, the allotment society told me they'd be paying up this week, so don't feel bad about chasing them if they don't. I know they've got the money, because they've just had a big raffle to raise funds for their Christmas party, so they've got to be rolling in it at the moment. Though not rolling in any of the soil from that stinky allotment. Imagine going to all that trouble just to be able to grow bigger marrows…which he won't have the chance to do, now that they've slung him off his patch. Serves him right; their bylaws clearly stated that no noxious substances were to be used, and it doesn't get more noxious than spraying liquidized turkey manure all over the place.'

Mavis made sure she spoke warmly when she said, 'You did a good job there, Annie; and it cannae have been pleasant hanging about in various sheds, at night, until you spotted who was doing it.'

Annie grinned. 'Nah…it only took two nights, Mave, and Tude came to keep me warm, ta. Anyway…like I was saying…I met Pauline when I was doing that. Well, when I was buying supplies and snacks in

Brecon itself, before I settled into the first shed. She was buying some bits and bobs in the little corner shop too, and I helped her pick up a few things she'd dropped onto the floor. She was wearing a brace on her wrist, and one on her ankle, and she was using a walking stick, so it wasn't a surprise that she'd dropped stuff. Of course we got chatting, as you do…'

'As *you* do, Annie,' said Carol, with a warm smile.

Annie winked. 'Yeah…as I do…and I commiserated with her about her injuries. I asked her what had happened, and – when she told me – I said something like she needed someone to watch over her to make sure she didn't have so many accidents…and that's when she dissolved into tears, and I had to get the bloke out from behind the counter to bring her a chair so she could have a sit down and a proper cry. That was last week, and I know I told her what we did, and gave her one of our business cards…and she rang me yesterday to ask if we could help. As luck would have it, I knew we had a bit of a lull coming up, so I'm glad we were able to agree to see her today. Ta for that, 'cause she seems to think she's really…in danger.'

Mavis felt herself tense up. 'Danger? This is the first I'm hearing of this. Explain yourself, Annie.'

Mavis accepted the slightly withering glance that Annie shot in her direction, and answered it with a much more effective one, that sent Annie's eyes back to her phone's screen.

She read, 'Pauline feels that she's not just suffering a series of unfortunate accidents, but that she's being targeted by "someone" who's making these things happen to her. She told me, on the phone, that the more she thinks about it, the more certain she is that she hurt her wrist when she fell not as the result of a slippery bit of pavement, but because someone pushed her. And she also reckons that she twisted her ankle not because a slab of curbstone was loose, but because she was tripped up. Now, I don't know if this is all in her head, or if it's real – but what's definitely real is the fact that these accidents have negatively impacted her ability to earn her living. Her customers are turning away from her – canceling appointments and so forth – and she's not picking up new business in the way she's done before.

So – whatever the root cause – she needs help. Fast. Or her business will collapse, and she'll have to move on.'

Christine said, 'Move on? In what way, Annie?'

Annie nodded. 'Right. She lives on a narrowboat. It's currently berthed in Brecon, but she's only been there for about six months – since the early summer – and she can move on to anywhere else whenever she wants to. Well, not to anywhere at all, but to anywhere that a narrowboat can be berthed. But she said she likes Brecon, and she was doing well there – had built up a good clientele.'

Mavis asked, 'And what does she do, Annie?' She was imagining that any number of jobs that involved a 'clientele' could be impacted by a dodgy wrist and ankle: hairdressing was the first that came to mind.

Annie sighed. 'See, that's the problem, Mave…she's a fortune teller, and people tend not to trust a fortune teller who can't avoid bad things happening to them. See? No wonder her clients aren't showing up – I mean, if she can't foresee that she's going to have to be careful when she's crossing the road, they're hardly going to take advice from her on…well, whatever it is they're asking her about.'

Carol snorted. 'What – she's a real-life fortune teller? Tea leaves? Crystal balls? That sort of thing? How on earth does anyone manage to make a living doing that?'

'I have a low overhead, and no need for fancy things in my life. And I'm good at it – so people trust me, and keep coming back to me.'

All four of the WISE women turned to see who was shouting angrily from the door to the barn. Balanced on a stout cane, stood a woman who Mavis suspected was approaching fifty, with long magenta hair that was being tossed in the wind that was spattering her with rain.

Mavis shot off the sofa. 'You must be Pauline Thomas. Do come in out of the weather. Annie here's just been telling us all about you.'

She approached the potential client knowing that Carol's words might have already convinced the woman that they weren't as professional as they might be…and she didn't like the idea of losing a client before they'd even got them. She hoped she'd be able to rescue the situation, and set about doing so.

CHAPTER THREE

Althea Twyst, Dowager Duchess of Chellingworth, was feeling her age. She'd had a poor night's sleep, and had done her best to appear as bright as possible when she and Mavis MacDonald had shared breakfast, but she knew – in her heart of hearts – that she wasn't her usual self. Maybe it was the prospect of seeing Oswald again…

Oswald Featherington had – quite literally – swept Althea off her feet almost sixty years earlier, and she'd never quite got over the impact the man had made on her life. Back then, she'd been a mere slip of a girl, and quite determined to make her mark in the world of musical theater, in spite of the hopes of her parents that she'd put her classical dance training to what they'd always called 'good use'. Oswald had been the principal male dancer with a company she'd joined in the West End of London…and she'd fallen for him. Hard. She'd been partnered with him during the audition process, and his ability to make her feel special had allowed her to elevate her performance sufficiently that she'd been hired to be a dancer for the run of a show she'd hoped would be her Big Break. Which was exactly what it turned out to be – though not in the way she'd imagined; she'd left the company to marry a duke – her Chelly – and her life had never been the same again.

Althea had been a professional dancer since the tender age of sixteen, which wasn't so unusual in those days, when leaving school at sixteen was an option taken by many who didn't excel in academia. As Althea had always known she hadn't. No…what she'd wanted was to be on the stage. Her parents had supported her dreams, allowing her to study ballet and tap-dancing, as well as what had then been called 'movement and modern' – the sort of interpretive dance that was quite popular with the cognoscenti of the day. But Althea had yearned to be specifically on the West End stage, and to work toward becoming what was coined as a 'triple threat' – someone who could sing, dance, and act very well. She'd had the dancing sorted before she'd turned twenty, and worked on the singing element by earning enough money to pay for a significant number of lessons. But she'd found it difficult to gain any experience in the acting department.

Which was why she'd been so delighted to get the part she had, because the named role – yes, she was due to have her name printed in a theatrical program with a character's name beside it! – had a few lines attached to it. A speaking part, no less. Oswald had been assigned as her partner on stage, and had become a good chum off it. They went everywhere together, and she'd learned a great deal about London…after the theaters had spilled their audiences and performers out into the night. Unbeknownst to Althea, there existed in the back streets of west London, the sort of establishments where one had to know someone – who knew someone – to be able to gain entry. The sort of places that didn't even open until gone eleven at night, and then continued to serve drinks – and, sometimes, even food – until dawn. Oswald had been well known for some years by those responsible for allowing entry to many such places, and Althea became his 'plus one' throughout the rehearsal period, and well into the run.

Rearranging her snowy, wispy hair as best she could – given there was now so very little of it – Althea mused upon how terribly naïve she'd been back then, and how ridiculous she must have appeared to the rest of the cast when they saw her gazing longingly at Oswald as they danced, and when she followed him like a smitten puppy wherever he went. Oh dear. What a silly girl she'd been.

Althea selected a wide, cerise velvet headband and placed it on her head, trying to create an effect of height, and volume. Yes, that was better. And the color went very well with her mustard silk shirt, and eau-de-nil tweed skirt – a highly unusual color for a tweed. Yes, that all looked much more jolly.

Without Mavis around to be her 'speaking clock' – which was what Mavis invariably became whenever the pair had a timed appointment – Althea realized, with a jolt, that Oswald was due to arrive in just a few moments. She decided to make her way downstairs to the morning room, which she felt would be the most appropriate setting for their reunion to take place.

As she took her time on the stairs – her red patent shoes had a stout heel, but could prove rather tricky – Althea recalled the rather surprising way in which she'd discovered that, while she might have become somewhat attached to Oswald, he was never likely to become attached to her…nor to any other female, saving – perhaps – his mother. She'd taken a wrong turn at the end of a dark and winding corridor in a basement club in Soho…and there he'd been. Or, rather, there they'd been. Oswald and Ralph – pronounced 'Raif' – had appeared to be inseparable in that moment and had, adorably, thereafter remained so.

At least, that's what she'd discovered just last week, when a series of telephone calls and text messages had led her back to him. Oswald Featherington had been living in Brighton for the past two years, it appeared, having left his beloved London because he couldn't bear to see places that reminded him of his dear, departed husband. Althea had been delighted to learn that the most couply-couple she'd ever had the good fortune to know had at least been able to legally marry before cancer had taken Ralph to the great proscenium in the sky, where she had no doubt he would be entertaining rapt audiences as surely as he'd thrilled those who'd attended his magic shows around the regional theaters of the United Kingdom.

The magician and the dancer really had been together until death had separated them. But Oswald was no longer a dancer; indeed, she'd discovered that he'd managed to move from hoofing, to choreographing, to stage directing, and now – when even that profession was no longer available to him, at the stately age of eighty-three – she found he was just the right person, with all the right experience, to be able to help her achieve a goal of her own.

Finally ensconced in her favorite armchair, with her aged but sprightly Jack Russell, McFli, at her feet, the dowager, who'd met her duke at the stage door of the theater where she and Oswald had been performing, was ready to receive her chum from her past life. A life she'd walked away from without hesitation, because she'd known right away that whatever Chelly had asked of her, she'd give it. She might have been a lovesick puppy following Oswald about, but she'd known that she'd found The Real Thing with Chelly.

When the doorbell chimed, McFli's entire little body quivered with anticipation – and Althea found herself to be in much the same state.

She reminded herself that she'd planned to remain seated when young Ian Cottesloe knocked the door to present her visitor, but she dashed across the room to greet the man she hadn't seen for an age.

When the hugging and kissing was over – of which there was a great deal – and once McFli and Oswald had been properly introduced, and tea had been delivered, and praise for the elegance of Althea's home had been given, and politely received – the chums sat mute for a moment, sipping tea from fine bone china, being viewed with interest by two beady little doggy eyes.

Althea was making her own observations: Oswald had shrunk in terms of height but had more than made up for it in a broadening of his beam; he was now almost round. His three-piece suit had been tailored for a slimmer man, that much was obvious, but it hadn't quite reached bursting point. However, what should have been straight lines in a Prince of Wales check, running down the front of his waistcoat, were more like waves bulging around buttonholes that were threatening to fly open. His once fine features had blurred with age, weight gain, and – Althea suspected – the odd drop or two of Scotch, which she recalled he'd always quaffed with the enthusiasm of a man dying of thirst. She felt some sympathy for his choice to wear a toupee; she'd been thinking, just that morning, that she might consider a wig herself, if her hair got much thinner. But she wished he'd chosen a shade that would have been more believable for a person of his age; that copper color was quite close to how his own hair had looked decades earlier…but now? The aggressive nature of the color wasn't…quite right.

Oswald's voice hadn't changed; it was still a commanding baritone. 'You're looking good for your age, Alth. For *our* age. Though I think I've got a couple of years on you, if I remember correctly. And I do, you know. I still remember things correctly. Nothing wrong with this.' He knocked on his head with his knuckles. 'You still remember what day of the week it is, who the Prime Minister is, how to tell the difference between a rhino and a giraffe – all that sort of stuff?'

Althea smiled so that her dimples showed; she'd always known exactly how to create that effect, and she wanted Oswald to see she'd lost none of her charm. 'Friday; don't care; and…short, fat, and pointy, as opposed to tall, thin, and licky. Will that do for you?'

Oswald laughed, a sound that took Althea back to…motes of dust and Leichner face powder dancing in a key light.

He said, 'And there was me thinking it was Wednesday, the PM's just another talking blob that's only lying if its lips are moving, and that rhinos are boringly gray, whereas giraffes have a proper bit of pattern. Good to see you're still the wit you once were, my dear. We had some good times, didn't we?'

'Indeed we did, Ossie, indeed we did. I was sorry to hear about Ralph's passing. I hope it wasn't…too dreadful for him, or you.'

'It was bloody awful, and it has been every day since he's gone. Same for you?'

Althea nodded. 'I miss my dear Chelly like I'd miss the air, or salt. It never gets any easier, though – of course – I've kept going. I don't want to think about the alternative.'

'I've got a bottle of pills with me, all the time. If they ever tell me I've got what Ralph had, or if I ever reach the point when I don't know that a giraffe is the most perfectly designed and decorated creature on the face of this earth, I'll just get myself an excellent bottle of Scotch and say ta-ta to all this…and hello to the great performance space above. The best sort of exit…though not, I hope, pursued by a bear.'

Althea couldn't help but smile. 'Oh, dear me no…not a bear. Remember that chap who used to make roaring noises at that club just off Grosvenor Road? He was rather bear-like, I always thought.'

Oswald laughed again. 'He was…and just as furry. All over.' He winked.

'Ossie…you're awful.'

'I was awfully…popular. For quite some time. Then along came Ralph, and the only person I wanted to be popular with was him. We had a good life, Alth. Considering. Was it difficult for you, fitting in with this lot? Ralph and me never fitted in. Didn't ever try to, I suppose. But by the time we knew he was very ill, it seemed that – finally – people were prepared to treat us as…well, just another old, married couple. That made a difference. Not being accepted for most of your life makes one…choose to operate on the fringes, I suppose. I could see you were besotted with your Chelly, and he with you…but were you ever really accepted? With your background.'

Althea gave her response some thought. 'To begin with, Chelly was the only one whose opinion mattered to me, as you recognized in your own relationship. But it was important for me that our children were accepted – that people didn't just think of Henry and Clementine as "less than" the child Chelly already had from his first marriage, to his late wife. So, once Henry was born, I decided to put some effort into becoming a proper duchess – not just a wife, hostess, and then mother. I applied myself, until it felt natural. It all seems to have worked out quite well, thank you.'

'No children for us, of course. So you have more than one child, you say? Sorry, Alth, I lost touch with you, and you weren't really on my radar all these years. I know nothing about what you've been up to.'

Althea smiled. 'No reason why you should, Ossie. And I'd like to hear a lot more about your life for the past…well, however many years it's been, too. I have my Henry, yes, who became the duke after my dear Chelly's death; his older half-brother, Devereaux, died unexpectedly. And I also have a daughter, Clementine, and she'll be coming to stay at the Hall quite soon, so you'll have a chance to meet both of them, and my grandson, Hugo, too. He's rather adorable…though I'm afraid he's going through a grumpy phase, at the moment. His mother's good with him though; Henry also married a woman without a title…a "commoner" was the term they all used when referring to me. She's intelligent, loving, charming, and incredibly hardworking. I don't want to make it sound as though I'm giving her a job reference, but if I were, I couldn't have hoped for a more suitable person to be duchess to Henry's duke.'

'Bit of an ass, is he?'

Althea couldn't tell if Oswald was joking; she'd forgotten that about him – that he had something of a cruel streak, that could present as spite, or troublemaking.

Choosing to believe he was trying to be amusing, she replied, 'No more than his mother.'

Oswald pulled a face. 'God help him, then.' They shared a chuckle. He leaned forward. 'So, tell me what I can do for you, ma'am. Or is it Your Highness?'

Althea decided that Oswald was now most definitely being jocular, and countered with: 'Actually, it's Your Grace, but only the staff use that, and members of the public, and…well, everyone except family, and special friends, I suppose. I'll mention to Henry that I've told you that you don't need to take any notice of anyone's title while you're my guest – so you don't have to worry about that.' She made sure she dimpled after she'd spoken.

He said, 'Oh yes, it's definitely taken with you, this duchess thing. So, lovie…you want me to put on a panto for you and your subjects? What's it to be…*Aladdin*, *Cinderella*, or *Puss in Boots*?'

Althea grinned. 'Bless you…at least you know me well enough that you've given me a choice. However, to be honest, all of those pantomime stories are a bit…well "problematic" is the word that comes to mind. *Aladdin*'s off the agenda, because we have almost no one in the area who isn't lily-white, and you just cannot have anyone wearing dark make-up to play the titular role – it's so disrespectful. Then there's *Cinderella*: I don't think we want to be telling young girls that their entire life's worth and future happiness rely solely upon being picked out of the crowd by a man at a dance. And as for the fact that she's happy to go off with a man who announces his highly questionable intention to marry any woman whose foot fits into a particular shoe…well, I won't even go there, Ossie. No, I've been thinking about it, and I rather like the idea of *Mother Goose*. It's based on an ancient Greek play – so has heritage beyond, say, the Brothers Grimm – and it's about a woman who learns, the hard way, that money, beauty, and appearances aren't as important as the love of those around you…which is a good lesson.'

'You've given it a lot of thought, Alth. Always were a thinker, weren't you? And you'll have seen from my website that I have a *Mother Goose* production all ready to go. Did you read the script? Like it?'

'I did, and I do. I was delighted to discover that you, of all people, now write, direct, and produce pantomimes, when that was exactly the range of services I was looking for. Though I do have a request: could you make a few changes so that the entire thing is most definitely set here, in Anwen-by-Wye, in Wales…not in some invented place. I could help with local knowledge to make some of the jokes more relevant.'

Althea was pleased to see Oswald's face light up. 'I'd like nothing more. A completely bespoke script it is…though that will take some time. When had you seen Opening Night? How many performances?'

'The day after Boxing Day – the twenty-seventh of December – with one performance only. I expect many of the locals will be in the production, so we're going to have to work hard to sell tickets in the wider area. While there's certainly an argument to not exclude anyone from attending because they can't afford the tickets – I do fear people might not turn up if it's "just" a free performance. So there'll be a nominal fee, with free tickets for deserving cases, and all the proceeds will go to a charity I'm involved with.'

Althea noticed Oswald fidget for a moment, then he said, 'I…um…I wish I could do all this *gratis*, old thing, especially because it's you, Alth…and now the charity thing, too…but it's how I make my living, and there are always wretched bills to pay.'

Althea recalled how fond Oswald had been of padding his bank balance in sometimes questionable ways, back when they'd been in and out of most of the late-night clubs in London on a regular basis.

She replied softly, 'I saw your rates on your website, and insist upon being treated as any other client. Of course, you'll stay here, as my guest, throughout the rehearsal and performance period…and I think you'll enjoy meeting my housemate, Mavis. She's also deeply invested in the charity in question – both in terms of her professional input, and emotionally. She'll be back for tea, which is at four, of course.'

'Don't people like you have "companions"? I thought that was required casting.'

Althea didn't like how Oswald's comment had made her feel, but did her best to shrug it off. 'Mavis is highly companionable alright…when she wants to be. I think you two will get on like a house on fire.'

Or else you'll be at each other's throats in hours.

CHAPTER FOUR

Carol noticed that it was taking longer than usual for Mavis's soothing techniques – honed by years of developing an effective bedside manner during her long career as a nurse – to calm down the rather put-out Pauline Thomas. Annie added her efforts to those of her colleague; she was the only person in the room the potential client had ever met, and also someone Carol knew to be an expert soother. However, in Annie's case, she hadn't had the advantage of working with subjects who were usually stuck in a hospital bed – oh no, Annie's charges had been city types, who needed to be corralled and organized by her in her role as head receptionist at a firm of Lloyd's brokers, which Carol thought might have been even more challenging, in its own way, than being an army nurse.

Carol had remained on the sofa, looking as miserable as she felt – which she hoped would make Pauline, and her colleagues, realize how much she regretted her unguarded comments. Christine had busied herself making a fresh pot of tea, and had even broken out the bourbon biscuits.

The concerted effort worked – eventually.

Finally settled with a piping hot cup of tea, and more biscuits on the plate in front of her than Pauline Thomas could possibly have eaten even if she'd stayed all day, Annie was finally able to open more formal proceedings. Carol noted, with interest, that Mavis appeared happy to cede her usual role of leading all client meetings, and she wondered how Annie would manage the whole thing. She wasn't surprised when her friend of many years – many more than they'd been working together – began in her usual, breezy manner.

'As you know, Pauline, I was talking about you when you got here – thanks to Carol opening her mouth…and putting her foot in it.'

Carol made sure that Annie saw the smile of thanks she threw her way. She didn't like it when Annie called her Car, rather than Carol – nor when she referred to Carol's son as Bertie, rather than Albert – but she knew that Annie invariably changed people's names however she chose, and Carol had got used to that. However, she was grateful that she'd been properly introduced in this business setting; she felt that was an important detail.

Carol said, for about the fifth time, 'I'm so sorry, Pauline, I didn't mean to be rude.'

Pauline finally unclenched her jaw, and her entire body too. Carol hadn't realized how physically 'wound up' the poor woman had been – as well as emotionally overwrought – until that moment; Pauline Thomas looked as though she were deflating when she slumped into the sofa.

The potential client sighed heavily as she relaxed. 'It's alright, I know exactly what you mean, and…well, that's why I'm here, right?'

Carol noted the strong Liverpudlian accent – yes, it was definitely from Liverpool, like Paul Baker's at the Dower House, not from Wrexham, like Janet Jackson's, who now ran the Lamb Tearooms. She'd assumed the woman would be Welsh, like Carol herself and about ninety percent of all the people in the area. Annie had said that Pauline was living in Brecon – not a place noted for its cosmopolitan nature.

Annie suggested, 'We're all ears, if you'd like to tell us about it in your own words. But it's helpful if you tell it like a story – with a beginning, and middle…and then run it along until you get to today, if you see what I mean. Do you fancy doing that? Or would you prefer me to start, and you just chip in as I go?'

Pauline now seemed to be embedded into the sofa, and looked quite comfortable. She said, 'It's alright, thanks, I'll do it myself, but, to be honest with you, I don't really know when it started…so I'll start from when I noticed that things were all going a bit too wrong for me.'

Annie clapped. 'Go for it, doll…the floor's yours.'

Pauline smiled contentedly. 'What you were saying when I got here, Carol, is about right: I read tea leaves, I read palms, I use Tarot cards, and I do use crystal balls, sometimes. Am I a fake? I dare say that's what you're all thinking, because it's what most people think. And the answer is no. I do get…feelings…but I'm not as in control of them as I'd like to be. That means that – sometimes – I have to…give a reading a bit of a helping hand.'

Carol noticed that Christine didn't seem to be able to keep still; she was wriggling like a small child who needed the loo. She flicked her eyes toward her chum; she hadn't known her for quite as long as she'd known Annie, but certainly knew her well enough to shoot an accusing look. What was Christine playing at? Carol sighed with the recollection of her own pregnancy; Christine might just be sitting in such a way that it was impossible for her to get comfy. Carol herself had felt that way on many an occasion, so told herself to be sympathetic.

Finally, Christine waggled a hand.

Just as Carol was thinking that her colleague was about to excuse herself, Christine asked, 'Did you do the tea leaf reading thing at the charity ball they held to raise funds for the kids' hospital wing in Chelsea last year? You look ever so familiar. Are you Madame Paulina?'

Pauline Thomas blushed all the way to her magenta roots. 'I am. I did. Did I read yours? Sorry – sometimes at things like that I don't even notice the faces of the people I'm reading for.'

Carol was surprised when Christine's mouth fell open. 'You told me I was going to get pregnant. And I did. And you said the father would be tall, dark, and handsome. And he is. You must be good.'

Carol wanted to say so much…but she didn't dare, because she'd already belittled this potential client before she was even fully through the door – so didn't feel it helpful to point out that an attractive, single, young woman at a posh charity ball in Cheslea would – at some point in her future – be likely to bear a child. And as for the tall, dark, and handsome thing? Well, most single young females would like to hear that, wouldn't they? Carol knew she would have done at that age, though the chances of her being at a posh charity ball back in those days would have been next to zero; the daughters of sheep farmers from Carmarthenshire aren't usually found at fancy Chelsea anythings…let alone an event where the entire point of being there is to put your hand into your pocket as deeply as possible, and pay up.

Carol wasn't surprised that Mavis dared, 'Aye, well – that's as mebbe, Christine, but we'll let Pauline get back to her story, if you don't mind.'

Pauline said, 'I'm pleased you feel I did a good job. A satisfied client is a wonderful thing. And that's my problem. My clientele is worried that, if I'm not able to foresee my own misfortune, then how can I warn them about theirs? You see, what I did at that ball is one sort of thing…a sort of generic reading. But when you have clients who've chosen to see you, they tend to come with a specific problem, or because they have to make a choice of some sort. Even if it's not specific, it's usually about a certain part of their life, or a relationship – I get a lot of those, of course. But they expect me to not just tell them about how well things are about to go for them if they do this, or do that – they also expect me to warn them about dangerous outcomes of potential decisions or actions. So sitting there all strapped up, like I am, tends to…well, undermine their confidence in me.'

Annie asked, 'And when was it that you realized that you were…more unfortunate than you were used to being, shall we say?'

Carol silently applauded Annie's approach.

Pauline pulled her phone from her pocket, and scrolled. 'It's almost the middle of December now; I did my wrist three weeks ago, and my ankle the week after that. Last week it was my right eye; I woke up and it was all pink and swollen. It had only just gone back to normal the day I met you, Annie. But – knowing I was coming here – I've been thinking about a few other things that I didn't mention to you when we talked, so here goes: back in September, all my tomatoes died, overnight – and, no, it wasn't an unusually cold night, or anything like that. They were lovely when I went to bed; I grow them in pots on the top of my narrowboat and take as many as I can for salads and so forth. They were coming ripe at that time, and I was eating a lot of them…then one morning they were all dead: they'd sort of collapsed, and the leaves were all brown. I didn't think much of it at the time, except to suspect that some kids might have thrown hot water on them, or something like that – but that was one thing.'

Carol asked, 'Do you happen to have an exact date for that, Pauline?' She realized as she spoke that she was likely to be drawing Mavis's ire, because they were supposed to charge for the time they spent being more fully briefed by a client once the client had signed their contract.

Pauline nodded. 'The twenty-sixth of September that was. Night of. I found them all dead on the morning of the twenty-seventh; I was having people over for drinks that evening. Had to go out and buy tomatoes for the salad, which was annoying.'

Carol muttered, 'Thanks,' and scribbled down the information, while avoiding making eye contact with Mavis.

Pauline continued, 'Then in October – on the sixteenth, Carol – I was out at a lunch, and returned to my narrowboat to discover that all my washing – which I put on a clothesline to dry when it's a nice day, which it was – was in the water. The clothesline had broken at one end, and everything was trailing in the canal. It was all a right mess. Some of my things couldn't be saved. And – before any of you ask – no, I didn't check to see if the clothesline had been cut, because, at the time, I just assumed it was an accident. Though now…I'm less sure.'

Carol jotted some notes.

Annie asked, 'Anything else, before your fall when you hurt your wrist?'

Pauline shook her head.

Carol felt she did so with some disappointment.

Mavis asked, 'Was that a slippery bit of pavement, that caused you to fall, and you put out your hand to save yourself, as Annie told us?'

'I thought I'd slipped on some leaves, at the time; it was a wet day, and I was rushing about, and it happened in a split second. I hurtled forward – I was walking fast, because I was late – and I automatically put my hand out to save myself. I was lucky I didn't break my wrist, though the sprain is bad enough. As I mentioned to Annie – when I had that little meltdown in that shop – thinking back on it, I believe I was jostled as I was walking, and that's what made me topple over. Same thing with my ankle; I saw the uneven curbstone, and I even stepped aside to avoid it, but I managed to sprain my ankle by falling off it sideways in any case, and I think, now, that I was tripped.'

'And what about that swollen eye you got?' Mavis leaned forward. 'Any sort of interaction ahead of that happening?'

Pauline shrugged. 'It came up overnight. I'm single, and there wasn't anyone else on the boat with me that whole afternoon, evening, or night. But, in the morning, it looked just awful. I went out to get an eye patch to cover it up because I had clients I didn't want to cancel.

One of them was a first-timer, and she didn't even stay…didn't even get onto the boat. I'd managed to balance myself quite nicely on my stick and my good foot, and I always welcome clients aboard with a jolly "Welcome to my trusty vessel" – which usually goes down very well. But all she did was ask me where my parrot was, then she flounced off. I don't know what she was on about, because I haven't got a parrot. Not even a budgie. I wondered if she might have been allergic to birds.'

Annie spluttered tea, clamped a hand across her mouth, and appeared to be about to explode, if her eyes were anything to go by. Carol could see Mavis looking daggers at her colleague, but also saw how Annie's reaction played with Pauline…she was looking completely puzzled. *Oh dear…*

Christine passed Annie a pile of tissues she pulled from her pocket, and Carol had to work hard not to laugh out loud, so pretended to cough, to be able to cover her face. Mavis stared at Annie, whose shoulders were heaving as she waved her free hand at Pauline. She held the tissues over her mouth, with tears streaming down her cheeks. She managed to blurt out, 'Stop…please,' before she finally attended to her face, and managed to compose herself.

When she was eventually more her normal self, Annie croaked, 'Gordon Bennett, Pauline, if you'd had an eye patch on in that shop that day I'd have said the same thing to you myself.'

Pauline appeared confused. 'But…why?'

'Stick, balanced on one foot, eye patch…your trusty vessel? A parrot? Nothing? Oh, come on…pirates? Oo-arrr.' Annie waited for Pauline's reaction.

Carol watched as the light of realization dawned in Pauline's eyes. 'Oh…I see. I get it…now.'

Carol suspected that Mavis was trying to regain control of the meeting when she asked, 'And there are no other instances of misfortune, Pauline?' Pauline shook her head. 'Good – so we have details, and a timeline. Now – what about folks you think might want to do this to you? Any disgruntled clients? People who might feel you "deserve" some sort of "punishment" for…something?'

Annie said, 'I told Pauline to think on that before this meeting. You come up with anything?'

Pauline seemed to sink back into the sofa again. 'There are so many negative comments and bad reviews online, that I don't know where to start, to be honest. There's always the odd one, of course – something I suggested would happen, didn't…or not in the way the client thought I'd meant it would. Or things took longer to happen than I'd suggested when I'd given no timeline, that sort of thing. I'm used to that. But this is…different. There are lots more reviews, and ratings, and so forth – across multiple sites and platforms – than I've ever had before. And they seem to be from different people – they have different names, in any case. And you know what that's like, it's never an actual name, but some sort of "handle" – that's what they call it. But they're all spiteful, or snide, or just plain bad. Some are so general that I can't tell if they might be from a client I actual read for, but some are quite specific, and are definitely fake. And it's not just the reviews and initial comments that are bad; other people then pile on who I know aren't clients – they're just happy to have someone to say mean things about. And some have been quite threatening. The general effect is that I'm just not picking up new clients the way I used to, and even existing clients have started to cancel. And the thing is, my narrowboat is a part of the charm of the service I offer, so it's always been pictured on my website – which means it's not really that difficult to find if someone wants to follow through on some of the threats they've posted. So I wondered if maybe those online trolls are the ones who've been targeting me in real life. I'm scared. That's why I'm here. I need to know what's going on. And I want to keep myself safe, too.'

Mavis spoke gently. 'You know we're no' a security firm, right? We cannae offer protection as such. Nor are we the police – we have no standing to enter people's homes, or access their computers, to find out if they're the ones who've been hurting you – if that's what's happened. Have you thought of taking your concerns to the police?'

Pauline tutted. 'I did. They said that the online stuff doesn't reach the level required to send it to the cybercrime people. There aren't specific threats, you see. They said I might have a case for libel, if I can find out who's been lying about me and my work online, but there's no credible threat to my personal safety they can discern. They believe I've suffered a series of misfortunes and have said there's very little they can do unless, or until, there's a specific threat, or an action taken against my person. Which isn't a very nice thought. I've had an alarm system fitted to my boat, and I've changed the existing locks, as well as having locks fitted onto all the windows and entry points that I can. I don't know what else to do…for myself. So, when Annie told me what you do – that you dig about to find things out – I thought I'd see what the professionals would propose. So what can you do for me? And how much would it cost? I'm not made of money, but if I can't sort this out, I'll have no business at all; all my online work will dry up, as well as my in-person stuff. I can move the narrowboat to help bring my skills to the attention of a new group of face-to-face clients, but the online work I do – video readings and so forth – that's a lot of money, and it's international, too. So this is an investment. Within reason.'

Carol, Christine, and Annie all looked toward Mavis, who said, 'That's right, we are professionals, so the next step is for us to discuss your case, come up with a proposed plan of action, an assessment of how long it would take us to do what we propose, and then we tell you how much that would cost. If you agree with our proposal, you sign a contract, and we get going. How does that sound?'

Pauline scratched her head with her good hand. 'Sounds like a plan. But, if I'm doing this, I want to start soon.'

Mavis said, 'If you were to leave us now, we could send our proposal to your email address by…shall we say half past three?'

'Today?' Pauline sounded pleasantly surprised, thought Carol.

'Indeed,' replied Mavis. 'We wouldn't want to wait to get going, either, Pauline.'

'Now that's what I like to hear. If you could give me a hand up from this sofa, then steer me toward the loo, I'll be off. Thank heavens I drive an automatic, because I can just about manage it; if I needed to change gears I'd be stuck using taxis or whatnot everywhere. But I'll definitely need to get rid of all that tea before I leave you, thanks.'

CHAPTER FIVE

Annie knew she'd be for it the moment Pauline left the office, and Mavis didn't disappoint. She largely tuned out the lecture about professionalism, until she finally felt she had to say, 'Right-o, Mave – I get it. Sorry. Don't react when a client says something that…amusing…ever again. Anyway, she's agreed to look at a proposal, so could we get going with that now, please, because I'd like to get back to the pub, where I promised I'd help Tude in the kitchen.'

Christine asked, 'You're helping him in the kitchen these days? I didn't know you could cook.'

Annie bit. 'Oi you…I'll have you know I've managed to feed myself all these years quite nicely, ta. Even though I made do with a lot of take-aways, when I lived in London. But you know what it's like around here: no take-aways, no deliveries, nothing. So I've had to learn what's what in a kitchen. And it's fun to play around with food…sometimes. Anyway, Aled's not in today, so Tude asked if I could lend a hand.'

Carol asked the next question, which Annie had been half-expecting. 'I thought Aled was trying to work all the hours God sends. That's what you said. Has he got…somewhere better to be tonight?'

Annie knew very well what Carol was getting at. 'If you mean "has he got a date?" the answer is that I don't know. And if you're wondering who he might have a date with, if he had one, I also don't know that. Though –' she couldn't help but smile – 'it'll be interesting to see who comes into the pub tonight, with him not being there. It might be Sharon Jones, or it might be Joan Pike…or it might be neither…or both. Only time will tell.'

Mavis snapped, 'Ach, we cannae be thinking about what you choose to call "The Anwen Love Triangle" at this time, Annie. So, yes, let's get on. I think we need a short, sharp effort by all of us on this one. Dare I ask, Annie – do you have a case name in mind yet? And it had better have nothing to do with pirates…or parrots.'

Annie giggled. 'No worries, Mave. The Case of the Unfortunate Fortune Teller. Not a difficult one to come up with, really.'

'I'll set up a case folder on our shared drive, with that name,' said Carol, tapping at her keyboard as she spoke.

Annie loved the way that Carol was so…'efficient' wasn't really the word. Her chum got things done: she was a loving mother to her infant son; she supported a husband who worked sometimes long and strange hours; she worked some pretty long and strange hours herself; and she managed to do everything that needed doing to set up and maintain her home – and it all ticked along, very nicely.

She wasn't surprised when Carol added, 'I'll pop all the notes I've taken, as well as the links I've already found for the platforms where Madame Paulina is getting slammed into the folder – so it's there, ready to go, if she signs the contract. But, for now, let's give that our attention; I promised David I'd be home by half three, because he's been holding the fort and taking care of Albert so that I could come here, today.'

Annie dared, 'Have you settled into your new home office alright, Car? It must be nice having a room for just work, then being able to shut the door on it, and focus on your family life.'

Carol smiled, and Annie was pleased to see the real warmth in her friend's expression. 'You have no idea how wonderful that is. It's almost on a par with having a dishwasher, for the first time ever. They're both life-changing, in their own way. And yes, thanks, everything's unpacked for the office. I've even flattened all the boxes so I can walk around my desk, if I need to think.'

Christine stood. 'Speaking of walking around the office, I'm going to do that right now, while I think and talk, if you don't mind. I've got a bit of wind under my ribs that won't shift.'

Annie couldn't resist a quiet, 'Just as well it didn't shift when Pauline was here, or you'd have got it in the neck from Mave, like I just did.' She chose to ignore Mavis's steely gaze. 'So – cameras everywhere for Pauline, is it?'

Mavis nodded. 'She owns the boat, we can put cameras on the exterior and interior. We should propose that. But we should also watch-and-follow, too, I believe. From what she said, the "danger" has shifted from property vandalism to personal injury, so we'll need to keep an eye on her as she comes and goes. I'd propose that Annie and I take that duty. Christine, you're pregnant, and we want no repetition of the incident where you sustained that nasty injury to your eye and face – which, I have to say, is now looking almost completely healed, by the way. And, Carol, you're going to be busy with what I suggest should be the third prong of our proposal – online trawling through bad reviews and nasty comments, and so forth.'

Christine called across the office, 'So what will I be allowed to do exactly?'

Annie grinned. 'If we're using cameras, you can monitor them from the safety of this place, while Mave and I freeze off our you-know-whats following Pauline about, wherever she goes.'

Christine laughed. 'Annie, if you don't want whoever it is who's already following Pauline about to spot you, you'd better come up with some good disguises.'

Annie was about to put Christine in her place, but Mavis jumped in. 'You're no' wrong, Christine. We're all aware that there are few people in this part of the world who are Black, like Annie, so it's true that her undercover skills are best utilized when we have cases in cities or towns where she…blends in a bit better. But – we are who we are, and this case is based where it's based, so…'

Annie felt herself sagging. 'Oh no, Mave…not more sheds, overnight? Are you going to put me on stakeout duty when she's in her boat? In the dark…somewhere.'

Mavis nodded. 'I think it's for the best, don't you? We'll have to find out how we can make that work – given that you have no car, because you don't drive. And what are you doing about that, by the way? Anything useful?'

Annie didn't want to let the cat out of the bag yet – she'd decided to surprise her colleagues with what she hoped would be good news, for Christmas, so replied, 'Sorry, Mave…I'll think about it. But I could talk to Tude. He doesn't sleep much, and he was really helpful in the shed at the allotments; maybe we could use his car, so – if anything happens – we could follow any suspects in that.'

'If he would do that, we should pay him, Annie,' said Carol.

Annie was surprised. 'None of our helpers get paid, Car…never have been, anyway.'

Carol turned to Mavis. 'Annie's right, of course; I know there are times when each of us gets a helping hand from someone else, but I don't mean that – what I mean is in this situation: without Tudor's help, we wouldn't be able to offer this option for our potential client – so Tudor should be paid.'

Christine had finished one circuit of the barn. 'If only you'd all let me help…more…I could do it. I wouldn't mind doing stakeout duty – I mean, it's not dangerous, is it?'

Annie sucked her teeth. 'That's what we all thought about you just popping into a client's home to pick up some bits and pieces, and look what happened. Nah, Chrissy, you've got Lumpy to think of, and – anyway – none of us could manage to stand up to that Alexander of yours if we let you do it; we all know he's a bit handy, when it comes to looking after himself.'

Annie thought Christine overdid things a bit when she replied testily, 'He's a very placid person by nature. He wouldn't hurt a fly.'

Annie thought it best to say nothing.

Mavis stood. 'I'd say the full camera package for a week, personal oversight for three days and nights, and a full online data trawl – agreed?'

They all agreed.

Carol looked hopefully at each of her colleagues. 'Right, standard terms, I'll get this all emailed to Pauline, and we'll wait to hear, okay?'

Mavis nodded; Christine did the same.

'Fine by me, doll.' Annie was pleased that she'd be able to get away soon; though she wasn't quite sure what Tudor had planned for her in the kitchen at the Coach and Horses, she was looking forward to doing whatever it was, because it would be time spent with the man she loved.

CHAPTER SIX

Mavis was glad to get away from the office: the rain was now flying sideways, meaning it was impossible to stay dry, so when she parked her Morris Traveller at the Dower House, glad to be home in good time for tea, she scampered from the garage to the entryway without an umbrella. She hated the feeling of the rain that was dripping down her back, it having sneaked into her collar when she'd performed the same maneuver when leaving the barn.

As she closed the front door behind her, she heard Althea's voice. 'Yoo-hoo, Mavis, we're in here.'

Mavis called back, 'I'll no' be a moment – but I'm wet, so hold your horses, dear. I'll be there in a tick.' She unbuttoned her trusty gaberdine, shook it off, and hung it up. Then she checked her watch, and wondered, *It's only twenty to four…is someone here early, for tea? And…is that a…tambourine I can hear?*

She was surprised by the sight that met her eyes when she entered the room: Althea was dressed bizarrely, even by her standards – she was swathed in some sort of red velvet cocoon and was waving about a moth-eaten, vividly emerald feather boa as she twirled in front of the fireplace, with McFli yapping at her heels. She had the full attention of an elderly man who was wearing an eye-wateringly checked suit and a top hat…who was holding a tambourine.

Mavis couldn't help but say, 'Do you no' think that feathery thing's a bit too close to those flames for comfort?' She realized she had no idea who the chap in the hat was, so wondered if she'd been just a bit too informal with the dowager, so quickly added a mumbled, 'Your Grace'.

Althea giggled. 'Oh Mavis, don't fuss so, I'm perfectly safe.' She stopped twirling. 'Come and meet Ossie. Ossie, this is Mavis. Mavis, this is Ossie.' Althea plopped onto a chair, where McFli settled at her feet and didn't remove his gaze from her face; he was panting.

Mavis struggled to make sense of the scene as she reached down to shake hands with the seated 'Ossie'.

'Pleased to meet you,' she said politely.

'Ossie knew me in my gilded youth, Mavis. We've just been recreating a little number I used to perform oh…probably back when you were in infant school, haven't we, Ossie?'

Ossie looked at Althea with what Mavis felt was a decided twinkle in his eye. 'When this one was the prettiest girl in the chorus, and even had a speaking part, in the West End, don't you know.'

Mavis hovered. 'Aye, she's mentioned that to me.'

Ossie boomed, 'She should have more than merely mentioned it, Mavis – this one was on the path to stardom, no question about it. Until that duke of hers spirited her away from us, of course. I was bereft when she left us for…well, I daren't say "just this", dare I?'

'Indeed,' replied Mavis, thinking it was best if she kept her responses short. She wondered, *Has Althea invited him for tea? Was this what she was going to 'reveal' to me? An old theatrical chum?*

Pondering these questions as she stared at a pink-faced Althea, Mavis also wondered if it were appropriate to ask them aloud. 'It's wonderful to meet someone from Althea's time on the stage. I've heard so much about it all – though mainly about the professional aspects of her time back then, rather than the…personal side of things.' She hoped that would give Althea an opening to shed some much-needed light on this man's presence in what she very much thought of as 'their' sitting room.

Althea waved the feather boa toward the sofa. 'Come on, settle down, Mavis, and I'll tell you all about Ossie.'

'Don't you dare do that, Alth…she might be an undercover police officer, for all I know.' He laughed – too loudly, for Mavis's taste.

'I can guarantee you I'm no police officer,' said Mavis tartly, not caring for the man's comments…nor his use of the 'Alth' thing.

Althea giggled. Again. Mavis noticed that the woman's dimples were working overtime. 'No, Mavis isn't a police officer, but she is a detective. I am too, sometimes, aren't I, Mavis?'

Mavis smiled. 'Aye, that you are. And – sometimes – you're a good one.' She couldn't help but take some pleasure from the fact that her statement had led to some of the color draining from Ossie's face.

He spoke uncertainly, 'A detective? What do you mean, exactly?'

Mavis rose, and handed him a business card. 'The WISE Enquiries Agency. We're a firm of investigators. All trained, and qualified. Always highly confidential. There are four of us, and we run our business out of a converted barn, here, on the Chellingworth Estate.'

'WISE? Like owls, you mean?' Ossie seemed flummoxed.

Althea giggled again – which irritated Mavis more than it should have done. The dowager wittered, 'Oh no, Ossie, not like owls – though they are, indeed, all truly wise women. No, it's a thingy thing: Carol Hill, now she's Welsh – such a lovely girl, with a wonderful husband and an adorable little boy. She was raised on a sheep farm, in Carmarthenshire, of all places, and she's so clever with computers it makes my head spin. Then there's Christine…she's a Wilson-Smythe, daughter of the Viscount Ballinclare, and such a beauty. Brains and looks, she's got, and I think she believes she'll live forever – the way people do, when they're young. She's not yet thirty, you see, so it's all ahead of her. Got the most delicious fiancé…who's a bit of a dark horse – and a bun on the oven.' Mavis tutted – she couldn't help herself. Althea ignored her, pointedly. 'Then there's Mavis here. You tell him about yourself, Mavis – go on…then I'll tell him about Annie.'

Mavis glared at Althea, with no effect. 'Army nurse, my whole career. Started late, worked my way up. Was Matron at the Battersea Barracks when I retired.' She didn't care to share any other information with the man.

He, sadly, lived down to her expectations of him when he quipped, 'You must have retired very early, in that case, Mavis, because you're still just a young thing.'

Mavis had no intention of sharing her age with the man, so satisfied herself with a polite smile.

Althea bubbled on, 'Then there's Annie Parker. Oh, Mavis – what can I say about Annie? She's so…well, Ossie, let's just say that I like Annie a great deal. She's intelligent, warm, really quite funny – even when she doesn't mean to be – and she'd fight anyone, tooth and nail, to help a friend. Just the woman to have in your corner if you find yourself in a tight spot. And there you are. Oh no, did I mention that Annie's a Cockney? Well, she is. So you have four women, one of whom is Welsh, one Irish, one Scottish, and one English. W.I.S.E. See? That's it…it's an acronym, that was the word I was looking for. Does that happen to you a lot these days, Ossie? Words just…evaporate when you want them?'

Ossie looked quite thoughtful, then said, 'They do, on occasion. But, since I am now a wordsmith – mainly – by trade, I do my best to grab them when I can and type them into my trusty laptop.'

Mavis decided to pounce. 'You're a writer, Ossie?'

Althea beamed. 'Of course, I haven't told you, have I, dear? Ossie writes pantos, and he's going to adapt one for us.'

Mavis understood every word Althea had uttered…but still couldn't make any sense of what she'd said. She turned her attention to Ossie. 'You write pantomimes? Scripts for pantomimes to be performed on a stage?' He nodded. 'And when Althea says you're adapting one for "us" she means…who exactly?'

Althea tutted aloud. 'I told you when we were at the Grand Opening of the renovated village hall – at the harvest supper – that I liked the idea of there being a local panto. Well, this is me making sure my idea happens. I knew we'd need a proper producer, a director, a script that I'd want to be adapted, and someone who could take complete control of what I hope will be a highly professional production – allowing for the fact that it will be performed by amateurs…people from the area, here. I heard a whisper that Ossie was writing pantomime scripts, and – when I finally tracked him down, via his website – imagine my delight to discover that he would be prepared to fill all the required roles. He'll be able to achieve exactly what I want – and he's just one person, whom I know rather well. It's perfect. Don't you agree?'

Mavis had no doubt that there needed to be a lot done to allow a panto to appear on a stage, but hadn't given the matter the slightest thought since Althea had first mentioned it. 'And when would this happen, exactly?'

Ossie boomed, 'Now, dear lady. Now. Alth wants one performance on the twenty-seventh of December, and I know I have the ability to accommodate her wishes. Which means there's not a moment to lose. So we were planning to discuss the specific aspects of the script that she'd like to tweak over tea. And, of course, I'd be happy to take any input you might care to add, Mavis. Would you see yourself treading the boards, by any chance?'

Mavis had absolutely no intention of coming within a mile of doing any such thing. 'Not everybody is cut out for everything, I've found, Ossie. Though, of course, if I could be of service in other ways, I'd step up.'

'All the money's going to be for our charity, dear,' said Althea quietly. 'The MacDonald Trust could do with a bit of extra income – so you can plan how to do even more good.'

Mavis noticed a shift in Ossie's facial expression; he was seeing her in a different light. 'What's this? You said your housemate was an interested party in a charity – not that she has her very own. What's it for, Mavis? Cats? Or maybe dogs, like this old fleabag here?'

Mavis noticed a slight glower pass across Althea's face; she couldn't imagine that anyone had ever had the temerity to refer to McFli in such a way before. Even McFli himself seemed to realize he'd been defamed – he lifted his head from his paws, and gazed up at his mistress, who rewarded him with a ruffling of the fur behind his ear.

Deciding to remain polite, Mavis replied, 'It's an outreach program for those suffering addiction to prescription medications. We have cells of professionals who work within the community, and we liaise centrally with a network of support services, and groups, around the country. It's important work.'

Ossie deflated a little. 'I'm sure it must be. Though maybe if doctors were better at their jobs there wouldn't be as many pills and whatnot in circulation. My poor, dear Ralph was fobbed off by his GP for months with pills and potions for dyspepsia, when what they needed to do was take a look inside him. If they'd spotted that damned cancer sooner, he might have made it…though they all said that wasn't the case. They all cover for each other, these medics. I bet you've done it yourself, Mavis…getting some over-worked nincompoop of a doctor out of hot water.'

Mavis decided to tread carefully; she wasn't sure who this Ralph might have been, but understood only too well how those left behind after the death of a loved one often sought solace by apportioning blame – and the medical profession was, quite frequently, where it landed. 'My condolences, I'm sure…but, no, I've never covered up malpractice, though I have been known to pass on words of advice to doctors, when appropriate.'

'Mavis is never afraid to point out when someone – anyone – could be doing something better than they are.' Althea dimpled. Mavis nodded her agreement.

A knock at the door was followed by a short period of silence among the threesome as Paul Baker delivered tea, and ensured that all Althea's special requests had been met.

He noted, 'Cook Davies sent a seed cake over from the Hall, as you requested – and as you can see – and I've made sure that the scones were fresh out of the oven half an hour ago. They'll be just right, by the time you get to them. Now, Your Grace, shall I pour…or will you be doing that?'

'Mavis can take care of it, Paul, thank you,' said Althea airily. 'Is this the jam from the Hall that they made this year, or is it last year's?'

'This is the new batch, Your Grace.'

Mavis had to work hard to not smile when Althea said to Ossie, 'Last year's jam was very seedy…and, while I adore seed cake, I don't care for seedy jam. So they made up a special batch for me with fewer seeds this year. Very good of Cook Davies to get them to strain it for me. Thank you, Paul. I'll ring when we've finished.'

As the door closed behind Paul, Mavis felt her skin crawl when Ossie whispered, 'Handsome devil, that one. Love the hair. He'd make an excellent Demon on stage…I bet he has the presence for it. Slight air of the Elvis of the late Fifties about him. Very…alluring.'

'Down, Ossie,' said Althea, playfully. 'He's attached – to a woman – and you're far too old for him, anyway. I'd have thought you're far too old for anyone…I know I am, and you're even older than me.'

'Only by a hair, Alth. Besides, I'll never be too old – at least to look, and imagine – until I'm under the sod, with my dear Ralph. He and I always allowed the other to at least imagine, Alth…don't rob me of the only excitement left to me in my dotage.'

Mavis decided to start the proceedings. 'Indian tea, Ossie?' He nodded. 'Milk?'

'Not for me. And weak, rather than strong, dear thing. And – even though these darling cups are small – just half fill it, would you? Thank you. One doesn't care to be up and down all night, if you get my drift. But there'll be an *en suite*, will there Alth? Or doesn't this pile of yours run to such modern luxuries?'

Mavis felt herself tense up, quite involuntarily. 'Will Ossie be staying with us?'

Althea beamed. 'Indeed. Until the performance is given…and the after-party's been enjoyed, of course.'

Mavis realized this was quite a big surprise that Althea had managed to keep all to herself…or had she? 'And staff's been over from the Hall to prepare a room for him?'

'Yes, dear. He'll be in the peacock room, which I thought would be most appropriate.'

Althea grinned, and Ossie guffawed.

Mavis queried, 'That would be the peacock room next door to mine?'

'Yes, Mavis – as you well know, not even this place can run to two peacock rooms; there are only eight bedrooms, after all.' Althea petted McFli, who was showing more than a passing interest in the seed cake she'd loaded onto a plate. 'You must try this, Ossie. It's a recipe from the eighteenth century, and it's quite wonderful. Cook Davies makes it up at the Hall. I had her send one down, especially for today.'

Ossie glared at the cake; Mavis wondered why he appeared to be regarding it with such suspicion. 'Not keen on seeds, myself. Not of any sort. I might stick to that strained jam your chap spoke of. Probably safer, with this plate of mine.'

He grinned widely, and Mavis was almost dazzled by a set of clearly false teeth that appeared so large in his mouth that she was amazed she hadn't spotted them before. Now, she found she couldn't take her eyes off them.

Althea tutted. 'At least you've got a full set, Ossie; I still have my own, but not all of them. It's a bother, sometimes. Just stick to the scones if you prefer. Mavis – seed cake for you, I assume?'

Mavis nodded dumbly. She felt that things were about to change at the Dower House, and she suspected it might not be for the better…which unsettled her greatly – though she was pleased to see that Althea had some sparkle about her. So, if it took a visit by an old colleague and friend to give Althea some of her old vigor back again, then Mavis would accommodate any changes that might befall what she'd certainly come to think of as her home.

CHAPTER SEVEN

Annie had expected the bar at the Coach and Horses to be empty when she returned from the office; the afternoon lull was always a great opportunity for Tudor to catch up on…whatever needed catching up on, and there was always a list on the go. So she was surprised to find Marjorie Pritchard and Iris Lewis at a table close to the fire, which was built unusually high. Tudor himself was scuttling between the table at which they were sitting and the bar when Annie arrived; he was carrying a tray of bowls.

'Hello Marge, Iris. You been having a spot of late lunch here today? Not like you two, is it?' Annie breezed past them, kissed Tudor on the cheek, and made her way toward the stairs that led up to the couple's flat.

Marjorie called, 'Hello, Annie. We came to tell Tudor the news as soon as we heard. It's critical that the social committee gets to work on this as soon as possible.'

Annie stopped, her foot on the bottom stair. She turned. 'Tell Tude what?' As she spoke, it became immediately clear from the barking that broke out in the flat above that Rosie and Gertie – the couple's yellow and black Labradors – had heard Annie's voice.

Iris said calmly, 'There's an impresario staying at the Dower House, and we're going to have a panto, at the village hall.'

Annie was torn: the girls needed to smother her with licks, upstairs, but, in the bar, the man that she loved clearly needed to be rescued. It wasn't a difficult decision. 'Right-o, you all stay there. I'm going to dump my mac, because it's soaking, and change my shoes – ditto – then I'll be back down so you can all tell me about it for ten minutes. Then me and Tude have to get into the kitchen if anyone's going to have any food to eat here at all tonight. So practice how to make a long story short, alright, Marge? Back in a tick.'

Annie stomped up the stairs, and spent three glorious minutes being fussed over by her girls. Having pacified the dogs with treats, she braced herself for the inevitable Pritchard Onslaught when she returned to the bar, only to discover that Marjorie and Iris had left.

She peered around. 'Oi, Tude – did I manage to frighten them off?'

Tudor appeared from the kitchen, grinning. 'Sort of. I wish you'd come back an hour ago and done it then; they've been at that table since one o'clock…right through the lunch rush, and, as you know, Aled's not in today. Marjorie even had a clipboard with her. She almost put people off eating.'

Annie laughed aloud, and hugged Tudor close. 'Oh, Tude, she's been doing that for years, I bet – and worse. So, now that they've gone and this place is empty, let's do what we need to in the kitchen, and you can tell me all about it.'

'Deal. Though there is someone here: Joan Pike's in the snug. She's on her own, and drinking…well, more than I've ever seen her drink before. I wondered if you might have a word? You know Aled's been working not only all the shifts I've asked him to, but he's been begging me for extra ones too?' Annie nodded. 'Well I thought that might be because he wanted to be here, in the pub, more often, so he could see more of Joan. I mean, it's not easy for Sharon to get away from her shop, and Joan…well, I know she works from home a bit, but she's mainly her mother's carer…so her time's a bit more flexible. So Aled and Joan have been in each other's company quite a bit. But now he's gone off for the day, and she's in there. See what I mean?'

Annie's heart fell. 'So Aled's off somewhere with Sharon Jones? He picked Sharon, not Joan? Oh dear. Well, I suppose it was always going to be one or the other of them that was let down. No, hang on…he can't be with Sharon – I just saw her winding the awning out a bit further at the front of her shop.'

Tudor shrugged. 'Well, if he didn't take the day off to be with either of them, where do you think he's got to?'

Annie had no idea. 'I've got no idea,' she said, thinking it sensible to say so under the circumstances. 'Do you think Joan's in there drowning her sorrows, believing he's off somewhere with Sharon?' Tudor nodded. 'Right-o, then, I'll have a quick word, let it slip about Sharon being over at the shop, and see how that goes. You start whatever needs starting in the kitchen, and I'll come back to help as soon as I can.' She kissed him on the cheek. 'Young love, eh?'

As Annie approached Joan, she could see the girl was glassy-eyed and looking decidedly miserable. No…that wasn't right; Annie reminded herself that Joan was in her mid-twenties, so really a young woman, not a girl. She had a book with her which she'd placed on the table, face down, its spine almost completely cracked. The sight made Annie feel queasy; she'd always believed that books were precious objects that deserved to be treated with respect. However, she resisted the urge to 'save the book's life' by closing it – she had a young woman's happiness to focus on.

She decided on what she hoped would be the best approach for the situation. 'Hello Joan, how are you? And your mum, of course. Is she still having more good days than bad with that nasty old MS of hers?'

Joan looked up, and Annie wondered if she'd actually swayed in her seat. 'Mum's fine.' Annie noticed how Joan's inflection suggested that someone other than her mother wasn't doing as well.

Annie pounced. 'Aww, you sound a bit down, doll. But, there – at least you're dry, not like poor Shar at the shop. I just saw her get soaked when she was grappling with that old awning of hers. I bet she's looking forward to shutting up today, and having a nice warm bath.'

Joan definitely swayed in her seat as she said slowly, 'Sharon's at the shop? But…but it was shut when I came in here…I thought she was…that her and…' Joan's voice trailed into silence.

Annie persisted. 'She has to put up the closed sign if she needs more than a quick break; I know she doesn't do it often, but you must have seen that little clock thing she's got on the door that says when she'll open up again. I mean, she's there on her own – she needs a little time to herself, now and again. But she's there now. And wet, as I said.' Annie hoped that would buck Joan up enough that she'd go home…and sleep it off.

Joan slurred, 'Yes, you did.'

Annie gave one last push. 'It looks like it's easing off a bit out there at the moment, and there's still a bit of daylight fighting through the clouds. I bet if you nipped back home now you wouldn't get too drenched. Why don't I help you get into that big old waxed cotton coat of yours? There you go…oh dear, that's tricky; I happen to know that if you run a household candle along that zip, it'll work a lot easier. There you are…now, off you go, and I'll keep an eye on you as you go back home for the evening…which I dare say you'll be spending with your mum, while Shar spends hers in the bath.'

Having finally dispatched Joan Pike on her somewhat unsteady way across the village green, Annie joined her beloved Tudor in the kitchen, where she found him surrounded by dozens of jars and bags of spices, as well as a good number of saucepans.

'Gordon Bennett, Tude…what's all this in aid of then?'

'Curry Night.'

'Curry Night?'

'Curry Night.'

'And what's that when it's at home?'

Tudor wiped a hand on the chest section of his full-body apron. 'We're doing alright with the food, Annie, and we both know what a difference that converted horsebox and gazebo have made in the beer garden, but the weather's definitely turned now, and we need to bring people from farther afield into the pub – and what better way than to tempt them with food? I thought a curry night would be a good way to start.'

Annie surveyed the scene. 'And you're planning to make curry from scratch?'

'Not just one type – a whole menu full. You can't just offer one curry, can you? So I've got the ingredients here to be able to follow recipes for korma, jalfrezi, and vindaloo. I'll put them with chicken, lamb, and beef…and Bob's your uncle, a decent menu. My research suggests they're the three most popular dishes, so I thought that's where I'd start.'

Annie grinned. 'And what "research" is this, Tude? Did you phone that old school friend with an Indian takeaway in Penarth?'

Tudor winked. 'You know me so well, Annie, and we Swansea boys have to stick together, you know, wherever we end up.'

'But I thought you said that…was it Jay…Jay Singh?' Tudor nodded. 'I thought you said that he used all his mother's recipes, and that she'd made him swear to never share them. He hasn't, has he?'

Tudor chuckled. 'Not on your Nellie. But I did talk to him, and he's given me a good bit of direction. He told me where to find recipes he thinks have the potential to make good dishes. I don't want to offer customers something they can make at home, so I'm not going to just slap a bit of meat and veg into a bottle of shop-bought sauce, see?'

Annie's heart warmed. 'I do see, Tude, and you're right – we agreed that everything we offered here would be authentic…so what's the plan for tonight?'

'Tonight is sauce night; Jay said that's what's critical, so if I can crack the sauces, the rest of the dish will come easy. We should get at least two done, if not all three. He's coming over tomorrow around eleven-ish, so it should be quiet, and Aled will be here, anyway. He's going to taste them all and give me a bit of feedback. Nice of him, isn't it?'

'Lovely. It'll be good to meet him – I've heard so much about him. So, what's my role, now?'

'You read out the recipe, and we'll both try to spot the spice. You might have noticed that I've arranged them in alphabetical order, here on the counter.' Tudor waved his hand across the array of spices as though they were the prizes on a game show, and he a toothy model.

Annie laughed aloud, then looked at the labels. 'Impressive, Tude.'

'Ta muchly. Anyway, once we've found the ingredient, you tell me how much, and I'll measure it out. Okay?'

'And can you tell me what Marjorie Pritchard was going on about while we do it, please? If she and Iris were prepared to camp out in your bar all afternoon, it must be something important. So spill your guts – but not these spices, because they'll make a right mess.'

'True, so, let's start with the korma. First ingredient, if you please, maestro…'

Annie enjoyed the next hour or so; Tudor only had to leave to serve a half of dark mild when a regular came in early – saying it was cheaper for him to sit beside Tudor's fire than to turn up his own heating, which pleased Tudor so much that he threw on an extra log.

By the time five o'clock came around, Annie's mouth was watering because of the wonderful aromas of the three sauces that were now simmering on the stovetop, so she helped herself to a bowl of the lamb stew for which Tudor was rightly famous, as he cleaned up. That was their deal: she'd help in the pub kitchen, but clean-up was all Tudor's responsibility. It was only then that he finally got around to telling her about all the excitement, because the sauce-making process had needed both of them to be fully involved at all times. Indeed, it took so much concentration, and careful attention to detail, she was surprised Tudor hadn't gone off the entire idea of preparing curries.

As Tudor tucked packets and jars into two old biscuit tins he'd managed to find, he filled her in. He began, 'As you might imagine, Marjorie did most of the talking.'

Annie asked, 'Did Iris even get a word in edgeways?'

'Not often,' conceded Tudor. 'Just so you know, Marjorie's source was someone called Wendy – who is not Iris's granddaughter Wendy, but another one – which Iris was at pains to ensure I understood.'

'Got it.'

'This particular Wendy is a part-time cleaner at Chellingworth Hall, and Mrs Davies Cleaning, at the Hall, had been asked by Althea Twyst to send someone over to the Dower House to make up a room for a guest who'll be staying through Christmas and possibly as long as the New Year.'

Annie stopped eating. 'Really? Staying there?' Tudor nodded. 'Oh heck, I hope that doesn't put Mave's nose too far out of joint. She told us that Althea had someone coming for tea today – and she even knew that Althea was up to something. But I bet she wasn't expecting the person in question to come for tea today, and then not leave for weeks.' She returned her attention to her stew, then paused. 'So what's all this about a panto?'

Tudor hunted about for space where he could store his precious biscuit tins, opening and closing cupboards, all of which appeared to be already full. 'Word is, Mrs Davies Cleaning managed to wangle out of the dowager that the person coming to stay is a famous theater producer from London, who's done panto with some of the best; she mentioned Danny La Rue, and John Inman – but I think that was Marjorie embellishing. The thing is, there's a plan to have a panto here, at the village hall, over Christmas. Which could be good for us; I know that the bloke in question will be staying at the Dower House, but there could be some other people coming here to be in it too, and our rooms are ready to go now. So that could be good news for us.'

'Oi, hang on a minute – one of them rooms is spoken for; Eustelle and Rodney are coming, don't forget that. And we also agreed we won't take a penny from them for it. It's the first time ever, in my whole life, that I've been able to have my parents come to stay with me for Christmas…every other year, since I left home at sixteen, it's been me going to them. I more than owe them one.'

Tudor smiled warmly. 'I know, don't panic. And I know what you're like – they're coming for the run-up to Christmas because you and your mother agree that there's more fun in looking forward to it, than the event itself. It'll all be exactly as you want. Anyway, the thing is, Mrs Davies Cleaning told Wendy, who told Marjorie – at church – that there'll also be parts in the panto for locals. You know, a community involvement. Hence the importance to the village social committee. Marjorie thinks we should ask to be formally involved, to make sure the village gets what it needs out of it. So…what do you think?'

Annie had finished her stew, and was enjoying the warm, full feeling it always gave her, as she replied, 'Well, Tudor Evans, you wonderful man…I think this could be your big break – I could just see you as Widow Twanky in *Aladdin*, or as one of the Ugly Sisters in *Cinderella*. Do you think they'll hold auditions, that sort of thing? Or might it just be that the villages get to go on stage as…well, villagers?'

Tudor laughed and wiped his hands dry; he'd washed them after finally stowing away his spice collection, and turning off the heat under his saucepans. 'I have absolutely no desire to begin a theatrical career in my late fifties, thank you very much – though I'd lend a hand off stage, if such were needed. But that's the thing, see? We need to know, don't we? Do you think Mavis might know more? Could you ask her if we could talk to Althea about it? Or maybe ask if we could talk to the bloke himself?'

Annie kissed Tudor, pulled back, and whispered, 'You only want me for my contacts, don't you?'

CHAPTER EIGHT

Henry gazed with wonder at his son, who was – finally – sleeping peacefully in his pram in the small dining room at Chellingworth Hall. His poor wife looked exhausted, and didn't appear to be terribly interested in the beef consommé they'd been served.

'I do think you should try to eat at least this, Stephanie. You need to keep your strength up. You're still very much eating for two, my dear.'

His wife's tired eyes met his. 'I know, Henry, and it does smell tempting. But, I don't know…I'm just not feeling…well.'

Henry felt his tummy flip. 'Well, in that case, we'll get the doctor in to see you. Do you think you might be developing a head cold, that sort of thing? Or is it elsewhere that you feel poorly?' He thought it unseemly to make more specific enquiries.

'It's not a head cold, I don't think, though I do feel a bit lifeless, and I wasn't terribly well this morning. Maybe stomach flu?'

'Oh, I say…we should most definitely at least speak with the doctor. Is it safe for you to feed Hugo if that's what you have? I mean…would it pass from your body to his?'

He noted the darkness of the circles beneath his wife's eyes when she smiled. 'It's perfectly safe, Henry dear, don't worry. In fact, if my body is fighting off an illness it'll be producing antibodies, and it's good for Hugo for me to pass those to him through my milk. But the whole process is feeling rather…draining at the moment.' Stephanie laughed. 'Which it is, of course…but I'll keep it up. Don't worry. But, yes, you're right, maybe I should telephone the doctor. I'll do it in the morning, if I feel no better.'

'Please do. I know there'll be the kerfuffle that invariably accompanies Clemmie's visits and, of course – this time – Julian will be with her. Her husband. My sister's husband. My brother-in-law.' Why was Stephanie looking at him so strangely?

'I know who Julian Treforest is, Henry. What's going on? Is there something you need to tell me?'

Henry had finished his consommé and was rather looking forward to his guinea fowl; Edward had informed him it was to be served roasted, on a bed of celeriac mash, with carrots, and a prune sauce. It happened to be Henry's favorite way to enjoy the lovely little gamey birds. 'No more of that for you, dear?' His wife shook her head at the glowing, clear broth. 'In that case, I'll ring for the next course. I do hope you'll manage to do it justice, Stephanie…you have to keep eating, even if it is stomach flu. You need goodness inside you…for you, and Hugo.'

Henry thought that his wife brightened a little when she replied, 'Yes, I do rather enjoy this preparation of guinea fowl.'

Finally ready to begin his main course – he and the duchess didn't have more than three courses unless they were entertaining guests – he tried to push away his worries about the impending arrival of his sister, and especially of his brother-in-law, by chattering on to his wife, urging her to bring him up to date with how the revitalization work in the village was progressing. But Stephanie's replies weren't peppered with her usual pithy observations, nor with her natural wit and charm. He was, however, pleased to see that she managed to eat most of her meal.

Sitting back, she finally initiated a topic. 'Do you know if Clementine and Julian have any specific plans during their stay with us?'

It was a reasonable enough question, and Henry knew that – under normal circumstances – he'd probably have begun to moan about how utterly unpredictable his sister was capable of being, so there was little point in discussing the matter. But he felt desperate to engage his wife, so told her about the telephone call he'd received from his brother-in-law.

He was delighted when he heard a little spark in his wife's voice when she said, 'That sounds very odd, Henry. He wouldn't speak to you then, on the phone, about it? Said it needed to be face to face?'

'As I said, the term he used was "one-to-one". Might that have a meaning of which I'm not aware in the world of business? I know he's an artisan blacksmith, but he's grown up in a family embroiled in the world of big business…an arena where you shone so brightly, before you came here to run our public relations effort, and then agreed to become my wife.'

He beamed at the remembrance of their courtship, and was pleased when his wife beamed back.

'No, Henry, it just means what it says. Though it clearly implies that Julian wishes to speak solely with you, rather than with us, as a couple. He gave you no clue as to what the topic of this conversation might be?'

Henry shook his head. 'Not money, I shouldn't have thought. But, maybe…Clemmie?'

Stephanie sighed. 'Oh dear…yes. Well, you'll find out soon enough, Henry. Maybe he'll take you to one side as soon after they arrive as possible, then we can both stop speculating. You know, I rather enjoyed that. Is it quince posset for pudding? I do like that.'

'It is. Oh, that's good…that you feel a little better. Maybe it was something that's passing already, dear. Shall I ring?'

'Indeed.'

14th DECEMBER

CHAPTER NINE

Christine Wilson-Smythe stood back as her fiancé, Alexander Bright, lugged a hard-sided, wheeled case toward what was – it turned out – a rather jolly-looking narrowboat moored at a wharf in the center of Brecon. The bottle-green hull was topped with a sunflower yellow cabin structure, and all the trim was red.

As they approached the boat, Christine observed, 'Good for Pauline Thomas – she's got a semi-trad stern; they're the best.'

Alexander stopped wheeling. 'She's got a what?'

Christine laughed. 'A semi-trad stern. See…that bit there, at that end of the boat. It looks as though the cabin goes almost all the way to the back, but it's enclosing an open area where you can socialize. Some designs have a cabin that really does go right back there, but then you only have a tiny bit of deck to play with. Alternatively, there are great big open areas – they call them cruiser sterns. They're more popular with the sort of narrowboats that are hired out to holidaymakers. But Pauline's got the best of both worlds. I'm looking forward to seeing the inside, now. Come on, not far to go…though these cobbles along the towpath aren't helping, are they?'

'No, they're not. So how come you seem to know all about narrowboats? I had no idea you were up on all the terminology.'

'I once spent an excruciating week on one with some chums from school. You'd think it would have been fun, but it wasn't…which is why I learned so much about the boat, and all the others we saw as we sailed. I was bored out of my mind, so decided to take charge of getting us from A to B every day. The other girls seemed to think we were on a seven-night pub crawl…which, I suppose, was basically what it was.'

Christine loved the sound of her fiancé's laugh, and enjoyed seeing him so…happy. Gone were the brooding looks, and the sorties to parts unknown where she was convinced he was involved with some shady dealings. Since he'd found out about her pregnancy, and she'd endured that extended period in hospital following her latest injury on the job, Christine felt that Alexander was finally putting his absolutely legitimate business dealings front and center, and leaving his other – more questionable – contacts behind.

Alexander asked, 'She knows we're coming, right?'

Despite the fact it was a chilly morning, Christine could see that Alexander had perspiration on his brow. She felt a little guilty, but reminded herself that he was the one who'd insisted upon her not lifting a finger, informing her that he'd install all the cameras that it had been agreed would be needed by this client.

'Yes, though we're a few minutes early. Just as well she warned us we wouldn't be able to bring the car all the way to the boat. At least we were able to allow time for you to do…this.'

As Christine was speaking, Pauline Thomas's magenta head popped up from the part of the cabin at the rear of the boat to which Christine had already drawn Alexander's attention. It having been agreed the previous afternoon – well, around six o'clock in the evening – that the proposals put forward by the WISE Enquiries Agency were acceptable, it had then, rather hurriedly, further been agreed that the installation of the camera package would happen the next morning.

Pauline called, 'I've got coffee going. Can I give you a hand on board with that?'

Alexander assured Pauline that he could manage, and Christine watched him use what she suspected was every ounce of his determination to lift the unwieldy case from the towpath to the higher level of the boat, while avoiding all the metal bars and railings, and ropes, that seemed to be in the way. Eventually, it was done.

Pauline said, 'It should be safe there, but I'll close the cover over it, to be sure…then why don't you come in and get the lie of the land, so to speak? You can decide where you want to put what. But first – coffee.'

Christine asked, 'I'll just have a peppermint tea, thanks. I carry my own teabags, so I only need hot water.'

Pauline paused in the entryway. 'Why on earth do you carry peppermint teabags with you?'

'As is only too obvious, I'm pregnant, and I find it soothing. I have a couple of cups a day, and that suits me.'

Pauline looked from Christine to Alexander and said, 'Oh, I hit the nail on the head when I said the father would be tall, dark, and handsome, didn't I?'

Christine giggled.

'What's that?' Alexander sounded puzzled.

'I'll tell you later,' whispered Christine; she'd forgotten to mention her previous encounter with 'Madame Paulina' to him.

As the couple settled down, and Pauline provided refreshments, Christine noted, 'Your saloon is spacious, and you've decorated it all so beautifully. Do you do your readings here, at the dinette table?'

Pauline looked impressed. 'You know all the proper terminology, Christine. Have you been swotting up?'

Christine told her client about the time she'd once spent on a narrowboat, without mentioning the pub-crawling aspect – though she suspected that Pauline had inferred as much, given her smirk when she replied.

'I know these boats are popular with groups. Mine only berths four, in two bedrooms, which is why the saloon is so large. I had the bulkheads moved when I bought her, to suit me; this reverse layout – with the galley and saloon at the back end of the boat – means I can welcome clients at the rear, which is better, because they don't have to pass any of the more "private" areas. So I have one guest room, and that's it. Not that it's ever been used a great deal, but it means I can have friends to stay, when I'm in their area. People like to experience a night or two on the water, even if I'm only in their general neck of the woods.'

Hoping she might glean some helpful insights, Christine asked, 'Do you have any friends in this area who've come to stay?'

Pauline shook her head. 'Not here. This is fresh turf, for me. I don't move around a great deal – though, over the years, I think I've probably managed to cover most of the UK's inland waterways. I like stopping, getting to know a place…and building up my clientele there, as I told you. But I rarely make friends, except for the sort of acquaintance that I might meet up with here, then bump into – not literally, of course – if I'm somewhere else. The friends I have around the country are friends from before I took to the water, and I don't have any of those here.'

Christine tried again. 'You haven't got to know any of the local gongoozlers?'

She wasn't surprised when Alexander almost choked on his steaming coffee, then asked, 'What on earth is a "gongoozler"?'

Pauline and Christine shared a smile, and Christine allowed her client to answer. 'They're like train spotters…but for canal boats. They hang around wharfs and locks, taking photos of narrowboats, making lists of names of boats they've seen, and noting all the details of each one. Length, colors, designs – that sort of thing. But no, Christine, I haven't got to know any of them here; though there's a gaggle of them who like to visit this wharf when a boat arrives, they mainly go out to the active canals, to see more boats that way. Once you come into this wharf, you usually stay for a while…and they're all about collecting details of vessels that are new to them – or in seeing "old friends" again – by which I mean boats, not people. They don't…engage with people, much.'

Christine caught her fiancé's rolling eyes as he replied, 'It takes all types.' He placed his empty mug onto the table. 'Now – about these cameras. We seem to have an awful lot of them for what's really a small space. How wide's this boat?'

Pauline replied, '*Gracie*'s a newer boat, so she was built a little less than seven feet wide – the maximum width for a narrowboat, so that she fits in all the locks. She's fifty-five feet long, and just about perfect.'

'Did you name her "*Gracie*" after someone special?' Christine asked.

'Mum. Named after Gracie Fields. Mum came from Rochdale, like the original Gracie. My gran had a thing about Gracie Fields; used to hum her songs all the time, she did. "Sally" was her favorite.'

Christine tried to recall the song, but couldn't. 'Nice. Well, as Alexander said, we'd better get on. As agreed, we'll set up the cameras to give coverage of the entrances and exits to your boat, but we won't be invasive…no coverage of private areas, as such – though you'll have to try to remember that you could be recorded as you…go about your business.'

Pauline laughed. 'You get used to the idea of having – potentially – no privacy on a narrowboat, what with people walking past and being able to see inside, if they choose. The shower has no windows, of course, nor does the toilet compartment – but I'll remember to make sure my nightie hasn't ridden up before I go from my berth to anywhere else, of a morning. Thanks for the warning.'

Christine noted, 'This is your property, so we can use cameras for security reasons, but we can't just go pointing them wherever we like. Why don't you stay there, and I'll let Alexander get on with the internal set-up, while I go outside and check the best locations for our purposes. I'll also check for suitable mounting spots, so that we don't damage the structure of the boat at all.'

Pauline said, 'With you warning me about running around in my undies, I'll warn you about moving around the exterior of the boat: watch your footing, don't forget there can be unexpected movements – if someone chooses to sail past, for example…though that's unlikely, here – and always bear in mind that even flat surfaces can be slippery. As you might imagine, with my ankle and wrist in this state, I haven't been up top at all – I'm only going in and out, and that's tricky enough.'

The following half an hour saw a relatively seamless installation process achieved, then the threesome met up in the saloon again, where Christine checked that all the cameras were working properly, and that she was able to access every feed.

Christine was finally satisfied. 'Thanks, Pauline. Leave the rest up to us. Will you be leaving the boat today?'

Pauline flushed. 'I'm not planning on it. I have a client due here at two, and it's such a palaver for me to go anywhere that I stay put as much as possible. Besides, the weather's not exactly brilliant, is it? If the sun would only break through those clouds it wouldn't be warm, but it wouldn't be as dark inside this place, either. If I do decide to go out, is one of you lot going to be following me, wherever I go?'

Alexander whispered, 'Don't ask, and we won't tell.'

He winked.

Pauline giggled. 'Oh, you're quite something, aren't you? I tell you what…how about I just give you a short reading; I bet those palms of yours could tell a few tales. On the house…boat…of course.'

Christine noticed how swiftly Alexander withdrew the hand he'd been offering Pauline to shake. He said, 'It's a very kind offer, but I really think we need to be on our way. I'm overseeing a big job in Anwen-by-Wye – a complete refurbishment of the old school there – and I can't be away from the site for too long, or they'll all slow to snail's pace, and we won't get the job finished on time.'

Pauline sounded puzzled. 'They're working on a Saturday?'

Christine could see Alexander mentally slapping his forehead. 'Some specialist trades will work any day,' he lied. 'You ready, Christine? I'll give you a hand over onto firm ground once I've got there myself.'

By the time the couple were buckling themselves into Christine's Range Rover, she'd made a Big Decision. 'You grabbed your hands away from Pauline a bit sharpish back there, Alexander. Don't you want her telling you if Lumpy's a boy or a girl? Or are there other things you don't want to know about your future?'

Alexander began to pull out of the car park as he replied thoughtfully, 'The palm reading thing isn't all about the future, Christine, it's also about the person, and their character. And I've no desire for anyone to know anything about my character, especially anything that might signify my past deeds – as you might imagine. My past, and everything I did back then, is where it should be – behind me. The youth who moved illicit items around south London on behalf of the high-ups in the local criminal fraternity has grown from being the shadowy Izzy, to the successful developer, landlord, and entrepreneur, Alexander Bright. Let's keep it that way, shall we?'

Christine agreed. 'Yes, please. Just keep on the straight and narrow, my darling – and we'll be grand, so we will. Ignore those texts and calls you get from your shady contacts which I know still come through to you, because…well, you can't stop them getting in touch with you…and…oh hang on, here's a text from Pauline.'

Christine read, then clicked links, and swore.

Alexander didn't take his eyes off the road when he asked, 'So what is it? Has something happened in the fifteen minutes since we left her, and before Annie and Mavis have begun their stakeout?'

'Not really – it had already happened before we left. It happened yesterday, in fact. Someone's been posting photos online of Pauline getting into her car yesterday, as she was on her way to see us. She knows it must have been then, because of what she was wearing. She's concerned that someone's been that close to her, who might mean to do her harm. Though it looks as though they've already done quite a bit of that. The photo of a fortune teller looking as though she's been in the wars is gaining quite a bit of traction online, she says. And the client she was due to see this afternoon has phoned to cancel. Oh dear, I'd better let all the others know; we might have to all push just a little harder, and faster, on this one, than we'd thought.'

CHAPTER TEN

Mavis MacDonald never found herself to be lacking comforts when she fulfilled an overwatch duty; she ensured a sufficient number of snacks and drinks were packed into the capacious rear of her beloved Morris Traveller, and she'd long ago mastered the art of sitting comfortably, while keeping her head as low as possible in the driving seat. Her only real challenges were the temperature, and her bladder. By turning the engine – and, thereby, the heater such as it was – on and off, she managed to regulate the temperature quite well. She also always had access to a beloved, old, crocheted blanket, given to her late mother by a friend who'd managed to incorporate every color under the sun into the thing; it usually managed to take the edge off the cold. She was bundled up in it as she sat in a scrubby parking area on the side of the wharf opposite to where Pauline Thomas's boat, the *Gracie,* was moored.

As for her bladder? Well, that was always in the lap of the gods…though she more than understood the usefulness of a decent incontinence pad, and found them to be reliable, in dire circumstances. But that wasn't her concern, at this precise moment. No, what she was worried about was the fact that her client appeared to be about to leave the relative safety of her boat to head off…somewhere. They'd agreed with Pauline that she'd let them know if she was planning to leave, but there'd been no message, nor any texts. Mavis felt peeved. *What was the point of the woman saying she'd help the WISE women to help her…if she then didn't do so?*

The greasy rain that had been falling for the past hour had eased off, and Mavis could tell that Pauline was taking her time with her walking stick and dodgy ankle as she navigated the cobblestones. Then the woman stopped, pulled her phone from her pocket…and Mavis heard her own phone ding with a text alert. She checked her screen. It looked as though Pauline had finally remembered that she was supposed to report her whereabouts; she'd sent a text saying: **Getting milk mines all gone 15 mins**

Mavis pulled out her long-lens camera, which had a good zoom capability and looked a bit less suspicious than simple binoculars; if challenged, she usually claimed to be a birdwatcher, or something similar. She observed Pauline hobble along the towpath – noting that, these days, it really was simply a path, mainly used by walkers, joggers, and people exercising their dogs. A woman walked by with a double pushchair, a man wearing a puffy jacket and a flat cap pulled down over his face hurried past, then along came Pauline with her vivid magenta hair. Mavis was pleased she was so easy to spot, though she hoped she wouldn't have to follow her in a crowd at any time; Mavis wasn't tall, which she found to be a disadvantage under such circumstances.

Surprisingly, Pauline entered a building Mavis knew to be an arts center, of sorts. Maybe they had somewhere in there that Pauline could buy milk? Mavis thought it highly unlikely, but she'd never been into the place herself, having only gleaned the purpose of the brick-built structure from her digital map. With her lens trained on the door, Mavis waited. And waited. Ten minutes later, Pauline hadn't emerged.

Mavis felt torn: because the building was on the opposite side of the wharf, in order to get there she'd have to walk along the bank on her side of the water, then over a bridge, then along the path Pauline herself had just taken. She reckoned it would take her about ten minutes. If Pauline came out of the building at any point during that time Mavis wouldn't be able to see her, because of a bend in the waterway…but reasoned she'd already lost sight of her quarry for that same amount of time already, so might be no worse off.

Tossing aside her blanket, and stowing away her camera, Mavis gathered everything she'd placed on the passenger seat into her capacious bag, and pulled a scarf around her head and face to guard against what turned out to be a biting breeze. She scurried along the gravel path on her side of the water, labored up and over the bridge, then kept up a good pace until she reached her destination. Luckily, the place had glass double doors, so she could see in to what appeared to be a small cafeteria, with a counter at one end, and refrigerated display cabinets.

Mavis froze: Pauline Thomas was on the floor, in a corner, being tended to by two wide-beamed women in blue overalls. She strode through the doors and put on a very good act of being a normal patron, who'd happened upon an unexpected incident, hoping that Pauline would remember the agreement that – were she to ever spot any of the WISE women when she was out and about – she was to act as though she didn't know them.

Mavis opened with: 'Ach, dearie me. Has there been some sort of an accident?' She rushed to Pauline's side.

'This lady here took a tumble,' said the shorter of the two women attending to Pauline.

'Done it before, too, by the looks of her,' said the other.

'I'm fine, like I said,' snapped Pauline. When she caught sight of Mavis she added, 'What are you doing here?'

Both women gave their attention to Mavis, who responded, 'I saw the place and fancied a coffee…then thought I'd come to the aid of a stranger.' She hoped Pauline would take the hint.

She did. 'I don't need any more Good Samaritans, thank you very much. I just need a bit of space, and maybe a hand to get up.'

All three women lent a hand, and – eventually – Pauline took a seat on one of the bentwood chairs, and caught her breath.

Mavis asked, 'What happened?' She needed to know.

'Lady took a tumble. This floor can get slippery when it's wet,' said the tall woman with a bad perm. 'I keep saying we ought to have signs, but you'd think we were asking for gold-plated ones, the time it's taking for them to get them to us. I did write a note and stick it to the door – but notes blow off, especially when it's windy like that outside.'

Pauline glanced at Mavis, then looked away. 'I suppose that must be it…but I wondered if someone tripped me up. I know I caught myself on the table when I went down.' She touched the skin on her right eyebrow very gingerly. 'I wouldn't be surprised if I ended up with a black eye. Same eye, too.'

'Same eye as what, my dear?' The short woman looked confused.

Pauline glanced at Mavis. 'Oh, nothing…I'm just getting over an eye infection, that's all.'

'Well, maybe that's it then. You're really in the wars, aren't you? Pins not too good, slippery floor, and your eyes not working quite right. Bound to go over when you're like that.' The tall one seemed delighted to have fully explained the incident. 'Were you coming in for a coffee? I could bring one to you if you like – no need for you to come up to the counter.'

Mavis could see tears welling in Pauline's eyes; she mentally attributed this to shock.

Pauline managed to say, 'That's…very nice of you, but I came in to get some milk. I know you've usually got some.'

The short woman tutted. 'Oh, you're on that boat out there, aren't you? I should have recognized the hair. I've seen you about a bit. Of course you can have some milk – but would you like one of us to walk you back to your boat…if that's where you're going? Maybe a bit of a lie-down would be a good idea.'

Mavis pounced. 'You two have responsibilities here, but my time is my own. I'll walk this lady back to…wherever her boat is.'

Pauline's gratitude showed in her eyes, and Mavis sorted out a carton of milk, which she stuffed into her bag, then steered Pauline to the door, and back out into the elements.

As the pair made their way – with great care – toward the *Gracie*, Mavis took advantage of their close proximity to carry on a hushed conversation with her client.

'Tell me everything, Pauline…but, firstly, tell me about the exact nature of your fall: what did you hit, and how hard did you hit it? I can come into your boat and perform first aid…though you've not broken the skin anywhere on your face, which I believe is a good sign.'

Pauline wobbled along and hissed, 'I didn't slip, I didn't trip…I think someone kicked my stick away when I was leaning on it. There were about half a dozen people in there when I got there, and they were all milling about. A couple were coming back to the entryway from the direction of the toilets, then they all left together. I…I think I saw someone come in as they were all wrapping themselves up in their scarves and whatnot…then I started to head toward the counter, and down I went. I felt the edge of the table hit my eyebrow, or just above it, and I felt a hard thump. I didn't even have time to put my arms out to save myself – though we all know how well that went last time I did it.' She raised her injured wrist in Mavis's direction.

'Well let's get you inside your boat, then I can take a look at you. I can perform a basic assessment of head injuries, and I'd just like to run a few field tests for a concussion. If I really were a stranger, I don't think it would be odd for you to invite me inside – under the circumstances.'

Pauline managed a weak chuckle. 'You mean I wouldn't be blowing your cover?'

'Exactly. But let's concentrate on you keeping your footing as you get onto the boat for a moment, shall we? Then we can speak privately, inside, and I'll make you a nice, hot, sweet cup of tea…which really does make everything better.'

As they reached the boat, Mavis was touched by the intense gratitude in Pauline's eyes when she grabbed her by the arm and said quietly, 'Thank you for being there, Mavis. I felt terribly vulnerable, lying on the floor like that…knowing I wouldn't even be capable of getting myself up without rolling about like a flipped-over tortoise. I…I don't like this feeling at all.' She sighed. 'I shouldn't have gone out, but I needed milk. I…I can't live like this, Mavis.'

Mavis's heart went out to Pauline. 'Now come along, there's no point having this conversation here, in this nasty wind; let's get into the warm, then you can have a good old cry…which works wonders almost as much as tea.'

15th DECEMBER

CHAPTER ELEVEN

Annie Parker didn't want to get out of her snuggly bed, but she knew she had to; it was almost eleven, and the Sunday roasts down in the pub usually meant an extremely busy lunchtime, that could sometimes extend all the way from noon until three in the afternoon. She'd promised Tudor she'd be able to lend a hand, even though she – and he, bless him – had spent the entire night sitting in his car, keeping watch on Pauline Thomas's boat. She was glad – and amazed – that Tudor had managed to get as much sleep as he had; even if it hadn't been her job to be alert, she'd have found it impossible to sleep on those seats of his, but he'd snored for hours, which meant he'd been relatively fresh when they'd got back to the pub, by six. He'd napped in bed until eight, before heading out with the dogs and getting things going in the kitchen. At least, Annie knew that had been the plan.

Gertie and Rosie were curled together on one of their two dog beds on the floor at the foot of Annie and Tudor's 'human bed', which was how Annie had started to think of it since she'd acquired Gertie. As she stirred, so did the dogs, and she allowed herself a moment or two to enjoy the frantic tail-wagging and thorough licking that they offered her. With both of them up on the human bed, beside her, she found it difficult to untangle herself to escape to the bathroom, but she made enough fuss of them that they finally let her go…and she got on with the start of her day.

As she showered, Annie hoped there'd be a chance for her to nap later on, before she took over again from Mavis at ten o'clock; she couldn't stop yawning. She knew she wouldn't have time to think, let alone rest, until the last of the roasts had been carved, and the final Yorkshire puddings had been ladled full of gravy. She pulled on her chocolate-colored corduroy jeans, then a cozy red V-necked sweater, that looked seasonally appropriate but was really lightweight; she hoped she wouldn't get too hot as she dashed about between the bar, the kitchen, and the snug, serving food…and making sure people had collected all the cutlery, napkins, and condiments they needed – which they never did, somehow.

When she arrived in the bar, it was already quite busy, which was good. The smell of roasting meats made her mouth water instantly, and she realized she was famished; how was she going to be able to serve food to people if she was drooling all over it? She'd have to grab something before she was needed. Tudor was in the kitchen, stirring and twirling. He grinned when he saw her, which delighted Annie.

They managed a peck on the cheek before Tudor announced, 'I'll do you a roast beef sandwich, with your hot sauce instead of horseradish, of course. That should get you through lunch. Okay?'

'Horseradish is fine, ta, Tude…though never tell my mother I said that. She'd wonder what had happened to her daughter if she knew I'd eaten anything but her hot sauce…even if I admit to you that I can manage without it on everything, all the time.'

Tudor feigned mock shock. 'I don't know about your mother fretting over what's become of her daughter's tastebuds, but I'm wondering if the Annie Parker I'm living with is the same woman who wouldn't ever go anywhere without a bottle of hot sauce in her handbag.'

Annie chuckled. 'Don't panic, it's in my handbag, alright, but that's upstairs – as are all my other bottles of it – and I haven't got the energy to go back up there to get it. It took me ages to settle Gert and Rosie. So just slather on the horseradish – the really fierce one. I'll be fine.'

Feeling a little more human, Annie fulfilled her role alongside Tudor and Aled, ferrying food from the kitchen to the eager customers. As all three servers acknowledged the surprisingly good turnout for what was, after all, a pretty bleak day, Annie spotted the arrival of Wendy Jenkins – Iris Lewis's granddaughter – in the company of a man she knew she'd never seen before. Both were bundled up against the elements, and they made their way toward the table where Marjorie Pritchard and Iris herself were seated.

'Is that a family member coming in with Wendy there?' Annie asked Tudor as she reached for an extra knife and fork to take to a customer who'd dropped theirs on the floor, splattering gravy on their trousers as they'd fallen. She also reached for a wodge of napkins, to address that problem.

Tudor looked up from the beer he was pouring. 'No idea. Never seen him before. Oh blast, now look what I've done.' The glass he was holding had overflowed, and he grabbed the tea towel from his shoulder to clean himself up.

'I dare say Marjorie will inform us,' said Annie, as she headed off to help the man who now had a large stain on his pale khaki trousers, that she suspected he'd never get out; Tudor liked to make his gravy with a good amount of beef dripping, meaning it was lusciously fatty, and flavorsome. He also wasn't afraid of using a great deal of gravy browning, so the beef gravy was almost black. Ah well, it would give the bloke a chance to buy a new pair of trousers, and Christmas wasn't too far off, if he had to wait to be given them.

Within five minutes, Marjorie was standing at the bar, ordering food for four. Annie didn't dislike Marjorie – they'd been affable next-door neighbors for some time, until Annie had moved into the flat above the pub with Tudor. And she'd certainly done more than the odd favor for Marjorie, over time. It was just that Marjorie never knew when to stop talking, or telling a person how they should do…anything, and everything. However, Annie knew she had the perfect excuse to have no more than a brief exchange with the woman that day – anyone could see how busy they were.

'All come in for a nice roast, Marge? Who's that with Wendy, then? Someone from Iris's family?'

Marjorie preened. *Oh dear.* 'That's Oswald Featherington, the famous London theatrical impresario.' Marjorie's tone suggested that Annie must be incredibly stupid to not have recognized the man. 'He's staying at the Dower House, and will bring us the opportunity to present our very own village panto. Wendy's doing the music – selecting the songs, leading the musical rehearsals, and then getting together a group of professional musicians to play at the performance. Isn't it exciting?'

Marjorie then more than surprised Annie when she turned toward the customers in the bar and declaimed, 'All the world's a stage, and all the men and women merely players.'

Everyone stopped talking and stared at her, Annie included. The man sitting at the table with Iris and Wendy clapped loudly and shouted, 'Brava! Excellent projection, ma'am…have you ever trod the boards, perchance?'

Marjorie twittered, 'Isn't he amazing? So, all that for the four of us…and would you bring our drinks over, Annie, please? I couldn't possibly manage them myself. Thank you…I must get back.'

Annie didn't have the opportunity to remind Marjorie that table service was for food only before the woman wafted her way between the jostling tables and plopped herself back into the seat she'd vacated – next to Oswald Whateverhisnamewas – where she proceeded to wave her arms about in the most bizarre manner, and laugh operatically every twenty seconds for no apparent reason.

'What's got into Marjorie?' Tudor indicated the table where the round man in the loud suit was sitting. 'Is she having some sort of fit?'

'Nah, showing off to that bloke from London who's going to be putting on that panto. I reckon she's angling for a part. What do you reckon, Tude – would Marge make a good Wicked Stepmother in *Sleeping Beauty*? Or what about the wolf – or even the grannie – in *Little Red Riding Hood*?'

'It's *Mother Goose*.'

'Pardon?'

Tudor dropped a slice of lemon into each of three glasses. 'The panto. It's going to be *Mother Goose*.'

'How do you know that?'

'Wendy phoned me this morning; she's doing the music.'

'So Marge just informed me. You didn't say.'

Tudor paused, a bottle of tonic in his hand. 'Haven't exactly had the chance, have I? And there's a chicken with no stuffing, and a lamb with extra mint sauce for table six ready for you back there; you'd better get your skates on, or the gravy'll grow a skin, under those heat lamps.'

Annie mugged a salute. 'Sir, yessir,' and did her duty.

As a keen, and happy, observer of human behavior, Annie couldn't help but notice how people changed over the next hour or so, as word got around that the man doing the casting for the panto was lunching at a table close to one of the front windows. People began to move circuitously to and from the bar, necessitating a detour close to his location, it appeared. At which time, most folk paused to politely introduce themselves…after which there was usually some sort of weird behavior on the part of people who Annie had believed – until that moment – didn't have the slighted interest in a single one of any of the performance arts. When three brothers who jointly owned a local sheep farm spontaneously burst into a close-harmony rendition of 'We'll Keep A Welcome In The Hillsides', Annie was less surprised than she would have been on any other day, though the sight of Janet Jackson, who ran the Lamb Tearooms, tap-dancing up to the bar did give her pause.

'They've all gone mad out there Tude,' she observed on what she hoped would be one of her last trips to collect loaded plates from the kitchen. 'Someone's going to be giving a full-on rendition of *Hamlet*, or flinging themselves about the place doing a tango, before you know it. Do you think this happens to this bloke wherever he goes? People trying to attract his attention to their hitherto undiscovered talents.'

Tudor dropped a massive Yorkshire pudding onto a plate. 'That's the last of those, and the beef's gone. Though we've still got lamb, and about two servings of chicken, I'd say.' He checked his watch. 'I think I judged that all about right, today. What did you say?'

'Never mind…you finish up that plate and I'll take it out. Does it go with that lamb there?' Tudor nodded. 'Okey doke.'

By the time four o'clock rolled around, Annie's feet were throbbing, and she was feeling totally exhausted. Tudor handed her a gin and tonic as she sat at the bar of the now almost deserted pub. 'It's a short measure…but I know you're probably fancying one.'

'Ta, Tude. First of the day…and probably the only one, given that I'm on duty tonight. Is Aled staying on, so you can take a break too?'

Tudor nodded. 'As agreed. He's got someone to give him a hand this evening, while I get a bit of shut-eye.'

Annie made sure they couldn't be overheard, then whispered, 'Joan Pike, or Sharon Jones? And…did you find out where he went the other day? With neither of them.'

'He didn't say and, to be fair, it's none of my business. But I happen to know it's Joan who's helping him this evening.' He rolled his eyes toward the snug. 'She's in there, the other side of the bar, already.'

Annie whispered, 'Keen…like me, but I'm keen on putting my feet up, or maybe even taking a proper nap on the bed. Then we could set an alarm, and take the girls out for a walk to wake ourselves up properly before we head off to Brecon. What d'you reckon?'

Tudor grinned. 'Sounds like a plan. I've made us up a couple of Ploughman's…with a bit of cold lamb, not ham, because that's all I had. I'll bring them up, then we can spend a bit of time with the girls, and have a snuggle, alright?'

Annie could think of nothing better. 'I'll go on ahead of you, and keep the girls off you when you come up…or they'll have you over and that food inside them before you know what's happening. Oh, and – by the way – did you break that teapot on the front windowsill? You know, the one with the flowers in it. Maybe when you were doing that bit of dusting?'

Tudor looked puzzled. 'Teapot? The cracked one, with no lid?'

'Yes. The one I use as a vase for those dried grass things. I noticed it wasn't there, and wondered if there'd been…a little accident.'

Tudor shook his head. 'Not me, I promise.' He flung up his hands in mock surrender.

'Not that it really matters. Like I said, it was cracked, and the spout was terribly chipped. Oh well, maybe it'll turn up; someone might have moved it to put something on the windowsill…oh, hang on…this is Mavis phoning, I'd better take it.'

Tudor disappeared into the kitchen.

'Hiya, Mave, how's it going? Everything alright? She hasn't gone out and taken another tumble has she, our Pauline?'

Mavis spoke tersely. 'As far as I'm aware, she hasn't left her boat all day…but I heard sirens not too long ago, and an ambulance and a police car have just driven along the towpath, to Pauline's boat.'

Annie felt her tummy clench. 'Gordon Bennett, Mave…what's happened? Do you want me and Tude to come over there now? We can…we're just clear of the rush here.'

Annie heard Mavis gasp.

'What? What's happened? What's the matter?' Annie could feel her frustration shoot through the roof. 'Don't just make noises, Mave – tell me what's going on…and in more ways than the "Oh God" that you're muttering.'

'What's up?' Tudor emerged from the kitchen with a plate loaded with bread, cheese, apple slices, pickled onions, and cold roast lamb in each hand. 'Anything wrong?'

Annie tutted. 'I don't know. It seems Mavis has lost the power of speech. Mave? Mave – are you still there?'

Annie heard a sob, then: 'They're pulling what appears to be a body out of the water…can you and Tudor come here, now? I'll get hold of Christine while you're on your way, and you bring Carol up to speed. Maybe our cameras and the recordings they made will be able to help in what I believe will soon be a police enquiry into a drowning…or a death, at least.'

Annie asked, 'Can you see who it is? Is it…Pauline?'

'I don't know. But I fear it might be. Oh Annie…we've failed our client in the most dreadful way. She hired us to keep her safe, and she's…dead.'

Annie didn't hesitate. 'Mave – you don't know that, so let's hold our horses, alright? We'll be there as fast as we can be – and, yeah, you get hold of Chrissy. Don't panic…okay?' She disconnected the call. 'Tude – sling that food into a couple of plastic containers, grab a few cans of something wet and sugary, and get the car sorted – Mave needs us. We're off to Brecon. Now. Well…as soon as I've been to the loo.'

CHAPTER TWELVE

Mavis stood behind the tape the police had used to cordon off the towpath alongside the waterway. There were a few other people on the scene who'd been making their way home after a walk; they appeared to be more annoyed that they'd have to take a long detour to reach the bridge that was just yards beyond the tape than saddened by the sight before their eyes. Mavis wanted to point out that if they'd initially gone out for a walk, now they had the chance for a longer one, so they really had nothing to complain about, but stopped herself from saying anything of the sort, just in time. Twice.

There was a great deal of activity happening just beyond where she could see — that blessed bend in the waterway wasn't doing her any favors. Again. Lights were flashing in the deepening darkness, and she was aware of people moving about…and there was a certain amount of splashing. She hadn't recognized any of the faces of the first responders when she'd been watching from her vantage point in the little car park on the opposite bank. She'd dared to hope that Constable Llinos Trevelyan might have been called to the scene, but she hadn't arrived so far. For all that Mavis knew, the young officer wasn't even on duty. She texted Carol – who was quite pally with Llinos – to see if she could get in touch with the constable, and possibly gain some more insight into the situation that way.

Mavis hovered, getting colder and damper by the minute. She was relieved when Annie and Tudor arrived, and felt gratitude wash over her when Annie announced, 'I told Tude to shove some cans in a bag to bring with us, but he brought a Thermos too. Fancy a cuppa?'

Mavis patted Tudor on the arm. 'You're quite an extraordinary man, Tudor Evans. Always ready, willing, and able, to save the day. Thank you. I'll be honest and admit I don't usually care for tea from a Thermos, but I'd take anything hot and sweet right now.'

Annie and Tudor appeared amused. Annie said, 'You might have mentioned – once or twice – how tea from a Thermos isn't to your liking, Mave, so Tude's brought hot water, and teabags…and china mugs. It won't taste of stale chicken soup and plastic, alright?'

Mavis managed a chuckle herself. 'Ach, I dare say my mother's to blame for my attitude toward Thermos tea. We only had the one when I was growing up – like every family I knew – so it was used for everything. I dare say that the flavors lingered as the years went by. And those little plastic cups that you screwed onto the top? Tasted of a conglomeration of every drink that had ever been put in them. I appreciate your thoughtfulness. Thank you.'

'Annie, Mavis…Tudor? What are you doing here?'

The threesome turned to see Constable Llinos Trevelyan, in full uniform, standing behind them.

Mavis sighed. 'Ach, Llinos. It's you. Wonderful. We're trying to find out what's happened, but no one's come along this way, and your colleague there – keeping us all away from the tape – won't say a word. Is there any chance you can tell us what's happened?'

Llinos acknowledged the male constable who was pacing just beyond the tape. 'All I know is what came over the comms: female found in the water. Deceased. No determination of a cause of death yet, though drowning is presumed.'

Mavis asked, 'Is it Pauline Thomas? The woman who lives on the narrowboat named *Gracie*?'

Mavis saw Llinos stiffen. 'No name released yet. Why, Mavis? Do you know…the person you just mentioned?'

Mavis sighed, and judged how much she should say. 'I was watching her. She…feared for her safety, and we were hired to keep an eye on her. Christine and Alexander installed a good number of cameras on her narrowboat just yesterday – all the recordings are yours for the asking, of course. If there's anything we can do to help, we'll do it. I can tell you Pauline hasn't left her boat since yesterday afternoon. We've been watching her boat that whole time. I've spoken to Christine and she's trawling through the recordings from the cameras to check to see how on earth Pauline managed to end up in the water without me seeing her leaving her boat. I was…shocked to see what was happening. Saw them pull the body from the water myself.'

Mavis felt Llinos's arm around her shoulders. 'Mavis, like I said, I don't know the name of the victim, so don't go jumping to conclusions. Let me go and have a word with my boss, and I'll come back to you…if I can. Do you all mind waiting here for a bit?'

Mavis assumed that Annie and Tudor had agreed to stay, because she felt herself being steered – on surprisingly wobbly legs – toward a low wall. She was pleased to sit down, even though the wall was wet.

She said quietly, 'Sorry, Annie – I can only think I'm feeling so bad because my inattentiveness has, somehow, led to our charge losing her life. My entire professional career has been dedicated to saving lives, to bringing people comfort…and now…this. It's all my fault.'

'Oh, Mave, no it's not.'

Mavis was aware of being squashed by Annie's long arms, and felt her face get buried in her colleague's wet coat. It smelled vaguely of beer and…curry? She pushed Annie away. 'Sorry, Annie, but I can't breathe. Let me have my tea…and a moment to my own thoughts.'

She was glad that Annie and Tudor stood aside, even if they were whispering to each other. She felt herself warming from the inside, thanks to the tea, and gradually started to regain control of her limbs. A moment later she phoned Christine, for the second time. Her first words were: 'Anything on the camera feeds?' Mavis didn't have time for niceties.

'Hello Mavis, I'm in front of two screens, watching as fast as I can…but if I speed things up too much, I might miss something. Like I told you, I was keeping an eye on them all day, and I didn't see anything out of the ordinary.'

'The critical time was around four this afternoon. Have you looked at all the feeds from that time?' Mavis suspected she was snapping, but she felt snappish.

Annie drifted toward her, and asked, 'Chrissy seen anything useful?'

Mavis shook her head. 'Have you viewed all the feeds for the couple of hours before that, Christine?'

Christine replied sharply, 'We put twelve cameras in and on that boat. So, no, I haven't watched twenty-four hours' worth of recordings yet. You only asked me to do this twenty minutes ago.'

Mavis looked at the time on her phone. Had it really only been twenty minutes since she'd spoken to Christine?

She sighed. 'Ach, you're quite right, of course. Please phone me the minute you have something…anything.'

'Will do – now let me get on.'

Mavis looked up at Annie. 'She'll phone when she has something.'

Annie nodded. 'Another cuppa?'

Mavis declined. 'There aren't any public loos around here, so I'd better not, thank you. That one was probably enough. Oh look, there's Llinos. Let's see if she's got any news.'

Llinos motioned to Mavis and Annie to approach the police tape. She remained on the secure side of it. 'I've been cleared to tell you this much: the victim is not Pauline Thomas. She's still on her narrowboat, and is being questioned as a potential witness to what is still an undetermined incident.'

Mavis felt dizzy…she reached out, and felt Annie's arms around her. 'It's not Pauline? Our client's alive? Safe?' She looked up at Annie, who was beaming down at her. 'She's not dead, Annie.'

'Yeah, I heard. Mave. Thanks for that, Llinos – you can see how much that information means to…both of us.'

Mavis added, 'Whatever Christine might find on the camera feeds could still be useful to your investigation. When did the victim go into the water? I saw them pulling her out at about a quarter past four.'

Llinos nodded. 'That's yet to be determined, but it's clear that the body's not been in the water for days, or anything like that. So, when did you put up those cameras?'

Annie replied, 'Yesterday morning. Do you lot want all the recordings? Oh…hang on…my phone's going. Oh, it's Chrissy.'

Mavis was puzzled. 'She said she'd phone me if she had any news. Why's she phoning you?'

'Maybe she misdialed? I'll ask her. Hiya Chrissy, doll. Mave thought you were phoning her – and I've got Llinos here, too. Good news at this end – it wasn't Pauline they pulled out of the water…though, obviously, it's not good news for anyone who knew the actual dead woman, nor the dead woman herself. What have you found?'

Mavis waited as patiently as she could while Annie listened, her brow furrowing as she did so. She asked, 'What? What is it, Annie?'

Annie waggled an arm and said, 'What – all of them? All twelve?'

Mavis said, 'Put her on speakerphone, Annie.'

Annie waggled again. 'Right-o, I'll tell them. Nothing at all? Okay. I'll text you if they want them. Ta, doll.'

She disconnected.

Mavis asked quietly, 'What's wrong, Annie?'

Annie addressed both Mavis and Llinos. 'The cameras all functioned perfectly up until about an hour before the body was found – then all twelve feeds went blank. There's nothing at all after that time. And they haven't come back online yet. Christine can't explain it. Possibilities are: a power malfunction – some sort of surge that fried everything; or some sort of jamming device was employed, so the cameras stopped transmitting. There might still be recordings on the hard drives within the cameras themselves, if it wasn't a problem with the hardware…that's our only hope of there being anything to see. Llinos – you might want to tell your tech people about this. Christine asked me to text addresses or numbers to which she could send a plan of the boat showing installation points, so your people can get to all the hardware.'

Llinos's phone pinged. Mavis watched as she read a text, her brow furrowing as she did so.

Mavis liked this even less than when she'd been watching Annie do much the same thing. 'What is it, Llinos?'

The constable pocketed her phone. 'I can't say.'

Mavis and Annie exchanged a desperate glance.

Annie said, 'Go on, doll, it's us. You can tell us. We won't say a word.'

Llinos nibbled her upper lip. 'In the spirit of reciprocity – tell Christine to send all those recordings to me. Let me have your phone, Annie – I'll text her an address.'

'Then you'll tell us?' Mavis hoped the answer would be yes.

Llinos replied, 'Once I know those recordings are in my cloud. But I want to see them there before I say a word more.'

Mavis pulled out her phone and also texted Christine herself, making it clear she was to upload the recordings immediately.

They all waited. To Mavis, the minutes felt like hours. She felt her shoulders shudder when Llinos's phone pinged again, shuffled from foot to foot as the constable checked her screen, and could feel the anticipation build in her belly as Llinos nodded and smiled as she texted a reply.

'All done,' she said.

Mavis demanded, 'So what can you tell us?'

Llinos leaned in. 'Pauline Thomas was asked if she could identify the body. She could.' Llinos checked her phone again. 'She identified the woman as one Sylvia Jenkins, of Pontypool – a past client of hers. My colleagues made a quick search of records, and the ID appears to be correct. The thing is…Sylvia Jenkins was seeking to take out an anti-harassment injunction against your Pauline Thomas, via a solicitor in Pontypool…and Pauline Thomas was seeking one against Sylvia Jenkins via a solicitor in Brecon. I think you know Rhodri Lloyd?'

Mavis nodded. 'We've done a fair bit of work for him. Do they know anything more?'

Llinos shrugged. 'When confronted with this information, your Pauline said that Sylvia was trying to ruin her life. Pauline claimed that Sylvia had been scammed by a man with whom she'd formed a romantic attachment – which Sylvia claimed she'd never have done, had it not been for a reading that Pauline had given her. Pauline claims she hasn't been harassing Sylvia at all – that she's simply been responding to texts, emails, and online comments she's received from the woman, on a like-for-like basis. It might come as no surprise to you that Pauline's going to be taken to the station, to make a statement. My boss has his…suspicions, shall we say? But I didn't tell you any of this. Right?'

Mavis felt her strength return to her in an instant. 'So Pauline Thomas was taking legal action against a woman who's now been found dead, right beside her boat?'

Llinos nodded. 'Yes. It sounds a bit suspect to me.'

Mavis felt hot. 'Pauline was using us to…she lied to us….and…'

Annie grabbed Mavis's arm. 'Hang on, Mave – calm down. Maybe Pauline needed evidence of harassment. Maybe she believed this Sylvia

Jenkins was the one who was tripping her up, or pushing her over, or whatever, and Rhodri Lloyd told her she needed more than just suspicions? You can't deny she's managed to have a few too many accidents recently.'

'As you mentioned when you briefed me,' said Llinos.

Annie added, 'And you were pretty sharp there, too, Constable Trevelyan…getting us to send you all those recordings, when they might end up condemning our client.'

Llinos said, 'Annie – they'll only show the truth. And you're always telling me that's all any of us ever want. All of you WISE women work to bring the truth into the light, as I do.'

Mavis could tell Annie wasn't impressed with the constable's tactics. She checked, 'Your people will be taking Pauline away now, Llinos?'

Llinos smiled. 'We'll be as thorough as we can be at the scene, of course, and sometimes that means we're not exactly like greased lightning…so it might take a while, but it'll be done tonight, yes. I think they're going to treat the narrowboat as a possible crime scene, even though no crime has been determined. It's because of the litigious nature of the relationship between the victim and…well, a person who was literally found at the scene of an unexplained death.'

Mavis made a decision. 'Very well. You have the recordings, and we all have homes to get to. Annie – I'm perfectly fine to drive, though you might be so kind as to give me a lift to my car, which will save me a considerable walk. I'll give you directions. We'll say nothing about what you've told us, Llinos, outside our group…and we'll all accept that Tudor will tell no one, either.'

Tudor nodded toward Llinos, mimed zipping his mouth shut and tossed an invisible key into the darkness.

Mavis straightened her back, and felt much more herself when she said, 'We'll no' bother you any longer this evening, Constable Trevelyan. Thank you for your…professionalism.'

Once Mavis was safely installed in the back seat of Tudor's car, she announced, 'I'll admit that all this has unsettled me a great deal. At first, I'd feared a tragedy which would most certainly have called into question my professionalism, and possibly any future I might have had as an enquiry agent. Now it's plain that we face a tragedy of another sort: we've been dragged into a situation about which we were intentionally misinformed by a person who might well have resorted to violence, rather than seeking a legal resolution. I'm devastated by the thought of what that might do to our business reputation. If Pauline Thomas has been dealing with Rhodri Lloyd, maybe he can shed some light on the matter. I shall speak to him about this first thing in the morning. Leave it to me.'

CHAPTER THIRTEEN

Stephanie Twyst was enjoying motherhood a great deal. She was keenly aware that her experience was being cushioned by the knowledge that – when it came to advice, help, or supplies – anything she or her son required could be provided, and that it would always be the best of its type. Such were the enormous advantages of her having become a duchess, and her son being a future duke. However, as she gazed at her darling baby Hugo, her feelings were purely that of a mother toward a beloved child: she felt absolutely and utterly responsible for him in every way, and loved him with a deep devotion, and fervor. Whatever her circumstances might have been, Stephanie knew her child's interests would have been her highest priority.

However – as a duchess – there were other people, and matters, that also required her attention, and she had recently begun to feel that she was being stretched too thinly, without the emotional or physical capability to be as attentive to her son as she'd have liked, nor to really be able to…enjoy him.

And her husband wasn't helping matters.

Stephanie loved Henry, that much was true, and she more than accepted his foibles; indeed, they were a part of his charm. But his relationship with his sister had always been a challenge, and just this past half an hour as the couple was dressing for dinner had shown her that Henry's antipathy toward his sibling was developing to include her husband – a man of whom Stephanie possessed as little knowledge or experience as her spouse.

Stephanie removed Hugo's foot from his mouth, and marveled at his perfect little toes, just as Henry said, 'And that's the thing…Clemmie never understands how her flightiness impacts others.'

Stephanie considered a sharp retort, then satisfied herself with a more measured answer. 'Henry – Julian has asked to speak to you, not skin you alive. You have no idea what he wants to speak to you about. If you occupied your mind with other things, you might not dwell on the prospect of one conversation with your brother-in-law so much.'

Realizing immediately that her tone had been much sharper than she'd intended it to be, she added hurriedly, 'I'm sorry to speak so bluntly, dear, but I hate to see you working yourself up into such a state over this. I wish you could set the matter to one side until we know what we're dealing with. We discussed this at dinner last evening, and we're simply repeating ourselves. We could talk about something else. Indeed, I suggest we should. What about the gentleman your mother's bringing to dine with us, for example?'

Henry muttered, the way he always did when his feelings had been hurt, 'I don't know anything about the man, other than that he's even more ancient than Mother. They used to dance together, that's all I know.'

'Your mother's rarely spoken, in detail, about her time on the stage. Maybe we'll find out some secrets from her past with this chap on the scene. Is he staying for a couple more days?' Stephanie asked.

Henry fiddled with his tie. 'Until the New Year, I think.'

Stephanie was surprised. 'That long? Good heavens, when Mrs Davies Cleaning said she'd have to allocate some additional help to cover extra duties at the Dower House, I imagined she meant only for a brief period. So he'll be here through Christmas? While Clementine and Julian, as well as my parents, will be here at the Hall?'

Henry rolled his eyes at his wife's reflection, while she applied her lipstick. 'Apparently. "'Tis the Season" and all that.'

'Not that Mum and Dad will mind – they just want some quality time with Hugo. I shouldn't imagine that you and I will see a great deal of them.'

Henry sounded sullen when he said, 'I hope things are a great deal less…momentous…than when they were last beneath our roof.'

'I agree.' Stephanie could have said much more, but didn't see the point. 'So this chap's a great friend of your mother's? I don't think anyone's even told me his name. Do you know it, dear? Is he someone we should know something about?'

Henry was regarding the final effect of his labors in the grand mirror in the corner of his dressing room. 'Arthur Feathers – I think that's it. Featherson? Something to do with turkeys, anyway.'

'Pardon?'

Henry smiled; Stephanie judged he was pleased with his appearance. 'When Mother told me, I recall thinking that his was the sort of name one would give to a turkey in a children's book.'

Stephanie sighed. 'Not terribly helpful, Henry. Anyway – we'd better get Hugo down to the library, and installed in his pram, ready for drinks. They'll be here in a few moments.'

'I say, you look rather wonderful tonight, my dear. That burgundy dress is one of my favorites…but you have even more than your usual rosy glow about you.'

Stephanie felt her face get warm. Henry's compliments were so genuinely spontaneous that they touched her heart every time. 'Thank you, dear. I'm trying a new shade of lipstick, which might account for it. But I have to make something of an effort, because my husband cuts such a dashing figure, don't you know.'

It was a beaming duke and duchess who descended to dinner, with Stephanie taking great care as she carried Hugo to his pram, which was ready and waiting in the Great Hall. Once he was comfortably tucked in, she wheeled him into the library, and accepted the ginger beer she'd requested from Edward, just as Althea and her guest entered, accompanied by a happily yapping McFli.

'And how's my handsome grandson this evening?' Althea rarely acknowledged either her own son, or Stephanie, before she cooed over Hugo. Stephanie rather liked that; it was as it should be.

Althea added, 'Come and meet Hugo, Ossie. Isn't he edible? Especially those cheeks of his. Henry's were much the same at this age, I recall.'

The man did as Althea had instructed, which gave Stephanie a chance to look him over, before they were introduced. His dinner suit was a little shiny, and tight; his shoes had been polished for many years; his bow tie was large, and patterned in purple and green; his 'hair' had to be a toupee, because a head that age didn't grow a thatch that lush, nor that shade. Stephanie felt apprehensive, but wasn't sure why.

Althea was certainly attired appropriately for what was, essentially, a family gathering with an honored guest, though Stephanie thought it unfortunate that Althea's copper taffeta ballon skirt was almost exactly the same shade as her escort's 'rug', while the dowager's purple blouse and jade jacket appeared to reflect the colors of the man's bow tie; the overall effect was to make the pair look unsettlingly 'couple-like'. Stephanie didn't like how that made her feel.

She was somewhat pleased that Henry seemed to be oblivious to her inner turmoil when he said, 'So tell us how you two first met, Mother?'

Althea had taken a seat, relinquishing her spot beside Hugo to the man accompanying her. She was holding a glass of sherry with her little finger poking out – which Stephanie knew for a fact was something the dowager never did. Indeed, Althea had remarked upon others she'd seen do the same thing and accused them of an 'affectation'. Stephanie also noted that Althea was just a little more declamatory than usual in her manner of speech, and was waving her arms about a great deal as she recounted her nerves when she'd auditioned for a certain stage role, and the wondrous way in which she'd felt herself blossom in the arms of such a gifted dance partner.

Althea closed her reminiscences with: 'By the way, Ossie, you'll have gathered that this is my son Henry, and his wife Stephanie, but I haven't introduced you properly yet. This is the great Oswald Featherington, once of London's West End, now semi-retired to the delights of Brighton. We were confidantes almost sixty years ago, and I don't think he's changed a bit since then.'

The man replied, 'Oh Alth, you flatter me.'

Stephanie was taken aback. *Alth*? She glanced at her husband, who looked as though he'd heard McFli speaking – at least, he was staring at the dog, and his mouth was moving, but nothing was coming out.

Fortunately, the gong sounded, and Stephanie was able to begin to fuss over Hugo and his pram, and encourage Althea and Oswald – she didn't intend to refer to the man as 'Ossie' – to make their way through to dinner, leaving Henry clutching his tumbler of Scotch, and eyeing the bottle.

'Come along, Henry dear,' she called, bouncing the pram gently as she pushed it. 'We don't want anything to get cold, do we?'

Henry's flat delivery of: 'It's smoked trout terrine,' wasn't helpful.

When the foursome was finally installed at the dinner table, and Edward had receded into the background, Stephanie felt she should take control of the conversation, because the look of dumbfounded incredulity hadn't left her husband's face since the Featherington person had referred to the duke's mother as 'Alth'. Stephanie felt that suggested a level of intimacy between the pair she hadn't expected. She didn't dare imagine what might be running through her husband's head, but believed the only way to get him to snap out of it was to focus the conversation on the present, and the future, rather than allowing the entire evening to become a litany of remembered, and shared, moments.

She decided to open the conversation. 'I understand you'll be staying for an extended period, Oswald. Is this a welcome escape from the cold seaside air to the less bracing climes of the countryside?'

'Good God, no,' said Oswald, having already all but polished off his first course. 'I'm here for the panto, of course.'

Althea said, '*Mother Goose.*' Her tone suggested it should explain everything.

From Stephanie's point of view, it just made the situation more opaque. She raked through dim memories of her annual trips to the theater to hiss and boo at the panto baddies, cheer the principal boy's high jinks, and scream, 'He's behind you!' when the 'baddie' loomed over the 'goodie', threatening harm. No, she couldn't recollect that one at all.

She said, '*Mother Goose*…the pantomime?'

'Yes dear,' said Althea. 'It's the least offensive and morally confusing of all of them. Revolves around an old woman thinking her life will be a bed of roses if only she were rich and beautiful. Needless to say, she discovers that's a load of twaddle, and that love, family, and community are worth more than a bulging purse, or the smoothest skin and most luscious lips. It's quite…uplifting.'

Stephanie asked, 'And you're going to appear in a local production of this, Oswald?' She still couldn't put two and two together.

Oswald had vacuumed up his entire dish before he replied, 'I shall produce, direct, and choreograph the production, and Alth has asked me to tweak my original script so that it better suits its Welsh bucolic setting. Lots of local jokes, that sort of thing.'

Stephanie looked at her mother-in-law, who was dimpling alarmingly, and said, 'Althea – please explain.'

Althea tutted. 'I thought I'd mentioned that I was hoping to mount a pantomime to be performed in the village hall. Oswald will facilitate, as he explained.'

Henry finally entered the conversation with a terse: 'You mentioned no such thing, Mother. I should have remembered if you had. Do you also have a collection of wandering troubadours coming to stay at the Dower House to mount said production, Oswald?'

'The people from Anwen-by-Wye will be in it, dear,' said Althea sweetly.

Finally, Stephanie and Henry's eyes met, and she could see the panic he felt. She had to take control.

She ventured, 'What a wonderful idea, Althea. So…Oswald will cast the parts, then plan and rehearse the production, I see. I dare say you have detailed plans in place already, Oswald. Please do tell us about them. Henry, I think you can ring for the main course now, dear. It's lamb with a port wine reduction, roasted root vegetables, and mashed potatoes. You'll enjoy it very much, I'm sure.'

She was pleased to see her husband perk up a bit. 'Indeed, I shall.'

Althea commented, 'What a shame, Clementine adores lamb, and we can't possibly have it twice in two nights. What shall we have for dinner tomorrow, when she and Jools are here?' She turned to Oswald. 'Did I mention that my daughter and son-in-law arrive tomorrow? We can all dine together. Won't that be fun?'

Stephanie noticed that Oswald didn't even try to hide his eagerness to have his empty plate replaced with a fresh one that was to be covered with more food. As his eyes danced from one serving dish on the sideboard to another, he said absently, 'But Alth, I'll be holding auditions tomorrow evening, at the village hall from five until nine, remember?'

'Oh drat, that's right,' said Althea, sounding much more disappointed than Stephanie might have expected, or hoped. 'Ah well, you'll be here until Christmas, so we'll have lots of opportunities for many get togethers. One more, or less, won't make a difference.'

Stephanie had an actual physical sense of her spirits falling, and the look on Henry's face suggested to her that he was experiencing much the same, despite the way that Edward was drizzling sauce over his lamb and vegetables.

Althea kicked off the dinner conversation. 'I've suggested to Ossie that he considers Marjorie Pritchard to be stage manager; what do you think, Stephanie? You know her current capabilities better than I.'

Stephanie chewed a piece of parsnip as she considered exactly what she should say about the idea.

16th DECEMBER

CHAPTER FOURTEEN

Mavis had endured a poor night's sleep and a challenging day, and the dismal prospect of having to take tea with Althea and her 'good old chum Ossie' was on the horizon, making her feel as though she were staring into an abyss. She decided that the only antidote was to convene a full meeting of the women of the WISE Enquiries Agency. She'd been planning to type up a report of her day's findings and email it to everyone, but realized she could possibly avoid tea if she organized an online get-together.

Via Ian Cottesloe, she passed word to Althea that she had a pressing business engagement so would take tea in her room; she suspected the dowager would hardly miss her presence, given her embroilment with all things theatrical. Having sent emergency texts, Mavis filled her time as she waited for replies trying to find a pair of small sewing scissors that her late mother had given her; shaped like a stork, the long, thin bill of the creature created by the blades was exactly the sort of shape suitable for snipping off hard-to-reach ends of cotton – which was just what she'd spotted inside the lapel of her trusty gaberdine. She rummaged through every drawer in her room, seeing the object in her mind's eye so clearly that she knew it had to be there…somewhere. Her frustration grew exponentially when it dawned on her that it was the only pair of scissors she possessed that could do the job.

When a 'ding' alerted Mavis to activity on her laptop, Carol appeared seated behind her new desk, in her new home office. The rather overwhelming – if artistically pleasing – blue version of William Morris's 'Strawberry Thief' wallpaper behind Carol was something Mavis realized she'd eventually become accustomed to seeing…and something the entire team had agreed was an apt background for a member of an investigative agency to use.

Christine's background told Mavis she was using her laptop while sitting on the sofa in her apartment above the office, while Annie was at her kitchen table, in her flat above the Coach and Horses pub.

Mavis welcomed everyone. 'Thank you all for agreeing to this impromptu gathering. I thought it best to speak to you all, so I could convey the facts as I have them, with their proper weight.'

Annie quipped, 'Sure you're not trying to get away from that Ossie bloke, Mave?'

Mavis had great admiration for Annie's powers of perception – except when they were used against her. 'I might manage to have tea with the pair of them yet,' she replied, as noncommittally as possible.

Carol noted, 'He's made quite a splash down here in the village, I know. Even my dad said he might go to the auditions this evening.'

'How are your parents settling in, Carol?' Mavis thought she'd better ask.

Carol lowered her voice. 'They brought…well, a bit more stuff with them than I'd imagined they would. But we're still not sure how long it's going to take them to find somewhere to live, now that they've sold the farm. So I suppose Mam's right when she says they'll need a good selection of clothes but…no, I'm sure things will sort themselves out. David's in his office doing an online trawl for the sort of place they say they want, which might bring up a few more alternatives than the two they got the details about from an estate agent in Swansea.'

Annie chipped in. 'Tudor says he's heard good things about those flats down at the Swansea Marina…nice location, though there's some sort of scandal about some of them not being watertight, so tell Dave to be careful about that when he's recommending places.'

Carol chuckled, 'Thanks, Annie – I'll pass that on…to Dav*id*. Anyway – I've got loads of stuff here I can talk about regarding Pauline Thomas's online life, most of which I emailed to you all yesterday afternoon, before the…developments. But do you want to speak first, Mavis? How did it go with Rhodri Lloyd this afternoon, when you saw him at his office?'

Mavis rearranged her shoulders at the recollection of the meeting. 'Aye, mebbe it's best I do. I have to say, before I begin, that I've found the past twenty-four hours to be something of a worrying time, but now, I believe, we have a way ahead. Let me begin with this: Pauline Thomas is no longer our client, but Rhodri Lloyd is. He has agreed to act as Pauline's solicitor in the matter of the police investigation into the death of Sylvia Jenkins. He has retained our services to gather data that might help him better represent his client's interests.'

Mavis saw Annie lean toward her camera. 'Are they charging Pauline with murder?'

'No, because no murder has been proven,' replied Mavis tartly. 'There hasnae been a post-mortem, yet, meaning they don't even know how the poor woman died. So let me be clear in this – what we know, so far, is what follows: Pauline was seeking an injunction against Sylvia, and vice versa, each woman claiming that the other was harassing them. Rhodri Lloyd had, indeed – as you surmised last evening, Annie – instructed Pauline that she would need evidence of harassment in order for her application to succeed, and that was why Pauline retained our services. She has told Rhodri that she did not inform us of this additional reason for our investigations because she didn't want to sway our findings. Everything I am about to tell you is information that Rhodri's client – Pauline Thomas – has given him permission to share with us. It is, needless to say – though I am, in fact, saying it – completely confidential. Understood?'

All three heads nodded.

Mavis continued, 'Very well. Pauline claims that many of the online taunts, bad reviews, and downright unpleasant comments she's been bombarded with came from the now deceased Sylvia. The information that Carol sent to us yesterday does not – on its face – bear that out, though I know she has more to tell us today, and we'll get to that. But, by way of background, what I have learned from my meeting with Rhodri today is this: approximately nine months ago, Pauline Thomas took on Sylvia Jenkins as a client, when Pauline's narrowboat was berthed close to Sylvia's home in Pontypool. Pauline was asked by Sylvia to give her readings pertaining to her love life, which Pauline says is not unusual. Sylvia Jenkins was a divorcée in her late forties, and was trying to decide if she should launch herself into the world of online dating. Pauline says she worked with Sylvia through a number of alternative reading methods, including Tarot cards, tea leaves, rune stones, and crystal-gazing. I suggest that we don't discuss our feelings about the usefulness of any of these methods, but stick to what concerns us…which is that – in every instance – Pauline says that the indications were that Sylvia would open herself to positive new opportunities if she took the leap. Which is what Pauline claims is exactly what she told Sylvia. Pauline has stressed to Rhodri that she also warned Sylvia that she would have to use her sharpest judgment about her decision-making when it came to potential partners. This is the basis for Pauline's claim that she cannot be held responsible for anything that happened to Sylvia after she chose which man to communicate with once she'd joined a dating app…nor for what transpired as a result of that selection.'

Christine asked, 'Any concrete evidence of Pauline actually having done that, Mavis? Does Pauline record her sessions, for example?'

Mavis sighed. 'The sessions are private, so not recorded in any way, except in terms of notes that Pauline makes – in some sort of code of her own making – in a notebook; this to aid her should she ever see a client again after a period of time has elapsed. The police have the notebook. Other than that – if the notebook actually helps at all – there was no evidence of exactly what Pauline said to Sylvia…though it would appear from what Sylvia said to her solicitor that she claimed she received no such "supplementary" advice from Pauline.'

Annie said miserably, 'She-said, she-said, with one of the "shes" being dead, and the other one on the scene where the body was found. Not looking good for Pauline, is it, Mave?'

Mavis tutted. 'It's no' looking too promising, I'll grant you – but that's where we come in. Rhodri's shared more details of the situation in which Sylvia Jenkins found herself embroiled: Sylvia had an angry confrontation with Pauline and told her some of what follows, and Rhodri's own enquiries with Sylvia's solicitor in Pontypool have unearthed the rest. The "facts" gathered by these means are that Sylvia did, indeed, join the online dating community, via an app-based private service, and found herself faced with several potential "matches". The specific process then involved her deciding whether to open communications with any or all of the potential matches – the suggestion made by the service being that all communication should begin online, and progress until the participants felt they were ready to meet in person. Rhodri has checked the "Terms and Conditions" of using this particular company, and they quite clearly state that they are not responsible for anything that transpires as a result of connections made through their service; they have "completely covered their backsides against any eventuality" was the phrase Rhodri used. Sylvia Jenkins chose to communicate with two of the contacts she was offered. With one man, the communication fizzled out rapidly, with another it reached a point where Sylvia agreed to meet him face to face. The assignation took place at a pub in Cardiff, at lunchtime; the dating service in question suggested parameters that might make initial personal contact "safer" for their users, so Sylvia picked a large pub near the rugby ground, because she'd been there before matches, in the past, and felt safe there. Approximately two weeks after that date, Sylvia Jenkins had "loaned" the man she'd met approximately seventy-five thousand pounds – which she believed would allow him to complete a cash purchase of a house on the outskirts of Pontypool; he told her he had the rest of the money required. Sylvia obtained the sum by taking out a second mortgage on her own home. She handed a bankers' draft for the amount to the man, in person, at the same pub where they'd originally met. The man, and the money, disappeared. Despite numerous attempts to track him down, Sylvia quickly realized that the man "didn't exist" in the way he'd portrayed himself. Believing she would get back the money that she'd loaned the man – when the sale of his existing property in Cardiff had been successfully completed – she'd over-extended herself. Her threats to Pauline began when it became clear she would lose her home, which she did just a matter of weeks ago.'

'Gordon Bennett, Mave – she gave a bloke she'd only met once something that's basically as good as cash? How could she possibly claim that's Pauline's fault?'

Mavis shrugged.

Carol said, 'A banker's draft means he needed a bank account in the name of the person the draft was made out to. What was the name?'

Mavis said, 'Llew Merton.'

Carol said, 'Not such a common name. There must have been a way for Sylvia to trace him, via his bank.'

Mavis said, 'Rhodri's not very clear about what Sylvia did and didn't do to try to locate the missing Llew Merton; he only knows what Pauline told him…which she says she was told by Sylvia. I dare say that a detailed report of what steps she'd taken was not top of Sylvia's mind when she accosted Pauline at a craft fair, where "Madame Paulina" was plying her trade…which is where the confrontation took place, by the way.'

Christine said, 'So, in a nutshell…this bloke – Llew Merton – got away with Sylvia's money, Sylvia eventually lost her home, and blamed Pauline for her situation. Then Sylvia mounted this campaign against Pauline…and was found dead in the water, close to Pauline's narrowboat yesterday afternoon. Well, isn't that just grand.'

'A fair summation,' said Mavis. 'Carol, have you been able to make any progress since I informed you of Sylvia Jenkins' identity? Have you been able to gain any online insights that would support Pauline's claims that Sylvia was the source of all the complaints, poor reviews, and so forth, with which she was bombarded online? Or, maybe, have you been able to confirm this was definitely not the case?'

Carol nodded. 'Okay, you've all got what I sent yesterday, before I knew about Sylvia Jenkins' existence…or her death. I won't repeat what I said in my report, but you could all see that I confirmed Pauline's claims that she was receiving an unusually high level of negative reviews and comments, and that many were also high on the "angry" scale. Once Mavis informed me of Sylvia's name, I did a bit more digging, and analyzed the data I'd collected in a different way. And, no, Annie, I won't bore you with any of the technical details, so don't panic about that. I know that all you want is to hear my results.'

Mavis watched with satisfaction as Carol and Annie shared a grin of fellowship.

Annie said, 'Go on then, doll…do your thing.'

Carol winked. 'There are clusters I can spot, sent from a few locations – which I mentioned in my report – but maybe the fact that one of the locations is a library in Pontypool takes on new significance, now that we know that's where Sylvia Jenkins lived. These particular clusters of posts were all created during library opening hours, which, of course, isn't a surprise, but I've also identified other clusters posted later in the evenings, which were made from two other addresses. It took me some time to find them, but I can tell you that one is a pub in Cwmynyscoy, the other a café in Griffithstown – both of which are suburbs of Pontypool. Since I got her name, I've also trawled Sylvia Jenkins' socials. If you check your inboxes, you'll find the best photos I've been able to find of her. I've also established that she belonged to many online groups, some of which were also groups in the real world, often involved, in some way, with walking, hiking, or rambling. At least, she was active within their online presence until about seven months ago – which lines up with what Mavis has told us. Since then, she's been exceptionally quiet, and even unresponsive, online.'

Mavis anxiously opened the file Carol had sent, and found herself gazing at the slightly blurred figure of a woman who was wearing wintry attire and a large backpack, standing beside a stone wall with a clear sky above her. She was of middling height and weight, and had mid-brown hair poking out from beneath a bobble hat. Yes, she was smiling for the camera, but was unremarkable in any way…except for the fact that it was her body Mavis had seen being hauled out of the water the previous day.

Mavis said, 'Thank you, Carol. Your newer findings suggest that it probably was – or at least could arguably have been – Sylvia creating those clusters of online trolling that you've identified. If Pauline had only been more transparent when she briefed us, we might have been able to discover this earlier, thereby preventing…whatever transpired yesterday. Though, of course, we do not yet know what happened, and we mustn't make assumptions. I'll pass all this to Rhodri. Before we open the floor, is there anything else, Carol?'

Carol shook her head. 'I know my way around banking systems, but I don't think I stand much chance of finding out anything useful about a man, possibly named Llew Merton, from – again possibly – the Cardiff area. But there might be avenues Rhodri could pursue, via the dating service, for example. They might have information that could be used to locate Merton that Rhodri could access – information that would not have been available to either Sylvia, or myself. If they choose to cooperate, he might be able to get something useful quite quickly. If they want to put barriers in his way to slow things down, they could.'

Mavis said, 'He told me that he's already taken steps on that front, given the nature of Pauline's situation. He – and I dare say, we – believe that tracing this Llew Merton might be of use only insofar as it might throw light on whether Sylvia ever managed to connect with him again after she'd told Pauline about having lost touch with him…though, I have to say, I think it unlikely.'

Annie said, 'Even if we could find him, what's the point of that, Mave? Do you think…what, that Sylvia found him and then…he shoved her into the waterway right where Pauline's boat was berthed? I mean that's…well, to say it would be a "coincidence" would be stretching even that word's use.'

Mavis said, quite bluntly, 'Pauline has instructed Rhodri to tell us that she believes that finding this man will help clear her of any possible charges in this case. Rhodri was…less than supportive of Pauline's assertions, but has passed them on. He hasnae choice. He muttered something about her having a "revelation" while in custody. His tone suggested to me that Pauline had used tea leaves, or some such, to come up with the idea. However, I cannae say more than what he's told me, so – whatever Pauline's reason for doing it – Rhodri, has instructed us that we should make our best efforts to trace the Merton person.'

Christine asked, 'Our fortune teller's "revelation" aside, what's Pauline told Rhodri about what happened yesterday afternoon, Mavis?'

Mavis replied, 'Pauline's story is that she was in her narrowboat from the time I helped her there after her "fall" two days ago until she emerged to investigate why she could hear sirens. She claims she's not seen Sylvia Jenkins since the woman accosted her at that craft fair, and had no idea why Sylvia would have ended up dead at all, let alone where she did. This is what she's told the police, and Rhodri.'

Annie asked, 'Who found the body, Mave? My money's on a dog walker, but Chrissy reckons a jogger. What about you, Car – any bets?'

Carol smiled. 'I think you two've picked the leading contenders.'

Mavis managed a wan smile. 'I'm sorry to disappoint you, ladies. On this occasion, it was a small child and his grandfather who spotted the body. They were trying to find "treasure" with a large magnet on a rope which they let down into the water. They were making their way along the towpath and…encountered the remains. I gather that the child was less upset about the discovery than the grandfather, who phoned the emergency services and took his grandson for an ice cream. I also understand that the first sighting was just the other side of the bridge, so it would have been out of my sight.'

'Does that mean the body drifted on a current until it reached Pauline's boat?' Annie sounded eager. 'If it did, it could have gone into the water some way away from where it was found, right? Car – can you find out about currents and so forth along that stretch of water?'

Carol replied, 'A map of the area shows me that all that's beyond that bridge is a wider part of the canal – a sort of turn-around spot, I suppose, for the boats – and then it ends. I can't see why there'd be any particular current from that end.'

'How's that Albert of yours, Carol?' Surprised, Mavis turned to see Althea standing in the doorway with a winsome smile on her face, and a piece of cake on a plate in her hand. The dowager added, 'I brought this for you, Mavis. I didn't want you to miss out on Cook Davies's seed cake. I say, Carol, nice wallpaper. Is that your new office? And does that mean I won't see anything more of young Albert when you're videoconferencing with Mavis?'

Mavis wanted to ask Althea why she hadn't knocked before coming into her room; Mavis valued her privacy, but had to admit that she was no more than a long-term guest in Althea's home – the dowager could go where she pleased, whenever she chose. For the first time ever, Mavis considered the idea of locking her door; it had the ability to be locked – maybe she should find out if a key existed.

Carol giggled. 'Thanks, Althea. It's very nice wallpaper, courtesy of the Chellingworth Estate, and put up about twenty years ago, I believe. There's a lot of life left in it yet; I don't think this room was used much by…anyone. It's pristine. And, yes, one of the marvels of having my parents to stay is that I'm in here, David's in his office, and Albert's being spoiled rotten by his grandparents, who finally have a chance to get to know him properly – and just as his personality is starting to show, too. The only member of our family who hasn't worked out that we're much better set up here than at the last house is poor old Bunty…who misses her Aga, and can't seem to decide on what will become her spot. Though, being a calico cat, my money's on that being whatever she decides is the comfiest place in the house.'

Althea placed the cake beside Mavis's laptop. 'Do give them all my love, Carol. I look forward to meeting your parents…soon, I trust.'

Carol asked, 'Are you going to the auditions later on with Oswald Featherington?'

Althea dimpled. 'Wouldn't miss it for the world.'

Carol chuckled. 'In that case, you might meet at least my dad. He said he fancied the idea of getting involved with the panto; they don't know how long they'll be with us, see, so Mam and Dad both decided to throw themselves into things, so they don't feel like "just visitors". Until they can find a suitable place to buy.'

Mavis could feel the excitement radiating off Althea's small body. 'Oh yes, that's such a good idea. Ossie said I can help him with the casting, and I'm sure it'll be great fun. I've only ever experienced it from the other side of things, when it's a tortuous business. It has to be much easier to choose, than to hope to be chosen.'

Mavis muttered, 'We need to get on, please, Althea. Will you no' need to be getting ready for this evening, anyway?'

Althea looked down at herself. 'Why? Will this not do?'

The dowager's bottom half looked as though it were about to saddle a horse – at least, Mavis assumed the peculiar khaki trousers were jodhpurs – whereas her top half appeared to be heading to a summer day's garden party, that being the impression given by her hyacinth blue, floral, chiffon blouse.

Mavis thought it best to say, 'Will you no' be a wee bit chilly in the village hall like that, Althea?'

Althea tutted. 'Don't be silly. I have a coat, Mavis. That red woolen one is rather jolly, don't you think?'

'Aye,' said Mavis, wondering how a knee-length coat and jodhpurs would work. 'But we do need to get on, here, if you don't mind.'

Althea peered at Mavis's notes. 'Is it an interesting case?'

Mavis snapped, 'Althea – you're fully involved with this panto thing, can you no' let us get on with our work, please, dear?' Althea pouted, but Mavis determined she would not be swayed. 'Besides, it's all highly confidential, dear, best you don't know.'

Althea twiddled her fingers toward Mavis's screen. 'Very well; if you think I don't know how to keep a secret, I know where I'm not wanted. Tell your father to introduce himself to me this evening, Carol.'

Mavis was glad to see the back of the dowager, and even more pleased when the woman closed the door firmly after she'd left. She said, 'Where were we?'

'I think we need to decide who's doing what, next,' said Carol. 'And while my parents might be happy to be with Albert, I can tell – even up a flight of stairs and through a closed door – that he's losing interest in them. So, let's make a plan, please.'

Mavis said, 'Right. Carol, please continue with your online efforts to see if you can finesse any of the information you already have, now that we know about Sylvia Jenkins, and Llew Merton.'

Carol grinned. 'Already ongoing. I have an idea that might let me at least see what Llew Merton looks like, even if we don't know who he really is…but it might not work out, so I'm not going to promise what I might not be able to deliver.'

Mavis thanked Carol and wished her luck. 'Christine: liaise with Rhodri regarding our camera recordings, please. He wants them all. And maybe find out if there are any other cameras in the vicinity?'

Christine replied, 'Yes, I can do that. And I'm continuing to go through everything we captured, in case there's something helpful. I'll also try to find out when we can get our kit back, then arrange with Alexander to collect it.'

Mavis added, 'And Annie — while I liaise with Rhodri and feed information to everyone as it arises — could you please take the photograph that Carol found of Sylvia Jenkins and find out if anyone around the general canal area saw her, either on the day of her demise, or at any time beforehand. You're so good at that.'

Annie chuckled, 'Sure, Mave — I'll get Tude to drive me over there, and pick me up.'

Mavis tutted, 'Annie, your inability to drive is a real problem for us, on occasion. I don't know how often I have to raise the topic, but I feel I must, once again.'

Carol offered, 'I'll get you there and back, Annie. You don't have to drag Tudor away from the pub. We'll come up with a plan between ourselves, alright Mavis?'

Mavis had to accept Carol's suggestion. 'Right then, we can all make a fresh start in the morning. Please ensure you account for your hours in the usual manner, ladies; you know what a stickler Rhodri is for log sheets. Now — good afternoon, all.'

Mavis felt the meeting had gone rather well, then bit into her seed cake, as she wondered if she might have used her stork-shaped sewing scissors downstairs at any point, and that maybe Althea had 'acquired' them. She'd ask…but not until tomorrow.

CHAPTER FIFTEEN

Henry was pacing in front of the library fireplace. Upon the arrival of his sister and brother-in-law at Chellingworth Hall just before luncheon, Julian had whispered, 'After tea, in the library,' as he shook Henry by the hand, and half-hugged him.

It had been an awkward moment for many reasons, not the least of which was that Henry was contemplating a marked difference in his sister's appearance since he'd last seen her: she looked as though she were in training to become a nun, so plainly was she attired. He wasn't sure he'd even been aware that her natural hair color was gray-brown, nor that her skin, without make-up, was so…sallow.

His sister's altered appearance, his screaming son, his hugging brother-in-law hissing at him about what sounded like a lovers' tryst…it had all pushed him off balance in the most irritating way. And now here he was – waiting, and pacing.

Eventually, Julian loped in, then made sure the door was properly closed behind him. He approached Henry with the threat of another hug gleaming in his eyes; Henry wasn't a small man, by any measure nor dimension, but Julian dwarfed even him, so bear-like was he in appearance. Henry noted that he'd regrown his full, bushy beard since his nuptials, and thought the man looked rather better with it than without. But hugging was not something with which Henry felt comfortable, so he stuck his thumbs into the pockets of his waistcoat, and made a stand at the hearth – all elbows – as he nodded toward a seat.

'Have the one nearest the fire, Julian. It's a chilly day.'

Julian took the seat offered. 'Not half as cold here as it is up at the house in Scotland. Not only is the weather a lot more fierce there, but I don't think there's a window or door that fits the hole it's supposed to fill in the entire place. I wear more clothes indoors there than I've ever done. Except when I'm actually in the smithy, of course, when I'm glad of a bit of cooling air.'

Henry wondered if he should enquire about how Julian's artisanal blacksmithing was going, but decided better of it. He replied to Julian's observation with a noncommittal, 'As you say, no doubt,' and rolled on his toes, to pass the time. Best to say nothing, he reckoned.

'Thanks for agreeing to talk to me,' began Julian.

Henry wanted to point out that he felt he'd been given no choice in the matter, but politeness demanded that he, once again, said nothing.

'I'm in a bit of a pickle, Henry. Totally bewildered, to be honest, and I don't know who else to turn to.'

Henry pulled a face that he hoped matched his words. 'I'm sorry to hear that. What's bothering you?'

Julian began, 'It's Clementine…'

Henry knew it: of course it was. It was always Clemmie's fault…whatever it was. He blurted out, 'What's she done now?' He hadn't meant to sound as angry as he did.

Julian seemed not to notice. He was studying his rather large feet. 'She's of an age…and I'm of an age…well, you know, we're both over fifty, so the idea never occurred to me…in my youth, then maybe…but I hadn't thought it possible…hadn't even considered it…'

Henry had no idea what the man was blathering about, but drew his own conclusions. 'Has she met someone else?'

Julian stared up at Henry, a look of shocked amazement on his face. 'Good God, Henry, no. Almost the exact opposite: she wants a baby.'

Henry's brain couldn't come to terms with what he'd heard. 'In what way do you mean?'

'Exactly,' was Julian's confounding reply. He sat mute, staring into the fire for what seemed like an age, with Henry hoping he'd explain. But he said no more.

Henry applied himself to thinking through possibilities: maybe Clemmie wanted to…no, there were no possible explanations. 'Do you mean she wishes to bear a child – conceive and be delivered of a child? At her age? Is that not…beyond the realm of possibility?'

Julian sighed. 'A Spanish woman gave birth when she was sixty-six, and two women in India did so in their seventies…it appears women are having children just for the heck of it well into their dotage.'

Henry noted the edge in his brother-in-law's voice. True, he hardly knew the chap, and conversations over a few lunches and dinners with the fiancé of a sibling were hardly the way to assess character, but Henry couldn't help but feel that Julian's obvious anxiety was not the norm for him. Henry reasoned that a blacksmith would be constantly hammering and beating hot metal, so must have many opportunities to vent their frustrations in a productive way – but it seemed that this topic had Julian on the ropes.

'So, to be clear, Clemmie actually wants to give birth to an actual baby?' Henry thought it best to check.

'Exactly.' More silence followed. Eventually, Julian exploded, 'I don't want children, Henry. I've never really wanted children. I didn't expect that a marriage at my age to a woman of Clementine's age would ever lead to children. I don't think that's an unreasonable assumption. Do you think that's an unreasonable assumption?'

Henry was immediately wary; he suspected that anything he said at this juncture might be hurled back at him, or shouted about him, at any future incendiary clash between his sister and her husband, or himself, and he didn't want to get caught in any crossfire.

Henry dared, 'Was the topic discussed in any way prior to your marriage?'

Julian returned his attention from the fire to his feet. 'Not as such.'

Henry pressed, 'Not at all? Never mentioned…not even in passing?'

Julian leaped out of the chair, giving Henry quite a start. 'No…not to my recollection. I mean she'd coo over bundles in pushchairs, but all women do that, don't they? I didn't think that was some sort of code. And now she's…well she's devastated that she hasn't got pregnant yet.'

Henry felt a sourness in the pit of his belly. His sister. Julian. The idea that… He found he'd uttered a quiet, 'How awful,' before he knew what had happened.

'So she says,' responded Julian, causing Henry even more perturbation. 'She's now insisting we seek medical intervention. What do you think, Henry? You're a new father. Well, Hugo's not one year old yet. And you're a little older than me. How is it? Or is it different for you? I mean, being the duke, did you always expect to…well, know you'd need to produce an heir. Is that why you did it?'

Henry wanted to crawl up the chimney. Or wake to find himself safe in bed, after having eaten too much cheese. But the fire crackled noisily in the hearth, and he'd not been able to find the Stilton he was sure Cook Davies was hiding from him somewhere in the kitchen, saving it until Christmas Day.

Henry sighed, and chose to face his fate head on. 'I fell in love with Stephanie, we married, and nature took its course. As for your situation, I honestly don't know what to say, Julian. Though, given Clemmie's age, when compared with Stephanie's, I rather think that seeking medical advice might be a good idea. The doctors might suggest that it would be unwise, or even impossible, for my sister to conceive.'

Julian added, 'Exactly what I said – but Clementine tells me there are ways around most of the aspects one might think would be a hurdle to conception. She's said she'd be open to using donated eggs to avoid the potential problems associated with relying upon her own, for example.'

Henry felt both hot and cold, simultaneously. He decided he had to speak up. 'This is all beyond my comprehension, Julian. It's clear to me that you and my sister have had some detailed discussions on the matter, and that you're both a great deal better informed than I about the…technicalities involved. Maybe my dear wife would be able to add to your process, but I fear I cannot. I have no insights whatsoever.'

'But you know your sister, Henry. Will she be swayed by science, or medicine, or even good old-fashioned common sense? Or will she never budge? Worse still, if I fight her on this, will I make her rush into something she might otherwise have had second thoughts about?'

Henry saw a straw, and grabbed at it. 'Ah, yes – Clemmie herself. I can help you with that. She's stubborn and fickle in equal measure, which is quite infuriating. You've already seen how she'll dig her heels in…but you might not have experienced how quickly she can be just as certain that she wants to do something else entirely. I'll be honest with you, Julian, and dare to let you know that I had wondered if you wanted to discuss a possible split with my sister – that she'd made it clear she was tired of playing house with you in the snowy wastes of

Scotland, and was going to leave you there to work at your ironmongery while she returned to the bosom of her loose-living art set in London. That wouldn't have surprised me at all…though I must admit I hadn't seen her desire to become a mother on the horizon. However, I dare say that none of us can really see into the future, can we?'

For some reason, Julian appeared to have been shocked by what Henry had said; the portion of his face that was visible above his whiskers was turning quite pink, Henry noticed. And he was clenching those enormous meaty fists of his, which never looked quite clean.

Henry didn't dare move backwards, fearing his rear end would be in danger from the flames, so he took a couple of hops to one side, putting a little space between himself and his brother-in-law. He ventured, 'I'm quite warm through, now, and I dare say it's time we repair to our respective apartments to prepare for dinner. You and Clementine will be joining us, I trust?'

Julian was still turning scarlet, and scowling, and clenching, when he muttered, 'Not this evening. We'll dine alone. Clementine is tired.'

Henry was delighted. He answered, 'Jolly good, so we'll see you tomorrow evening then.' He moved as swiftly as possible to the door, crossed the Great Hall without turning back, and took the stairs two at a time…until he couldn't manage that any longer.

Henry closed the door to the private suite of rooms designated as being for the exclusive use of himself, his wife, and his son, and leaned against it, panting, for a moment.

Stephanie was at his side in an instant. 'Don't slam about so, Henry – Hugo's asleep.'

'Sorry, dear.'

Stephanie stood back and hissed, 'Are you quite well, Henry? You look…stressed.'

Henry felt he had no choice but to take his wife into his confidence. 'Have you spoken to Clemmie, since she arrived?'

'I saw her arrival, as you know, but, other than that, no. I assumed we'd all dine together and catch up at the table. Is something the matter with Clementine? Where've you been?'

Henry took a seat and did his best to unburden himself. 'Julian wanted to speak to me, as you know, and I'm rather…bewildered. As is he. He tells me that my sister wants to have a baby – as in actually give birth to one. Herself. Julian doesn't think he's up for it. That's the gist.'

Henry was relieved to see an expression of incredulity appear on his wife's face. 'But, surely she's too old for childbearing, Henry. She's more the age to be pre-menopausal, or to even have started menopause. She's your junior by only three years. That's…not…do you mean she's undertaking special medical treatment to be able to have a child?' Stephanie sat beside her husband, and reached for his hand. 'This knowledge has unsettled you, hasn't it dear?'

Henry nodded. 'Julian says she's set on it, Stephanie. And you know what Clemmie's like when she's set on something. I suspect that Julian didn't see her sudden desire to move her entire life to Scotland from London as such, but that would be a good example. If this is only the second time he's seen Clemmie on a mission, maybe he's still not come to terms with how she operates. I've warned him of her nature, but – when I did – he appeared to start to…boil with anger. I fear this matter might be raised at the dinner table, tomorrow evening, when they join us. It'll just be us this evening, dear…so we have a little time before we might have to…discuss it. Clemmie and Julian appear to have investigated medical options, though not by consulting an actual physician. I fear their conversation might become rather…pictorial.'

Henry enjoyed watching his wife smile, and laugh…but not when he feared it was at his expense.

'Oh Henry, dear, you wouldn't be comfortable with that at all, would you? Well, maybe I can steer things in a direction that's theoretical, rather than practical, if the topic comes up. So was Julian seeking your input on how he should deal with Clementine in this matter?'

Henry shrugged, because he still wasn't terribly sure. 'He asked what it was like to become a father at a later stage in life, and then whether trying to dissuade Clemmie was a good idea. I told him that having Hugo in our lives was wonderful, and that telling Clemmie she shouldn't do something was likely to be counterproductive.'

'I think you did very well then, Henry, because that's exactly right – on both counts. But you should start to get ready for dinner, dear, because time's marching along. And let's cross our bridges when we come to them. We'll have to think about how best we can help with the…Case of the Bewildered Brother-in-Law, eh?'

Henry sighed. 'Not even slightly amusing, Stephanie.'

17ᵗʰ DECEMBER

CHAPTER SIXTEEN

Mavis was rather looking forward to her breakfast, and she wasn't even put off by the sight of Oswald Featherington already slathering butter onto toast when she entered the dining room.

'Good morning,' he called as Mavis considered her choice. 'And what a beauty it is.'

Mavis looked out at the heavy rain, and leaden skies. 'Aye, if you're a duck.'

'Even ducks deserve happiness, Mavis,' chided Oswald cheerily. 'Ah, there she is. Come along, Alth – it's not like you to be a slug first thing. Most important meal of the day, breakfast, right?'

Mavis glanced at Althea, who looked, she thought, a little pale. 'Are you feeling quite well?'

The dowager nodded, though without vigor. 'Not too bad. Ossie and I had a bit of a late night.'

'And a few warming brandies, eh?' Ossie chuckled.

Mavis felt concern for her friend; Althea was spry, and in good health for her age – but wasn't used to late nights and large quantities of brandy…though Althea was never short of an excuse or two to enjoy the odd tipple. Mavis suspected that Ossie poured with a heavy hand, and on a frequent basis. Maybe she shouldn't have avoided the pair when she'd heard them return the previous evening.

'I can't say that one late night will hurt, Althea, but you've had a few on the trot now. Maybe a light dinner and an early night tonight?' Mavis felt a duty of care toward the octogenarian for whom she had a deep, and genuine, affection.

Althea tutted. 'As long as the tea's good and strong this morning, I'll be tickety-boo, thank you Mavis. You don't need to fuss. How do you feel, Ossie? Any ill effects from that final drop of port you fancied?'

Mavis gave the man an acid look, which he didn't see because he was poking about in the jam pot. 'Is this strawberry, or raspberry?'

'It's blackberry and rhubarb, from the garden,' said Althea. 'Sounds awful, tastes heavenly. Try some. The sugar might help, but don't say I didn't warn you about that port.'

'I'm in the rudest of health, Alth. No need to worry on that count. Is that all you're having, Mavis? Still, I suppose a piece of dry toast is still better than porridge…which I believe you Scots are rather keen on.'

Mavis didn't react. 'How did the auditions go?' She suspected that all she'd have to do was start Oswald on the topic, and there'd be no stopping him, which would have the exact effect she desired: to not have to carry on a conversation with the man.

Oswald proved Mavis right by expounding about the hours he'd spent in 'Alth's' ethereal company, and of how he'd managed to do a good job of fulfilling all his casting requirements. He concluded, 'Of course, the titular role will be my own. It's the only panto where the dame is the lead, you know – best part for a panto dame ever written. I've given it before, and shall do it again. Too big a responsibility for an amateur to pick it up in such a short time.'

'Do you know all the characters in *Mother Goose*, Mavis?' Althea appeared sufficiently revived by her third cup of tea to join the conversation.

Mavis was enjoying the spoonful of scrambled eggs that she'd placed beside her 'dry toast', so shook her head. A mumbled, 'Mmh-hmm' was all she could manage.

Althea waved a hand. 'Never mind. Anyway, suffice to say that Ossie has his cast, and so many people are going to be in it, and it's been decided that Joan Pike and her mother Gwen will make the costumes; I didn't know that Gwen Pike had been a professional seamstress until that dreadful multiple sclerosis robbed her of the reliable use of her hands, did you, Mavis?'

Mavis admitted she hadn't.

Althea continued, 'And I'm going to talk to Henry about him painting the scenery.'

Mavis thought she'd misheard. 'Your Henry? To physically paint the scenery that will appear on the stage?'

Althea smiled. 'You know what a wonderful artist he is, and he's always complaining that he doesn't have enough time to paint. Well, if he volunteers to paint the scenery, he'll have an excuse to paint for days…and it'll do some good, too. Ossie's wonderful "Panto Package" already contains all the designs, because he knows what the production needs. I'm sure Henry will say yes. To his mother. Oh, and Marjorie Pritchard has been confirmed as stage manager. I have a feeling she'll be very good at it.'

Mavis wasn't at all sure what a stage manager did, but was glad she was going to be well out of the chaos that was bound to ensue. Marjorie and Oswald working together? She'd never met two people who thought they were so right, so often; she wondered what would happen when they disagreed. She dared to ask, 'Who else will be involved?'

Oswald said, 'I have a list, but I'm not familiar with everyone's names. Alth, you tell Mavis, there's a dear.'

Althea did. 'Elizabeth Fernley, and Emyr – Carol's father, who has the most delightful baritone, doesn't he, Ossie?'

Oswald nodded. 'The portly chap with the good voice? He'll go down well. I might ask him to do a good solo turn – I've noted that, and I'll speak to Wendy about adding in something suitable. End of the first act, I'd have thought.'

Althea looked surprised. 'Well, if you think so, but I'd have thought he'd do better as part of an ensemble. Carol's mother joined her husband at the auditions, Mavis – for a bit of support, you know – and she's going to be taking a small non-speaking part, too. Then there's Aled from the pub; he's got a good part – Mother Goose's son, and Sharon from the shop will play his girlfriend. Their wedding's the big finale. Young Ian Cottesloe will be very good in his role, and I know that Janet Jackson will probably overdo it, but she and our lovely Paul Baker did a duet last night that I have to say went down very well with everyone who was sitting about waiting to do their own bit. You said you'd make sure they got to do something together, didn't you, Ossie?'

Ossie laughed. 'That "retro" couple? Absolutely – hot as mustard those two. I might kick off the second act with them.'

Althea wittered on, 'Iris is going to be in it – but her part allows her to sit down all the time, and I managed to talk Tudor into being the prompt; it means he won't have to attend rehearsals, just sit in the wings with a script during the performance keeping up with what everyone's saying, and help them out if they forget their lines. Oh, and your Christine's Alexander said he'd supply some muscle for moving the scenery, and he's organizing the props, and sound – wasn't that it? Yes. Oh, and there's a chap from the woodworking barns at Chellingworth Hall who's going to do the sound with Alexander. Oh dear, even I've forgotten his name. Gary? Gareth? Grant? I think it's G-something.'

Mavis observed, 'It sounds as though almost everyone in the village will be involved. So who's going to actually pay to come to see it? There's no one left.'

Oswald cackled. 'That's where you come in, Mavis.'

Mavis stiffened. 'Me?'

Althea dimpled. 'You know all the money we make is going to the MacDonald Trust…so I thought you'd be the best person to put in charge of ticket sales.'

Mavis sat back in her seat. 'Ticket sales?'

Oswald said, 'We're having them printed; pukka tickets, perforations and everything. The Anwen Players Present…etcetera.'

Mavis said, 'The Anwen Players?'

Althea twinkled. 'I thought that was rather good, myself.'

'I dare say,' was all Mavis could muster.

Althea added, 'It'll be really important to spread the sales far and wide; we need the money to come in from outside the village, otherwise we might as well just ask everyone who lives in Anwen to make a donation to the charity, and not go to the bother of all this. But, no, that's not the point; the panto will build community – that's the reason I wanted us to do it – the money from the tickets is a bonus. It might not amount to much, because we won't be charging a great deal, but it'll be more than nothing. You'll do it, won't you, Mavis?'

Mavis felt she had little choice but to agree, which she did.

Althea squealed. 'I told you she would, Ossie. Ossie said you wouldn't, but I know you so much better than he does. Thank you, Mavis. Maybe you could find a printer who could do the job for us?'

Mavis felt her eyebrows rise. 'I thought you said you'd already arranged that, Oswald.'

'I believe I said we're having them printed – which we will be, when you arrange for it. And I'd like samples to approve.'

Althea nodded. 'And you'd better liaise with Josie – the woman with all the retired greyhounds – because she's organizing the printing of the commemorative brochure, which we'll sell at the performance; she said she thought she might know of some people who'd even like to buy advertising space in it. She's such a live wire, that woman…I'm not surprised that she and Annie have become such firm friends.'

Mavis was puzzled. 'Annie and Josie? I know they were in cahoots about getting that horsebox all dolled up so that Tudor could use it as an additional bar in his beer garden, but I didn't realize they still saw much of each other.'

Althea waved a hand. 'I've seen them a few times out and about in Josie's car, that's all. Maybe a common interest in dogs – who knows. Anyway, she's the one you should talk to about that.'

Mavis had finished her breakfast. 'I really should get away to the office, so I'll say good morning to you both.' She stood, ready to leave.

Oswald said, 'You'd not fancy being the goose would you, Mavis, by any chance, old girl? Priscilla's the best skin part in the entire pantheon of pantos…and you're about the right size to fit into the costume. It's the only one the Pike women aren't making – I own it, and I'm only too happy to rent it out – at friends' rates, of course, Alth.'

Mavis asked, 'A "skin part"?'

Althea said, 'He means you're in a goose costume the whole time – until the curtain call, of course. Mind you, some Priscillas don't ever reveal themselves, preferring to allow the children in the audience to continue to believe in her as a goose.'

Mavis was genuinely lost for words, so she walked out, and left them to it.

CHAPTER SEVENTEEN

Christine was just coming out of the shower when she heard unusual noises in the office below her apartment. 'Who's there? Is that you, Mavis?'

'Aye, it's me. I'm early. I'll put the kettle on.'

Christine peered down the ironwork spiral staircase. 'I wasn't expecting you at all, to be honest. With Carol and Annie out showing Sylvia Jenkins' photo around, and me glued to these blessed screens, watching recordings, I'd have thought you'd have preferred to work from the comfort of the Dower House.'

Mavis replied somewhat cagily, 'There's a lot going on there, at the moment.'

'Ah, you mean Oswald? Yes – he was puttering around the village on Sunday, after his lunch at the pub, talking people into doing all sorts of things. He phoned Alexander at about eight last night and got him to agree to do…a lot. He's very persuasive, and I think Althea told him that Alexander was a bit of a soft touch. I managed to stay out of it, thank goodness.'

Mavis smiled. 'You've no desire to tread the boards, as they say?'

Christine chuckled. 'Not me. And especially given my current girth. But I do have a desire to get dressed and warm myself up. Let's share a pot of tea, then we can both get cracking. Okay?'

Mavis agreed, and Christine finished her ablutions, which allowed her the chance to study how her body was changing, given her pregnancy, and to examine the scar she'd acquired as a result of her most recent injury. At least she felt it added a little interest to what had – for her entire life of almost thirty years – frequently been referred to as a flawlessly beautiful face; an observation that had become incredibly annoying. Finally, she stroked her fingers across the mark of that gunshot wound, which she knew, now, would never fade. As she dressed, she hoped she wasn't ever going to add to her collection of scars, because – if she kept going at this rate – she'd look as though she'd been run over by a bus before she knew it…and she didn't want that. A little interest was enough.

The tea Mavis had made was strong enough to allow an entire chorus line of mice to trot on it, which led Christine – naturally, she felt – to the topic of the local panto.

'Ach, let's no' talk about that, Christine. I've just had my fill of it over breakfast.'

Christine was familiar with Mavis's somewhat dour personality, and liked her very much both because of, and in spite of, it…in equal measure. Mavis never sugar-coated anything, but was, at heart, a woman who saw the good in the world, and felt compelled to speak out about the bad, which Christine believed was an excellent trait. Mavis's entire life had been one of service to others, and the rapidity with which she usually pointed out people's flaws or shortcomings was, Christine knew, matched by her judgment of her own self – which was why Mavis always worked so hard to do her best, and to get others to do theirs. But this morning? Christine saw a true lack of spirit in her colleague.

'Okay – as Annie would say: Mave, there's something wrong. Spill.'

Mavis cracked a smile. 'Aye, that would be Annie. I'd no' say this to her because she'd feel she had to do something about it – in a good way, of course – but I will to you, because you understand how to let things lie. It's Althea. She's…well, all a-twitter isn't unusual for her, as we all know, but this time it's different. I've really only known her for a wee while – just a few of her eighty-odd years. But this Oswald fellow, who she knew when she was young? He's bringing out a side of her I didn't even know existed. She's got a reckless air about her. To be honest, Christine – and I hope you don't take this the wrong way – she's putting me in mind of how you can get, sometimes. I know we've spoken of it before, so it won't surprise you to hear me say this, but you have been known to act as though you think you're immortal – and you have the scars to prove it. And that's what I'm seeing in her. She's mentioned her life before meeting Henry's father on numerous occasions, but I'd never got the impression that, back then, she ran with such a racy crowd.'

Christine laughed. 'Is Oswald "racy" then? How does a man in his eighties manage that?'

Christine watched as Mavis sipped her tea and furrowed her brow. 'There's bound to be an amount of "remember when we did this, or that" between them, I know, but that's not what I mean. There's something about the man I cannae put my finger on. He rubs me up the wrong way, and there's an undercurrent of…maybe spite in his whole manner.'

Christine admitted, 'I haven't met him, yet, though I dare say I will, given what Alexander's agreed to do. In fact, I sort of half-promised to meet the two of them at the Coach and Horses for a spot of lunch today. I need to get away from these screens for a proper break…my eyes go all peculiar, if I don't. I'll firm up that plan with Alexander, and I'll spend my time appraising Oswald, Mavis – how about that? I'll look at him the way Alexander does a potential piece of Swansea pottery, okay? The full examination, inside and out.' She chuckled. 'Well, maybe not inside.'

Mavis shrugged. 'The Case of the Disagreeable Director? Do you think Annie would like that one?'

Christine rose. 'I won't tell her if you don't, because you know what she's like if we all decide to do case-naming without her. But this isn't a real case…is it? You're not asking me to do a little bit of digging into Oswald Featherington on the side, are you, Mavis?'

'Ach no, I'd never do that. And I dare say I should tell you, specifically, to not do anything of the sort. Though you could tell me what you think of him, if you meet him for lunch. Besides, if I wanted to dig into his background, I could do it myself. Carol's taught us all a lot about how to gather data on a person from online sources over the years, and I'm no slouch when it comes to a bit of digging on my own.'

Christine paused. 'So you've already started?' She didn't really have to ask.

'That's as mebbe,' said Mavis, rather enigmatically, 'but we'd best get on. We've both a lot of work ahead of us for Rhodri and his client.'

Christine hauled herself up the stairs, clutching a fresh mug of tea…wondering how she'd manage to do such a thing when she was fully nine months into her pregnancy. She told herself that she and Alexander would be moving into Honeysuckle Cottage before that –

though she simultaneously had to tamp down her rising frustration on that front; it seemed that it wasn't as easy as she'd imagined it would be to decorate a small cottage in exactly the way she'd planned within a short timeframe, and on – of all things – a budget. It was a word that she and Alexander had been introducing to their conversations of late, and not something she was wildly happy about, though she understood the reasons: they'd be a family of three, soon, and they needed to ensure a sound financial future for that family.

The allowance from her trust was adequate for her needs, and she knew that Alexander's business interests had made him wealthy, but planning her personal finances with a view to the future hadn't been something she'd ever done before. She'd even had to rethink using her chum Nat to design and paint a mural in the small dining room at the cottage, once she'd received the quote for her work. And she'd only just begun to discuss schools for Lumpy with her mother: the fees had been a wake-up call.

Putting aside such irritating thoughts, Christine settled herself on her sofa and took in the screens of three laptops, which were positioned in a semi-circle on the coffee table. Having given her attention to the internal camera feeds initially – and thereby having established that Pauline Thomas had, indeed, been inside her narrowboat from the time that Mavis had helped her back there until the time all the cameras had shut down, she'd at least been able to write up a report to that effect, for Rhodri Lloyd, and send it off with a log of relevant movements. Of course, that didn't clear Pauline of any encounter with Sylvia Jenkins in the period immediately prior to the discovery of the woman's body, but she'd done all she could on that front; it had been a relatively straightforward, if tedious, task. However, the cameras giving a view of the exterior area surrounding Pauline's boat were presenting Christine with a much more daunting task, because she had to slow to normal speed every time a human being came into view on one of the feeds, and give her full attention to the person, or persons, involved to do her best to establish their identity.

Logic dictated that, since she had footage of Pauline inside her boat, she couldn't have been, simultaneously, outside the vessel. However,

Christine was aware of the possibility that the victim, Sylvia Jenkins, might have been in the area ahead of being found in the water – and not just in the time immediately prior to the discovery of her body, but at any point during the period since Christine and Alexander had installed the cameras. Christine was amazed by how well-used the towpath, and even the surrounding areas of grass and the bridge – which could be seen from two of the cameras – had been. She was beginning to recognize 'regulars'. Did people really walk their dogs that often?

Mr Puffy Red Jacket had a liver-and-cream spaniel; Mrs Twins had a double buggy and a pair of dachshunds, one tan, one mottled…or would that be 'brindled'?; Grandpa Barbour and Grandson Patterned Backpack had no dog, but the child carried a stuffed Snoopy. Christine spotted rhythms, and patterns, and was constantly reminding herself of what Sylvia looked like…though a number of figures she saw were completely unidentifiable, other than by judged – or guessed – gender. These she logged with a camera source and time code, for further investigation. She'd got as far as just around eleven o'clock on the night before Sylvia's body had been found, and saw Mrs Twins out with the dachshunds, but no pushchair; maybe Mr Twins was doing the childminding while his wife had a carefree saunter? But no…it wasn't carefree, because her tiny dogs were getting quite upset about something.

Christine paused two screens and focused on the one with all the doggie kerfuffle. Mrs Twins was holding onto the two leads in one hand, and waving her other arm at…what? Was there someone just out of the range of the camera…off in the darkness? Christine checked her plan of all the cameras' coverage. Camera seven might help. She accessed the feed, ran it forward to the appropriate point, and yes…there was a figure in the darkness, though she couldn't quite make it out. Would the person step into the light from the lamp standards along the towpath? Mrs Twins clearly wanted them to.

Christine was absolutely thrilled when Mrs Twins chose to use her considerable common sense and initiative when she pulled out her phone, and trained her torch-light app on the person lurking in the dark. She was so ecstatic when she saw Sylvia Jenkins' scowling face that she yelped aloud.

She heard Mavis call out, 'Are you alright up there, Christine?'

'Yes – and I've found something. Come on up and see for yourself.'

It took a few moments to get Mavis installed beside her on the snug sofa, but then Christine ran through the recording she'd found, and they watched together as the feed continued.

There was a clear exchange between Mrs Twins and Sylvia, with both of them doing what they could to calm the dogs, who were scampering around Sylvia, their leads getting entwined around each other's, and around Mrs Twins', legs. The two women spoke for a couple of minutes, then Mrs Twins continued along the towpath, and Sylvia appeared to saunter off in the opposite direction.

Christine sorted the feed from camera nine: it showed that Sylvia had loitered, rather than departed, then she had turned and made her way toward Pauline's boat, but walked past it, without stopping. Mavis and Christine followed Sylvia's progress beyond a gap in the coverage – due to the structure of the bridge and a bend in the waterway – until she appeared again on the bridge itself, crossing to the other side of the water. They knew that Annie had been inside Tudor's car, parked in the same spot where Mavis had spent the day.

'Annie'll have seen her,' said Mavis. 'Why did Sylvia Jenkins' presence on the towpath not end up in her report? That was important.'

Christine replied, 'To be fair to Annie, when she was on watch at the time, not only did we not know that Sylvia would turn up dead…we didn't even know she existed. Look, I've got Annie's report here, and she does note all this activity: "Ten fifty-seven: dog walker and woman interact; not close to boat, both walk past it, but not together". That's exactly what happened, but neither Annie, nor we, recognized the significance. Until now. We were focused on Pauline's boat – on anyone who might come close enough to harm her. But Annie's notes also mention that there were no other vehicles in the car park, so – if Sylvia crossed the bridge to that side of the water – how did she leave the area? Did she have a car parked elsewhere, close by?'

Mavis noted, 'There's very little parking around that way. All designated for residents only, except that wee spot on the waterfront. She'd have had a decent walk from there to get to a place where she could have left a car.'

Christine had a thought. 'Might she have been staying in the area? Local B and Bs, that sort of thing? She might have been stalking Pauline in the real world, as well as online. It's a possibility, you have to admit.' She felt quite pleased with herself.

Mavis stood. 'I'll look into that, while you continue with your viewing of the feeds. But we should let Carol and Annie know about this sighting – and about your idea; it could help them with their enquiries in the area…give them more to go on, to jog people's memories. They might even encounter – what did you call her? – Mrs Twins?'

Christine chuckled. 'Yes, well…double pushchair – twins. And that's an excellent idea, Mavis, because she should be pushing her twins along the towpath in about half an hour; I'll text them so they can be in position to ask her about the exact nature of the interaction she had with Sylvia. I'll do that, while you start on the B and Bs.'

'Let's get them on speakerphone, Christine – you should have the chance to be praised.'

Christine called Carol, because she reckoned Annie was likely to be in full flight, chatting with someone or other. Carol had agreed to go along not only because she was able to get Annie to where she needed to be, but also because she'd be able to deal with anyone who spoke only Welsh, or who chose to only speak Welsh in the presence of an Englishwoman who was peppering them with questions. Carol answered on the second ring, and sounded excited.

'Hello Christine, I'm glad you phoned, because I was about to call you. I have news, and it's a bit unexpected.'

Christine nudged Mavis. 'Sounds like we're all making great strides. Excellent. Shall I go first?'

'Is it Chrissy?' Annie's voice boomed through.

'Yes, it's me – and we've discovered that Sylvia Jenkins was in the vicinity of Pauline's boat around the eleven o'clock mark the night before her body was discovered. You noted her presence, Annie, but we didn't know who she was, then. She was the woman who had a bit of a chat with Mrs Twins.'

Both Carol and Annie chorused, 'Who?'

Christine said, 'A woman who's got twins, and two dachshunds.'

Annie said, 'Oh her…yes I saw that. Was that person she was talking to Sylvia Jenkins? Wow. Didn't know that. Anyway, did Carol tell you her news yet? She's been noodling around on her tablet while I've been doing my thing, and she's only gone and found that Llew Merton, haven't you, Car? Go on, tell them how you did it.'

Christine felt disappointed that her discovery hadn't made more of a splash, but knew that everything they were all doing added up. 'How did you manage that? All I had to do was make my eyeballs sore by staring at screens – what wizardry did you use, Carol?'

Carol laughed. 'No wizardry, just following trails. I checked the social feeds of the pub in Cardiff where Sylvia and Llew met. I knew approximately when they'd met, both times, from the report Rhodri Lloyd sent through. And then I did my thing. I followed trails to the social feeds of people who'd attended gatherings at the pub, tagging it in their posts, and managed to find Sylvia in one shot…which meant I could focus on a specific date, so I ploughed that furrow, until I saw the man Sylvia was with. I then did a search for photos that looked like him, and I found him. Though he's called a variety of names, they're all variations on a theme: Llew Merton, which we knew about, but there's also L.L. Merton, Lal Merton, L. Llewellyn Merton…you get the picture. Speaking of which, there's a variety of photos of him, too. I'll send them all, shortly. I'd say that he hasn't just preyed upon Sylvia; it looks like he's pretty expert at this sort of thing. Scam artist scum.'

'Yay you,' managed Christine.

'Yay you, Chrissy, too,' said Annie. 'We don't know if tracking this bloke down is going to get us anywhere, but you've actually found the victim, near where she died, the night before she did…which has to be significant.'

Christine felt warm inside. 'I wondered if Sylvia might have been staying in the area. You haven't found yourselves knocking on the door of any B and Bs or the like, have you? If Sylvia had lost her home, she might have been living in a vehicle, but Mavis reckons there's nowhere to park near Pauline's boat, other than the car park you and Tudor were in, Annie. Any thoughts on that front?'

'Good thinking, Christine,' said Carol. 'I'm not aware of any other parking.'

'As I said,' added Mavis. 'But, look – you get that information about Merton to us, Carol, and share it with Rhodri too, would you? We'll do the same with our findings. Between us, we've made great strides. This is excellent work all round, ladies. Thank you.'

A few moments later, Christine heard her phone ping, alerting her to an incoming email. Carol had attached a link to their cloud account, where Christine found a collection of photographs of a man striking various poses, wearing different types of outfits – from sharp suits to cozy sweaters. In each one he'd also adopted a slightly different persona: clean-shaven, with a serious expression above his charcoal suit and crisp white shirt; giving a warm smile, with a goatee above a snuggly tan woolie. But in all of them, he was the same man. And Christine recognized him; she'd known him as Larry Merton, when he'd been an unscrupulous and very much under-the-radar headhunter for a recruitment company in the City. She wasn't exactly surprised to discover that he was seeking a different type of trophy, these days. She punched Carol's number into her phone as she called down to Mavis. She even knew where he lived – at least, she knew where he'd once lived – because she'd been to his house for dinner on one occasion, before she'd twigged to his oiliness, and it wasn't in Cardiff...it was in Clapham.

CHAPTER EIGHTEEN

Henry was bereft: Stephanie was feeding Hugo; Bob Fernley, his Estates Manager, was at some sort of gathering at the village hall, as were several other members of his staff – with his wife's blessing, it appeared; Cook Davies had banned him from the kitchen because she was doing something there he wasn't allowed to see – which he hoped bode well for dinner; he hadn't seen hide nor hair of his sister, nor his brother-in-law…not that this gave him cause for concern, indeed, that was something to be pleased about. Nevertheless, he felt as though he were absolutely superfluous to anyone's requirements.

When his mobile telephone rang in his pocket, he observed, with interest, that his mother was calling him…which was not like her, at all; the two of them usually communicated via Edward, unless they were in the same room as each other.

'Hello, Mother. How are you?'

'Very well, thank you Henry. But I'll be a lot better if you'll agree to doing a small favor for me.'

'If I can.'

'You're most certainly capable of it, dear. The question is whether you're willing.'

Henry bridled. 'If I have the time, and it is – as you believe – within my ability, I'll most certainly consider it. What would you like me to do?'

'I'm afraid it would involve rather a lot of painting, dear. How would you feel about that?'

Henry felt his mood lift a little. 'You know I always welcome the opportunity to exercise my artistic side. Though I'll admit that I'm not terribly good at capturing people; noses and hands are especially challenging, so a portrait would be a non-starter, I'm afraid.'

'Don't worry, dear. This would be for landscapes and a few interiors.'

Henry felt his spirits soar. 'My pleasure, Mother. Though…what do you mean by "a few"? Is this a commission for a series of paintings?'

Henry felt quite excited by the idea; it would be something he could get his teeth into. He could position a series all around the interior of the folly where he had his studio, maybe even working on a few pieces at a time. It would need a bit of organizing though…and Stephanie would have to know that he had a Big Job on. A commission? Recognition, at last.

He asked, 'Who's the job for, Mother?'

'It's for Ossie, and the Anwen Players, of course.'

Henry paused. 'You mean that your Oswald Featherington wants to commission a series of paintings by me? And who on earth are the "Anwen Players"?'

'Not paintings in the small, normal sense, Henry – but something on a grand scale. Something everyone would get to see, as though your work were at an exhibition. Yes, that's it – an exhibit, with your art in the spotlight. Wouldn't that be wonderful, dear?'

Henry felt his tummy clench. 'An exhibit – of my work? And what do you mean by it being on a "grand scale"? You obviously have something in mind, Mother. Could you be more clear, please?'

'I'm sorry, dear, Ossie is calling me, I'll ring you back. Please think about it – it really would make your dear old mother very happy if you said yes. It might be my only chance to see the joy on the faces of so many members of the public as they gaze upon your wonderful paintings. Bye bye, dear. My love to Hugo, and Stephaine, of course…and Clementine. Never mind, I'll see you all at dinner.'

Henry gave his attention to the small watercolor hanging on the wall in the Estates Office that he'd painted of the view toward Chellingworth Hall, across the ha-ha, from the meadow. It was rather good…but it was rather small, too. A 'grand scale'? How might he have approached his subject differently if he'd been working on a piece that had been maybe four times the size? Or…maybe even larger? Yes, he'd need a great deal more detailed work in there, on the Hall itself…but what fun he could have had with the sky.

Maybe he should go through the same thought process for some of his other works? Several hung in his private apartment of rooms. Yes, he'd take himself up there and have a think about it. He was sure that Hugo must have finished feeding by now – he'd been gone for…gosh, was it that long?

As Henry crossed the Great Hall he was keenly aware of the spring in his step…until he looked up and saw Julian descending toward him; the man was crying. Henry's spirits plummeted.

'Hello, Julian.' He hoped the man would be unwilling to engage beyond basic niceties, given that he was so clearly distraught.

'Henry, it's all blown up again. She's told me to get out of her sight. I…I don't know what to say, or do. Please help me. I'm so…confused. I feel as though I'm not…enough for her. A husband should be enough for a wife, shouldn't he? This is all so…beyond me. I bash metal for a living. All this emotional angst is so unexpected…so alien to me. I don't know whether I'm coming or going. Though Clementine made it abundantly clear that I should be going.'

Henry didn't know what to say, so blustered a reply. 'Clemmie's always been rather fond of ice cream. Maybe Cook Davies has some you could take to her? I used it on many occasions to win her over, when we'd had a tiff. Especially when Mother would tell me that I had to apologize to Clemmie – even if the entire problem in question had been of her making, which it usually was, of course. Yes, ice cream might do the trick.'

Henry believed he'd had a very good idea indeed, but Julian's expression made him suspect that the man didn't share his opinion.

'My wife has told me she cannot stand the sight of me because I will not support her desire to bear a child in her mid-fifties, and you think a bowl of ice cream will smooth things over? Henry – Clementine isn't six. This isn't a spat over a broken toy, or a disagreement about who won a game of…hopscotch, or cricket. We're adults. These are huge life decisions. You two are as bad as each other. I don't think either of you ever really escaped your nursery, or that blessed Nanny Thingummy of yours that Clementine's always going on about.'

Julian continued his descent, wiping away tears that Henry feared were now borne of anger, rather than sadness.

'We had a number of nannies,' Henry called.

The look that Julian cast over his shoulder suggested to Henry that his brother-in-law didn't care how concerning this might have been for the siblings.

He confirmed Henry's suspicion when he shouted back, 'And they were obviously all bloody useless.' Then Julian stomped out into the darkness…without even stopping to get a coat, or an umbrella.

'Most extraordinary.'

'What is, Henry?'

Henry looked up the stairs again, to see his wife standing at their head. 'Nothing, dear. At least, nothing that I feel I should speak of here. Let's go to our rooms; I think we should have a bit of a chat before dinner.'

Once they were safely closed away from the world, Henry described his encounter with Julian.

Stephanie looked concerned. 'This is obviously quite serious, Henry.'

'I agree.'

'Clementine and Julian appear to have reached an impasse.'

'I agree.'

'We should probably do…something.'

'I agree.'

'Stop agreeing with me, Henry.'

Henry was confused. 'But I do agree with you, on all counts. Though as for what exactly we should, or even could, do about it…I have no idea. It's not really the sort of matter that involves persons outside a marriage, is it?'

'Indeed. But Clementine's your sister, so at least she's your blood. I think you should speak to her, Henry. Otherwise, dinner might turn into a…well, who knows what might happen.'

'The way Julian slammed the door – as best you can when a door's that large and heavy – suggests to me that he might not return for dinner. He ran off once before, prior to their marriage, if you recall.'

'But that was different – that's in the past. This is very much in the present…with implications for the future. Neither of us has spoken to Clementine herself about the matter. There might be…elements we know nothing about.'

Henry nodded. 'You're quite right, of course, but I have to say that I don't believe I'd be the right person to discuss this with her. Yes, we share blood, but it's so often bad blood that we've barely ever had a civil conversation as adults. She tries my patience within an instant, as you know. And I hers, as she's told me on many an occasion.'

The duchess sighed. 'That's true.'

'Besides,' added Henry, rallying to the topic, 'there must be many aspects of this entire having a baby thing that lie exclusively within the realm of female understanding. You'd be much better at talking to her about it than I.'

Stephanie nodded. 'A woman's insight…yes. Of course I'm a mother, but I wonder if it might help Clementine to have a tête-à-tête with someone who's currently pregnant? How would you feel about inviting Christine and Alexander to dinner this evening, Henry?'

Henry's immediate reaction was panic. 'Have a pregnant woman in the same room as another who's desperate to be so? As well as Hugo being there in his pram? I'm not sure that's…wise. Wouldn't we be rubbing Clemmie's nose in it? I don't have many positive feelings toward her, but she is my sister, as you said, and that would be…harsh.'

Stephanie did the thing with her eyebrows that always told Henry she was thinking hard. Eventually she pronounced, 'I believe that the topic will be raised, and there will be upset, whether Christine – and Hugo – are there, or not. So let's have it out, Henry. We need to solve the mystery of why Clementine is so set upon having a child…and I believe this is the best way to do it: to ask her.'

Henry slumped in his chair. 'You and Christine are chums; I think you'd better warn her when you invite her.'

Stephanie rose to get her phone. 'I shall, Henry…and I shall couch the invitation so she understands that, although this might not be a real "case", she would be helping us get to the truth of a matter that…matters.'

'Indeed.'

CHAPTER NINETEEN

Annie Parker hovered in the middle of the village hall watching Marjorie Pritchard and Janet Jackson as they stood within inches of each other, wondering who'd blink first. Her money was on Janet, and she was proved right.

The woman who'd only been running the Lamb Tearooms for a few months finally said, 'Have it your way then, Marjorie. But I'm telling you now, it won't look as good as my suggestion.' Janet flounced off, and Marjorie smiled.

Annie could see that Janet was genuinely upset, and followed her as she headed toward the ladies' loos. 'Don't let her get to you, Janet, her bark's worse than her bite.' She tried a winning smile.

Janet looked pretty downhearted. 'She's loving every minute of this. It's like all her Christmases have come at once. She doesn't seem to understand that she can throw herself into this panto full-time, but a lot of us have businesses to run all day before we come here. And this is only the second day of rehearsals – for her, too – and she's telling us what to do like none of us have ever performed in our lives. Me and Paul know what it is to be on stage; we've done a fair bit of karaoke in our time. Won prizes, and everything. Oswald obviously loved our audition. He came into my place this morning and almost begged me to talk to Paul about us doing a turn. Of course I – we both – said yes. But now I find I'm having to deal with…her. Besides, I've had a day of it. I don't know if you're the same as me, but I like to use certain things for certain jobs – it makes them go easier – and I've lost my favorite vase. It's nothing special, and no one even notices it, really, but I've taken it with me from place to place, and it's always beside me when I greet people. Like an old friend. But it's gone. I was wondering if a customer had knocked it over, didn't like to admit it, and just cleared it away. There were never real flowers in it, only dried ones – it had a crack and wouldn't even hold water – but it had a nice, friendly shape to it. Unless I've put it…somewhere. Like I said, I was busy at the tearooms today…lots of people buzzing about, and wanting to natter over a pot. This panto could be good for business.'

Annie smiled. 'Well, good luck with it all, Janet. I'm a bit run off my feet, too – but I'd better do what I came here for, and find my Tude. You haven't seen him, have you?'

'Not since Paul and me were in for a pint on Sunday night. Sorry. Hope you find him. I'm off to break it to Paul that our duet will be done in front of the curtain, while the set's being changed, not on the set itself. He won't be pleased. Bye.'

Annie took in the chaotic scene around her, strolled toward Marjorie Pritchard and dared to ask, 'How's it going, Marge? Everyone doing as they're told, are they?'

Marjorie gripped her clipboard. 'Once people understand that they have to listen to what the stage manager says, things will run a lot more smoothly.'

Anne said, 'I'm sure they'll get it, Marge. And I know you've got a lot on your plate but…I wondered if you'd seen Tude? I came back from Brecon, and he wasn't at the pub. Aled said he'd told him he was coming here, and that he'd be back in half an hour. But that was two hours ago. So – any ideas?'

Marjorie looked a little pink around the gills. 'Do you have any concept of what a stage manager does, Annie?'

Annie hung her head. 'No, Marge, not a clue.' She reckoned she was about to be told.

'Everything. And I mean that. I call all the rehearsals: we're supposed to have the full company coming together tomorrow evening, and I'm still waiting for my final cast list, and the list of dancers…main choreography is in two days' time. And I have to make sure everyone has a script, and sheet music, and tell everyone where to be and when, and I have to know what's going on with the lighting, and the music, and the stage direction. I have a bible containing details about…everything, Annie. That's what they call it – a "bible" – it's that important. Not that folks take any notice of what it says, of course. I mean just look at that chap – he's glaring as though he's about to squash everyone he looks at. I don't even know who he is.'

Annie followed Marjorie's gaze. 'That's Julian Treforest, Lady Clementine's husband. They're down from Scotland.'

Annie noticed that Marjorie's expression immediately softened. 'Oh, well…in that case, it's very kind of him to volunteer to help…even though he does look like a drowned bear. But, as you can see, I'm run off my feet. Now do you understand why I might have no idea where a random pub landlord might be at any given time?'

Annie felt her neck get warm. 'Now hang on a minute there, Marge. Tude's volunteered to help out with this panto out of a sense of community spirit, and because of the kindness in his heart. Oswald's told him he's going to be the prompt, so he won't have to come to rehearsals and can get on with running his pub – which he'll have to put even more hours into now, because Aled will be over here all the time, swanning about like a lovesick puppy in his…role, whatever it is. If Tudor came here, it was because he needed to, which means you must know why he came, if you're in charge of everything…with a bible.'

Marjorie sighed. 'He came to collect a copy of the script, which he'll have to study – in his own time, at the pub, at his convenience. But that was some time ago. I gave him the script, explained his duties – he'd asked to meet when it was quiet, after his lunch period. I assumed he'd left.'

Annie looked around. 'I've been in the kitchen, and backstage, and he's nowhere. And…what are all these people doing here, anyway?'

Marjorie said, 'Just a moment, Annie.' She stepped away and grabbed something off a table that Annie couldn't quite make out. The next thing Annie saw took her aback: Marjorie had a loudspeaker, through which she announced, 'Tudor Evans to the stage manager's desk. Now.' There was a deafening squeal, then Marjorie put the instrument of torture back in its spot.

The hush that had befallen the buzzing village hall gradually built back to a thrum of chatter. But there was still no sign of Tudor.

Annie gave up. 'If you see him, tell him I've gone back to the pub.'

Marjorie replied sharply, 'I'm not your messenger, Annie.'

Annie grabbed the loudspeaker, clicked the ON button, and shouted, 'If anyone sees Tude, tell him Annie's back at the pub.' She stared at Marjorie, and left.

Annie set off toward the Coach and Horses, circumnavigating the village green, which was completely sodden. The rain had stopped, and she saw Joan Pike pushing her mother in her wheelchair in the distance. Annie risked cutting the corner of the green to get to the women to ask if they'd seen Tudor…and she almost made it, but skidded on muddy turf about two feet from the road, windmilled her arms to try to get her balance, then spun and landed flat on her back on the thick, wet grass.

She allowed herself to lie there for a moment, silently cursing. Joan's face appeared above her. 'Are you alright, Annie?'

Annie nodded. 'Yeah, I'm fine.' She hoped she was.

'Want a hand?'

Annie considered how useful a slim, twenty-something-year-old and no more than five foot three tall might be in helping her haul her considerably meatier, six-foot frame to an upright position. Annie reasoned that her back must be completely soaked, so why worry about her knees, or the rest of her front.

'I'll do it on me own, ta.' She rolled over, got to her knees, and pushed up. Yes – drenched, front and back. She was glad that Carol had moved from a house that overlooked the green to one that had only a partial view of it, and hoped all the other residents had been too busy doing something else to notice when she'd taken her little tumble.

'You'd better get your mum, she looks anxious, and tell her I'm fine.' Annie imagined she must look a sight, so decided to ask about Tudor, then get back to the pub to clean herself up.

Gwen Pike still looked concerned when the threesome met on the relative safety of the road. 'You and Tudor are both having clumsy days. He took a tumble at our place earlier on, didn't he, Joan?'

'Tudor's been over at your house? Today?' Annie was puzzled – she couldn't imagine why he'd have needed to go there at all.

Joan nodded. 'He left about twenty minutes ago, said he was popping into the shop for…something, then heading back to the pub. I don't think he was expecting you'd be back from Brecon until later.'

'I finished up there a bit earlier than I'd expected,' said Annie. 'I must have just missed him. But why was he at your house?'

'He wanted to see the costume for Priscilla, the goose,' said Gwen, with a grin. 'He's very diligent, isn't he?'

Annie nodded. 'He is, but I still don't understand. He's doing the prompting for the panto — what's the goose costume got to do with that?' She couldn't make head nor tail of it.

Joan said, 'He'd seen in the script that the goose doesn't speak, but Marjorie has told him that if the goose forgets to do something it's supposed to — you know, like nod at a certain point, or waggle a wing, that sort of thing — he has to prompt it to do that too. So he came to see how the costume works — so he'll know if the goose is doing what it's supposed to do, the way it's supposed to do it. It's got strings inside it to make parts of it move — the wings, the tail feathers, the beak and so forth, and we're doing all the costumes, so Oswald had it delivered to us. He even dropped by himself to check that it had arrived safely, and everything. He's quite a force of nature, that Oswald, isn't he?'

Annie accepted the strange explanation, and said, 'Oswald? Oh yes, you could say that. I don't suppose Tudor tried the costume on himself, did he?' It was the sort of thing Tudor might do.

Gwen laughed heartily. 'Good heavens no, Annie. He wouldn't fit into it — it's for a much smaller person. Well made, but it looks to have a good few miles on the clock…and quite a few feathers missing. I'll tart it up the best I can, so Priscilla looks pristine on the day.'

'I didn't know it had a name, other than Mother Goose,' said Annie.

Joan said, 'Priscilla isn't Mother Goose — Priscilla is the goose that lays the golden eggs, and she's given to Mother Goose by the Good Fairy, so that Mother Goose — who's very poor, and can't afford to pay her rent, so she's going to be evicted in the middle of a cold, cold winter — can be rich, and be happy.'

Annie realized she'd clearly completely misunderstood the basic premise of the story. 'I though the goose that laid golden eggs was in *Jack and the Beanstalk*. Isn't it?'

Gwen said, 'No, that's a hen that lays golden eggs, not a goose.'

Annie was still confused, but decided that she wanted to get away, and get dry. At the remembrance of her clumsiness, she asked, 'Thanks for that…so tell me, how did Tude manage to take a tumble at your place then?' She reckoned she could do with some retaliatory ammunition if she was going to have to face Tudor looking as though she'd been hosed down.

Joan tutted. 'He was helping us, of course. He's so lovely, isn't he? Anyway, we'd misplaced a box full of thimbles; they're all in a small, old, dented biscuit tin…always have been, since Mam's days as a seamstress – I used to play with it when I was little, like it was a musical instrument, didn't I, Mam? But we couldn't find them, could we?'

Gwen shook her head. 'Poor Joan's been all over the house looking for the blinking thing, and we did wonder if it might have gone down the back of the sideboard, but that's so big that neither of us could shift it. Tudor said he'd have a go, and he pulled and pulled, but it wouldn't budge, would it, Joan? Then it finally gave-to a bit, and he fell right backwards. Lucky for him he's quite well padded. But the tin wasn't there. Anyway, he managed to push the sideboard back into its place very nicely. No harm done, we hope.'

Annie was glad to hear that Tudor hadn't damaged himself, and she was quite sure she'd hurt nothing but her pride; they'd had two lucky escapes. She felt a drop on her face. 'I think it's going to rain again – best we all get back inside…well, it'll make no difference for me, because I don't think I could get any wetter, but you two are nice and dry. I'll see you both soon. Thanks for all the info, and I hope that tin turns up. Bye for now.'

Annie didn't think she could do any more damage by crossing the green, but was now wary of the slippery grass, so stuck to the road. When she got to the pub, she sneaked up the stairs, hoping to avoid Tudor altogether – she could hear him in the bar, and that was enough for her to know there couldn't be that much wrong with him.

CHAPTER TWENTY

Stephanie could feel the tension in her midsection; she'd been dreading dinner since breakfast time, and now it was almost upon her. She'd spoken with Christine about the possibility of her joining the group, with Alexander, and had taken some time to explain the situation – as she understood it – regarding Clementine and Julian.

Alexander had already promised his evening to Oswald Featherington, it seemed – along with half the village, by the sounds of it – so Christine had offered to come alone. Stephanie had readily accepted, so she knew she'd have one ally in the room, though Christine had warned her that she might not arrive until just before dinner was due to be served as she had a great deal to get done at the office.

Thus, Stephanie feared, the most potentially dangerous part of few evening was likely to be the time when everyone was mingling, and drinks were being served. Which meant she had approximately ten minutes of calm to enjoy before any storms broke out. Maybe even a hurricane. She knew Clementine well enough to fear that.

'Henry, however much we don't want to, we really should go down. It always takes a while for Hugo to get settled in his pram, and I think we should be ready for incoming family on time. I suppose that – with my parents being stuck in Spain for an extra day – at least it's just us this evening…which might help. I can't imagine it would be productive to have them in the mix, too.'

'I don't see why having John and Sheila here would hurt. They're my family now, as Clemmie is yours, and they're both very good at talking common sense, which I think is what my sister needs to hear.'

Stephanie loved her husband a great deal, and never more than at that moment. 'That's a very kind thing to say. Thank you, dear.'

Henry appeared to glow. 'Is it? Well…good. And you're quite right, we should go down.'

Hugo was still refusing to settle into his pram at the bottom of the staircase in the Grand Hall when Althea and Mavis arrived. Stephanie was happy to cede her duties to Hugo's grandmother for a few moments as she pushed a curl into her chignon, and smoothed down her claret gown – the serviceable, slightly stretchy one, that really didn't crumple too much when she carried her son in her arms. As she did so she noticed – to her horror – that the seam had split just on her right hip, where she usually supported most of Hugo's weight. All she could do was hope that no one would notice, and make a mental note to check if the seam could be mended.

With Althea having been able to work some sort of magic on Hugo – so that he was now happy to coo and blow bubbles, rather than scream until he looked as though he might explode – the foursome, plus Hugo, made their way into the drawing room, where drinks were served by Edward.

When Clementine and Julian joined them, Stephanie did her best not to act as though she were expecting a disaster to befall, and was delighted when Althea made a tremendous fuss of her daughter and son-in-law, whom she'd not seen in some time.

The dowager kissed her daughter and stood back to observe her for a moment. 'I had no idea your hair was that color, my dear. Is that how it appears when it's *au naturel*? I think it rather suits you. You look less…drained…than when it's a solid, dyed shade. Good for you, Clementine; a brave choice, and a good one. What made you do it, dear? Not able to get the right sort of hairdressing treatments close to the house in Scotland?'

Lady Clementine Twyst nodded graciously. 'It's quite amazing, but true; my girl in London warned me about the challenges I would face when I moved, but I had no idea things would be so…difficult up there.'

Stephanie was surprised; in her life before she'd taken up the position of PR manager at Chellingworth Hall she'd traveled extensively in Scotland, both on business and for pleasure, and she'd never got the impression that the Scots were particularly lacking when it came to matters of fashion, or beauty treatments. However, she reasoned that the Twysts' house in Scotland was remote, and suspected that the villages in the surrounding area didn't cater for what she could only suppose were Clementine's somewhat exotic expectations.

Henry asked, 'Haven't you been to London at all since you moved, Clemmie?'

Clementine shook her head. 'All that's behind me, now. I want it to fade away.'

Stephanie felt her back stiffen…was this going to be the start of it?

'You're as hirsute as when we first met,' said Althea to Julian. 'I thought you might have kept the clean-shaven look after your wedding; I thought it rather suited you.'

Stephanie saw Julian draw breath as if to reply, but Clementine jumped in. 'Julian's chin got terribly sunburned in Egypt, and then he couldn't shave at all, so his beard had grown in before we even returned to London. He made a decision to keep it.'

Stephanie could quite clearly hear the accusatory tone in Clementine's voice, but no one else seemed to. Something for which she was grateful.

Henry whined, 'It is something of a bore to be constantly having to shave, Clementine. Though I wouldn't expect a woman to understand.'

Oh no, Henry…

Clementine spoke sullenly, 'I agree that there are so many things that women don't understand about men, Henry, but there's also a great deal that men don't – and, apparently, will never – understand about women.'

Stephanie blurted, 'And isn't it wonderful that we're all so different? Life would be so boring if we were all the same. And did you know that your mother has a good old friend staying with her at the moment, Clementine? He was invited this evening, of course, but had a prior engagement – a rehearsal at the village hall, isn't that right, Althea?'

Stephanie noticed a strange glint in Althea's eye when she replied, 'Yes, Stephanie, that's true. But I expect you've heard all about Ossie from your Julian, Clementine. Isn't it wonderful that he's agreed to fashion some sort of device that will allow the lighting in the village hall to be more versatile for the performance?'

Stephanie could tell that Clementine had no idea what her mother was talking about when Clementine asked, 'Ossie? And what have you offered to do, Julian? Would someone please explain what's going on.'

Stephanie sighed with relief when Althea immediately began to witter on about her past friendship with Oswald Featherington, and to explain why he was staying at the Dower House, and the reasons for, and nature of, the panto. She hoped the topic would carry them through drinks and even beyond being seated at the dinner table.

Clementine's face was a picture as her mother talked: Stephanie watched her sister-in-law's reactions – shock, delight, surprise, horror, glee – and Stephanie went so far as to hope that these obviously genuine emotions would defuse any potential threat of incendiary conversations later in the evening. However, Stephanie also noted that Clementine had been completely caught off-guard by the news that Julian had volunteered his services; she wondered how that might play out.

Edward rang the gong for dinner.

Round One over…with no incident. Hurrah!

An outburst from Hugo while he was being pushed from the drawing room to the dining room – when he seemed determined that every limb should be freed from his blankets and waving in the air, all at once – meant that danger came close, because Clementine offered to settle him, and even hold him. Stephanie felt all she could do was offer assurances that Hugo would settle if only he were re-covered – and that he needed to learn that noisy attention-seeking would garner him no such thing. She was gifted with stern and puzzled looks by both Althea and Mavis. However, she didn't care if they thought she'd lost her mind, as long as she managed to avoid an opportunity for Clementine to exercise her broodiness before they were all seated.

Despite a slight delay, the table was eventually surrounded, wine and water were served, and the company set about enjoying their warm split pea and ham soup, which Stephanie had requested, knowing it was one of Henry's favorites. Given her husband's propensity for discussing food while he was enjoying it, Stephanie hoped the entire evening's menu would give many opportunities for Henry to expound, thereby delaying any talk about pregnancy until the end of the meal.

Edward announced the arrival of Christine, which bolstered Stephanie…until Christine walked into the dining room. Not having seen her chum in the flesh for several weeks, Stephanie hadn't realized the extent to which Lumpy was making its presence known by…well, living up to its name. Christine's pregnancy bump had been small – remarkably small, Stephanie would have said, when compared with her own experience with Hugo – but now Christine looked as though she might deliver a child within moments. It seemed that Lumpy had decided to expand exponentially within, what, five weeks?

Julian's face as he looked up from his soup – that which was visible above his beard – showed horror.

Clementine's response was more…enigmatic. She asked Christine, quite calmly, 'Is your dress from that little shop close to Borough Market, in London? They charge through the nose at that place, and with good reason: it's the most exclusive and sought-after maternity clothing for those who have any fashion sense at all, and don't want to look like an overstuffed sofa while they're pregnant. I had no idea you were expecting.'

Christine replied with a simple, 'Yes, I am.'

Althea smiled. 'Didn't I mention that, Clementine? Oh yes, Christine and Alexander are having a…Lumpy, you're calling it for now, isn't that right?'

Christine returned Althea's smile. 'Yes, Lumpy.'

'I think you've made a good choice to not know the gender until the birth,' observed Mavis.

Christine nodded. 'Alexander and I have decided that the nursery at Honeysuckle Cottage will be gender-neutral, as will anything else we get for the baby before its birth, so not knowing won't make much of a difference.'

'Though you'll have to be discussing names suitable for boys and girls, of course,' said Althea, dimpling. 'Or will you be playing safe and going for gender-neutral on that front, too? Anything decided, yet?'

Christine shook her head. 'Not yet. But…it's early days.'

Clementine said, 'It can't be early days, you're enormous. When are you due?'

'Mid-February.'

Clementine burst into tears.

Stephanie felt everything clench.

Althea's puzzlement was clear from her tone and question. 'What on earth's got into you, Clementine? We're all delighted for Christine, as is she; pregnancy isn't the end of an independent life, it's the start of a new phase entirely. There, there, now, Clementine, no need to get so upset about…well, I don't know what really. Good girl, that's right, dry your eyes.'

Clementine did.

Mavis's complete lack of knowledge about Clementine's situation also became clear to Christine when she added, 'We've all been making sure that Christine's been mainly doing desk-bound duties since we found out. Oh…by the way, Christine, any luck on finding someone who could check on that address in Clapham you had, for the Merton person?'

Christine nodded. 'Alexander's colleague, Geordie, is going to pop by there, on our behalf. As soon as he can.'

Mavis glanced around the table. 'Sorry to talk business over dinner, but this case of ours is really quite a serious matter.'

No one was looking at Clementine as she snuffled, except for Julian, who reached out a hand of comfort, only to have it batted away by his wife.

Henry asked airily, 'What are you all up to now?'

Stephanie added, 'Oh yes, please, tell us all you can.'

Mavis and Christine shared what Stephanie judged to be a significant glance.

Mavis answered, 'Our client is a solicitor, and we're acting on behalf of him, for a client of his…so what I say cannae go beyond this room, and I'll no' be able to give any details anyway. Is that acceptable?'

Stephanie noted that even Clementine nodded her head, along with everyone else.

Mavis continued, 'Suspicion has fallen upon an ex-client of ours in the case of a death from, as yet, an undetermined cause. Rhodri Lloyd, a solicitor in Brecon, is now acting on behalf of our ex-client. We are doing our best to unearth information that might exonerate Rhodri's client…or at least discover the truth surrounding the sad demise in question. Following a direction given to us by Rhodri, our investigation has led us to an address in Clapham where another…person of interest might be located. The seriousness of the situation in which Rhodri's client finds herself is not yet clear; though she has been "helping the police with their enquiries" for many hours, she's back at her home now, pending further investigation.'

Henry grumbled, 'That doesn't sound terribly exciting.'

Christine replied, 'Sometimes detective work is more of a slog, and less of an entertaining performance.'

Mavis concurred, 'Aye, you're right, Christine – but this is an important case. The future of a woman's life hangs in the balance, and we have a responsibility toward her, via Rhodri Lloyd.'

Clementine asked, 'Is she a mother, Mavis? Because then her children's lives would also be impacted by your success, or lack thereof.'

Mavis appeared puzzled. 'She has no children, so that's no' a consideration.'

Edward served the main course, leading to a natural discussion about ingredients, presentation, and flavors. Henry waxed lyrical about the delights of buttery mashed potatoes and the way they went so very well with the wild salmon steaks and tender broccolini, draped with glistening hollandaise sauce.

Stephanie was pleased that the chatter, and compliments, continued for a while, until Clementine observed, 'Salmon's rich in omega-3, which is excellent when you're pregnant. I intend to eat a great deal of it between now and whenever I conceive.'

The next few moments were a flurry of activity, as Edward rushed to the aid of Althea, who fell victim to a bout of severe choking. Eventually it was ascertained that the dowager wasn't choking on a bone, and the meal continued – in stony, and tense, silence.

Stephanie knew it couldn't last for long.

It didn't.

Replacing her water glass, from which she'd been sipping since her bout of choking, Althea said, 'Forgive me, everyone, for giving you all cause for concern. I'm afraid I misheard Clementine, and…reacted rather foolishly. My dear, I thought you said you were planning to…conceive. Now, what was it you really said?'

Clementine placed her cutlery to signify she'd finished picking at her meal. 'I've decided to have a baby, Mother.'

Althea sat back in her chair. 'Yes, that's what I thought you said. But surely that's not something you're physically able to do, dear. You must have at least started The Change by now. You're…' Althea paused and employed her fingers to count. 'Yes, surely by now you're beyond it.'

Clementine spoke firmly. 'I am not. I am capable. All I need is for my husband to participate and there should be no problem.'

Stephanie's heart sank. Henry paid an unreasonable amount of attention to removing his fish from its bones. Christine put down her napkin. Julian sagged. Mavis sat forward, alert, and shrewdly attending to Althea…who laughed her tinkling laugh.

'Good heavens, Clementine – are you feeling quite well? Surely you and Julian discussed the fact that – at your ages – you wouldn't be having a family once you married. His preparedness to provide his part of the equation involved is absolutely not something for discussion at the table, but your desire for a child is…well, it's something I think we should talk about. Are you quite serious? You want to physically bear a child? Isn't that dangerous – for both you, and any potential offspring? Mavis, you're a nurse – tell us about it.'

Stephanie saw Mavis stiffen. 'My knowledge isn't sufficient in the matter; as an army nurse you might imagine that I had few pregnancies to deal with. My own were unexceptional, I'm pleased to say, and the field is not one in which I've ever had a sufficient personal interest to lead me to read, or keep up with, research, beyond my general knowledge that the eggs a woman has have been with her for life…so the older she is, the more chance there's been for them to have become either less viable, or – if viable – then potentially less able to allow for a perfectly healthy child to develop from them. But I'll no' give advice beyond this: consult a specialist, and be honest with them.'

Mavis sat back, and Stephanie was touched by the way Althea patted her on the hand.

'Exactly what I've been saying,' muttered Julian.

The silence stewed…like tea in a pot.

It appeared that Clementine knew when she was beaten. 'Very well then – we'll find a doctor who'll work with us, Julian.'

Stephanie was about to say that she didn't think that was what Mavis had meant, when she was saved by the bell…though the bell took the form of a warbling sound in Christine's handbag.

'I'm so sorry – I didn't turn it off because I was hoping for a call,' said Christine as she tried to retrieve her phone before it stopped ringing. She punched a button. 'Hang on.' She appealed to Henry, 'Do you mind if I take this here, at the table, Henry…it's such a palaver to get up and move about, these days.' Henry nodded his assent, now having completely dissected his fish.

Christine continued, 'Hello, Geordie, any luck?' Stephanie wasn't surprised that everyone at the table – even Clementine – showed an interest in Christine's face as she listened. 'I see. And did they say when this was?' More silence. 'I see. Well, anything you can find out would help.' Another pause. 'Yes, I see. Thanks, Geordie. I really appreciate this. I'll keep checking for texts, or emails. Yes, thanks. Bye.'

Stephanie wondered what Christine's furrowed brow signified.

Mavis asked, 'Was Larry Merton at his house, still?'

Christine nodded. 'Yes – and no. He still lives there…at least, he did until he died.'

A concerned murmur passed around the table.

Mavis was now as upright as a board, Stephanie noticed. 'And when was that?'

Christine replied, 'A few days ago. The same day that Sylvia Jenkins' body was found.'

Althea perked up. 'Two dead people? Oh come on, Mavis, now you must tell us more…is your client – sorry, Rhodri's client – a double murderer?'

18th DECEMBER

CHAPTER TWENTY-ONE

The women of the WISE Enquiries Agency had agreed to meet at their office at noon: Christine greeted Carol and Annie with a pot of tea when they arrived – they'd traveled together in Carol's car – then Carol watched as Christine made a second pot, ready for Mavis's arrival.

Christine threw a general, 'How's it going?' in Annie's direction, which opened the floodgates for Annie to explain – in detail – about how annoying Tudor was being when it came to his role as panto prompt. Carol had endured Annie's grumblings about how Tudor was driving Annie around the bend all the way from the village; apparently, he was constantly muttering to himself because he was taking his role incredibly seriously and had decided to try to memorize the entire script, along with all the stage directions.

Carol could imagine how infuriating that might be…but Annie's multiple examples of how he was fraying her last nerve, ahead of the imminent arrival of her parents, was – as far as Carol was concerned – equally annoying. Still, as Carol kept reminding herself, she'd been able to leave the house knowing that her mother and father were looking after Albert, so that David could focus on his work. At least, her mother was taking care of Albert, because her father was at yet another rehearsal at the village hall; she had no idea what he was up to, but he'd flung himself into the panto with gusto, whereas her mother had backed out of being in it at all. Carol hadn't been informed by her parents why this might be the case, and had decided not to pry.

Once the foursome was settled, and Annie had finally run out of pithy comments about Tudor's ability to be both wonderful and annoying, they all sat waiting for Christine to update them.

Which she did, succinctly. 'Larry Merton died on the fifteenth of December. Geordie was able to extract this information from Larry's next-door neighbor, by suggesting he might be a cousin of the deceased man. When he passed this information to me, I was at dinner at Chellingworth Hall. Mavis and I were together. We agreed I would do what I could to find out more before this meeting. Thanks for all coming here; I'll admit it's getting more difficult for me to be comfortable driving, so staying here, when I can, is helpful.'

Mavis prompted, 'And what more have you discovered?'

'Geordie was able to discover that, tragically, Larry Merton died when he fell into the path of an oncoming London Underground train, and I found out that the incident took place at approximately eleven in the morning on the date in question. Larry was about to board a southbound train on the Northern Line at Borough station; presumably heading to his home near Clapham Common. It was busy there at the time: Borough Market would be a popular place for folks to be doing their pre-Christmas shopping, so the pause in service of the trains due to the tragedy was widely commented upon across social media.'

Carol blurted out, 'So, hang on, Christine…Sylvia Jenkins was fished out of the water around four, in Brecon, and the man who'd lied to her – who'd scammed her, leading to her losing her home – died just a few hours earlier, on the same day, in London?' Christine nodded. Carol thought it best to just add a quiet, 'Wow.' She was trying to work out how unlikely that might have been.

'Gordon Bennett, that's a turn up,' said Annie. 'So…do we know if he jumped, or was he pushed…or was it a terrible accident? Chrissy – anything?'

Christine shook her head. 'Not at the moment, but I do have a connection to someone in the British Transport Police; a friend of a friend is married to one of their officers. I've done what I can to make a direct connection, and I've passed the information to Rhodri Lloyd, though he feels he's unlikely to be able to access anything confidential, given the fact that he's not really able – in any meaningful way – to connect the death of Larry Merton in London to his client in Brecon…except via Sylvia Jenkins. And he reckons that's pushing it. But he'll try.'

Carol opened her laptop and began to tap keys. She wondered if she might be able to help. It wasn't that Christine was any slouch when it came to online research, but Carol did so much more of it. She kept her head down, and only half-listened to her colleagues' conversation as she wandered the highways, and many, many byways, of the internet.

Mavis asked, 'Did Rhodri say he'd been given the post-mortem report for Sylvia Jenkins yet?'

Christine replied, 'He hasn't received it. He's aware of its importance, but – given that Pauline is now back safely on her narrowboat – he's not pushing for it. He says there's no point; he'll get it when he gets it. Meanwhile, he's advised his client to stay at home, to mix with no one, to refer anyone who approaches her asking for a comment – be they law enforcement, or the media – to himself. That advice does not extend to us. We're free to talk to Pauline, and Pauline's free to talk to us – to the extent she's prepared to do so.'

Annie said, 'I know we think we know the whole story about this Sylvia and her scammer…but, look, it's not just me, is it? Don't we all think it's a bit…funny…that Pauline sent word via Rhodri that we had to look for the bloke who scammed Sylvia as our priority? 'Cause I do. I don't think you could look in the bottom of this cup of mine and tell me anything at all about me, or my life…or anything else except, maybe what sort of tea leaf was used to make the pot it came out of. Reading palms? Well, I reckon there's something to be said for the sort of life you lead, or even the job you do, making its mark on your hands, so there's that – but it's all rubbish, right? So how come Pauline set us off looking for this bloke – then it turns out that not only is he dead too, but he died on the same days as Sylvia? I mean…come on. That's…fishy. Innit?'

Mavis replied, 'I don't know about "fishy", but it's certainly something that we could ask Pauline herself. Do we think it's worth our time to meet with her, personally? Mebbe not all of us, though.'

Carol waggled her hand. 'Okay, I think I've got something here.' She looked up, and saw three eager faces beaming at her.

Annie nudged her. 'We all know when you're off down your rabbit holes, Car. So – what have you got for us?'

Carol smiled, though she felt she'd let her colleagues down. 'Sorry, I haven't got anything for you that I found online – though I'll do a bit more work there, later. No, this just pinged into our cloud inbox – it's from Rhodri. He's got the post-mortem report and it says that Sylvia Jenkins died of drowning – there was water in her lungs. They've sent the water for testing – to make sure it was water from where she was found – and they're also waiting for a full toxicology report, though the initial report says she had alcohol in her blood; not much – a couple of drinks' worth, but some. They've put time of death as being between approximately noon and three in the afternoon, on the fifteenth of December.'

Mavis asked, 'Is that it?'

Carol nodded. 'Rhodri didn't send us the report, but an email summarizing it. I can ask him for the full version. There's no harm, is there?'

Mavis nodded, and Carol tapped a note to Rhodri as Christine said, 'Well, even if Merton was pushed in front of a train, it couldn't possibly have been Sylvia Jenkins doing the pushing: there's no way to get from Borough Station in London to where her body was found in Wales that fast, unless you can sprout wings. So, however much she might have wished him dead, Sylvia Jenkins definitely didn't kill Larry Merton.'

Mavis added, 'And Pauline Thomas is also in the clear, in terms of the killing of Larry Merton; we know she was inside her narrowboat when he died.'

Annie said, 'True, but she's still in the frame for Sylvia. We now know that Sylvia drowned, and when. We also know she had a drink or two in her. But we don't know if she'd have been off her face after two sherries, do we? Someone could have got her to drink and given her a shove…or maybe even a small amount of alcohol could have made her so wobbly that she fell into the water of her own accord.'

Mavis replied, 'But it couldn't have been Pauline who made Sylvia drink either, because we know she was inside her narrowboat until the camera feed cut off, which was about an hour before that grandfather and his grandson saw the body in the water. Oh…yes…I see: Pauline could have encouraged Sylvia to take a couple of drinks, and then – theoretically – she could have let nature take its course, or have given it a helping hand. The post-mortem says that the time of death was approximate, after all. Oh dear.'

Carol said, 'We need to draw up a timeline, so we can focus on what we need to know. So – stop me if you think I've got anything wrong. I'll type as I talk. We have Pauline Thomas on camera inside her narrowboat until the cameras cut out at three minutes to three. Rhodri's other input tells us that the nine nine nine call, stating that a body had been sighted in the water, was logged at eleven minutes to four. From our point of view – and I don't mean this to sound heartless – we either need to prove that Sylvia died some time before three, or else we need to prove that between three minutes to three, and whatever "approximately three o'clock" actually means, Pauline Thomas was not out and about, either encouraging Sylvia to drink, or hurling her into the water. It's…well, it's a relatively small window of opportunity. If the post-mortem can't confirm Sylvia's time of death with any more accuracy, it's up to us, right? With what we have so far, Pauline could still be in the frame for it, as Annie said. It all depends on how certain the pathologist is that Sylvia was dead by three o'clock. I'll send a note about that to Rhodri, too – though I understand that he'll have already put two and two together. Now let me play devil's advocate for a minute: if Pauline somehow managed to "cause the death of" Sylvia Jenkins around three in the afternoon of December the fifteenth…what do you think the odds would be of the man who'd made Sylvia's life a misery meeting his end at the hands of another person on the same day?'

Annie clapped her hands, giving Carol a fright. 'What if Pauline was working with someone? She was being trolled, and maybe even stalked, by Sylvia, and she'd had enough. Rhodri had passed her to us, because he didn't think she'd get an injunction without evidence, and she just snapped. She knew all about Sylvia's Larry Merton, and had tracked him down…somehow…and she sent someone to kill him at the same time she was killing Sylvia. What about that? That could work, couldn't it?'

Carol didn't like to say anything; she was usually the one who had to tamp down Annie's unbridled enthusiasm, so she thought she'd give Mavis or Christine a chance to be the one to throw cold water on her chum's ideas.

Mavis began, 'I think it highly unlikely, Annie.'

Christine added, 'I think that's a bit…farfetched, Annie, don't you? Really? This isn't like that Patricia Highsmith story – you know, where strangers do each other's murders, to get away with it…which, by the way, wouldn't have worked, because Pauline had a good reason to want Sylvia dead, and was right there, on the spot, when she died.'

Annie pouted; Carol did her best not to crack a smile.

Annie said, petulantly, 'Well how did Pauline know? How did she know to tell us to look for the scammer? We found him, and he's dead. That…that must mean…something.'

Carol said, 'I bet it does, Annie, but I don't think any of us understand exactly what it might be. And another question might be…if Pauline's such a hot-shot fortune teller, how come she didn't know Larry was dead? But I think our real focus has to be: what do we plan to do next? While it appears that the post-mortem suggests it would have been touch and go for Pauline Thomas to have been able to kill Sylvia, it's still a possibility we cannot ignore. If our brief from Rhodri is to undertake enquiries that might lead to the discovery of evidence of Pauline's innocence, do I take it that you all think we need another face-to-face with Pauline?'

Three heads nodded.

Carol asked, 'Okay, then, so who do we think is the best person to do that?'

Carol was already looking at Annie; Mavis and Christine's gazes met hers there.

She grinned at her chum. 'You're it, Annie, though I'll give you a lift.'

CHAPTER TWENTY-TWO

Mavis was pleased that Carol and Annie had left her alone with Christine at the office, because she wanted to take the chance to discuss a concern she'd been harboring.

'Christine, since we cannae be doing much while we wait for anything the interview between Pauline and Annie might reveal, I wondered if I could have another little chat with you…no' about a case, as such, as I've said before, though it does impact on someone I care about: Althea.'

Christine replied, 'Of course I can, Mavis. As you say, we'll let Annie work her magic, and I'm free of Alexander's presence for the foreseeable future; Oswald Featherington – and Marjorie Pritchard – have him running in circles at the moment, juggling the blessed panto, and the renovations at the old school, all while he's determined to oversee the work that's going on at Honeysuckle Cottage. He says I'm not to go near the place at the moment because it's full of paint fumes…though I thought we'd agreed to use that paint that doesn't have any at all. So – what's the problem? Althea hasn't been poking her nose into our business again, has she?'

'The boot's on the other foot for once: I've been poking my nose into hers. As I mentioned to you, I have concerns about her chum "Ossie", and I've been looking into his business interests, and not liking what I've found. I know I told you that I was happy to carry out my own investigations into him without your help – though I am rather sorry you weren't able to arrange to have lunch with him, after all – but I do wonder if I'm…overreacting to what I've discovered. Which is why I'd welcome a second opinion, if you don't mind.'

'Not at all. Fire away, Mavis – what have you got so far?'

Mavis opened her laptop, then accessed the file she'd already built concerning Oswald, and handed the entire thing to Christine, who took it to her own desk. Mavis cleared away the tea things as she waited for Christine to read through everything she'd assembled in the folder.

Eventually Christine said, 'Why don't you pull up a chair beside me here? It'll save me moving, if you don't mind.'

The two women sat huddled together, with the screen of Mavis's laptop illuminating their faces in the darkening office.

Christine said, 'I can see why you weren't able to gather any more financial data for his so-called "company", because that's not what it is at all. Oswald is a sole trader, so his financial records are largely hidden. Though, to be fair, that's not so unusual. How did you manage to get the photos of where he lives?'

Mavis replied, 'I started with his website and thought the location sounded rather posh: "Grand View" as an address gives one…expectations. But he clearly lives in a flat above a boarded-up corner shop. The building might once – about a hundred and twenty years ago – have had a half-decent view, but now it's a sad little back street, and I suspect he lives in a sad little flat. I cannae imagine anyone with a thriving business choosing to live there.'

Christine asked, 'Had Althea given you the impression that she believes he's doing well? Thriving, as you said?'

Mavis nodded. 'She speaks of him, and acts around him, as though he's some great impresario, scattering his largesse as he goes, and deigning to step away from his theatrical empire to help out our poor little village panto production. All I can see is a website offering rather cut-price – when compared with the alternatives – panto scripts, a seedy flat, and a man who gives himself airs, yet wears clothing that's thirty years out of style, and looks as though he's been wearing it since he bought it…when it was in fashion.'

Mavis was gratified when Christine said, 'I get it, Mavis. But isn't he actually performing a service for Althea, for which she's – presumably – paying him a fair rate?'

Mavis sighed. 'You see, this is why I wanted to talk this through with someone. From what I'm aware, Althea is, indeed, paying a fair rate for a fair service. She's throwing in free room and board, but – in all honesty – she's enjoying Oswald's company a great deal. I've never seen her so…effervescent, and that's saying something, for Althea. My concern is…well, I dinnae like it that the man is misrepresenting himself to her. The way he acts you'd think he'd turned down umpteen offers to direct a panto in multiple locations around the country. He's always talking about all the famous people he's worked with – what it was like to have tea with this star of the theater, or that. Althea laps it up, her eyes alight with…well, maybe thoughts of a life not lived, I suppose.'

Christine mumbled, 'Always a consideration.'

Mavis pressed on. 'And that's my other concern, Christine. When Oswald has gone – and that will be in the New Year, I believe – what then? Will Althea's spirits plummet? Will she feel her current life isn't exciting enough for her? I hate the idea that this man's presence, and influence, is going to wind her tight like a spring, then, when he goes, she'll just unravel, and collapse. It's all…preening, and folderal, and my money's on none of what he says being true. I'm so worried for her. She's…well, she's no' as young as she once was, and – though she's spry, mind you, and active, because I do my best to make sure of that – she's a little less than she was even when we first came here to live. She's diminished physically, of course – she's shrunk in height, and she's lost a little body mass, but that's to be expected, now she's in her eighties – but I dinnae mean that. Now? Now she takes her rest because she needs it; she doesnae fight me when I encourage her to have a nap. That's different. And she's even grown an interest in a slightly healthier way of eating, though I'll never be able to wean her off her beloved cakes and biscuits, I know. Of course, the fact that we have an honest to goodness baker doing all our cooking for us means he sneaks baking in there whenever he can; I've recently spoken to him about how much pastry was creeping onto our plates because of all his pies, and so forth, and I think we'll strike a good balance, soon.'

Christine laughed. 'I can't remember the last time I ate pastry…but, there, I think I only have to look at most foods these days to get indigestion. When Lumpy finally comes out to see the light of day, oh, it'll be grand to eat whatever I fancy again.'

Mavis chose not to disabuse Christine of her expectations, despite the fact that she herself had found that her taste had never returned to the way it had been before she'd had her first son. She knew that experiences differed for every mother, so thought it best not to spoil Christine's positive outlook.

Instead, Mavis remained on point. 'So, do you think I should talk to Althea about…my concerns? I must admit, I'm in two minds.'

Christine arched her back, as best she could. 'First of all, now that I can see what you've got, let me have a little noodle around; the theatrical world needs backers, and I know that Daddy's put a bit of money into a few things…he might know someone, who knows someone, who knows something more about Oswald. But, whatever we find out, Mavis – do you think she'd listen to you? Althea can be…well headstrong is being polite – downright stubborn is closer to the mark. Tell me more about what she and this Ossie chap are like when they're together.'

Mavis did her best. 'She witters on at the best of times, but when she's with him it's a constant stream of "do you remember so-and-so doing such-and-such?" and "what about the night when we went to this place and that place?" She goes on and on about the things they did together. To me, it sounds as though they were joined at the hip, and got up to all sorts. I had no idea she'd been so very…well, um…active. Not in a bad way, I don't think – though I have to say it sounds as though she drank like a fish, and possibly swore like a sailor. And she ran with a set where there didn't seem to be a lot of money, but there were always parties.'

'Might that be normal, for people who were on the stage, back then? I know that theatrical people have a…certain reputation – I mean, think of all the stories about the famously drunk actors like Richard Burton, Peter O'Toole, Richard Harris, and the like. I can't imagine it was just the well-known ones who came off stage after a performance then wound down with a bottle in one hand, and a list of places where they could party the night away in the other.'

Mavis wasn't sure what to think. 'But even so – that was then. This…is now. And he's lying to her, Christine. What if she finds out and then she's disappointed. She doesn't handle disappointment well; she's had so little of it to cope with since she became a duchess.'

Christine spoke gently. 'Well, that's not exactly true, is it? She lost her beloved Chelly, and she managed to bounce back from that. And she sort of lost Henry to the dukedom, when he had to take his late-brother's role, and couldn't be an artist – I bet that was a bit of a loss for her, though probably not as much as it was for him; she must see how Henry feels burdened. And, of course, there's Clementine; I get the impression she's always disappointed Althea a little…never reached her full potential. By the way, what do you think about this thing with her wanting to have a baby?'

Mavis knew exactly how she felt about that. 'Despite what I said to her last evening at dinner, I was being circumspect, as you might have guessed. I think it's a poor idea at best – and might suggest the woman needs some sort of counseling. Your mid-fifties is no time to start thinking about having a baby – the human body wasnae designed for it. To have a burning desire to give birth might be a sign of something else…so I do think a doctor might be the best place to start. In that respect, I gave the best advice I know. You're pregnant, so you know how you feel; could you see Clementine going through this, at her age?'

Christine chuckled. 'If I'd known then what I know now – and despite the fact that Alexander and I are very much looking forward to becoming parents – I'd have been a great deal more mindful of our contraception's effectiveness. This is not for the faint of heart…and I mean that both figuratively, and literally. The strain being put on my body is…well, I hadn't expected it to be this much hard work. I feel as though I'm carrying a person around with me all the time. I know I am, but it's like there's a five-year-old child attached to my front…not what might amount to only eight or even ten pounds' worth of baby, when Lumpy comes out. Gaining ten pounds in weight, and being pregnant, have no more in common with each other than riding a bicycle and driving a Ferrari.'

Mavis had to smile. 'I'm with you. Though when you give birth I dinnae think you'll be calling it "only eight or ten pounds". My first was less than six pounds; that was more than plenty.'

Christine shook her head. 'Okay, that's enough, Mavis, thanks.'

'Aye, it is…and I've taken too much of your time with this.'

'I think you have to follow your intuition, Mavis…unless something happens to bring things to a head. You've got excellent instincts. Listen to what they're telling you.'

Mavis's body felt a little more tired than usual when she rose and started to pack her laptop away. 'Aye, I'll watch over her, and him…not that I see much of him these days. If you think Alexander's spending a lot of time at that village hall, you cannae imagine the hours they're putting in at the place…and then they dissect everything when they do get back to the Dower House. I'm looking forward to enjoying a meal without there being a constant list of notes being made and discussed about this character, or that, and what they could or should be doing differently. It's mind-boggling.'

The women hugged, and Mavis made her way back to her trusty Morris Traveller, to drive back to the Dower House, where she suspected she'd be alone – at least for a while.

CHAPTER TWENTY-THREE

Carol and Annie were only about ten minutes away from getting back to Anwen-by-Wye when Annie exploded; Carol had expected it to happen much earlier. She'd felt Annie fuming beside her in the car since they'd left Pauline Thomas's narrowboat, and Carol fought to keep her eyes on the road as her friend and colleague let rip.

'How on earth can Pauline expect us to do the best we can for her if she won't tell us everything, and goes on and on about clouds in the crystals? I mean, come on, Car, what a load of old tosh.'

Carol didn't bother to say anything. Indeed, she realized she might not be required as a participant at all in the conversation Annie was about to have with herself.

Annie proved her right by continuing, 'She had no excuse for not telling us about Sylvia Jenkins to start with, but, yeah, she made a bit of a case about that I suppose, though I still don't like it. We wouldn't have been swayed by her telling us; we could have done a better job if we'd known. Then there's all the details she just let slip about Larry Merton. Alright, I know she didn't know his actual name, because she says Sylvia never told her – but she knew what he looked like…though I suppose "tall, dark, and handsome" is a bit of a tried and trusted one…but at least you'd have known you weren't trying to spot a little bloke with blond hair when you went trawling through all those zillions of photos, wouldn't you?'

Carol said, 'True.'

'Exactly. Then there's the fact she didn't tell us that she was aware that Sylvia knew where her boat was moored. We could have done with being told that right off the bat. Though…what would we have done differently than what we did? Eyes-on oversight, and cameras everywhere is about it, really, in't it, doll? Short of actually sitting right next to her every hour of the day and night. Yeah. So…well, I suppose that's it, really. I think that's just a few hours of my life I'm never going to get back, because we didn't find out anything new, except that Chief Inspector Carwen James knows that we're working for Rhodri and trying to find evidence that'll get her off a possible murder charge. And both you and I know that's what Carwen flipping James will be trying to do, don't we?'

'Possibly.'

'Yeah, well, it's all well and good the pathologist's report saying it's touch and go that Pauline could have killed Sylvia…but that doesn't really help either Pauline or the police, because I bet both sides could rustle up the odd expert witness or two to speak about how accurate science can be when it comes to determining exact time of death. So we've got to keep going…but I don't trust her to have told us everything, even now, Car. I think she's holding something back, don't you?'

'Not sure.'

'Well, I am. Did you notice what she did when I pressed her on that? Exactly – started on with all that mumbo-jumbo that she'd seen something in her crystal ball about whoever it was who'd scammed Sylvia. In her crystal ball? But, there, if she'd said that we might not have focused on tracking him down, and we'd never have found out who he was…nor that he died on the same day as Sylvia. And what did she have to say about that? Nothing, right? All she did was muck about with those Tarot cards. And what's all that about? I mean, I get that she put the card for Justice on the table first – because that's what we're all seeking here, right? But then asking me to shuffle those giant things? My hands aren't small, Car, but I know I made a right mess of that bit. Then picking out the cards? Trust me to pick out the flaming card for Temperance first. That made me laugh, right there – sorry, Car, I couldn't hold it in. Sorry. That came over as rude, I know.'

'It did, a bit.'

'Yeah. Well, I tried to make up for it by getting her to explain it all to me. And when she said that the Temperance card related to what was in the past, and that it meant people working together, in harmony, to achieve a common goal it made sense, sort of…because that's what we do at the agency, right? Then the card for what's going on at the moment was a bit…well…weird, really, right? I mean I know we'd been talking to her about Larry Merton being killed, but then for that Ace of Swords to come out, and upside down…well, she didn't have to say too much for us to know that was bad, did she? When she started bandying about words like destructive force, love denied, and the misuse of power, I knew she was talking about him…but what do you think she meant when she said it might also mean that I know someone who's very much involved with conception and childbirth. You're not expecting again, are you Car?'

'Most definitely not, Annie.'

'I'm not saying that Bertie wouldn't mind a little brother or sister, and you are getting on a bit, Car, so I suppose if you're going to do it, now's as good at time as any. You've even got built-in babysitters at the moment, haven't you? Anyway, like I said, that was…odd. Then when she did the future card, you could tell she was vamping. I mean, how can six sticks mean everything she said. Sorry, six "batons", not sticks. It's all well and good telling us that all our hard work will be rewarded, and that important news will come to us soon…but that's not…anything out of the ordinary really, is it? And I didn't like it that she told me off for handing it to her the wrong way. I mean – how am I supposed to know the right way? She never said. So then she goes on and on about how we should be on the lookout for someone who's a traitor…someone close to us. I mean – what use is saying something like that? All it does is make people who work together suspicious of each other. Tosh, the lot of it. Right?'

'Undoubtedly.'

'Yeah. And telling us that we should focus on finding out all about Larry Merton, because that way someone in a uniform would help get her cleared of Sylvia's killing? Rubbish. And I'm not buying, for one minute, that because "the clouds in her ball had parted" she saw someone push Larry Merton off that Tube platform as clear as…crystal.' Annie laughed aloud. 'Sorry, Car – couldn't resist that one. Get it – crystal ball…crystal?'

'I get it. And we're there. You wanted me to drop you at the shop. Well, we're there.'

Annie disentangled herself from her seatbelt and stuck her head back into the open door before she closed it. 'Thanks for the chat, Car – it means a lot. You're really sensible, you know? I'll type up a report and send it round to everyone. Tonight, probably. Talk later. Ta for the lift. Love to Bertie, and Dave and…well, everyone, you know? Bye.'

Annie slammed the door – too hard – and Carol pulled away, driving for at least two whole minutes before she entered the sanctuary provided by the high hedge that surrounded Tŷ Mawr, her new, and most wonderful home. Every window was alight with a welcoming yellow glow – some showing as a crack between curtains, some through blinds that were pulled down. A couple of the windows at the side of the house that looked over the lane that led to the church, and then to the Chellingworth Estate, seemed to be illuminated for…well, no good reason. Carol began to wonder why every window was lit up…it did seem a bit unusual.

The good-sized garden allowed for adequate parking, and there was even a separate garage, but, even so, Carol preferred to enter the house by the side door that led to the kitchen, so she hauled her bag out of the back seat, and dropped it onto the kitchen table as she passed through.

Before Albert had come along, both Carol and David would announce their arrival at their tiny flat in London with a cheery call of, 'It's only me,' whenever they got home. Since the arrival of a baby in their lives, they'd not dared to do it; instead, they'd both skulk around to be sure they weren't disturbing a fragile sleep. Carol crept into every single room, but there wasn't a soul in the house. Her parents' car was parked outside, as was David's. So…where was everyone?

Every light was on, as she'd seen from outside; as she checked that a room was empty, she turned off the light, and closed the door. Soon, she was back in the kitchen. Bunty was curled on a scruffy towel in the corner…where the Aga would have been, if they'd been in the old house.

Carol sat at the kitchen table and spoke to her cat, 'Where did they all go, Bunty? You'd tell me if you could, wouldn't you? But I dare say the easier thing to do is to phone my husband, eh? Yes, good idea.'

Carol punched the button to call David's mobile phone, but it went straight to his voicemail. She repeated the process with her mother's number, then her father's, and got the same result. 'Okay, Bunty – that didn't work. Any other bright ideas? What? Don't panic…yet? Okay, I'll work on that one, *cariad*, but I won't make any promises. Look for a note? Good idea. We haven't got a noticeboard, or a blackboard anywhere yet – so I should sort that out, soon. But…right, come with me, if you like, Bunty. There's nothing on the fridge. What about the mantlepiece, in the living room? Yes, people leave notes on mantelpieces, don't they? Let's look there. Nope, nothing there. Where else? Where would David, or Mam, think I would go when I got in from work? Oh, good idea, Bunty – I'll race you up the stairs to the bathroom. Good girl…you're not getting old at all, are you? Right – anything in here? No, I can't see any notes. But, while I'm here…'

Bunty accompanied Carol as she made her way back to the kitchen, and rubbed herself against Carol's legs when she sat at the table, so, of course, Carol picked her up and stroked her silky fur. It was just the comfort Carol needed at that moment, because she felt terribly alone…and a little wary. Where had everyone gone? And why had all the lights been on? And why was no one answering their phone? And…why were all their cars still at the house? Had they…gone to the pub? Gone to…church? That didn't seem likely.

Carol had it: they must all be at the village hall. She'd go to check; it wasn't far, and she'd most certainly leave a note before she ran off.

She put Bunty onto the floor, pulled her bag off the table onto her lap to get a pen, and that was when she saw the note.

'Oh Bunty, look at me – so silly. I dumped my bag on it and didn't even see it.'

I know you hate getting texts when you're driving, and I thought you'd like a note, like we used to do in the "old days". We're all off to the village hall. Your dad phoned and asked your mum to bring him his yellow jacket (?) and she didn't want to go on her own. I'm going with her, so Albert's coming too. I left Bunty in charge of the house – and I left all the lights on so it would look cheerful when you got here. See you…whenever (most likely, about five) Dx

Carol's watch told her it was twelve minutes to five; she must have just missed them. 'Right then, Bunty, shall I do a quick bit of work, or shall I start getting food ready? Nah – I'll take my bag upstairs, clear up my emails, then we can all cook together here in my absolutely massive kitchen with my incredibly big island, and my lovely kitchen table – that seats eight – and my dishwasher. Yes, Bunty…dish, dish, dishwasher, dish, dish, dishwasher…come on, follow me upstairs, there's a good girl. Dish, dish, dishwasher. Come on…sing along. Oh my word, Bunty – I am the world's luckiest woman.'

CHAPTER TWENTY-FOUR

Annie wondered if she was the unluckiest person alive. 'What do you mean, you in't got no super-sticky-glue stuff, Shar? You're the village shop; if you haven't got it, where am I going to get it? Builth Wells? Brecon? Hay-on-Wye? They're miles away. Eustelle and Rodney will be here tomorrow, and I've gone and chipped a flamin' china bowl that's supposed to have pride of place on the windowsill in their room. I managed to get all the pot-pourri stuff up off the carpet, and I even found the missing chip, but I can't find any glue anywhere in the pub. How can a pub not have any glue? And how can a shop have none neither? I knew I should have asked Car to stop in Brecon…but we were there for work, and I…well, I might have forgotten that I needed it, I was so flamin' angry with our client.'

Annie eventually noticed that Sharon Jones looked tired. She felt bad for having had a go at her. 'Sorry, Shar, doll. I'll shut up. It's my own stupid fault for breaking the thing in the first place. Maybe it'll teach me to take my time when I'm dealing with breakable things. Right-o then…have you got any Jammie Dodger biscuits? And I need some sticking plasters, too, please; when I picked up the bowl I nicked myself, and it won't heal properly unless I cover it up.'

Sharon managed a weak: 'Yes, Annie, I've got both of those. Is that it?'

'No,' said Annie firmly. 'You can tell me what's wrong with you. Come on, spill. You're not yourself. I'd have thought you'd have been over the moon, having some sort of thing to do with Aled in the panto. I've got that right, haven't I?'

Sharon nodded. 'I have. And I am. But…well, I never thought it would be this much work, Annie. Aled and me seem to be on and off that stage an awful lot, and it means we have to keep turning up to rehearse scenes with all different people. And that Oswald? He's playing the dame, you know that, right?' Annie nodded. 'Well, his costume is going to be this massive frock, so he's doing all the rehearsals wearing this hooped thing over his trousers, so we all get a sense of how much room he takes up on the stage. All I can say is that it seems to be his way of having most of the stage to himself, and all of us lot shoved off into a corner all the time. And who knows how big the goose costume is, because he's waggling another big hoop on a stick all the time, too, because that's where the goose will be. So it's all a bit fraught and…well, Aled and I aren't having as much fun as I thought we'd have.'

Annie wasn't sure what to say; she liked Sharon, and she liked Aled, and she liked Joan Pike too…but – of the three of them – Aled was the one Tudor relied upon to keep the pub open when he couldn't be around. To all intents and purposes, Aled was the under-manager of the place, and did a really good job of it. But Annie didn't want to make Sharon feel she wasn't valued – she was still trying to get over her mother having to leave the village under a cloud, after all, and Annie knew how close they'd been.

Annie offered, 'I dare say it'll all turn out alright in the end. Just keep rehearsing, and it'll be fine.'

'I don't know about that. I think I'm losing it, honestly I do, Annie. I'm supposed to be a bright young thing, but I can't seem to hold two thoughts in my head at once. The way people come in here? It usually goes in waves…there's a rhythm, but there are waves too. Never mind, I know what I mean. Anyway, yesterday, I had a wave: Marjorie and Oswald happened to bump into each other outside, and he came in with her when she was getting coffee and milk for the rehearsals, and they were talking about…the goose, I think…yes, because he was saying the goose only had to follow him about the stage, so they wouldn't need to rehearse. Anyway, I went out the back to get some broken biscuits – they're ideal for the rehearsals Marjorie says, because they're cheaper, and no one cares that they're broken, because they're getting them for free. Anyway, Marjorie was here, and Oswald, and then Iris came in to get some tea; and after they'd all gone then your Carol came in, I think; then Janet popped in for some cream…and after that, no one for half an hour. It's like that, see? Anyway, I'd got so overwhelmed by just having a bit of a rush that I couldn't think where I'd put Mam's headscarf.'

'The navy-and-white spotted one?' Annie knew it well.

'Yes, though I don't know why I call it Mam's – she hasn't worn it in yonks. I use it whenever I go out and it's raining. I need that scarf…but I must have shoved it in a pocket or something, because I ended up having to wear my old woolen one last night to go to rehearsal. Do me a favor and keep your eyes peeled for it when you're out with the dogs, would you? It might have blown away somewhere – that's the other thing I thought of. Anyway, there you are – plasters.'

Annie said, 'And Jammie Dodgers?'

Sharon tutted. 'See? I've gone *twp*, I have. Mam always said I'd go soft in the head, and it seems she was right. Oh, and I'm closing a bit early tonight. I don't think it'll matter because almost everyone's at the village hall anyway.'

Annie sighed. 'Really? Oh dear. That means the pub'll be empty.'

'I think people might be glad of a drink when they finish, to be honest, Annie, so look out for a late rush. I know I'll be fancying one myself, if last night's anything to go by. Though I don't think anyone will be offering to buy one for Marjorie. She's really enjoying being in charge.'

Annie chuckled. 'I bet she is…oh, hang on, there's my phone. Take this money and sort the change while I answer this, could you, Shar? Ta. Hello, Chrissy, what's up?'

Annie could tell that Christine was excited. 'I've got an update, but I can't tell you, you have to see it for yourself. Can you get to your laptop?'

'Can you give me…ten minutes?'

'Great. I'll get hold of the others – we need an urgent video call for all of us. Talk soon.'

Annie disconnected. 'No peace for the wicked, eh? Thanks for this, Shar, and good luck tonight…or am I supposed to say "break a leg" – I know that's a thing, isn't it?'

Sharon laughed. 'Apparently – but I don't think it applies to rehearsals. Ta. See you.'

Annie was at her kitchen table ten minutes later, with her laptop open, and two attention-seeking dogs scrabbling at her knees. 'Here I am, Chrissy. Hiya, Mave, Car…what's it all about?'

Christine was at her desk in the office, Mavis in her room at the Dower House, and Carol in front of her eye-watering wallpaper. Annie said, 'I'm doing my best to keep Gert and Rosie quiet, but they're excited, and they need a walk, so let's just get on with it, eh?'

Christine opened with: 'As you know, I was following a connection to a British Transport Police officer, and I got to him, eventually. All he could do was confirm for me that there would be cameras on the Tube platform where Larry Merton fell, but he couldn't tell me when – if ever – the recordings would be made available. I got hold of Rhodri, who managed to bring some pressure to bear, and he sent me the recordings. I'm not going to say anything but this: first of all, I need to warn you that it doesn't make pleasant viewing; secondly, it all happens very fast; third, Larry Merton is wearing a padded jacket and a flat, checked cap, with a plaid scarf…you'll see him in the bottom right of your screen. I'm going to share my screen with you, and play the recording with about a minute's run-up to the critical moment, so you can acquaint yourself with the overall view. Okay, here we go…'

Annie sat in silence – except for a few whimpers from Gertie – and watched with apprehension. She was about to witness the end of a man's life, and that immediately weighed upon her; she'd have to consider how this all made her feel, so she could discuss it with her counsellor.

Christine had been right, it all happened in an instant: there was the front of the train coming into sight, there was a general shift of bodies on the crowded platform, then the figure in the plaid scarf flew into the path of the train, and disappeared. Even though there was no sound, the shocked response of people on the platform was obvious, though Annie also noticed that people who were just yards away appeared to be completely oblivious to the whole thing until – she assumed – witnesses started screaming.

Mavis was the first to say, 'Could you repeat that whole thing please, Christine?'

Christine did. Then Carol said, 'And again, please.'

The third time around, Annie shouted, 'Stop it there!'

The recording blurred as it stopped.

'That's annoying,' said Carol, 'because I was trying to get a good look at a figure that seemed to be making its way toward Larry Merton immediately before the train arrived.'

Annie said, 'Yes, Car, me too…the person in a sort of knitted, lumpy jacket, or thick knitted thing – it looks as though it's brown, or burgundy – with double-breasted shiny buttons…that one.'

'I saw that person, too,' said Mavis. 'Does the recording go back further, Christine? Maybe a few more minutes? It's possible we might be able to spot the movements of both Larry Merton and the person in the jacket with the shiny buttons.'

Christine clapped. 'Thank you all – I thought it might just be me seeing things. Yes, let's all watch again.'

They did. Annie saw Larry Merton saunter onto the platform, then more people did the same, turning to spot a place where they could stand to wait. Annie knew the drill: she'd navigated London's Underground system for her entire life, and used it like a pro. 'Hang on a minute,' she said. 'Look, ladies, I don't want to be pushy, but let me tell you this, because I have a few insights here. You're looking at some people who know this station and platform well – they'd be local regulars – and you can spot them because they have a definite place they want to be. They'll know approximately where the doors will be when their train stops, and will know to keep away from the people getting off. Then there are those who might not know this station, but use the Underground regularly, and they might not know where the doors will be, but they'll look around to see where the people getting off the train will be heading, and they'll pick spot where they can stay back from the edge, yet get to the doors as soon as they can. But it's a Sunday just before Christmas, and Borough Market is a magnet for tourists and out-of-towners…so there'll be a lot of people milling about on the platform, not aware that there are good spots and bad spots. You'll see them because the experienced Tube users will sneer at them – and they'll probably be kitted out for Christmas. I'd say that Larry Merton knew this station: he walks in and heads straight for the spot he wants, and that's a great spot, by the way – he'd easily get into a carriage without having to cross a stream of people trying to get off the platform. That person with the buttons? They're not a regular – but that person is looking for someone. They pass empty spots, they aren't looking around for signs – they're bobbing and weaving – then once they see Larry, they head for him. Chrissy, if you could wind that back again, I think you'll all see what I mean.'

The four women watched in silence. It felt very strange to Annie that the sight of Larry Merton disappearing had already lost most of its dreadful meaning…but, at least with her mind clearer because of that objectivity, she was able to be the first to say aloud, 'She pushed him.'

Mavis asked, 'I saw something too, I think – but why do you say "she", Annie?'

Annie had to admit, 'I don't know why I know, but I'm pretty sure that's a woman. The way she moves – she's lithe, sinuous.'

'The button person is slight, and short, with mid-length, mid-colored hair.' Christine spoke with confidence. 'Sorry – I'd already watched this about ninety-five times before I showed it to you. And I'm also sure it's a woman. The thing is…I also have the pathologist's report on Sylvia Jenkins here, as well as the list of personal items they removed from the body. Sylvia was slim, short, had mid-length, brown-gray hair, and was pulled out of the water wearing a double-breasted knitted jacket. It was brown, with gold buttons.'

Carol said, 'But Sylvia was in Brecon when this happened in London. How can that be?'

Annie whispered, 'Gordon Bennett, Car – what did Pauline say to us this afternoon? "Hard work would bring its rewards, and important news was in the offing"? Well, she weren't wrong, were she? This is important news, that Chrissy found 'cause of all her hard work…but what does it mean? How could Sylvia Jenkins be in two places at once?'

19th DECEMBER

CHAPTER TWENTY-FIVE

When Edward alerted Henry to the imminent arrival of his in-laws, John and Sheila Timbers, the duke swung into action. His wife and son were already downstairs, so he made his way to meet them in the Great Hall, where the duchess had said she wanted to greet her parents.

Unfortunately, Hugo decided that was the exact moment when he needed to exercise his lungs; they were in excellent working order, Henry could tell. A cacophony of wailing infant and greetings between four adults – all working hard to be heard – lasted for several minutes, before Sheila Timbers decided to be a good grandmother and attend to her grandson, who promptly stopped screaming, and began to gurgle happily as though the world were not going to end, after all.

As his mother-in-law cradled Hugo, cooing and smiling into his now cherubic face, he noticed that his wife was…stroking her mother's back, with a look of great concern on her face. He wondered if he'd missed something important.

'You look done in, Mum,' said his wife. 'That canceled flight really messed you up, didn't it? I bet you'll be glad to have a lie-down.'

Sheila replied, 'And there was me thinking I looked not too bad for a woman who hasn't seen a bed for two days. Ah well, a bit of sleep and this tan will cover up most things, I suppose.'

Henry dared, 'You both look as though you've had a great deal of sun, but I dare say you were already well-toasted before you even got to Barbados for your break.' He still wasn't sure what a retired lumber merchant and his wife – who both lived rather indolently all year in Spain – needed a break from, but was aware that was how his wife always referred to her parents' annual sojourn to the Caribbean.

John cracked a smile – showing suspiciously white teeth. Henry couldn't imagine that they'd got bigger since he'd last seen the man, but…it really did look as though they had.

John said, 'We had a little trip to Turkey before we went over to Barbados. A bit of a flying visit, really – didn't get much done.'

He grinned again, and gnashed his teeth at Henry, which Henry found both puzzling, and a little alarming. He thought it best to just nod, by way of a response to John's peculiar observations.

'A lie-down would be lovely, Stephanie, darling,' gushed Sheila. 'We want to be in tip-top form for all the proper Christmas stuff. When are you having your do, when all the staff come in, and there's Christmassy stuff all over the place? Though it looks lovely already.'

Henry's heart sank as he thought of the staff party, and the carol singing, and the blessed speeches that would be involved…though he knew it was always well-received by everyone who worked at Chellingworth Hall, either on a full- or part-time basis. Apparently, it meant a great deal to the invitees that he and the duchess took the time to be with them as they ate and drank their fill – then disappeared into the background so that the staff could really enjoy themselves.

Stephanie replied, 'That's not for a few days yet, Mum – so there's plenty of time for you to get back to normal. Oh, but there's something you don't know about: we're having a panto in the village, and Henry's painting the scenery…though I haven't seen him do very much about it, to be honest.'

Henry was bemused. 'Stephanie, I don't know who told you that, but I'm doing no such thing.'

His wife turned to face him, a look of surprise – no, shock – on her face. 'You most certainly are. Not only did your mother tell me she'd asked you to do it, and you'd agreed, but Mavis has confirmed that your name's to appear in the brochure they're having printed to commemorate the event. In fact, I spoke to the woman who's organizing the brochure, to clarify exactly how you should be referred to within it. You are painting the scenery, Henry, and the panto takes place in just over a week, so I suggest you get hold of your mother and find out how you two have managed to miscommunicate, and to whom you need to speak so they can tell you what you need to do.'

Henry felt a bit wobbly. 'Mother has mentioned no such topic to me, I promise you. It's the sort of thing I'd have remembered. I mean, one's not asked to paint scenery every day, is one? Besides – why would she ask me? She knows that I've never painted anything on such a grand scale before…oh dear…a grand scale. Oh, I say…Sheila, John, please excuse me. I do rather think I should get hold of Mother straight away. I just hope she's not in one of those blessed rehearsals. Welcome, and have a good rest, after your break, and I shall see you…when I see you.'

Henry rushed into the library, where he hoped to find enough peace that he could speak to his mother with the vehemence that was required. He was now quite clear about what had happened: his mother had tricked him. And now he was stuck with…well, having to do something he didn't want to do, and a lot faster than it needed to have been done. Failing to reach anything but his mother's voicemail, he left a message, which he felt was suitably brusque, and ended by requesting that she return his call as soon as possible, because he needed to know – with some urgency – what was now required of him.

As Henry stood in front of the library's hearth, wondering if his message had been just a little too peremptory, even given the circumstances, he was startled by the entry of his brother-in-law.

Julian said, 'Ah Henry, you are here, good. I just met John and Sheila, Stephanie's parents. They were heading to bed…which I thought odd, but I let it pass. Stephanie said I could find you in here, and I'm glad I have. I wondered if we could have a little chat?'

Henry immediately felt the panic in the pit of his stomach. 'I have to rush to the village, unexpectedly, I'm afraid, Julian. To…to see about the scenery, for the panto.' It was the best he could come up with.

Julian nodded. 'Yes, I saw on the roster that you were doing that. Good for you, Henry. I'm rigging up something to help with the lights, myself. Went down there to escape this place for a while, truth be told, and offered my services. There's a woman – Marjorie Pritchard; she seems terribly well organized…found something right away that fits with my skill set. I've been out at your workshops doing a bit of welding. It's actually good fun.'

Henry had had been trying to avoid Julian quite unnecessarily, it seemed. 'Wonderful,' he said. 'But I must get there to see what's what.'

Julian replied, 'But of course, Henry. The stage is completely bare at the moment – I wondered when you'd be providing all the necessaries – and it looks as though there'll be quite a lot of necessaries to be provided. Will you be having everything built out at the workshops, too? I expect your team out there will be glad of a bit of overtime, with it coming up to Christmas.'

Henry paused and – for the first time – applied his imagination to what 'painting the scenery' might actually entail. And shuddered. He wasn't a great lover of theater, but had attended enough performances of various sorts to know that scenery was usually constructed of wood, and needed to provide a multi-layered backdrop for the entire stage. But…sometimes there were canvas treatments, too…and that village stage wasn't that big…was it? The panic had reached his gullet.

'I think I'd best get on, if you don't mind, Julian.'

'Don't let me stop you, Henry. I'll get back to my welding, and catch you later. But I wanted to tell you that Clementine's simmered down on the child front, and she's actually speaking to me again, so that's an improvement. But we'll talk later. Off you pop, and I'll get back to it.'

When Julian left, Henry sank into a chair. Realizing he knew nothing about set design, or construction, he decided to use the internet to find out what he could…but first, he rang for Edward.

By the time his butler appeared, Henry was absolutely certain that the job that lay ahead of him was probably beyond him, so he found himself snapping, 'I need to get to the village hall, post haste, Edward. Please arrange a car, and I shall need to return…when I am ready.'

'Indeed, Your Grace. Will that be all?'

Henry paused. 'Edward…do you, by chance, happen to know anybody who knows anything about scenery? Stage scenery – not the stuff that's outside the window, I mean.'

Edward replied evenly, 'As it happens, I do, Your Grace. Myself.'

Henry felt a range of emotions all at once. 'Really, Edward? You never cease to amaze me. But…how?'

Edward replied, 'My father was in service to a retired colonel, near Weobley, where I also trained. The colonel was very keen on amateur dramatics, and the patron of a local company. Of course, both my father and I volunteered our services to our colonel's efforts, and I worked on the construction of the scenery. I am not artistically gifted, Your Grace, so had no hand in the decorating of the constructed items, but I was called upon to come up with some inventive ways of allowing rather large items to be moved about in rather small spaces. Would that knowledge be of any service to you, Your Grace?'

Henry bounced up out of his seat. 'I say, Edward, you're absolutely splendid. Please make arrangements here so that you can accompany me to the village hall; you're about to become my right-hand man in a rather unusual realm of endeavor.'

Edward hovered. 'You'd like me to leave Chellingworth Hall?' Henry nodded. 'And to travel to the village, with you, in your car?' Henry nodded again. 'Well, I'm not sure about how…that wouldn't be the done thing, Your Grace. If you need me, of course I shall make arrangements so that I might meet you there. Would that suit, Your Grace?'

Henry saw that he was putting his butler in a difficult position, but decided to have his way. 'We'll travel together. You can sit in the front of the car, with whomever is allocated to drive me. But this matter is urgent, Edward, so I shall prepare myself in my apartment, and explain to the duchess what's happening, and we shall leave as soon as possible. Thank you.'

'Indeed, Your Grace.'

Henry felt a great deal less worried about the task he was facing than he had done just a few moments earlier, and found himself starting to envisage where, and how, he'd manage to paint large structures…then wondered if it might be normal to use house paints for scenery, or whether he might require gargantuan quantities of acrylics, instead.

CHAPTER TWENTY-SIX

Annie was having quite a morning of it. She'd been up and about since before six, hoping that would give her enough time to make sure that everything was as perfect as it could be before her parents were due to arrive in a taxi, from the train station. Tudor had offered to collect them, but Annie's father had been adamant – neither he nor his wife wanted to take Tudor away from his pub; he wanted everything to go along as it normally would.

Annie and Tudor had laughed about that, because their first Christmas at the Coach and Horses was turning out to be anything but 'normal' – at least, it wasn't anything like they'd expected it would be. And it was all because of the panto. The impact on the village had been profound: everyone Annie saw – or heard – was pacing about muttering to themselves, or incessantly humming, or mouthing words. And the amount of people she'd seen looking at their feet as they shuffled about, or who were waving their arms in the air for no apparent reason, made her think that if any visitors were passing through Anwen-by-Wye they might be forgiven for thinking that there was something in the water that was having a catastrophic effect upon the sanity of the people who lived there.

As she thought it, she actually wondered if it might be true…not that there was something in the water, but that everything was off kilter. Yes, a lot of it could be put down to the panto, but – even when they weren't panto-ing…if that was even a word – people weren't themselves.

'Are you through there, still, Annie?' Tudor's voice carried from the living room.

'Yes, just putting a few last-minute touches to their room. I'll be in for breakfast in a tick.'

Annie studied every detail of the room: the curtains were hanging just right; the bedspread didn't have a crease in it; the attached bathroom – tiny though it might be – was gleaming; and the whole room smelled fresh…the odors of paint, new carpet, and wallpaper paste had finally dissipated. She was satisfied. Except for the bowl on the windowsill; she hadn't been able to find any glue to cement the large chip back onto the body, so had done her best with sticky tape, and an artistic arrangement of pot-pourri. She hoped her mother didn't notice.

Joining Tudor at the kitchen table, she managed to gulp down her cereal so quickly that both their bowls were ready at the same time to be presented to Gertie and Rosie for licking, as usual.

Tudor said, 'I'll take these two around the green an extra time this morning, so you can get on…and be here in case your lot's early. I'll have my script with me, so I'll be fine.'

'Do you absolutely have to memorize every line of dialogue, and every stage direction, just so you can tell people what to do if they've gone wrong on the night, Tude?' Annie was worried about the way Tudor had become fixated on his task. 'I thought that the whole point of you agreeing to be the prompter was so that you didn't have to do anything but be there on the night with the script in your hand, and read from it as they all do…whatever it is they're doing. This seems like a lot of work.'

Tudor shrugged. 'It's not necessary, but you know I don't like to half-do a job. If I know what's supposed to happen next, I can be on the lookout for someone who seems to have lost the plot…literally. Then I can help them before anyone knows they've gone wrong.'

Annie stroked Tudor's arm. 'I'm concerned that you're not sleeping well, or even enough. You were babbling in your sleep last night – not snoring, but actually talking, though it didn't make much sense. This place takes it out of you, Tude – you're on your feet all day, in the bars or in the kitchen – and then you're doing all this panto stuff in what's laughingly called your "spare" time. And you haven't even got Aled covering for you as much as usual.'

Tudor sighed. 'It's not as though I'm run off my feet though, am I? I know that everyone's at the village hall, rehearsing all the time – or else doing their own thing in the comfort of their own home, like I am. But the big difference is that people are having snacks at home, instead of coming in for a proper bite. I know our beverage sales aren't too bad because we're picking up a bit with a late-night rush. But the food sales? Terrible. Not even the lunches are doing well. I just hope things pick up in the New Year – though that's when the reality of putting everything on the credit cards for Christmas hits home, isn't it? So, maybe not. I don't know, Annie – I'm not sure that introducing a curry night is going to cut it. We've got to offer customers what they want – because they don't seem to want what we're offering now. But what do they want? I've no idea. I mean, this is a pub, so our options are limited, aren't they?'

Annie was only too well aware that she and Tudor had played, and replayed, similar conversations when he'd been running the Lamb and Flag, as well as since they'd moved to the Coach and Horses.

She said, 'Look Tude, the Coach is doing much better business than the Lamb ever did. And that's because of you and all the effort and innovation you've applied to this place. But we both knew it would be a struggle. Anwen-by-Wye is a small, out-of-the-way village that doesn't bring too many people in from outside, especially in the winter, when Chellingworth Hall is closed to the public. But this panto? Mavis has told me she's doing her best to get tickets into the hands of people all over the wider area – from Builth, to Brecon, to Hay. Chances are, there's a lot of people who'll be coming here that night who maybe haven't been before, or else who haven't been for years. So what can we do to make them want to come back again? How can we make the whole village look so attractive that they'll want to see it in daylight? I think you should have a chat to Iris Lewis about that, because Marjorie's so involved with the production she hasn't got time to spit. There must be things we can all do to help. I know you'll be in the hall, hiding in the wings during the performance, but I don't mind not seeing the panto – especially since you're not actually on stage – so I can keep this place ticking over, as long as you leg it back, in case we get busy when everyone's off stage. Have you thought about a special offer for people after the show's finished? Get them to stop for at least a drink or two with the promise of free, or cheap…something or other? Or what about pre-panto snacks and treats?'

Tudor rose. 'You're brilliant, you are. I hadn't thought of anything like that. You're right…now, what could I do as a special offer, I wonder? I'll think about that while I'm out with these two; it'll make a change from repeating the lines that the greedy landlord has to shout at the poor widow, Mother Goose. I know that Oswald wrote the script, but I can't say he's done a brilliant job of it. It's got every cliché in the book…and the so-called funny lines don't seem at all funny to me. But, there, maybe it's all in the delivery? What would I know about all that? I dare say that's why people have to rehearse how they say things, not just memorize what they have to say, and where they have to stand when they say it…which is all I've got in the script. Oh, that's your phone, not mine – you do that, and I'll see you after I've walked the girls.' Tudor kissed Annie on the check as she answered her phone.

'Hiya, Car – how are you?'

'I've been thinking, Annie.'

'You never stop, do you? I love that about you, Car – brain always on the go. I'm surprised it doesn't overheat. Alright then, I'll bite – what's on your mind, doll?'

Carol sounded…anxious? 'If Sylvia Jenkins couldn't have been the person pushing Larry Merton off that Tube platform in London, then who was it?'

Annie said, 'Is this a serious question, or rhetorical?'

'Serious.'

Annie pondered. 'Sylvia's Evil Twin?'

Carol chuckled. 'Nice. But no soap opera resolutions for us, I don't think, Annie. If not an Evil Twin…then…any ideas?'

Annie gave it some thought. 'Okay, so Larry Merton was a scumbag. A liar, a cheat, and a thief. Not nice. Even Chrissy said that, about when she knew him in her City days – that he was slimy back then. So I don't think he's changed. Which means that this might not have been the first woman he took to the cleaners.'

'Are you thinking that we should try to find out if Larry Merton was ever "matched" with other women, whose lives he also made miserable, and whose money he also took?'

'Exactly.'

'Right, I'm going to propose to Mavis that I spend a bit of time on that angle. What do you think?'

Annie decided to say exactly what she thought – it was usually for the best. 'Rhodri's our client for this case, and his job is to work on behalf of his client, which isn't Sylvia Jenkins, but Pauline…the woman who might well be accused of having killed Sylvia Jenkins. Why would he want us to find out about who killed Larry Merton? I mean, isn't that the job of the London police, not us? Shouldn't we really be concentrating on – somehow – proving that Rhodri's client, Pauline, couldn't have killed Sylvia?'

Annie heard Carol sigh heavily. 'Yeah, I know you're making a good point, Annie – but I haven't got any bright ideas on that front. The post-mortem says it's technically possible for Pauline to have done it. Like you said, that will probably be argued for, and against, by both sides. It's medical, and technical – not our sort of thing at all. I can't see any way we can prove that Pauline didn't leave the narrowboat and shove Sylvia into the water; the cameras were down for an hour, she could have done it.'

Annie sighed. 'We checked, and there are no other cameras in the area, no way to prove she didn't do it, like you said. So if she *could* have done it, then our only hope is to prove she *wouldn't have* done it: we should focus on the motive, not the opportunity. But…she had a great motive; Sylvia was making her life a misery, to such an extent that Pauline was trying to get legal action taken against the woman, and even hired us to find evidence to prove she was being harassed by her. By the way, Car – I dare say it's not really necessary now, or maybe it's even counterproductive – but did you ever manage to prove that Sylvia was the one sending those clusters of negative online reviews and comments and so forth from the addresses you discovered? You know, the library, the pub, and the café, all in or around Pontypool.'

Annie could hear the smile in Carol's voice when she replied, 'You're terrible, you are. When do you think I've had time to do that? Besides, like you said, gathering evidence that Sylvia was harassing Pauline is now the job of the other lot – the Crown Prosecution Service, if it comes to that. Whatever Sylvia was doing to Pauline might not have been enough to get the cybercrime folks involved, but I bet they'll be all over it now, because that's how they'll prove a case for Pauline to have had a motive to kill Sylvia. So, no, I don't think Rhodri would be too pleased if we spent his money, and thereby his client's money, proving that Pauline had a strong motive to do harm to Sylvia…though, hang on now…if Sylvia habitually used the Wi-Fi at those locations, I wonder if she did so to contact Larry Merton, too. If she did, I could use that information to…okay, Annie, thanks for that. I'm going to just put half an hour of my own time into trying to trace any other women Larry Merton ruined, and we'll see what comes of that. Did you want anything else?'

'You phoned me, doll.'

'Right. Of course. Sorry. Things are a bit off here, today.'

Annie bit. 'What's up?'

Carol chuckled. 'Nothing really – except that I got home to an empty house…I didn't tell you last night, because Christine was full of it about those camera feeds from the Tube. Anyway, I knew Dad would have been at rehearsal, but Mam and David went too, and they took Albert…so there was no one here. Which was a bit weird. Then they all came home together, and of course everything was fine, except that Dad can't find his spare car keys anywhere. We've searched the house, but they just seem to have grown legs. He thought Mam had them, she says he had them – neither of them know where they are. Not that it's a problem, but spare keys are useful, aren't they? Not that his car uses a key…well, it does, but there's the fob too, you know. Oh well, maybe you don't.'

Annie retorted, 'Oi you, I do know my fobs from my keys, Car. But let's not get into that, alright? Talk later. Let me know how you get on. Bye.'

'Bye.'

An hour later, Annie was hugging her mother, who was one of the few women in her life who matched her in height, so it was always a unique experience…in every way. She also endured being properly squashed by her father for a good few minutes then – finally – she got the chance to show them around the new pub, with her wonderful Tudor at her side. She glowed as they made their way around the entire property and praise was heaped upon all her decorative choices, the general way the pub looked and felt, and then – the *pièce de résistance* – their very own room, upon which Eustelle immediately placed her stamp of approval. Annie was floating.

'I especially like the color of the curtains and the bedspread, Annie,' commented her mother as they all stood at the door of the room.

Annie jumped in with: 'Don't start, Eustelle. Me and Tude have been through this already. Several times. They are not green, they are not blue – they are both green and blue at the same time: the color is called teal. You know, the color they invented so that arguments about whether it's a blueish green, or a greenish blue, could be dragged out around the world forever, because there is no right answer. It's teal. I liked it as soon as I saw it, and knew it would be right for this room. It makes the place feel…safe. Homey. And, yes, I know I'll never, ever match it – which is why I bought four bedspreads: one's on the bed, one's been cut up and Gwen Pike made them curtains out of it, and I've got two more packed away for emergencies. So, yes, I am planning ahead.'

Annie noticed her mother's shoulders roll before she replied; always a danger sign. 'I was just going to say that the color is very much like the dress your grandmother made for your favorite doll when you were about three years old. And I know it's called teal, thank you. Which comes from the color around the eyes of a teal duck.'

Annie could hear the intake of air before Tudor said, 'If you fancy leaving your unpacking for a while, I've made some of my lamb stew – up here in the flat, just for you, not down in the pub; I thought you might value the privacy, so you can all catch up. Of course, you'd be very welcome downstairs, too – it's not very busy.'

Eustelle Parker grinned. 'You know how much I adore that stew of yours, Tudor Evans, and I'd love to have my daughter all to myself for a while. So how about you take Rodney downstairs to that bar of yours, and let him have a tot of rum? I know he's been dying for one ever since we got on the train this morning – he's mentioned time and time again how lovely it'll be to have a drop of rum with you.'

Tudor and Rodney shared a grin; Annie's heart melted seeing the two men she loved most in the world look at each other that way.

She said, 'Go on then, Tude…spoil him. He deserves it, I dare say, having to put up with this one getting ready to come here for Christmas. But don't return him as damaged goods. And, Dad, Tudor doesn't drink at all during the day, so don't go trying to talk him into joining you, alright? Best behavior, both of you.'

Once they were alone, Annie offered to serve her mother with lamb stew, but her mother refused. 'No Annie, I can't. Not now. I've had a bit of a mishap, child: I forgot to pack your father's Christmas present. I remembered when we were on the way to the station, but I couldn't say anything, could I? So – where can I get him something suitable? I know it'll have to be in the village, because you can't drive, and I'm certainly not getting on a bus, given how much traveling I've already done today. Should we go to the shop? Might that girl Sharon have something suitable?'

Annie replied, 'Not unless you fancy wrapping a packet of biscuits, or bacon for him to open, no. But there's the antique shop. How about that? Elizabeth Fernley keeps a very eclectic range of stuff in there, though a lot of it is furniture, and I dare say you'd prefer something smaller than a chair or a table, since you'll have to get it home with you on the train. But we could have a look there. How about that?'

Annie saw the worry on her mother's face. 'Well, if there's no alternative, it can't hurt to look, can it? Can we get out of this place without your father seeing us?'

Annie led the way.

When Annie and Eustelle Parker arrived at the antiques shop, the board was outside, announcing that the place was open.

Annie's mother observed, 'That's a bit of a mouthful, child. "Anwen Antiquities & Curiosities, curated by Coggins and Chellingworth". Doesn't roll off the tongue, does it?'

Annie chuckled. 'Nah, but the tourists love it, apparently. Let's go inside. Elizabeth will know her stock, I bet; you just tell her what you want, and maybe she'll find something suitable.'

Annie pushed open the door, but the place was deserted. The little desk that Elizabeth used for wrapping purchases, and so forth, was also unattended.

Annie said, 'That's funny – she's usually got a bell on this desk – big old brass thing, that you roll a little lever around. It sounds like a bicycle bell.' She raised her voice. 'Hello – anyone here?'

A voice wafted through the shop. 'With you in a minute – please, feel free to browse.'

Annie gave a courtly flourish. 'Browse away, Eustelle, and I hope you find something for Rodney…that you won't mind dusting for evermore.'

Her mother chuckled, and headed along a narrow path between tables and other bits of furniture that Annie couldn't imagine had any earthly use. Eustelle picked up a small pair of blue and white china geese, then put them down, then she picked up a bowl with a lid, and turned it over.

She asked Annie, 'Are there prices on any of these things? All I can find are little colored dots.'

Elizabeth Fernley appeared from a back room, and Annie and her mother – between them – stopped the lid from falling off the bowl and onto the floor. Even Annie had to admit it was a close call; of course, her mother blamed Elizabeth for making her jump, and lose her grip on the lid.

Elizabeth said, 'That would have been ninety pounds if that had broken. We're very much in favor of enforcing the "if you break it, you buy it" philosophy here.'

Annie wondered how her mother would react. She was surprised when Eustelle said, 'Well, of course you would be. That's only fair. Are you Elizabeth?'

Elizabeth smiled. 'And you'd be Annie's mother, I dare say.'

Eustelle replied, 'What gave it away?'

Elizabeth grinned. 'The fact that you two look like sisters – though I happen to know that Annie's an only child, so you've got to be the mother. Down from London for Christmas, are you? Doing some last-minute shopping?'

Annie watched with interest as her mother laid on the charm. 'I made a terrible mistake – left her father's gift at home. So now…well, I'm after something small, and preferably useful, as opposed to purely decorative. He doesn't go in much for useless things that look nice. And I don't want to spend too much money, this being his second present. How can you help me?'

Annie knew she'd talked to her mother on the phone about Elizabeth, explaining that her being the wife of the Estates Manager up at Chellingworth Hall had meant she'd taken on the role of "hostess" after Althea had moved into the Dower House, but before Henry had married Stephanie…and that Annie had, initially, thought that Elizabeth had a pole stuck up her back, and walked around as though everyone who lived in Anwen-by-Wye smelled of something unpleasant. Annie had revised her opinion of the woman since she'd got to know her a bit better…but she couldn't remember if she'd shared her updated views with her mother.

Realizing all this, Annie thought it best to say, 'Dad's not a bloke who likes folderol, is what Mum means, Elizabeth. So useful would be good. Useful for a man. Anything come to mind? You must know everything you've got in here – you're so good like that.'

She hoped her mother would take the hint. Elizabeth, too.

Elizabeth's expression softened. 'How about something he can put his bits and bobs into…money, keys, that sort of thing? I've got some lovely brass bowls – nineteenth century Indian, nicely patterned, but essentially useful. I think one of the dukes had them sent over for…some reason or another. They're just here, on top of…oh, no, they aren't. I thought they were. Now, where did I move them to? Just give me a minute, would you?'

Elizabeth weaved her way to the back of the shop, while Annie and Eustelle stayed where they were; Annie was glad of that, because – given the fact that almost every surface was covered with something breakable – she suspected it was safer. A few moments later, Elizabeth reappeared; her hair was out of place, and she was pink in the face. 'I've found one of them, but I've no idea what's happened to the other one. Would you be interested in a pair, Mrs Parker, or would one do?'

Eustelle asked, 'How much?'

Elizabeth turned over the bowl, which Annie had to admit was rather lovely; its outer surface had an intricate pattern chased into the brass.

Elizabeth said, 'A red dot means fifty, but I think that might have been for the pair. So, twenty-five?'

Eustelle replied, 'I'd have preferred the pair, so how about twenty?'

Elizabeth said, 'Of course. Would you like it wrapped? I do have paper suitable for Christmas, if you like.'

'Thanks, I'll wait.'

Annie was a bit taken aback by her mother's manner; Eustelle's usual warmth and general bonhomie was absent. She decided it wasn't the time or place to comment, but stood waiting, silently, as she and her mother watched Elizabeth expertly wrap what was, after all, a rather difficult object to deal with.

Eventually, with their purchase concluded, Elizabeth moved to open the door for them to leave. 'I'll be closing now,' she said – rather pointedly, thought Annie. 'I have a costume fitting, over at the Pikes' house. You're not getting involved with the panto, Annie? It appears that almost everyone here is doing…something.'

Annie shook her head. 'What with the agency, and helping Tude at the pub, nah, I haven't got the time, really. Though Tude's in it alright. I know he's just the prompter, but he's making sure he's doing the best job he can. What part are you playing, Elizabeth?'

The woman preened, just a little. 'I'm the Good Fairy. I hope they've got something nice for me to wear; it'll be a once-in-a-lifetime thing for me. I've never been on the stage before this. I had no idea it would be so difficult to keep all the lines straight in my head. And Oswald's got me doing a little dance. It's all a bit…daunting, but he's been such a treasure. He's done all the costume design himself, you know? He even got me to take my measurements, so that Gwen and Joan Pike could make the dress fit properly. He dropped by to pick up my details so he could brief the Pikes face to face. He's quite something. Not the sort of person we usually meet around here.'

Eustelle said, 'There's a panto? Here? At Christmas? Me and your father are going to be able to see a panto? Annie, you never said. And you're the Good Fairy, Elizabeth? Oh, how wonderful. Which panto is it? There are lots with fairies.'

Annie actually stepped back as her mother enthused…loudly.

Elizabeth appeared to be just as surprised by the rapid shift in Eustelle's demeanor. 'It's *Mother Goose*, I'm the Good Fairy who…'

Eustelle waved a hand. 'I know the story. I mean, who doesn't? One of my favorites, that one is. We saw it when you were little, Annie, at the Hackney Empire. Three times we went. You loved it. You must remember it. You laughed so much at Priscilla the goose that you…well, you were very young, I suppose, so accidents will happen.'

Annie couldn't believe what she was hearing. 'Eustelle, not now. And anyway, I never did.'

Her mother patted her shoulder. 'Look at you now, all grown up, and living in a pub in a Welsh village. Who'd have believed it? Well, anyone might have believed the bit about you living in a pub, I suppose. But in the Welsh countryside? Never. How's she fitting in?'

Annie wanted her mother to shut up. She sighed. 'I tell you what, Elizabeth, if you want to rehearse being the Good Fairy, could you just wave your magic wand now and make me disappear? Or maybe you could wind the day back by five minutes and I could have got this one out of here before she opened her gob. Eustelle, let's go.'

The three women shared a laugh, then Annie and her mother made their way around the green to the pub.

Eustelle observed, 'She seems alright, even if she can't keep track of where her antiques are, exactly.'

Annie said, 'She is, but, you know what – she's not the only person who's misplaced things around here. It's just dawned on me…I'll have a think about that while you put your feet up for a bit. But let's hide this gift from Rodney first, then I think you should have at least a taste of Tude's stew, because he'll be disappointed if you don't. Alright?'

Eustelle Parker hooked her arm through her daughter's. 'You make an old woman very proud, you do, Annie Parker.'

Annie laughed. 'I don't know about "old woman"; you're young yet.'

Eustelle replied, 'Heading for eighty doesn't feel so young, Annie.'

The realization that her mother was, indeed, not that much younger than Althea – who she was used to thinking of as a truly aged person – hit Annie like a sack of hammers. Were her parents really getting on in years that much? Oh…heck.

CHAPTER TWENTY-SEVEN

Mavis was pacing the office, wondering where on earth Christine had got to. She realized that her young colleague was finding it more difficult to get about these days, but she'd never been noted for her timely arrival at any location, for any meeting, anyway, so Mavis wasn't sure how kindly she should think about Christine's lack of punctuality on this occasion.

Deciding she should begin the emergency meeting without her, Mavis summoned up both Annie and Carol: Annie was on her telephone's screen because she was walking her dogs, in the company of her father; Carol was in her home office.

Mavis opened with: 'I cannae wait for Christine, so let's start without her. This is important.'

'Good,' said Annie, 'because I don't want to interrupt my time with Dad.'

Mavis understood only too well that the arrival of Annie's parents in Anwen-by-Wye was her chance to spend some rare time with them, because Annie had been at pains to point it out. She simply said, 'Well let me speak then.'

Carol said, 'Yes, go on Mavis. What's happened?'

Mavis said, 'The police have arrested Pauline Thomas on suspicion of murdering Sylvia Jones, as Rhodri had feared they might. He's gone to the police station to be with his client, and has urged us – in no uncertain terms – to come up with whatever we can to prove that Pauline didn't kill Sylvia. The case has reached a critical juncture…and here's Christine, at last.' Mavis rapidly repeated the news for her harried-looking colleague as she settled at her desk.

Returning her attention to her screen, Mavis asked, 'So do we have something? Anything we can point to that says she didn't do it? I have told Rhodri that – so far – we do not. Am I wrong?' Mavis hoped she was, but the glum expressions on the faces of all three of her colleagues told her she wasn't. 'Ach, we have nothing.'

Annie offered, 'I hate to say it, but I think we should have one more go at the door-knocking thing. I'm up for it – but we need a plan of action that means it's not just my ugly mug that's showing up at people's front doors all the time. Mave – might it be something you could give a go? I don't think we can expect Chrissy to be pounding the streets, and – sometimes – it's best if we let Car's fingers do the walking…you know, across the magic keyboards.'

Carol waggled her hand. 'I already have something, though it might not be what we need.'

Mavis said, 'Out with it – I think we should follow any avenues at this point, beyond door-knocking.'

Carol squared her shoulders. 'Annie and I were talking earlier in the day, and it occurred to us that it was unlikely that scamming Sylvia Jones was Larry Merton's first swindle. So I've been looking into his socials, and I think I've identified a specific person to whom he might have done the same sort of thing. I found an old profile of his, under the name of Larrie M. Llewellyn. There's not much content there, because I think he cleared it out…but there was a visit he made to a pub in Swansea, about a year ago, that was still pinned there. I checked the pub in question, and the date, and there was a wedding anniversary party being held there the same day. I waded through a lot of people's feeds, and found a photograph of our Larry; he had a beard at the time, but it's definitely him – and he's in the company of a woman. They're in the background of a few of the photos, and…you might not believe this, but it's true – she's wearing a knitted, double-breasted jacket, with big brassy buttons. And – even more interesting – the woman he's with was also in a couple of other shots, and she's actually named: it seems that someone at the anniversary party was at school with her, and they were surprised to see each other at the venue. The woman Larry was with is named Heather Summerville, nee Williams. I know this because the schoolfriend in question was bemoaning in her post that it's so easy to lose contact with old female chums who've changed their surnames when they marry. So Heather was Williams in school, and must have married a Summerville. I checked both names, and found several Heather Williamses on socials, one of whom is the same woman. It looks as though her account in that name began not long after the date of that meeting with Larry Merton. For about three months after that she was reaching out to try to find old friends in the Swansea area; her feed said she'd been living in England – in Somerset – for years, but was now back in Swansea following a divorce, and looking to get in touch with old acquaintances.'

Mavis jumped in. 'Carol, I cannae see how this is helping Pauline.'

Carol said, 'Hang on, Mavis. So – it looks to me like Heather Williams/Summerville went on at least one date with our Larry Merton, but he doesn't appear in any photos on her feed…until about nine months ago, when she started posting about how all women should beware of "slimy Lotharios" and she put up a photo of Larrie, aka Larry, with a caption warning women about him, by name. There are no more specifics, but, after that, her feed is empty.'

Mavis said, 'So you believe this Heather, in Swansea…is…what? A possible suspect in the death of Larry Merton?'

Carol nodded, and Mavis was surprised by the grimness of her expression. 'I do. There was a sense I got of the woman from her posts, and comments, that made me…wonder about her. I think she'd be worth investigating, and I've done a lot of the legwork. I dare say the police could track her down quite easily: I've found records of two homes in Swansea she owned – I think one of the addresses might be the old family home, the other is a flat, in Swansea Marina – where, coincidentally – my parents have been looking for a place. I checked: her flat's on the market…though it's not one my parents would consider, because it only has one bedroom. The price has been dropped twice in the past six months. It looks to me as though she needs to raise money. Maybe she, too, got taken to the cleaners by Larry Merton.'

Mavis gave what Carol had said some thought. As she did so, Annie said, 'You're brilliant, Car – I knew you could do it. Well done, doll. How about I give my old chum DCI Carys James down in Swansea a call? She might be interested in this.'

Mavis said, 'Good work, Carol, and mebbe you could talk to Carys, Annie, because this information could help with the Larry Merton murder case – but we're no further forward with the Pauline Thomas case, and we should be giving that all our efforts.'

Christine said, 'What more can we do for Pauline, Mavis? We've established that there is no camera coverage in the area, other than our own, and that was down for an hour before the body was found. Oh – for goodness sakes, I'll be forgetting my own name next: the tech blokes at the place where I took our cameras to be fixed said they'd all been hit by a magnetic charge. A big one. It messed up the electrics, but they've been sorted out now. We can collect our gear before Christmas, they said. But they can't tell me more than that. And there was nothing of any use on any of the hard drives; though the police had told us that, I checked, too.'

Mavis almost jumped when Annie shouted, 'That bloke who spotted the body, with his grandson – they were using magnets there that day. Weren't they fishing for metal things, in the water? Like treasure hunting. Given that they were the ones who found the body, what if they were somewhere along the waterside for the whole of the critical hour. You know – walk one way and helpfully knock out the cameras with their magnets, then walk back in the other direction and find the body. Mave, has Rhodri said he's talked to them? Or got hold of whatever statement they gave to the police? They might have seen something that they thought nothing of at the time…or maybe it would be even better if they saw nothing, because – given that they were right there, in the area – they would have seen Pauline if she'd been out of her narrowboat, and killing Sylvia. Pauline would have been quite noticeable what with her stick, and her wrist, and her ankle, and her magenta hair, don't you think?'

Mavis sat back. 'Now you're talking. Thanks for that information, Christine, and for the ideas, Annie…I'll send a text to Rhodri, that'll be the best way to reach him, because who knows when he might be able to take a phone call.'

Carol said, 'Good idea, Mavis. I can't be the only one who shouts at the telly when people phone, and leave a message, but will they send a text, that could get through, to be read and responded to, at the convenience of the recipient? Oh no. That's too much trouble.'

Annie laughed, 'Oh come on, Car, where's the fun in that? Those four-part telly things would all be two-parts then, wouldn't they? So, yeah, Mave, text Rhodri, and get him on that…and I'll text Carys, because we all know how slammed she always is. But I'll also send her an email – of the report that you're going to send to me, with all that information in it, right, Car?'

Carol grinned. 'Look, this is me sending it to you now. Watch me press send.'

Mavis beamed. 'And I'll come up with a schedule for going door-to-door in the area surrounding Pauline's boat – again. Ach, you're a good team. This was good work, this was. Thank you all.'

Annie quipped, 'Well, if what Pauline said to me and Car comes true, then we're due another important bit of information soon, and success. She definitely mentioned success…which is important for her, given what she's going through at the moment.'

Mavis said, 'Right, let's all do our best. And we'll all keep everyone updated. Bye for now.'

Annie shouted, 'Car – don't go – I just need a minute, please. Bye Mave, Chrissy.'

Mavis disconnected, then composed a text for Rhodri – using a pen and paper at first, so she got it right, then she sent it to him.

When she finally gave her attention to her colleague beside her, Mavis noticed that Christine was a bit pink in the face. 'Are you overheating? It's this place, it's so difficult to keep such a massive, open space at a decent temperature. Can I get you a glass of cool water? That might help.'

Christine stayed where she was, upright, on her office chair, and accepted Mavis's offer. As Mavis watched her sip, she wondered if Christine was finding these last few months of her pregnancy to be taking their toll on her.

She dared, 'Would now be a good time to talk about you mebbe taking more of a back seat at the agency, Christine? I know we've kept you basically desk-bound since your accident, and therefore your pregnancy – but now? Well, from now on you're going to get tired even more quickly, and you'll find yourself maybe getting a bit…well, they call it pregnancy brain for a reason. It gets hard to think in straight lines, let alone around corners, and our work is often about thinking around some very twisty corners. Not that any of us would want to push you out, of course. When do you think you'll be moving into Honeysuckle Cottage? Might that be an opportunity to take some extended time away from your role here? You know, get settled to be able to welcome the wee bairn?'

Christine burst into tears, a reaction with which Mavis had found herself having to become increasingly familiar over the past few months – hence the presence of a box of tissues on every desk in the office, and on the coffee table. She waited patiently, constantly glancing toward her phone just to make sure she hadn't missed a response from Rhodri. She hadn't.

Finally, Christine had composed herself sufficiently to be able to say, 'I talked to Alexander about it last night. We were here, and he saw how hard it was for me to get up that blessed spiral staircase. It's not that my legs aren't up to it, but I'm so…huge. Honestly Mavis, I can't begin to imagine how I managed to get so massive, so quickly. It's taken me by surprise. And everyone who hasn't seen me – in person – for a few weeks, too. And I am tiring more quickly, and finding it harder to do things I've been taking for granted. Getting into and out of my vehicle, and driving, is even more difficult, because I have to sit so far back from the wheel now, and my feet have to work harder on the pedals. And, you're right, my brain isn't as nimble as normal, and I'm getting frustrated with myself and…and…Lumpy.' Mavis saw a fat tear roll down her young colleague's cheek. 'And that's not fair to Lumpy. I've had to give myself a lot of good talking-tos about that. Mammy wants me to stop working now. But she's never understood why I do this, anyway. Daddy agrees with her, then secretly tells me I'm a woman who can make up her own mind.'

Mavis understood what it was for a parent to want the best for their child, and to have to stop themselves from telling them what they believed that to be. 'How does Alexander feel about the matter?' Mavis suspected it would be his opinion that would carry most weight with Christine.

'Alexander's making it all about the health aspect: mine, and Lumpy's. He's working long hours, so he is, what with the construction jobs in London, the rental property business, the antiques business in London, and here, as well as that blessed school renovation he's overseeing in the village. And now the panto, too. I hardly see him — and neither he nor I are happy about that. And, as you said, we've got the renovations at the cottage on the go, too…which were supposed to be finished by Christmas. Which they won't be. He suggested I go to stay in London, at Mammy and Daddy's house, where I won't have to lift a finger.'

Mavis could see the attraction of that; she knew that Christine's mother would make sure her daughter was well tended to.

'You're planning on delivering the bairn in London, aren't you?'

Christine nodded. 'Yes, we all thought that would be for the best. Even though the cottage was due to be ready in time, we still all agree that taking the baby back to the London house would be the right start for us all. So, yes, Alexander makes a good point; if I decamped to the London house now — or just after Christmas — I'd be on the spot whenever Lumpy decides it's time to put in an appearance. But the idea of sitting about there, doing nothing except getting bigger and bigger, with nothing to keep me truly occupied except for whatever plans Mammy might have for me is…horrifying. There. I've said it. But please understand that doesn't mean that I don't love my family; I just don't want to be stuck with them, and only them, for…months. I know I'll be there when I'm a new mum, but I want to keep on being me for as long as I can be. Even if I get bigger every day, and more tired every day…and, possibly — according to Alexander, at least — a bit grumpier every day.'

Mavis weighed her response carefully. 'I'm a mother of two sons, so I've never had to make this decision in real life. But, if you were my girl, I'd probably want you at home with me, so I could keep a good eye on you. I can understand why your mother feels as she does. But I'm no' your mother. I know you as a young, professional woman, with a good brain, an admirable work ethic, and a sound moral compass. I — and Annie and Carol, too — rely upon you as a critical part of this team of ours. We're stronger, and better, and more successful because you're a part of it — and we'd hate to lose you. But we've all come to terms with the fact that the early months of your motherhood will not be the same as Carol's. She's fortunate that David is able to work from home, but we're all aware that Alexander cannot. Any new mother will tell you that her life is made easier if she has a network of support around her, and you have a family in London that's prepared to give you that, in a way you cannae get here. So we've all accepted the idea that you'll be away from us for a wee while, and we'll do our best without you. If it's best for you and the bairn for that to be for several months, instead of a few, we'd deal with that, too. But, while we'll happily support whatever decision you make, we cannae make the decision for you. I'm sorry.'

Christine nodded her head slowly. 'I know that, Mavis – but thanks for letting me talk it through. You know, when Clementine announced to her mother that she intends to have a baby, I should have been more firm with her…or at least I should have talked to her honestly about the tremendous toll it takes on a mother's body. Maybe it's not too late for me to do that – I haven't spoken to Stephanie about it any further but, maybe, I can do some good…help someone face up to the realities of what they're imagining is a beautiful, pain-free dream. Which this isn't.' She patted her belly.

Mavis said, 'It can't do any harm, Christine, I don't think. I'm not aware that Clementine's ever been known for having a good grasp of reality, and maybe she'll listen to you, since you are, in fact, pregnant. But, for now, be kind to yourself, keep your feet up when you can, and rest whenever possible. Trust me…I'm a nurse, and a mother.'

'Is that your phone, Mavis?'

Mavis reached across the desk. 'Aye, a text from Rhodri. It's just basically a thank you. No information, at all.'

'Shame. But at least we know he got your text, so now he can act on his client's behalf. And that's what we've been hired to do in this case; help Rhodri, to help Pauline.'

'It's good that this is how we make our living – helping people – isn't it?'

'It is indeed, Mavis.'

20th DECEMBER

CHAPTER TWENTY-EIGHT

When Christine woke, she knew she'd enjoyed a better night's sleep than she had done for some time. Yes, it was still very early, and yes, she'd wriggled and writhed to try to get comfortable…and she must have done, because she'd actually slept. Alexander was snoring, softly, beside her. She gazed at his profile, silhouetted against the light coming from the bathroom, which they now left on, so she didn't trip in the night.

As ever, she was amazed by the perfection of his features – so symmetrical, strong, and yet not…too strong. She'd been drawn to him as soon as she'd met him…but she hadn't allowed herself to acknowledge that, and certainly not to act upon it. Indeed, she'd been as unapproachable as she could have been, and yet…here they were. Exactly where they were meant to be. Well, not quite exactly: they were meant to be in the process of moving into Honeysuckle Cottage, but the whole project had been held up because of her insistence that massive glass doors should be fitted on the house that folded back on themselves to open up – essentially – the entire front wall of the cottage to the garden. And there'd been delay after delay with the doors…so other things had to be pushed back, too.

However, now that they'd finally been installed, it wasn't just Christine and Alexander who felt that they entirely changed the nature of the cottage, but every single person who had been there to do…well, anything. She knew that Alexander was putting as much pressure on as many people as possible to get the place habitable…but not even he could work miracles, and – with Christmas only a few days away – she knew she wasn't the only person looking forward to a little time with her family; everyone working at the cottage wanted that too, so people had booked time off, and would be taking it.

Henry and Stephanie had very kindly invited Christine's parents to stay at the Hall for a few nights, and Christine had even bought tickets for the panto for them…and for herself; Alexander would be busy there. But, although she was looking forward to seeing her parents, she couldn't help but be disappointed that she and Alexander wouldn't, as they'd hoped, have one Christmas in their new home as a couple before they had a child. She knew – they both knew – they'd have many more happy times in the cottage, but she'd become just a little fixated on everything being perfect for this Christmas.

Should she get up? She finally felt comfortable, so decided to snuggle for just a little while longer…but her bladder had other ideas, as it often did, these days. Lumpy needed as much space as possible, which explained a great deal, and Christine feared that, despite slathering her belly with oils and unctions every day, she'd never again feel presentable in a bikini. What was she thinking? Her entire life, now, was about creating another human being. She and Alexander were still constantly worrying about how healthy Lumpy would be, due to her excesses before she'd known she was pregnant.

She wrestled with her conscience on that matter – yet again – as she wrestled with the coffee maker; she made a pot for Alexander every day just to be able to smell it, even though she wasn't drinking it. But coffee, and bikinis, were the least of her worries; her immediate concern was…well, she knew it should be the well-being of Pauline Thomas, but she also knew in her heart that she couldn't do much about that situation, whereas she felt she could do some good when it came to helping Clementine Twyst at what was, quite obviously, a difficult time for her.

Christine didn't claim to know Clementine well, though she'd spent enough time with her to have formed the opinion that she belonged to a particular 'ilk': young women of good breeding who had no particular purpose in life, and lacked the requirement to make a living for themselves. Christine – despite being the daughter of a viscount – had never been one of those; yes, she'd been fortunate to have received an excellent education but, after that, she'd had to apply herself to a profession, because her father was still in the process of trying to replace the family's fortunes that had been frittered away by his predecessors. Her father was intelligent, personable, and blessed with a persuasive turn of phrase, as was Christine, and both had built successful careers in the City of London, Christine as an underwriter at Lloyd's. But she'd known she wasn't happy, back then – not really happy – whereas now she was. Despite her aches, pains, general discomfort, and impending loss of independence.

But Clementine? Yes, she'd been well educated, and Christine had seen evidence of the woman's ability as an artist, but she'd turned her attention to becoming a patron of the arts, and artists, rather than developing her own creative path. Christine wondered if Clementine regretted that, now. Was this sudden and unexpected desire of Clementine's to become a mother a manifestation of her urge to create?

Most of the girls and women Christine had met who'd begun life like her and Clementine – titled, and with expectations that they'd breed the future titled males of long-standing families, due to a good match – had done just that. But those who'd followed their own path as Clementine had, or as Christine now was, by forming her own family with a man born so far from her own circle that he might as well have come from a different planet, were marginalized in 'their' world. Often spoken of with shrugs and raised eyebrows, or else given sideways glances dripping with disappointment, and tinged with disdain, at any social gatherings.

She felt she understood Clementine's type well enough to be of some help to the woman – despite their age difference, and their vastly differing life experiences. So, with a coffee pot to sniff in one hand, and a cup of decaffeinated tea in her other, Christine decided she'd talk to Clementine later in the day…whether Clementine wanted to hear her out, or not.

'Time for an intervention,' she said to the coffee pot as Alexander stumbled into the kitchen, rubbing the sleep creases from his face.

'What have I missed, Christine? An intervention? Who? Why?'

Christine realized why Alexander looked so panicked. 'Don't worry – it's nothing to do with Geordie's brother…no action needed on your part. I haven't heard any news about him that you haven't passed to me, so – as far as we're both aware – he's still in rehab, and he's still doing well. That's not what I meant. I was talking about Clementine Twyst.'

Alexander poured coffee for himself and sat on the sofa in the sitting room. 'I know I haven't been around much over the past few weeks, so what have I missed about Clementine? Is she here, at the Hall?'

Christine explained the situation.

Alexander's response was predictable. 'She's bonkers. A baby at her age? That woman needs to get a life.'

'I think she believes she can do that by making a new one.'

'Not what children are for. Trust me – this coming from a man who grew up with an absent and unknown father, and a mother who barely knew I existed, unless I was getting her a bottle of gin from the off license. Children are the biggest responsibility in the world, and that responsibility lasts for the entire lifetime of the parent.'

Christine smiled. 'So…if Lumpy here ends up looking as though they're going to make a poor life decision in fifty-odd years' time, would you hope they'd have people around them who might help them see there are other options?'

Alexander smiled his wonderful smile. 'Touché. Yes, of course I would. And that's going to be you, for Clementine, right?'

'Right. Today. I'm doing it today. In fact – I'm texting Clementine now, and I'll go up to Chellingworth Hall as soon as she'll have me.'

'And the pretext is? Because I dare say you're going to lie to her about why you want to see her.'

Christine grabbed Alexander's hand and gave it a squeeze. 'You know me so well. I think I'll say I want to get some inspiration from her about what to get you for Christmas.'

Alexander feigned shock. 'You haven't bought my gift yet? Yours is…as ready as it can be, at this stage. All I have to do is wrap it. But you don't have anything for me? You're cutting it a bit fine.'

Christine chuckled. 'I might have already made arrangements…but this is a cover story. However – if I hadn't yet got you something, what would you hope I'd be getting for you?'

Alexander stood, his coffee mug in hand. 'What I really need for Christmas is one day that lasts for at least forty-eight hours, so I can catch up on some sleep, and still have a whole day to enjoy with you, and Lumpy. As for what I'd want, as opposed to need…honestly, nothing comes to mind, beyond spending the day with you. That's it. So good luck with wrapping that. Now…I need to get into the shower, then get to the old school. Today's the last day the site's going to be worked on, so we've got to make the most of our time there, because, after what I reckon will end up being an early finish, nothing else will happen there until the new year. Same thing at the cottage – it's what's expected in construction. But, in a way, that's good, because then I get more time to focus on the panto, and us…and all the good things here…once I get back from London.'

'It's good of you to throw a party for all your people in London. I'm sorry I can't come – but the thought of the drive, then a party, is too much. I know you said Geordie understands, and he's the only person I'd really know, so that's okay – isn't it?'

Alexander finished his coffee. 'It's fine, like I said. Of course, it does mean you get to enjoy whatever it is that Althea has planned for the winter solstice, whereas I'll miss it; I'll expect a full report when I get back.'

Christine called after him as he disappeared, 'What do you mean? I haven't heard anything about any plans for the solstice…what's Althea up to?'

Enigmatically, her beloved replied, 'Not for me to say, my sweet…though if you take a look at the old school playground, you might get an inkling.'

Christine decided to text Clementine there and then, and that she'd pump Althea's daughter for information about the solstice, when she saw her…that could even become part of the reason for wanting to get together. Excellent. Now to compose a winning text that would get Clementine to agree to see her.

Christine was welcomed into Clementine's private apartment within Chellingworth Hall by Julian Treforest.

'Come on in, Christine. I'll leave you two to it – I'm just putting the finishing touches to something I'm working on for the panto. We should be able to get it installed later today, before this evening's rehearsals…if Marjorie can fit me in. She warned me it might have to be an overnight job. I do hope that's not how it works out but, well, she is in charge, so I'll have to wait to be informed. See you later – or, maybe not.'

Christine wouldn't have classified him as 'escaping', but it wasn't far off. 'Enjoy,' she called at his rapidly receding back.

She closed the door to Clementine's sitting room behind her, but she was alone. She called out, 'Hello? Clementine?'

'Through here, in my bedroom.'

Christine marveled at the maximalist décor surrounding her, and wondered how many *objet d'arts*, exactly, were crowded into each room. The impression was overwhelming, and somewhat claustrophobic. Christine couldn't fathom why she also felt so…safe. It was a disconcerting sensation, but a real one, nonetheless.

Clementine wasn't in her bed, but was lounging on it. Christine was pleased to see that the woman was fully dressed.

'Are you feeling quite well?' Christine thought she'd better check.

'I think I might have a bit of a cold coming on,' said Clementine, sounding a little stuffed up.

Christine gave the bed a wide berth. 'In that case, I'll sit over here, if you don't mind. The last thing I want is a cold.'

'A cold can't hurt a baby, surely.' Clementine sounded dismissive.

'The flu can lead to all sorts of problems, so I'm steering clear of you, even though I had the jab. I'm not taking any chances. Besides, a cold would be horrid for me…I cannot imagine having a cough and not being able to breathe properly; I'm uncomfortable enough as it is.'

Clementine snapped, 'If you've come here to tell me how miserable it is to be pregnant, you can leave now. I've read everything that's been written about being pregnant, and I know people who have children, so I'm aware it's no picnic, and I don't care.'

Christine was keenly aware that some of the goodwill she'd felt toward Clementine was draining away…rapidly. 'That's not why I came. I came, as a friend, to just have a chat. Like people do, at this time of year. I'm not mixing with people much at the moment, because it's so difficult to get about, like this. But we haven't seen each other – properly, and in private – in an age, and I really could do with a bit of advice from someone who's recently married, to someone who's in a relationship, about…gifts, and so forth. Oh – and do you have any idea what your mother's planning for the solstice?'

Clementine looked puzzled. 'Gifts? Really? I thought that was just a ruse on your part. It has to be, because what on earth would I have to say that would be helpful on that matter? Julian's getting a new tool that will allow him to get more heat, more quickly, onto specific parts of a piece of metal he's working on from me. Though it's being delivered to the house in Scotland, not here, since that's where he'll be using it. I sought advice from a blacksmithing friend of his – they all know what the other is lusting after, and this…thing…is apparently what's Julian's heart desires. And as for Mother? For the solstice? I've not heard anything. But whatever she might do wouldn't surprise me. You'd think this panto of hers would be getting her enough attention, but – you're right – if there's yet another opportunity for her to impose her will upon people, she'll take it. She always does.'

Christine decided to stop pussyfooting about, and go for the jugular – because she could tell that Clementine's mood wasn't going to allow for anything approaching 'a pleasant chat'…about anything.

'Very well – I'll say this: yes, my reasons for coming were a ruse. I really wanted to give you a chance to talk to someone sympathetic about your desire to have a child. It seems that everyone's telling you that you're too old for it to be either healthy, or practical – so I wanted you to have a chance to tell me why you really want a child. Because I don't think you're stupid enough to not realize that what everyone's saying is true: it's not safe for you, or a baby, for you to conceive at your age. And you are also capable of imagining what it might be like for a teenager to have a mother in her seventies. So…tell me what's really going on. I'll listen.'

Clementine rose angrily from the bed, and stomped toward the window. 'I won't come any closer, don't panic.'

'Thank you.'

'And I've only got a little tickle in my throat. I'm fine, really.'

'Just hiding?'

Clementine sighed. 'Maybe.'

'I'll wait…I'm listening.'

'Which is more than anyone else has done.'

'Have you given them the chance?'

Clementine shook her head. 'I suppose not.'

'Try talking it through. When did this desire…begin?'

Clementine shrugged. 'I don't know, really. Just after the wedding, I think.'

'Tell me.'

'We had a wonderful time in Egypt – except for poor Julian getting a terrible sunburn. It really wasn't very clever of him to shave off the beard he's had for years just before we were exposed to such strong sun. He suffered for it, poor thing. Though we've laughed about it since – and I prefer him more with his beard than without it; he had it when we met, so – for me – it's a part of who he is. But…when we decided to move to Scotland from London, that's when it began, I think. I wasn't seeing my old chums; I was having to manage staff who were new to me; and I had to get all the logistics of the move sorted out. Which…occupied me, but it wasn't at all satisfying. I thought that when I was surrounded by my things again, I'd settle there, but I haven't. I can't. I feel…as though I'm floating, or maybe in freefall, not tethered to anything – but not in a good way. My freedom has always been important to me, Christine; I've always been terrified of being tied down. But now I realize that I did rather enjoy being attached to people, and places, that meant something to me. But I don't have those touchpoints any longer.'

Christine decided that she should open herself up to Clementine…just a little. 'You and I have more in common than you might think, Clementine. It's not easy being the daughter of a titled family, knowing that the title will pass to your male sibling, and there being few expectations of you other than that you'll marry well and thereby add your genes to the stock of another titled family. But, these days, we really do have other options. I chose to move into the world of business where my father had blazed a trail. You followed your artistic inclinations. But we both still have to face up to the fact that we are who we are. I absolutely understand your desire for freedom, Clementine. I worried for ages about how trapped I might feel if I allowed my love for Alexander to change, and then define, my life. I believed that being half of a couple would mean I would become…less than I had been. And, while it's true that I'm certainly no longer the person I used to be, what I've discovered is not that I'm less, I'm just something I never was before. And discovering that I was pregnant when I, frankly, didn't mean to be – and didn't want to be – has led to even more compromises on my part. But I'm not here to tell you that you're being stupid by wanting a baby. What I'm here to do is challenge you to explain to me why you want one.'

Clementine thumped onto a slipper chair in the corner of the room. 'I just do.'

'You're not a child. Explain it to me.'

'I'm…I'm sure it will make everything better. For me, and for Julian, and our marriage.'

Christine's heart fell. 'Have you ever had this conversation when you were on the other end of it, Clementine? When a friend of yours said something like this to you?'

'Not really. I suppose I didn't really have any friends who would talk to me about such things. My friends and I tended to talk about art, and artists, and places we'd been, and things we'd done…or seen. Experiences, you know?'

'Do you have many friends with children?'

'Not really.'

Christine chose her words carefully. 'When I discovered I was pregnant, I talked to a few of my old chums who had children. To be honest, they were mainly girls I'd been at school with, though we hadn't really mixed much after that. Every single one of them told me the same thing, in her own way: children create problems, they don't solve them. They come pre-packaged with the sorts of challenges it's impossible to imagine until you've faced them, apparently. Though the other thing that every single one of them told me was – having the children they do – they wouldn't go back and change their minds about having them, even if they could. So hearing all that helped me decide that I wouldn't have this child. I'd already sort of made the decision before I'd talked to them, but thought it couldn't hurt to prove to myself I was right. And then I was certain that I was. Alexander and I never had what you might call a stable relationship, and I couldn't imagine that having a child in the mix would help.'

Clementine sat forward. 'But you are having it. And you're with Alexander. So…it's worked. Changing your mind has saved your relationship. And now – whatever happens between you and Alexander, you'll always have his child with you. You'll never be alone. And when you die…you'll be remembered. Always. By your children, and your children's children. Your legacy will continue.'

Christine saw Clementine's situation a little more clearly. 'Oh Clementine, a child isn't there to create a legacy for you; you're there to create a life, and a legacy, for it. You say that your mother seeks attention whenever she can; most people see her as someone who wants to help build community and support the people within it. You seem so bitter toward her that it appears to me you're determined to not be a part of her legacy; maybe her response to that is to work to build different memories within many more people who will speak of her achievements when she's gone. Henry's endeavors will always be remembered, because they'll be enshrined in the ducal histories. But Althea? A song and dance girl who married a duke? She's spent decades creating her own impact…as you have done. You're well known, and well respected, as a patron of the arts, and of artists. Yes, you've always had a reputation as a bit of a party girl too – let's neither of us even try to deny that – but you're more than that. Why can't that be your legacy? Why take the risk to have a child when there are other paths available to you? For example – if having a child in your life is important to you, you could adopt. There are so many with so little – and you really do have a great deal – you could change a life, or even lives, that way.'

'I'm too old for that.'

Christine sighed. 'You know what I do for a living now?' Clementine nodded. 'So I did some research; you can adopt, in Scotland, once you've been living there for a year, and they have no upper age limit for adoptive parents. Have you even looked into this?'

'No.'

Christine had to decide if biting her tongue were the right thing to do. She decided against it. 'Well you should. And I think you should stop stamping your feet like a petulant infant and take a long, hard look at the medical advice any specialist would give you about childbirth at your age. For once, use your brain, instead of your tantrums, to get what you want. And, by the way, if you think your marriage might not survive without a baby in it, I'm going to tell you it might not survive with or without one, the way you're going on. You need to talk to your husband about all this, Clementine – or the wedding you had on the summer solstice might not make it to the winter one. Julian seems like a good chap – though I hardly know him. But he's completely bewildered by this demand for a child, Clementine. Talk to him. Talk to a doctor. Research alternatives to childbearing. Maybe even talk to someone who can address the complicated psychological reasons that have brought you to this point. You seem to think that it's natural for the desire to want a child to suddenly develop, and I'm not sure it is. Work out how a child would fit into your life now…and not because you hope you'll have someone who'd have to love you in years to come just because you gave birth to them. Not all children feel they owe that to their parents; just look at how you and Althea interact.'

'I love my mother. How can you say I don't?'

'Oh Clementine – love is a verb. It's not just a state of being…it's also about actions. To say "I love you" is delightful, but it's a hollow sentiment unless your actions show how you mean it. So…love your husband: you've already chosen to take him into your life, and he's chosen to take you into his – act like that means something. Make plans together. Then you're more likely to spend the future together.'

Clementine pouted.

Christine's feet told her she needed to sit down, but she knew she had to get away…she was at her limit of telling Clementine to do all the things that she knew she should have done – and should continue to do – in her own life, but hadn't, and might not.

She said, 'Be honest with your husband, Clementine. I'm going to leave you to think about that. I have somewhere else I need to be, now…because we're trying to help another woman from possibly being convicted for something we don't believe she did. Call me if you want to chat about how things go between you and Julian.'

Christine left…having done more chatting along the lines of 'do as I say, not what I do' than she ever wanted to do again.

CHAPTER TWENTY-NINE

Annie was frustrated that the time she and Mavis had spent out and about trying to find someone who'd been in the area close to Pauline Thomas's narrowboat during the critical timeframe had borne no fruit, but the women were planning to repeat the process the next day, to cover the ground they'd not been able to get to already. However, she was glad that Aled was actually in the pub for at least a part of the evening, allowing Tudor to take a proper dinner break, so that he could join her and her parents for a meal together, with Gertie and Rosie in excited attendance, of course.

After dinner, her parents had decided to put their feet up for an hour – which Annie knew meant that they wanted to watch the telly in their room as they saw fit, which was fine by her. She'd cleared away and washed up, and now had to decide how best to use her time. There was no point wasting energy waiting for DCI Carys James to get back to her; she knew the woman had received both her text and email, because she'd texted Annie her thanks, and said she'd take it from there – which Annie hoped, and trusted, Carys would.

She decided to use the time to find a mustardy and brown silk pocket square – one of Tudor's favorites – that he liked to wear with his rust-colored waistcoat. He'd said he couldn't find it anywhere, so she checked the pockets of everything he had hanging in the wardrobe, and every drawer in the chest, and then in every unlikely place she could think of. But she couldn't find it anywhere. It was annoying, because it wasn't really fancy, and certainly wasn't new – so, therefore, probably irreplaceable – and yet it was precious, because it was loved. Like Sharon Jones's mother's old headscarf. And that nice old bell that used to be in the antique shop. And the bowl that was the pair to the one Eustelle had bought. And Carol's father's keys. And Gwen Pike's box of thimbles…and…

Annie felt a tingle in her neck. There were an awful lot of things going missing around Anwen-by-Wye. Not important things, or even obvious things – but cared for, loved, and used things. Like that chipped, old teapot that had gone from the pub…the vase that Janet

Jackson had taken with her everywhere over the years, that had disappeared from the Lamb Tearooms.

Annie sat up straight at the kitchen table; maybe she should make a list. And what if there were other things that had been 'misplaced' by other people that she knew nothing about?

'Want do you think, Gert? Shall I make a start, and see where we get with it?' Gert snuffled a suggestion that Annie should shut up and get on with it, so she did.

Half an hour later, Annie had all but covered the entire kitchen table with pieces of paper, each of which represented a mislaid item. Upon each piece she'd written what she knew about when the item had gone missing, and from where. Then she'd listed all the people who might have had access to the item in question within the appropriate time frame. There were some places where she obviously didn't know everyone who might have had the chance to take the item in question. When it came to the teapot that had disappeared from the windowsill in the pub downstairs, she realized that – between the time she could last recall having seen it, and the point at which she noticed it had gone – many dozens of people must have been in close proximity to it, and she couldn't even name them all. However, when it came to something like a person actually getting inside the house where Joan and Gwen Pike lived…well, that was a much shorter list.

And one name was on every list: Oswald Featherington. He'd been at the pub, he'd visited the Pikes, he'd been into Sharon's shop, the Lamb Tearooms, and the antiques shop. He'd been everywhere…and both Tudor and Carol's father had been with him, at various points, over at the village hall.

'Gert – what do you think? Should I talk to Car about it? Or should I talk to Mave? I mean…Mave knows Althea, and she's the one who's brought the man to the village. Yeah, you're right, I'll talk to Mave.' Annie was amazed that Gertie had been so eloquent, with just a few twiddles of her eyebrows.

Annie reckoned she still had half an hour or so on her own, so decided to take the plunge and talk to Mavis right then…though she wasn't sure she knew how she'd start.

Mavis sounded surprised that Annie had phoned her. 'Hello, Annie, what can I do for you? Are you no' with your parents?'

'They had an early dinner, with me and Tude, now they're having a bit of a lie-down, so I haven't got long, but…well, I need to talk to you about something.'

Mavis replied, 'Aye, well…before you do that, I was just about to send out an email, so I'll tell you what I've learned since I dropped you off at the pub earlier on. Rhodri got back to me regarding what the grandfather who found the body had to say for himself. It's nae good: neither he, nor his grandson, saw anyone at the side of the water that day, other than those who've already been accounted for by the police. They didnae see Pauline at all, which is good, but no' seeing her doesnae mean she wasnae there…it just means she wasnae seen by them.'

Annie couldn't help but ask, 'Have you been on the phone with people in Scotland, Mave? I reckon you're sounding a lot more Scottish than usual this evening.'

'Aye – my sons, and my grandchildren; it's the time of year that makes me realize I don't talk to them often enough. I slip right back into my accent when I've been talking to them.'

Annie thought she detected some sadness in Mavis's tone, and wondered how best to tackle the touchy topic she wanted to raise. She dared a question: 'And how's Althea doing? All okay with this panto thing, is she? I have to say she's been notable by her absence this past week or so. A bit tied up with it all, is she?'

Mavis tutted. 'Ach, the woman's more than tied up with it, she's completely immersed herself in it. She seems to be attached to Oswald…traipsing around the village together.'

Annie steeled herself. 'Mave…there's something I think I need to tell you. Something I wondered if you could broach with Althea. It's about Oswald Featherington.'

Mavis replied, 'Ach…what I've now chosen to name The Case of the Impecunious Impresario, you mean?'

Annie couldn't let that pass. 'Oi, what are you doing, going around naming cases? You know that's my job. And why's he even got a case title? Have you been up to something, without telling any of us, Mave? Come on, spill.'

Mavis tutted. 'Ach, Annie, you and your sayings. I might have done a little background research into the man Althea has opened her home – and her bank balance – to, aye. And I'll be happy to share what I've discovered in due course. But you phoned me, Annie, so I'm guessing you have something you want to tell me. I'm also guessing it might not cast a very flattering light upon the man's character, but I assure you, I can take it. So, please, tell me what you've learned about him.'

'It's a bit worrying, to be honest.'

'Aye, well, I've already found out he's misrepresented himself to Althea – so what else has he done?'

Annie felt buoyed: it wasn't just her who was worried about Oswald Featherington. The dam burst, and she explained to Mavis about the list of missing items, and the background she felt lay behind them. She finished with: 'There are at least two things I don't understand: why he would have nicked all those things, and how he managed it. Tudor swears blind the pocket square he's lost wasn't in his waistcoat pocket, where anyone could get at it; he'd dropped something on it, and didn't want it on display when it was dirty, so he'd put it in his trousers. And the trousers he had on are a bit special, because they've got pockets that zip shut. Which would make it impossible for anyone to get at it.'

Mavis replied, 'You can add sewing scissors shaped like a stork to that list of yours – I cannae find mine anywhere. And I've a feeling Oswald's been snooping about the place when I'm not there – at least, until I started to lock my door, that is. And Paul Baker was grumbling about an old jelly mold having gone missing from the kitchen at the Dower House – and, by old, I mean a battered old copper thing that was on a shelf, never used. And Ian Cottesloe has "misplaced" a pair of gardening gloves. All three items represent irritation, but not devastating losses, and none of the items have any intrinsic value.'

Annie nodded. 'Yeah. But still, Mave...they're all the same sort of things, like you say. So what have you found out about him?'

Mavis filled Annie in on her initial findings, then said, 'In addition to discovering the man's on his uppers, I've since been able to unearth the fact that he's behind with his rent on what are meager lodgings, and that he owes money around Brighton...in various pubs for drinks he's not paid for, and in many cases for items he's "needed for a production" – which people believe is code for things he wants for his own use. Oh, and he owes a minicab firm a fair bit, too.'

Annie gave the matter some thought. 'Look, Mave, I know that everyone's doing a lot for this panto for free – volunteering time, and so forth – but do you know of people who are spending out, and not getting paid back? Marjorie Pritchard must be putting her hand in her pocket if she's giving everyone at the village hall tea, coffee, and biscuits; and then there are the Pikes with all the fabrics and supplies they must have bought. Are they all sending bills to Althea...or what?'

Mavis sighed. 'I don't know. Though I think Althea's paying him, and he's supposed to be reimbursing them. I heard something about a producer being responsible for "petty cash" the other morning.'

Annie asked, 'So what do you think we should do, Mave? Or…what should you do? Because, to be honest with you, I think any approach to Althea on the matter would be best coming from you.'

Annie heard Mavis sigh for so long that she was surprised the woman hadn't run out of air completely. 'Aye, I should be the one to talk to Althea about all this. Though what good it will do, I don't know. But I do think she should know that Oswald is – probably – pinching things all around the village; whatever she might think about the man using her resources with abandon, I dinnae think she'd be impressed with him causing distress to the folks who live here. Leave this with me? I've had a bit of a chat with Christine about…some of these issues, and she's accepted that I should handle it, too.'

Annie felt relief. 'Of course, Mave. I trust your judgment completely. And I even give my stamp of approval to the title of The Case of the Impecunious Impresario…but don't get the idea into your head that you can go off naming cases all on your own, willy nilly, alright?'

Mavis chuckled. 'Agreed. Now, enjoy that time with your family you've been so looking forward to. You deserve it. Good night, Annie.'

'Good night, Mave, and thanks for taking this off my shoulders – I'm only sorry it's on yours, now. Good luck with it.'

21ˢᵗ DECEMBER

CHAPTER THIRTY

Annie did her best to creep out of the bedroom without disturbing Tudor, which also meant not disturbing Gertie and Rosie. She didn't succeed.

'You alright?' Tudor sounded sleepy, which wasn't surprising; the alarm clock told Annie it was only twenty past four.

'Go back to sleep, I'm fine,' she whispered.

'Can't sleep?'

'Not really. It must be all the excitement. I'll have a glass of milk and come back to bed soon. Night, night.'

Annie hovered in the doorway as Tudor snuffled and rolled over, then she padded as silently as possible across the creaking wooden floorboards of the ancient pub into the kitchen, where she grabbed a small glass of milk, and settled herself on the sofa, hoping her brain would stop whirring.

She was vibrating with…frustration. She'd wanted to spend the entire day on Friday with her parents, but, instead, she'd been out in the rain and biting wind with Mavis and Carol knocking on doors in Brecon in the hope of finding some sort of evidence that Pauline Thomas hadn't been outside her narrowboat during the critical period when Sylvia could have been killed, or that Sylvia had been seen in the company of someone other than Pauline at some point close to her death. When she'd set out the previous morning, Annie had even harbored some hope that they might find someone who'd seen some person – not Pauline – actually doing harm to Sylvia, but as the hours had worn on all hope had vanished, and they'd admitted defeat when they couldn't feel their toes or fingers any longer, and had covered every private and commercial building in the area surrounding Pauline's narrowboat berth.

By the time she'd got back to the pub, she'd managed to warm up a little, then she'd had a hot shower, and at least managed to have dinner with her family. But it hadn't been the day she'd hoped for, and she admitted to herself that she was still fuming about it, though she knew that she and her colleagues owed it to Rhodri Lloyd to work as diligently as possible on behalf of his client, who'd once been theirs.

'I hope you really did have milk and not something from the bar downstairs.' Tudor's voice made Annie jump. 'I know from experience that there's never a useful answer at the bottom of a glass. Trust me, as a pub landlord, I've seen enough people looking for one there over the years. What's wrong?'

'Oh, Tude…I had hoped I could take a bit more time to be with Eustelle and Rodney, but I had to work all day. I even had to cancel my…appointment with Josie. But that was only coffee. So it didn't matter, really.'

Tudor sat beside her. 'I know how much you've been looking forward to your mum and dad being here, but I also know you're a true professional, so I'm not surprised that you did the work you needed to do, instead of being with them. But why on earth did you make a date to have coffee with Josie when you knew they'd be here? That's…well, look, Annie, it's not for me to say, but you have been seeing a lot of Josie recently. She's a smashing woman, of course…I mean, if someone's going to dedicate their life to looking after retired greyhounds, what could be wrong with them? But you do seem to be popping off to see her a lot. I never knew you liked going out for coffee that much. We could go for coffee somewhere…you only have to say.'

Annie was shocked to see that Tudor's expression showed he was clearly hurt. She panicked. Should she tell him? No…she wanted to keep her secret for a little while longer.

She smiled brightly and said, 'Josie and I really struck up a friendship when the two of us were transforming that old horsebox into a bar-service vehicle for your birthday. There's not much else to do but chat when you're painting and stuff, and we promised each other we'd keep meeting up after we'd finished it. That's all it is. And, let's be honest, Tude, I'm not going to go off somewhere to another pub, am I? And what else is there to do around here other than go out for a coffee? She likes to drive and get a little time away from the dogs, when her volunteers are there, so she gets her break and I get to chat about something other than whatever case it is I'm working on. And we get along really well.'

Tudor shrugged, but Annie could tell he wasn't convinced. She hated lying to him, even though it was for what she knew was a good cause.

He mumbled, 'Well, if you've finished your milk, how about coming back to bed? The girls won't stay there snoring for long – they'll soon work out that their humans have left them alone, then they might make a fuss. We don't want to disturb your parents, do we?'

Annie felt the guilt in the pit of her stomach; Tudor's shoulders were down, he looked exhausted, and she hated keeping things from him. She couldn't stand the tension, so blurted out, 'Josie's teaching me to drive. I couldn't ask you to give me any more lessons because the ones we had were such a disaster, and I've tried all the proper schools within easy distance, and none of them worked for me. Josie offered, and I said yes. I was hoping to be good enough to be able to collect Eustelle and Rodney when they arrived at the railway station, but Josie said she didn't think it would be the best idea. I've just started to build up a bit of confidence see…and she thought that having my parents in the car might be a bit too much for me.'

Annie was taken aback when Tudor shot up off his chair and hugged her. 'Driving lessons? You and Josie? Oh, I'm so pleased to hear it.'

As the couple pulled apart, Annie wondered if Tudor's eyes were looking a bit…moist. 'You alright, Tude? I didn't know it meant that much to you, me seeing her so often. Didn't you like the idea that I had a new chum?'

Tudor laughed, quietly. 'What? Oh no. I didn't mind. Not really. I just wondered if…well, you seem to have been disappearing with her a lot, and I couldn't work out if…if you liked spending time with her more than with me. If you were starting to get a bit bored…because I'm always tied up. Because of the pub.'

Annie saw the worry in his eyes, the relief, too. 'Oh Tude, you silly sausage…I'm not bored. I'll never be bored with you. I love you, and

I love my life with you. I'm sorry I worried you – I had no idea that was how you felt. But I really do want to learn to drive. And soon, too. I know it'll take ages to get a test, but I want to practice as much as I can now, so that I can pass it first time. I hate exams, and if I fail…well, I might not have it in me to try again. You don't really mind that I didn't ask you, do you?'

Another bear hug followed. 'I love you too, Annie Parker, but we both agreed with each other that it would be better for our relationship if I never gave you another driving lesson, so Josie's welcome to you. I mean that lovingly, of course. And I bet you will pass – you can do it. You just needed to find the right person to teach you. And that person isn't me. We both know that. I'm glad that Josie's the one. And I'm also glad that I've solved The Case of the Confusing Coffee Addict, which was what I thought you were turning into…and it really was confusing because I know you prefer tea.'

Annie stood, and the couple embraced. She whispered in Tudor's ear, 'Not a real case, and a terrible name for it…but you're excused. And I'm sorry. I wanted it to be a surprise. But don't mention it to my parents, eh? When it happens, I really do want them to be blown away by my achievement. And nothing to Mave, Chrissy, or even Car, right?'

'Cross my heart. Now…come back to bed. And let's be quiet doing it; you know what they say about letting sleeping dogs lie, don't you?'

'Too right, Tude; we both know that if either of them stir now we'll end up having to take them out for a Jimmy Riddle, and it's cold out there – and trust me when I tell you that I've had enough of hanging about freezing my backside off for one day, thank you very much.'

'I'll wash that glass in the morning if you leave it there…you creep ahead of me. I'll do the lights.'

CHAPTER THIRTY-ONE

Carol couldn't sleep. She'd managed a few hours, she knew that, but her mind was restless, and now her legs were too. It was almost six o'clock, so she slipped out of bed, and padded past Albert's room, where she was pleased to see him sleeping soundly.

She closed the door to her office behind her and snapped on the desk lamp. She could still hardly believe that she had this wonderful space to call her own, and felt the energy surge through her as she woke up her laptop. She had a few hours, maybe, to call her own, and knew exactly what to do with them. She opened up several pages, and let her fingers fly, clicking on images, following routes and paths that appeared before her…enjoying the chase. Around the two o'clock mark earlier that morning, she'd decided that she wanted to continue to dig into the possibility of there being more victims that Larry Merton had scammed, and then she'd thought of all the ways she might be able to track them down, which was why she'd not been able to settle to a good night's sleep. She enjoyed doing what she'd been yearning to start on, and the next couple of hours passed swiftly.

A knock on the door brought her back to reality.

Her husband's head appeared. He smiled. 'I guessed this was where you'd got to. I brought coffee – any interest?'

Carol's heart melted: David's bedhead; his always slightly crooked smile; the love glowing in his eyes – the eyes she'd fallen for whenever they caught hers above his cubicle wall, or in her fancy corner office, back in the old days, in the City.

'You know the way to this woman's heart, *cariad*,' she whispered. 'Coffee would be lovely, thanks. Is Albert still sleeping?' Carol hadn't heard him fussing; he was sleeping rather well, these days.

'Fasto, as you always like to say, and your parents are creeping about downstairs so as not to disturb, him. Me too. But not for long, I don't think. But don't worry, you finish up what you're doing and enjoy this coffee; I'll take him down when he's ready and get some breakfast inside him. We'll all bundle up and go out to that thing at the old school later, right? Will you be able to join us?'

Carol stood, took the mug David was still holding and put it on her desk, then took her husband in her arms. 'David Hill, you are just about the most perfect man, you know that, don't you?'

'What do you mean "just about"? I thought I was completely perfect.'

The couple laughed, quietly. Carol whispered, 'What was I thinking? Of course you are. Absolutely perfect. And yes, I'll be coming with you – I wouldn't miss it for the world. But I do have to get hold of the other WISE women for a quick video call before we go. It starts at eleven, right?'

Her husband nodded. 'At least Althea didn't want it to start at dawn – that would have been an unpopular move, I think. With an eleven o'clock start, there's likely to be a good crowd there. If all your lot are going, you'd better summon them soon – it's nine already.'

With a peck on the cheek, he was gone, and Carol did what she needed to in order to get everyone online.

Like Carol, Annie was clutching a mug when she appeared on screen, Mavis had dark circles beneath her eyes, and Christine looked…surprisingly bright-eyed.

Carol observed, 'You look as though you had the best night's sleep of all of us, Christine.'

Christine tossed her chestnut curls. 'Alexander's in London, so I had the entire bed to myself, which makes a tremendous difference when you need to wriggle about to find a comfy sleeping position.'

Annie asked, 'What's he doing there, doll?'

Christine grinned as she checked her watch. 'At this precise moment? I suspect he's nursing the mother of all hangovers; he was hosting a party in a function room above a pub in Soho last night, for all his key staff. He mentioned fish and chips, but I dare say that gallons of beer were consumed too. He's staying there until tomorrow – by which time he should be safe to drive, I hope.'

Carol replied, 'I hope so, too. Look, I know we all want to get on, but I have something.'

Mavis was on full alert, despite the bags beneath her eyes. 'Something that might prove that Pauline Thomas is innocent?'

Carol felt herself sag a little, then forced a bright smile. 'No – I honestly believe we've done all we can in that regard. And I know that Annie's passed what I found about the Heather person, in Swansea, to DCI Carys James, but I wanted to…do more. And I've found another victim, and she might be the one who was in London last Sunday, shoving Larry Merton off an Underground platform.'

Carol had expected some pushback from Mavis, and it came swiftly. 'Ach, I thought we'd said we could do no more on that case, Carol. We agreed that all our efforts should be focused on Pauline Thomas, for Rhodri – our actual client.'

Carol forced another smile. 'It's only taken me a couple of hours, Mavis, and it was my own time. And it's something I think…well, I was hoping you might help, actually Mavis. If you would.'

Carol interpreted Mavis's loud tut as being at about a number eight on the scale of one to ten that she, Annie, and Christine had secretly categorized for their colleague – so, not quite as bad as it could have been.

Mavis said, 'And why would I do that?'

Carol explained, 'I know you really hit it off with the folks at The Lavender Hotel, near Tenby, when you stayed there with Althea, and this possible victim lives just outside Tenby – though the opposite side of the town when compared to the hotel. I also know you said that the people you met rather enjoyed helping you and Althea with your investigations there, and I think you said they styled themselves as The Lavender Mob? I thought they might be able to help us…if you were to give them a call. Wasn't there a chap named Siggy there? Something like that?'

Carol had spotted how often Mavis had mentioned a Siggy Welbeck, and a Dennis Moore, since her return from Tenby, and always with a bit of a twinkle in her eye; she wondered if Mavis might…bite.

Mavis said, 'Explain to us what you've discovered. I'll see if I can help, though I'm no' promising anything. And if I were to get in touch with anyone at The Lavender, it would be Uma Chatterjee I'd call; she's by far the most sensible person of the whole lot of them. So, fire away, and we'll see what we'll see.'

Carol did. When she'd emailed her report to everyone, she allowed them a few moments to read it while she finished her coffee.

Annie was the first to comment. 'Oh poor thing. You're right, Car, this one sounds like another of that Larry's victims. Goodness only knows why he went for Welsh women so much – not that they aren't lovely, like you, of course, Car, doll, but…it doesn't seem fair, does it?'

Christine said, 'He had a Welsh mother. Larry Merton. I remember him telling me that. Maybe she gave him the Llewellyn bit of his name? Maybe the Welsh targeting is because of that?'

Annie didn't sound convinced. 'Whatever. This one? This Hayley Taylor? She looks to be the same type as the others; a bit mousy, truth be told. And he's used the same approach – meet in a pub, roll out the sob story, fleece her for everything. Great job finding them photos, Car, and finding her, too. Mave, you should get your boyfriends in Tenby to track her down; Car's got the street name, but not the number. They'd do it for you, I bet.'

Carol saw Mavis's back stiffen. 'They're no boyfriends of mine, Annie,' she snapped. 'You've amassed some excellent information here, Carol. I dare say I could phone Uma to see if they might be able to help us out…though we could pass this to Carys James, to go with what we gave her about Heather Summerville/Williams.'

Annie said, 'Not her geographic area, Mave. Besides, if you got in touch with your Lavender Mob, you could tell them about the panto, too. I bet they'd buy some tickets.'

Mavis replied quietly, 'Aye, well, it's no' a bad idea. I'll give Uma a ring. They're a canny bunch, and they'd be up for a challenge like this, I dare say. Though I see no reason for me to tell them about the panto; the tickets have largely all been sold, thanks to some tremendous efforts on the part of all the members of the Anwen Players…and the majority have been sold to folks who don't live in the village. I understand that the area that was the playground at the old school is to become a temporary car park for the night, and that folks will be allowed to park around the green, in single file, of course.'

Christine observed, 'I dare say all that stuff in what will become the car park will have gone by the end of tomorrow, it being the solstice today. Will I see you all there at eleven this morning…ready for the shenanigans?'

Carol could tell that Mavis had no idea what Christine was talking about; she guessed she hadn't seen the old school yard, and wondered if she should spoil the surprise, or not.

Annie jumped in. 'I wouldn't miss it for the world. Though I have to say that the idea that people actually used to go out hunting for wrens and killing them is horrible. I mean, even I know they're just tiny little birds. I think this idea of Althea's is much better.'

Mavis clapped her hand to her forehead. 'Ach no, what's Althea up to now?'

Carol said, 'Another of her ancient Welsh traditions, Mavis. The Hunting of the Wren – to sacrifice it, to bring back the sun. Druids, sacrifice, killing the wren, the "King of the Birds"…all that; you have it up in Scotland too…well, you used to have a form of it. It kept going a lot longer here – it's well documented in Cardiff in the mid-1800s, even. And in Pembrokeshire they didn't kill the wren, but tied ribbons on it and then carried it in a box to everyone's house on Twelfth Night. Same sort of idea. Althea's organized a sort of "Wren Hunt" – but with tiny stuffed wrens hidden in man-made "trees". Sounds like you haven't seen them dotted around the old school yard. There's also going to be an Alban Arthan: she's got Ian Cottesloe to be the Holly King, and he'll have a mock battle with the Oak King, aka Aled from the pub. The Oak King – who reigns from midwinter to midsummer – will defeat the Holly King, who gets the other half of the year. Hasn't she told you any of this?'

Mavis shook her head wearily. 'She's no' said a word to me. Has this been in the works for some time, then?'

Annie nodded. 'Tudor told me about it about a month ago. Althea ran it past the village social committee and everything. We're providing mulled wine – though who'll want that at eleven in the morning is beyond me – and hot apple cider, the non-alcoholic type, so basically hot apple juice, which is disgusting. And we're all getting some mistletoe, to hang up at Christmas. Tudor's had a terrible time getting that, because we needed so much of it. In the end he managed to track down a woman who grows it for harvesting on the trees in her apple orchards just outside Hereford. He's even roped Eustelle and Rodney into tying it into little bunches for him. Mum's going on and on about how her and Dad have to be careful when they touch it, and not to let a single berry drop so the dogs might get at it, because it's so toxic. She's washing her hands every five minutes after doing it, despite the fact that she and Dad are wearing kitchen gloves whenever they touch it. So yes, Chrissy – I'll be there, and I'll be the one handing out the mistletoe at the end of it all. Wearing gloves.'

Mavis shook herself, like a dog. 'I know Althea's got the vicar doing another Carols by Candlelight service on Christmas Eve, and that she's being very supportive of the Mari Lwyd in the New Year – it seems that was very popular last time, so I think that'll keep happening, around here, for a while. But I had no idea she had this up her sleeve…as well as the panto. She really is trying very hard to…give the village lots of things to do together. Which is good, of course. But it's a lot for an older person to do, alone. I see, now, why this panto is so important to her; maybe if this Oswald of hers kick-starts some local enthusiasm for an annual performance, it, too, will continue, without needing an outsider to lead it.'

Carol said, 'I think it's all brilliant. There's a lot of villages that have nothing to get them working as a community these days; Anwen-by-Wye really does seem to be going from strength to strength, and that's largely down to Althea. I know we'll all be at the carol service…it's a lovely chance for families to enjoy the real spirit of Christmas, and the get-together at the church hall afterwards is always joyful.'

Annie chuckled. 'Yeah, Eustelle and Rodney are really looking forward to it, though I know Tude won't be there. There are still a few who prefer to nurse a half of mild on Christmas Eve, even if they do hum the odd chorus of a carol or two while they do it. Will your lot be here by then, Chrissy?'

Christine nodded. 'Yes, they're arriving some time around lunchtime on Christmas Eve – depending on the traffic, of course. They're leaving the London house first thing, then they'll stay for the panto, of course, and head back the day after that.'

Mavis smiled. 'So you'll be at Chellingworth Hall for dinner on Christmas Day, Christine? It'll be a pleasure to see your parents again…it's been a while since I've seen your father, especially. They'll have quite a large table there that day. A dozen adults, plus Hugo…but I dare say we shouldn't count him as the thirteenth guest.'

Christine raised a hand. 'I dare say Oswald will be there too – so that makes thirteen adults, a child – and don't forget Lumpy…a good crowd, to be sure.'

Carol felt it was up to her to draw the meeting – that had already morphed into something other than a purely professional gathering – to a close, since she was the one who'd called it. 'Look, it's lovely to chatter, but I have to get me and Albert ready to get to the solstice thingy – so we'll leave it that Mavis will get The Lavender Mob onto this lead in Tenby, and we'll all see each other in just over an hour at the old school. Thanks, Mavis.' She disconnected her feed before Mavis had a chance to say anything more.

CHAPTER THIRTY-TWO

Clementine Twyst lay in bed, wondering what to do. And not just what to do for the next ten minutes, but for the rest of her life. Julian had disappeared at an extraordinarily early hour – to prepare for the day, he'd said. Not having a clue what he was referring to, Clementine had rolled over and napped. But now? Now she was peckish, and knew that a substantial breakfast awaited her downstairs. But it was only just gone eight, and barely light outside, and she was so warm, and cozy.

A buzzing alerted her to the arrival of a text on the phone she had charging on her bedside table. She read it three times, but it still made no sense.

I'm the Holly King's page at the Alban Arthan at the old school in the village that kicks off after the Wren Hunt (starts 11.00) & it would be wonderful if my wife could see me dressed up. I think she'll like my outfit (no spoilers, but there are TIGHTS involved LOL!) Jx

Lady Clementine Treforest-Twyst had no idea what she'd be letting herself in for, but had to admit that – for all their 'discussions' of late – the idea of seeing her husband wearing tights, in public, sounded like a bit of a hoot…and she was in need of a good laugh. And – if she got a move on – there was no reason why she couldn't have a decent breakfast, then drive herself into the village in time to see…whatever it was that Jools meant by his note.

With her decision made, Clementine prepared herself to face the day, and chose a duck-egg blue knitted suit for the occasion; she'd been dressing rather drably, of late, hoping that would speak volumes to her husband about her state of mind…but to no avail. Apparently, he was oblivious to whatever she wore, always insisting that her 'inner light' shone through, which rather defeated the purpose of making mud-hued selections from her wardrobe. So the blue it would be. She was glad she'd packed it now; it had been an afterthought at the time.

Clementine breakfasted alone: her brother and sister-in-law were taking breakfast in their rooms with their son, her absolutely darling nephew, Hugo; her sister-in-law's parents, John and Sheila Timbers – who were pleasant enough – were not habitually early risers, Edward confided.

So Clementine enjoyed scrambled eggs, some mushrooms, and a single sausage, then drove herself to the village, where she was taken aback to find the entire place a-buzz with activity. Following the throng of what appeared to be the entire population of Anwen-by-Wye – plus a couple of dozen visitors, if the number of cars parked around the green were anything to go by – she found herself huddled in the crowd that was surrounding what had once been the tarmac playground of the old school. The school itself was encased in scaffolding and tarpaulins.

She could see Annie Parker and Tudor Evans ladling steaming liquid into china mugs that every attendee but herself appeared to have brought with them. There were several children present, only two of whom she vaguely recognized as belonging to a woman she thought she'd been told had moved away – a teacher of some sort? – who had, presumably, returned for this event…whatever it might be. And she couldn't fathom the purpose of the strange tree-like structures constructed of raw timber that were dotted along one edge of the open space, nearest the school building.

She spotted Henry and Stephanie, who had Hugo in a pram with them – *they could have said they were attending, then I could have shared their vehicle* – and saw Carol Hill with her husband and son, and two short, older people who were billing and cooing over the child in such a way that they had to be its grandparents. Christine was wearing a winter coat that almost buttoned over her distended belly; Alexander wasn't about. She couldn't see her own husband anywhere, despite the promise of the sight of him in hosiery.

Her mother – *of course it had to be her!* – blew a whistle, and all the children ran to her. She called out, 'Let the hunt for the wren begin', and off they all went rushing about the timber structures, squealing – some clambering up into the 'branches', some focusing on those they could reach from the ground. A yelp was let out by one of the children, and they ran to her mother, offering up something, which the dowager then shoved onto a stick – *what on earth was she doing?* – and held the entire thing aloft calling, 'The wren, the king of the birds, is dead.'

Clementine was completely confused by the whole undertaking.

Then, without further ado, her mother shouted, 'Let battle commence!'

Clementine was utterly bemused to see Ian, from the Dower House, arrive from behind a makeshift tented structure wearing an outfit that was all dark green with a red hat, and he was followed by…Jools – her Jools – who was carrying a massive – *is that a stick or a club?* – something on a cushion. Jools was also dressed in green, but, whereas Ian Cottesloe had managed to get away with a relatively ordinary-looking outfit – barring, maybe, his large, bulbous red hat – Jools hadn't fared as well: he was wearing red shoes, and green tights topped by a green-and-red-striped doublet, and a red hat with a large feather, that was bobbing about in the breeze. Clementine had no idea why this was happening, but she knew she needed to take as many photos of Jools as possible, so she made her way through the knots in the crowd until she could get a better shot of him, and snapped as though there might be no tomorrow.

Another pair dressed in similarly bizarre outfits, but this time in a fresher green, with brown ornamentation, moved into the open space from another tent at the other side of the…*arena?* Yes – both 'pages' were arming each of the two main characters with what was, indeed, a large wooden club, and they proceeded to dance around each other, hitting each other from time to time with what Clementine now hoped were fake, possibly rubber, clubs. This continued for a few moments, with the crowd cheering every time the not Holly King – she had no idea what he was supposed to represent – hit the Holly King himself, who eventually found it all too much, and fell to the ground, bringing loud cheers.

'The Holly King is dead, long live the Oak King,' shouted her mother. 'The old year has died, the sun will rise again – all hail the new year.' More cheering followed.

Once she heard his title, Clementine better understood the significance of the garb of the chap who wasn't the Holly King. Oak for the half of the year when the days were long, or lengthening, holly for the shorter, or shortening, days. It made sense…now. But she was still at sea when it came to the fake trees, and the fake wrens; maybe Jools would be able to enlighten her. It looked as though his duties as page were over, and she could see him peering around the crowd. She waved, and he made his way toward her.

As soon as he reached her, he gave her an all-enveloping hug, which wasn't something he'd done much of in the past few weeks. She felt…safe, and rather wonderful. As they pulled back from each other, her husband released his grasp of her and went down on one knee…which puzzled her a great deal. The crowd pushed back, giving the couple space, and Jools announced, 'You're my wife, Lady Clementine Treforest-Twyst, and we married at dawn on the summer solstice. Will you now renew the vows you made that day on this day, the turn of the year?'

Clementine was flabbergasted. She hissed, 'Stand up, Jools, everyone's looking at us.'

But Jools persisted. 'Exactly my reason for doing this now. A celebrant is waiting for your answer, Clementine.' He looked to one side, where Clementine spotted, for the first time, the Reverend Ebenezer Roberts in his cassock and collar.

Jools stood, and bent his head to hers, whispering, 'Whether it's just the two of us, or even if there's more of us, I want you to know that I love you, and I always shall. Let's speak our vows on the shortest day of the year, as we did on the longest, and cement them here, in front of everyone who knows your ancestral home…and your family.'

Clementine's hands were tingling, her knees didn't feel as though they belonged to her. *Oh what a wonderful thing for you to do for us, Jools.*

Her family members were making their way toward her; her heart was pounding…and she was both sweating and shivering.

Clementine looked into the eyes of the man she loved, and said quietly, 'Of course I shall, Jools. Nothing would give me greater pleasure.'

There was no service, as such, just a chance to speak aloud the vows they'd made to each other in Egypt, six months earlier. Clementine stumbled over a few words, but she'd spent a long time committing them to memory for their wedding, so was more than familiar with their core, even if a few of the phrases didn't come out quite the same way this second time around. When they'd both finished, the crowd surrounding them cheered and applauded, and Clementine knew that she and Jools had taken a significant step forward in their relationship, though she realized only too well that there were still a good number of hurdles ahead of them…well, ahead of her, in any case.

Jools kissed her, then pulled back and said, 'I have to get out of these clothes, and then I'm due over at the village hall to lend a hand with a few jobs they need doing there; it seems that a tall chap with a good amount of upper body strength is quite popular on a stage – though not, I'm pleased to say, with any expectations of me performing in any way. I should be back at Chellingworth by teatime.'

Clementine dared to ask, 'Could you do with some help? I'm not too bad at quite a few things…I could even make tea.'

Jools beamed. 'You might want to offer to help Henry.'

Clementine was surprised. 'What on earth is he doing there?'

Jools chuckled. 'It appears that your mother managed to talk him into agreeing to paint the scenery. Though he claims he agreed to do no such thing initially, he's now said he'll do it after all. You're as good an artist as he is any day of the week – and I bet things would be helped along by another proper painter being on hand. Though I would absolutely understand if you two didn't think it would be…productive if you were to share work on a project.'

Clementine gave the idea some thought. 'Henry's not used to such a massive format. I think I could help him gain the right perspective; I was involved in designing and painting the backdrops for a few fashion shows over the years…that's the same sort of thing. I'll talk to my brother about it. Wish me luck.'

Clementine very much enjoyed the kiss Jools gave her before saying, 'You won't need luck, Clementine, just use your charm. This is a team effort, and it would be wonderful to all be working at it together.'

Clementine waved at her husband as he left to rid himself of his bizarre costume, and headed toward her brother, and mother, who were waggling their arms at each other, both pink in the face. As she got closer, she could hear Henry saying, 'I just wish I'd had more notice, Mother,' to which her mother replied, 'None of us have the time we'd like, dear…but I have faith in you.'

Clementine decided to launch herself at the pair, and opened with: 'I'd be happy to lend a hand with the painting of the scenery, Henry; I have some experience with large-scale pieces, to be viewed from afar. I really do think I could be useful.'

Clementine was amused to see both her brother and mother hesitate, then fail to come up with a suitable response, then each glance at the other, looking panicked.

She finally said, 'Mother, Henry – please…use me. I can help.'

Her mother blinked first. 'I say, Henry, that's a wonderful idea…and to have both my children involved with a project that's so near and dear to my heart would just make my day…my year. I hope you'll accept your sister's offer, Henry, and thank you for giving it, Clementine.'

'I'll show you where the paints are,' said Henry, as he stomped toward the village hall. Clementine kissed her mother's cheek, and followed him, giggling.

Before she left the open area, she heard her mother asking, 'Has anyone seen our wren? Where's the wren gone from the top of that stick – it was supposed to remain here, as a part of the overall solstice celebration…Ossie? Have you seen it? Where's Oswald gone? Oswald? Carol, have you seen Oswald?'

Clementine caught Carol replying, 'No, and I can't stop to help you look for him, I'm sorry, Althea…I'm a bit backed up with work at the moment. I must get back to my office.'

23rd DECEMBER

CHAPTER THIRTY-THREE

Mavis had rather enjoyed what had felt like a somewhat normal Sunday; she and Althea had attended church together, as usual, and Oswald hadn't joined them, which hadn't surprised her one iota. However, she still chose to arrive at the breakfast table earlier than usual on Monday morning because she didn't care to break bread with the man – hoping to be able to eat and get away before he even arrived. But she failed; Oswald and Althea arrived within moments of each other and were giggling about…something.

Mavis rose to take her leave, and hissed at Althea, 'We need to talk, alone, after breakfast. Please come to my room, dear. Thank you.'

Althea brushed away Mavis's touch. 'Don't be silly, I shan't have time. Ossie and I are meeting people at the village hall at ten.'

Mavis said, 'Please, Althea – it's important.'

Althea took her seat at the table. 'Couldn't you just sit and tell me over a cup of tea? Ossie won't mind. You won't mind, will you Ossie?'

Oswald looked vaguely at Mavis, then the dowager. 'Mind? You two nattering on as I nibble my toast? Not at all.'

Mavis tried again. 'It's private, Althea.'

Althea countered with: 'I have no secrets from Ossie – eh, Ossie? No secrets between us, right?'

Ossie grinned as he buttered his toast. 'Secrets? Between us? Good grief no. You couldn't slip a cigarette paper between us, we're that close, Mavis. Say what you want – I've been on the stage my whole life, so I think you'd be hard-pressed to shock me.'

Mavis seriously considered blurting out her concerns about Oswald in front of the man, just to shut him up and – hopefully – get rid of that smug grin he always seemed to have. But she told herself that wouldn't be fair to Althea. 'Thank you, but I'll wait. When would it be convenient for us to have a meeting – just the two of us – Althea? I'll work around your…schedule.'

Althea looked bemused. 'My time is rather spoken for between now and…well, until the curtain comes down, I suppose…though then there'll be the after-party, of course. So no time would be convenient, Mavis. Besides, aren't you and your girls busy with some sort of case?'

Mavis was less than pleased to hear Althea using such a dismissive tone when speaking of Annie, Carol, and Christine, and the work they all did. She believed she could detect the influence of 'Ossie'.

Again, Mavis weighed her response. 'The case we've all been working on has nothing to do with the matter that I would like to discuss with you. It's personal, you might say.'

Althea paused, her teacup in front of her small face. 'Is this about Clementine wanting to have a baby?'

Mavis shook her head. 'It's not.'

'Good. I don't want to talk about that. At all. Well, look, if it's so terribly urgent – Ossie, would you be a dear and start without me this morning? I tell you what – I could ask Ian to run you down to the village alone, then he could come back to collect me. You know there'll be supplies there; we've made it quite clear to Marjorie how important that aspect is, so you could leave quite soon, make yourself a pot of tea when you get there, block out a few things, and I'd be with you a little later…still lots of time before anyone else arrives.'

It suddenly dawned on Mavis that Althea was spending an inordinate amount of time with Ossie at the rehearsal venue…and that early mornings were the norm, whereas she was pretty sure that rehearsals never started until after lunchtime. That was a puzzler…but she didn't dwell on that, instead pouncing on the offer Althea made, and doing her best to urge Oswald to wolf down his toast and leave.

Knowing that the man was going meant that Mavis was prepared to stay, so she watched him devour every greasy, jammy mouthful of toast, and slurp every last dreg of his tea before he finally left, and she and Althea were alone.

Althea poured herself a fresh cup of tea, and Mavis did likewise; Mavis felt that the silence in the room wasn't…a comfortable silence.

Althea's opening suggested she felt the same. 'You say you have something you want to talk to me about, and I suspect it pertains to Ossie. Am I right?'

Mavis nodded. 'Perceptive, as always, Althea.' As the words left her lips, Mavis realized that what she was about to tell Althea would show her she was anything but...and she didn't care for how that made her feel. But this had to be done.

Althea snapped, 'I dare say. But I further suspect that you're about to make me look like an old fool. Are you?'

Mavis sighed. 'There's no getting away from it, Althea dear, I have some unpleasant facts to share with you about Oswald: he's been lying to you. About everything. I'm so terribly sorry, my dear.'

Althea sipped her tea. 'Oh Mavis – I'm so terribly sorry for you, my dear. Have you found out that he's almost penniless, up to his neck in debt, and about to be kicked out of his lodgings…and likely end up – literally – living on the street?'

Mavis nodded. 'You…knew?'

Althea smiled kindly. 'I did. And that's why he's here. He doesn't know that I know, of course – that would never do. So you must promise to keep everything between us…and any of the other WISE women who might have been helping you with a bit of background research. I should have guessed you'd do it, because you're wonderfully protective of me – but, really, there's no need.'

Mavis felt some relief. 'In that case, why don't you tell me the truth about this panto thing – and him.' She nodded toward the remnants of a hurried breakfast that had been abandoned at the table.

Althea checked her watch. 'Very well, but I must be brief. You know I do what I can of a philanthropic nature…well, I don't do all that I could, but I do what I can. Anyway, I was having a look through some old photographs a few months ago, and it made me realize that – if they weren't dead – the people whose faces I was enjoying seeing again must now be old and wizened, like mine. Then I wondered about their circumstances; a life on the stage doesn't give you steady work, let alone the chance to save up or have anything but the state pension to live on when you're old. Which led me to look into what services there were for those who have retired after a life on the boards, and what charities existed, and so forth. I'm getting rather good at online research – thanks to you lot teaching me bits and pieces, especially Carol. Though I'll admit there are a lot of rabbit holes that a person can slip into, from time to time, and one finds that hours have simply disappeared. Anyway, I managed to find an old hoofing partner of mine, Aggie, who's almost ninety, and still planning to do the cancan – dressed as an angel, of course – in the Christmas show they're putting on at her care home, and she told me about Ossie being on his uppers. So I tracked him down through his company's website and decided to do this with him, and for him. He's all on his own now, and just needs a bit of help, to get him back on his feet. By doing this, I can make him feel he's not being given a handout, but is selling his professional services at a fair price…with a little bonus, because what I'm asking of him is so extraordinary.'

Mavis felt her heart melt just a little. 'You're a good woman, Althea…but I still think there's a thing or two you don't know about. You see, around the village…there've been…items…that have "grown legs" when he's been at a place. Quite a few people are upset – though nothing that's gone has been valuable, they're all items people are missing, in the true sense of the word.'

Mavis's heart fell with Althea's face. The dowager sunk into her seat. 'Oh dear, I thought that was a thing of the past. He used to do that all the time – said he couldn't help it. A powder puff gone from here, a shoe buckle gone from there; a headpiece that should have been somewhere, but wasn't; or a tie that disappeared from a dressing room. Ossie was known as "Featherfingers". I thought he'd stopped. He told me he had. Maybe since…since Ralph died, he's started again. I know he's missing him terribly. But for that to be happening here, in the village…well, that's not fair to anyone. I must speak to him about that – that must stop, and I shall tell him so. I dare say he still has everything he's taken, he always did have. Called them his "collectibles". Thought it was funny.'

Mavis was puzzled. 'You're taking this very…well, Althea. I must say, I'm surprised.'

Althea muttered, 'The older you get, the less often you'll be surprised, my dear. The word "normal" ceases to have meaning. You'll see.'

'I hope I don't,' replied Mavis, with all the feeling she could muster. 'So you think he's got my mother's sewing scissors hidden away somewhere safe? And Gwen Pike's box of thimbles…and Annie's teapot, and Janet's vase, and Elizabeth's bell?'

Althea dropped her chin and said quietly, 'Oh dear…Ossie.' She looked up, her expression grim. 'I believe he will. Somewhere. I'm sure we'll be able to return everything, undamaged.'

Mavis said, 'How does he even get away with it, Althea? My scissors are tiny, but the teapot Annie lost is…well, it's a teapot, so bulky is in its nature. And it was on a windowsill – in plain sight of everyone in the pub.'

Althea nodded. 'Did I mention that Ralph was a magician? Sleight of hand, diversion of attention, that sort of thing. Ossie would have picked up all sorts from him.'

Mavis understood. 'Well, I dinnae think it's a bad idea to help out an old friend, Althea, but this is…different.'

'Oh yes, I absolutely agree. But, listen…since my saying anything is likely to upset him – and we're so close to the performance – and he's under such a great deal of pressure…might it wait just a little?'

Mavis replied, 'I'm not so sure that's a good idea, Althea. What else might he take? What upset might it cause? It's a dangerous decision to make.'

Althea nodded. 'Well, I believe it's the right one. I shall act accordingly.' She returned her attention to her tea.

Mavis was in no doubt that there would be nothing she could say to dissuade Althea from her chosen course of action, so decided she should finally get around to phoning Rhodri Lloyd: her phone had been vibrating in her pocket while she and Althea had been…chatting…and she could see that Rhodri was rather keen for her to get in touch with him.

CHAPTER THIRTY-FOUR

Annie opened her eyes to discover that Tudor, and the dogs, had gone. The alarm hadn't woken her, and it was almost nine o'clock. She checked the clock: the alarm had been switched off. Tudor must have done it, but...why? Yes, the previous day had felt like a particularly long one; even for a Sunday, the pub had been unusually busy, but she'd managed to have a pretty early night, after all...so why the lie-in? She couldn't understand it.

The commotion she could hear in the kitchen told her the dogs hadn't gone far, and that both her mother and father were already up and about. Making use of every part of her bathroom as fast as she could, it only took her twenty minutes to join the throng, ready to face the day...though not, necessarily, the sight that met her eyes when she entered her open plan lounge-kitchen-dining room.

Yes, Gertie and Rosie were there, and both in a high state of excitement...and no wonder, because her mother was waggling sausages about, her father was brandishing bacon, and Tudor was doing something with potatoes.

'Gordon Bennett, you lot – what are you all playing at?'

The trio stopped and turned, and even Gertie managed a backward glance, before returning her attention to a bowl of eggs.

'We're spoiling you: it's a full, cooked breakfast for our resident brilliant detective,' said Tudor.

'I'm so proud, child,' said Annie's mother, sticking a fork into a sausage as though she meant it mortal harm. 'You're on the telly. My daughter's on the telly.'

Annie's father added, 'Our daughter, Eustelle. Your mother's already phoned all her friends back at home to tell them. It's only on the news in Wales, but she's telling them all in case they can get the Welsh channel on whatever system they use.'

Annie was more than a little confused. 'What do you mean I'm on the telly? The Welsh news? Me? But...why?'

Eustelle abandoned her attack on the plate of defenseless sausages and moved to hug her daughter; Rodney joined in.

Tudor continued to grate potatoes as he grinned like the Cheshire Cat. 'They didn't actually mention you by name, and they didn't show a photo of you or anything,' he said, as her parents continued their hugging, 'but they talked about the agency, and gave the name, and the location, and everything. Praised you to the heights they did. Rhodri Lloyd did, that is. They even had Carwen James's picture up there, and had him talking on the phone. He was full of compliments.'

Annie was glad when her parents let go, but still none the wiser. 'Alright, I give up – why? What was Rhodri on the TV talking about? The Pauline Thomas case?'

Annie's phone rang in her pocket. 'Hello Car, you alright?'

Carol's voice was barely audible. 'Did you see it?'

Annie waggled a hand at her parents. 'Did I see what, Car?'

'Them, talking about us on the telly?'

Annie snapped, 'No, I flamin' well didn't – but they're all going bonkers about it here. What's happened? Will you please tell me.'

Carol shouted, 'Pauline Thomas got a letter in the post from Sylvia Jenkins. It went on about how she knew she was really to blame for losing all her money to Merton, and that…well, it was sad, really, because it was a suicide note. But, you know, good for Pauline.'

Annie was astonished. 'That was on the TV? Mum – please – let me listen to Carol, will you? Is that what you're saying, Car?'

Carol spoke slowly. 'No, I've told you more than was on TV, because Mavis phoned me, because Rhodri phoned her. They didn't say anything about what the letter said, on the news, just that it exonerated Pauline – Rhodri's client. He got her over to the police station with the letter first thing, and then got hold of the TV people to interview him when they left, about half an hour ago. It was even captioned "Breaking News". I suppose he must have contacts. And he said lovely things about us, Annie. I've recorded it.'

'So I can see a recording?'

Tudor called, 'I recorded it too.'

Annie blew him a kiss. 'So is Pauline cleared now? Even though we didn't really find any proof that she didn't kill Sylvia – has this cracked it for her?'

'Seems so,' replied Carol. 'I'll see you later; don't forget we're meeting at eleven, at the office, so let's talk then. Got to go, Mam and Dad are over the moon about it. Talk later.'

Annie popped her phone back into her pocket. 'Right then, let's see this recording, please.'

As the sausages sizzled, and the potatoes browned, Annie Parker sat holding hands with her mother and father as she listened to the full minute of praise for the investigative skills of the WISE Enquiries Agency – a local firm run by four dedicated, professional women, based in offices on the Chellingworth Estate, that was now being used on a frequent basis by Rhodri Lloyd. Chief Inspector Carwen James, on the phone, agreed that the investigation into the death of Sylvia Jenkins had been contributed to by external parties, and – when pressed – said he had a high regard for the skills of the agency, though was unable to confirm their involvement in this tragic case.

Annie was on cloud nine by the time she sat down to indulge in the delicious breakfast, surrounded by her loved ones, and relished every mouthful, and every hug. It was one of the most wonderful experiences of her life…because she got to share it with everyone she truly cared about.

When Tudor poured her a third cup of tea, from the second pot, he said, 'I'll never forget today, I won't. We've got a star in the family. Your company – on the telly. Brilliant. Just brilliant.'

Annie nodded. 'I can't believe it myself. I mean…it came out of the blue. We were a bit stuck, to be honest – because we couldn't prove she didn't do it.'

Her father patted her arm. 'Well, that bloke, Rhodri, said that the police had found the dead woman's car in a lay-by – that she'd been living in it – and some of her stuff had examples of her handwriting, so the police knew that the letter was definitely written by her. Said his client was in the clear…that she could get back to her life, now.'

Her mother said, 'So what does she do then? Is she a hairdresser? She looks like a hairdresser. I bet people didn't want her doing their hair when they were thinking she'd killed someone. Who'd be wanting someone accused of drowning somebody to be the one pushing your head backwards into that funny sink thing? No one. They'll be queuing out of the door now, I bet...hoping she'll tell them all about it.'

Annie laughed. 'Well, she's no hairdresser, and she was losing business even before that poor woman died...because she kept having accidents, which we believed the dead woman was causing.'

'Injured, was she? Couldn't work? So what did she do?'

Annie's father chided gently, 'Maybe you shouldn't pry, Eustelle.'

Eustelle Parker rolled her eyes. 'Come on, Annie, she's innocent – you can tell us.'

Annie reckoned that circumstances allowed for it. 'Well...she's a fortune teller, and she'd had all these accidents, so folks stopped going to her – for obvious reasons.'

Eustelle leaned forward. 'Really? Is she any good?'

Rodney Parker slapped the dining table. 'That's a good one. Come on, Eustelle – you can't believe in all that rubbish.'

'I'm not saying I believe in it, Rodney – but I'm not saying I don't either. So, child...is she any good? Did she know she'd be...saved this way?'

Annie thought about it for a moment. 'You know what, Mum – she sort of did. She said she'd be saved by someone in a uniform, and the people who deliver the post wear uniforms, so I suppose she was right...though I dare say she's wishing that letter had arrived a few days ago. And there were a few other things she said that you could argue were true – though they were all a bit general for my liking. And there was a big one she got wrong; she's seen Chrissy, so knew she was pregnant, but she said someone else in our circle was pregnant too. I checked, and Car's not, so that's a big mark against Pauline's abilities, I'd say. And, just for your information, Dad – I think it's all rubbish, so we'll let Mum live in her own little dreamworld, shall we?'

Tudor said, 'It's not raining, and it's surprisingly mild for the time of the year – I was thinking we could all get out around the green, maybe even over to the duck pond, and have a bit of fresh air while we can...and give the girls a good walk.'

Eustelle stood. 'That's a good idea. We'll clear this when we get back. Let's get this star of ours paraded around that green out there.'

The walk was less of an opportunity for Annie's parents to be able to praise their daughter to the people of Anwen-by-Wye than it was a saunter with two rambunctious dogs, curtailed by the sudden onset of what Eustelle referred to as a 'spiteful shower'. With Aled not required to attend a rehearsal until the afternoon, Annie was delighted when Tudor offered to give her a lift to the office, but she took the one offered by Carol instead, since she was going there anyway.

When Annie and Tudor kissed on the back doorstep of the Coach and Horses that morning, she didn't think life could get any better – despite the rain that was now coming at her sideways as she took the short walk to Carol's new house, where she was greeted by Carol's husband, David, in the kitchen.

In a way, Annie missed Carol's old, small but cozy kitchen, though she understood the advantages offered by this new one – which was at least three times the size, and fitted with modern appliances and an island the size of a small continent. But it seemed to Annie that something was missing…the place was warm, but it was a different type of warmth than that which had come from the old Aga stove. Bunty seemed to be missing the old stove too – because she didn't settle at all while Annie was there, though the two of them had never been easy in each other's company; Annie put it down to the fact she must smell of her dogs.

Finally alone in Carol's vehicle, Annie said, 'So, come on then, I want all the details…or is that why we're meeting?'

'Not why we're meeting – Mavis said something had come up that she wanted our help with, so I dare say she'll tell us when we get there. I think she told me everything she's likely to know for now about the Pauline Thomas case: Sylvia's letter left no doubt in the matter – she meant to take her own life, had planned how to do it, posted the letter, took a load of pills, and was going to sit beside the water until she was ready to go into it. The letter also said that Pauline deserved to be punished for having suggested to Sylvia that love would find her, though she did accept that she shouldn't have given the money she did to Merton, which was why she sent the letter…so that Pauline would only have to suffer for a little while.'

Annie didn't like it. 'That's just…vicious. I believed Pauline when she said she'd warned Sylvia to use her judgment wisely, but I suppose that's easy to say, but not as easy to do. We've all done our fair share of stupid things in the name of love, I dare say.'

Annie noticed that Carol stiffened. 'I don't think I have; David and I have a very…normal relationship.'

Annie had to laugh. 'Hang on – is this the same woman who'd talk to me in wine bars in the City about the bloke she fancied but couldn't say anything to because he worked for her? The same woman who gave up a career so she would have a better chance of becoming pregnant? The same woman who's got her parents living at her house because she wants them to save money on rent so they can buy a nicer flat for their retirement? Oh, Car…you do things all the time because you love people, but, in your case, they all come over as sweet and lovely, because you're sweet and lovely.'

Carol giggled. 'I suppose you're right, Annie, as usual. Anyway – we're nearly there so, tell me, did you have a chance to talk to Mavis about what you were telling me about Oswald Featherington?'

Annie came back down to earth with a bump. 'Yeah, but she was one step ahead of me. She'd done a bit of digging into him herself, and didn't like what she'd found. She said she was going to talk to Althea about it all. Maybe that's why she called this meeting – I don't know. But, we're here now, so we'll soon find out.'

CHAPTER THIRTY-FIVE

Unusually, Mavis was the last to arrive at the office. Christine noticed Annie pointedly checking her watch as Mavis shook off her gaberdine and hung it carefully on a coat hanger before joining the trio at the coffee table, where she sat silently sipping tea for a moment. The looks exchanged signified how extremely out of character for Mavis this was.

With no one daring to speak, because Mavis had requested the meeting, Christine felt the tension build within the heavy silence. As Mavis placed her mug carefully on the table, the mood of expectation was palpable. 'Nice tea. You made that, didn't you, Annie?'

Annie nodded. 'I know you like it strong, and it's going to get us through this meeting…whatever it might be about.'

Christine admired Annie's guts.

Mavis sat back on the sofa and said quietly, 'We're here to…allow ourselves a moment of well-deserved congratulations. No' a celebration, exactly, because that would be in poor taste, but we should be satisfied with a good job, well done.'

Christine dared, 'And the mention we got on TV? That was grand, so it was…and it can't be bad for business, can it?'

Annie cooed, 'I was so happy that Eustelle and Rodney were here to see it with me. They were so proud. It was…great.'

Carol added, 'For me too. Mam and Dad nearly burst with pride, and Mam's probably still on the phone talking to people back in Carmarthen about it. David's said he'll keep the recording for Albert to see one day…which I think's a bit much, but it means he's proud, too. I bet Althea was all over you about it this morning, Mavis.'

'Althea is no' a devotee of television in the morning, and I've not even seen it myself. I was…otherwise engaged.'

'Pauline's post must be delivered very early for it all to have happened this morning,' said Annie. 'We don't get anything until about half eight, when on earth does she get hers?'

Mavis replied, 'Now that I can tell you: she was walking along the towpath to meet Rhodri to go to the police station…just a moment Annie…because the toxicology reports finally came in late last night, and showed that Sylvia Jenkins had ingested a large number of painkillers prior to her death; it turns out that they'd been crushed up in the alcohol she'd drunk, which didnae exactly clear anyone of having forced her to take them. However, the report showed that they were a specific type of painkiller that had been prescribed to Sylvia herself, and Rhodri felt this was an important finding, pointing to Sylvia having intentionally taken an overdose of her own tablets. He was going to accompany Pauline to be interviewed, with a view to getting her name cleared…publicly. The arrival of the letter was unforeseen, and highly fortuitous, as Rhodri put it. The postman gave the letter to Pauline at about ten past seven this morning, which allowed for the half past eight broadcast of the news. I dare say that it will appear in some form or other among the lunchtime news items too. So, yes, a good conclusion there.'

Christine added, 'And, hopefully, some business because of it.'

Mavis nodded.

Christine tapped her colleagues' legs to get their attention…with her foot. 'Mavis has something more to say,' she announced.

Everyone gave Mavis their attention. 'It's this Oswald person,' she began, which Christine didn't think bode well for whatever might come next. As she listened to Mavis's summary of her conversation with Althea, she understood Mavis's concerns, as did Annie and Carol, by the looks of it.

Annie was the first to jump in when it was clear that Mavis had finished her summary. 'Look, we did our best to crack The Case of the Unfortunate Fortune Teller, even though we didn't really swing it in the end. Sometimes, cases are like that, right? But we're still doing our bit to try to solve The Case of the Slimy Scammer – which is what I've decided to call the Merton thing, even though I know it's not really our case. I know Chrissy's been trying to help Henry and Stephanie with their Case of the Bewildered Brother-in-Law, by tackling what sounds to me like The Case of the Lonely Lady, so we're only left with The Case of the Impecunious Impresario, which I accepted as a suggestion from Mave. But it looks like it's out of our hands for now…and up to Althea to take it forward.'

Carol mused, 'If Oswald used to be known as "Featherfingers" donkey's years ago, then it sounds like he can't help himself. A form of kleptomania…sad, really. Though I'm glad that Althea sees that it's not a good thing to be happening around the village.'

Christine added, 'Daddy told me when I was younger that his family had a sort of general factotum at the house in Ireland who used to pinch stuff and sell it…but he wasn't psychologically compelled to lift things, he said it was because he never got paid, and felt he was owed it, so I see that's different. But I do share your concern, Mavis, that Oswald might do something truly regrettable before Althea thinks it's the right time to say something to him. Should we…I don't know, maybe mount an eyes-on operation until then? We're all available for parts of the time, so we could allocate shifts – maybe with you keeping an eye on him all the time he's actually at the Dower House, Mavis, and the rest of us keeping tabs on him while he's at the village hall. How about that?'

Annie said, 'It would be easy enough for me to take over if he came into the pub, but I'd volunteer for a few shifts. It's lovely having Eustelle and Rodney to stay, but we all need a little break from each other; they're both so used to having their own time to be…well, on their own.'

Carol grinned. 'Same with me and Mam and Dad. Dad's at rehearsals, so I could be with him, there, while Mam's with Albert – that would be good. And, Christine, Alexander's over at the village hall a lot too, I know, so neither of us would be particularly inconvenienced by having to be there. It sounds like a good plan, to me.'

Mavis sighed. 'Aye, not a bad idea, Christine, and it could work, as you say, because who knows when Althea will confront him. I have my suspicions that she'll wait until after the performance…she's keen that nothing upsets that.'

Christine said, 'Right, well, let's set up a rota now, and get going. I'll volunteer for today at the village hall, because I know Alexander's going to be there from one o'clock until early evening; he's helping Julian Treforest to install the new lighting rig thing he's designed and built.'

Carol offered, 'And Dad's going to be there this evening: he said it's a full rehearsal for the dance numbers, so I dare say that could go on for quite some time. They seem to be using some very odd music, if what he's been going around humming is anything to go by. It's very odd to hear my father rapping as he makes breakfast, but that's what he seems to be doing; it sounds as though Oswald has rewritten something that originated in some sort of American neighborhood. Weird.'

Annie laughed, 'I won't mind putting in some hours there, though I'll try to do it when Aled's able to be in the pub to support Tudor…who's just about driving me around the bend with his reciting of every single line and stage direction from that blessed script he won't put down. Am I the only one who's going to be glad when this thing is all over?'

Mavis replied, 'We all have a lot happening over the next few days, so, yes, let's sort out a rota for who will be keeping their eyes on Oswald and when…and don't forget, ladies, the man was married to a magician, so be aware of possible distractive techniques, and watch for sleight of hand…or he might defeat our purpose. And, by the way – not a word to Althea about this; she might have her secrets from me, but I have a few I think it's best I keep from her, too. And we'll allow for overlapping times when we hand off the responsibility, too – because he's a slippery one, there's no' much doubt about that.'

Christine couldn't help but grin when Annie grabbed her phone and stuck her arm in the air. 'Incoming call from Carys James, ladies. On video, no less – aren't we honored. Hello Carys – you've caught me at the office, and we're all here. Okay with you if I prop my phone on the coffee table so we can all see and hear you?'

When Carys appeared, she was wearing her habitual serviceable dark suit and white shirt. Annie jumped in. 'Thanks for seeing us, Carys. I bet you're busy, so…have you got news?'

Carys James beamed in her office, in Swansea. 'Thanks for the tip off – we've made significant strides. Heather Summerville has been interviewed, and – having made necessary checks – I can confirm she is not a suspect in the death of Lawrence, aka Larry, Merton.'

Annie looked disappointed. 'Oh, sorry, Carys, we thought we had her – thought we'd found a killer for you. How do you know it wasn't her? Did she have a fling with our Larry? Did he rip her off too? Is that why she's selling her flat? Sorry about all the questions – go on, please tell us what you can.'

Carys laughed. 'Oh Annie...I miss your candor, really I do. Okay, obviously there's a lot I cannot divulge, but we're grateful for you passing the information to us that you did, and we have a relationship which allows for some confidentialities to be shared, so I can tell you this: Heather Summerville couldn't have been on that London Underground platform when Mr Merton was pushed, because she was here, in Swansea, singing in a concert at the Brangwyn Hall. She belongs to a choir that was on stage at the time – they were giving a Christmas lunchtime concert – and the performance was video recorded, so we can actually see her there...as could several hundred people in the audience, and about fifty in the choir. So that's how we can be certain that she didn't push Merton. But don't look like that, Annie – there is more. Thanks to your agency's excellent research, we were able to show Heather the video from the platform that showed a woman matching her description at the scene, and she gave us some interesting information. We know that the deceased in your area – Sylvia Jenkins – was wearing a brown knitted jacket, and the person on the platform in London appeared to be dressed similarly; Heather Summerville has a brown knitted jacket that was given to her by Mr Merton. He had told her that he'd spotted it in a shop window and bought it on impulse for Heather. He then encouraged her to wear it whenever she met him. The jacket, therefore, took on a particular meaning for Heather when she was...smitten...with him, which has now...shifted. Yes, she too gave Mr Merton a banker's draft for a significant sum, and then he ghosted her. She still has the jacket he gave her. When she showed it to our officers it was in shreds. It seems she'd taken out her anger with Merton on the one thing he'd given her.'

Mavis said, 'I can see why that might be so. I take it you're suggesting he might have given every woman he targeted a similar garment?'

Carys nodded. 'We believe that might be the case. We're following a few leads to find where he might have bought them, and how many he might have bought. And that's where we are now. Carol is a wonder, but she's just one person, I have a whole team on it now, and we're working toward finding more women who were targeted by Merton. Personally, I think it's only a matter of time before we identify one or more victims. They will be interviewed – in the appropriate manner, and…well, we'll see what we shall see.'

Christine shot a glance toward Mavis and Carol, wondering if either of them would mention the potential victim Carol had identified near Tenby. She noted that Mavis signaled to Carol that she should speak.

Carol said, 'Carys, I know you told Annie that your team was on this case. But…well, I couldn't help myself – I just kept doing my thing, and I found another one, I believe. Mavis has…asked some contacts of hers to…look into the matter.'

Christine wasn't surprised when Carys replied sharply, 'I thought I'd made it clear that this was now a police matter. I have great respect for your abilities, Carol – and for the very professional work the rest of the team does – but, honestly, you all need to step back from this one.'

Christine wondered how Mavis might react – given that she could see the woman bristling. 'Aye, well, what's done is done,' replied Mavis, equally sharply. 'Carol unearthed a potential victim living near Tenby – and a lot quicker than your group of so-called cyber experts seem to have done, if I might say so. As you said, we're professionals, but we were unable to put the last piece of the puzzle into place ourselves, so I called upon the efforts of some folks I know who happen to live in that area. They, too, have a certain…skill set. I'll text you the contact details of one Sigismund Welbeck: I believe you'll find his background to be…interesting, and pertinent. He, along with a few others, has agreed to trace the exact location of one Hayley Taylor – Carol can send everything she's found out about the woman, so far…yes, she's doing that now, thank you, Carol. We realize that Tenby is beyond your jurisdiction, Carys, but please feel free to contact Siggy – Mr Welbeck – directly. As you ask, we'll step back from even this part of our enquiries, now.'

There was no doubting that Carys James was angry. 'Ladies, you can't just go letting whomever you choose go tramping about all over the place, sticking their noses in, when there's an ongoing police enquiry. We've spoken of this before, and I believed you were clear about where I stood on such matters. I really would prefer it if you contained your efforts to more…appropriate lines of investigation.'

Christine took up the reins as she replied daringly, 'Carys – we know, but we were trying to help. That's all we ever want to do. You know that, don't you?' She hoped that Carys would calm down a bit; she appeared to be getting a bit pink around the gills.

Annie chipped in. 'Carys, we're good at this, and Mave only asked for help 'cause none of us lot could get over to Tenby. But this Siggy bloke she's got on it? He's a retired spy, so he'll know what to do, right, Mave?'

Mavis sighed. 'Siggy used to work for the government, yes, Annie, but we cannae be certain that he was…what you said.'

Carys James held up her hand, and silence fell in the office in Chellingworth. 'Stop. Mavis – send me this man's details. Carol – I have your report. I'm now going to get back to my work – as a senior police officer, working on a police case, with a team of other police officers – and I suggest you all get back to working on…something else entirely. Is that clear enough for you all?'

All four women nodded.

Carys nodded back. 'Look, ladies, you did exactly the right thing handing this over to me – to us – when you did. But now you really need to let us handle it from here on. That's it from me – over to you for you to get back to your work, and I'll get on with mine.'

The connection was broken.

Christine said, 'She wasn't happy with us, was she?'

Annie chuckled, 'Nah…but I bet she'll be sorry that she got so shirty with us when she finds out who that Siggy of Mave's is, right, Mave?'

Christine thought that Mavis looked a little…tired. 'He's no' my Siggy, Annie, as I keep telling you. But, aye, she might be surprised…if she can actually find out anything at all about his background.'

26th DECEMBER

CHAPTER THIRTY-SIX

Carol reckoned that Christmas – for everyone she'd texted with, at least – had passed in the way most had hoped it would: families had spent time together, making memories that would last a lifetime; there'd been an amount of over-indulgence – followed by dyspepsia and promises to never repeat such excesses; there'd been a few spats among those who were close enough to say what they really thought, then wish they hadn't; there'd even been a hard frost on Christmas morning that allowed folks to praise the beauties of a 'White Christmas', without having to endure any of its inconveniences.

And then came Boxing Day, and the evening's dreaded dress rehearsal for the panto; Carol's father had begged her to go with him, because he was terrified, and knew he'd be alright if she were with him. She phoned Annie to see if she'd be going too; she knew that the dress rehearsal would be Tudor's First Chance To Shine As Prompt, so thought Annie might go along, but Annie told her that she and Tudor had both realized it wasn't fair to leave her parents alone to look after the pub. Tudor himself, Aled, Joan, and Sharon – in other words, anyone with experience behind the bars of the Coach and Horses – were all required at the dress rehearsal, so Annie agreed she'd miss it, and even the performance the following night, for the same reason. Carol promised Annie a full report after the dress rehearsal was over.

When she arrived, she could see her father across the village hall: he resembled one of those Oompa Loompas from that film, though at least he wasn't bright orange with green hair; he was just dressed similarly, as were several others – male and female. This appeared to surprise everyone as they mingled after changing – behind privacy curtains. Carol surmised the performers hadn't been told anything about their costumes. Elizabeth Fernley looked magnificent as the

Good Fairy – there was a definite bridal air to her ballroom-style gown – and Aled looked appropriately laddish as Mother Goose's son, while Sharon looked about ten years younger than she really was as his sweetheart.

Eventually, Oswald Featherington himself appeared, and Carol was impressed: he was dressed as a portly milkmaid, with a long plaited gray wig, and the hideous make-up as worn by all traditional dames…in other words, slapped on with a trowel, with vivid blue eyeshadow, comedically long eyelashes, and a lipsticked mouth of enormous proportions. Unfortunately, Carol reckoned she'd seen a young woman in Builth Wells looking not too dissimilar a couple of weeks earlier, which rather drained Oswald's pastiche of its sting.

Wendy Jenkins and her musicians played the overture – which Marjorie Pritchard explained would allow latecomers to take their seats without the performance itself being interrupted – then the lights in the hall were dimmed, and Carol watched as lines were delivered with greater, or less, conviction and confidence, and people she'd come to know in her daily life transformed into threatening cyphers, or jolly neighbors of the unhappy widow. Oswald himself really hammed it up as the widow, and Carol had to admit that his on-stage persona was much more winning than the person she'd met in real life. Carol booed when the landlord appeared, and shouted out 'They're behind you' when the landlord's heavies were looming over poor Mother Goose. She also enjoyed doing the whole 'Oh no he isn't, Oh yes he is' bit when Aled was telling Sharon about how sympathetic the landlord was being to his mother's plight.

When the Good Fairy gifted the goose that could lay golden eggs to the widow, Carol enjoyed the finale of the first act which was a song and dance performed by the entire company, and which finally answered her questions about why her father had been 'rapping' for days and days: Oswald had taken a song called 'Lose Yourself' by the Detroit artist Eminen, and had rewritten the lyrics to make it all about how Mother Goose now had the chance to change her life forever, which Carol thought was rather clever. Of course, the singers weren't all quite on the beat with everything, and Carol had to suspect that her father hadn't listened to the original version, but it was certainly a rousing way to bring the curtain down, and she suspected the audience would clap along to the thrumming beat, which Wendy Jenkins and her small group of musicians kept going very well.

The noises coming from behind the curtain during what would be the interval told Carol that the scenery was being shifted about somewhat, and that this was causing concern for people who'd not had to cope with such elements before. Eventually, at a signal from Marjorie, Janet Jackson and Paul Baker appeared, and gave a performance of the Elvis hit 'If I Can Dream' with Janet dressed as Ann-Margret basically singing backing vocals…which was a bit weird, but it gave people time to scamper back to their seats if there'd been a queue at the loos, she supposed.

Then the curtain went up again, and Carol was impressed by the work done by Henry and Clementine to depict the grand home in which Mother Goose was now living. The second act centered on the forthcoming nuptials of Aled and Sharon, which the widow could now afford, and the increasingly desperate need on the part of the widow to make herself look beautiful. It also made clear that her new-found wealth had turned her against those who'd previously been friends, who'd shared what little they had with her when she needed it most.…and her increasing alienation from everyone except her goose, whom she urged to produce more and more golden eggs.

However, the second act progressed a great deal less smoothly than the first; Tudor could be heard making frequent prompts from the wings. Carol felt the tension in the air: lines were fluffed; people bumped into each other; someone giggled nervously; then Sharon broke down in tears as she and Aled were singing 'Puppy Love'.

Marjorie stood in front of the stage and shouted, 'Everybody stop. Take a five-minute break. Come down here, take a seat, and gather your thoughts.'

Everyone did as they'd been told, and looked a bit surly as they were doing it. Only Mother Goose and the goose herself, Priscilla, remained on the stage; Carol suspected it wouldn't be easy for whomever was in the goose costume to get off the stage in any case. Then she witnessed something so strange, that she knew she'd have difficulty in relating it to Annie later that night: Oswald Featherington started swearing at Priscilla…loudly, and with more venom, and breadth of colorful vocabulary, than Carol had ever heard anyone use before. Priscilla stood there, silently, her beak in the air, reacting only with an occasional twitch of her tail feathers. It was…extraordinary.

Then Oswald stomped off the stage, turned around three times, walked back on and shouted, 'Now that's all over with, can we please press on to the finale?'

Everyone returned to their places on the stage and – miraculously – the wedding scene took place, with Mother Goose having realized that beauty wasn't important, that wealth could be shared, and that family and friends were critical to her future well-being. The closing tune – rendered with enthusiasm – was a reimagined version of 'My Way', with Mother Goose doing most of the singing, and the chorus echoing verses that emphasized the importance of community. Everyone took their bow – with Marjorie shouting 'Applause, applause' as they did so, then the curtain fell, and that was that…until the curtain rose again so everyone could leave the stage, which they did with what Carol judged to be relief and maybe even a little pride.

The goose had gone, Oswald was himself once again, and Marjorie asked everyone to go home, get a good night's sleep, and to be at the village hall, fully made-up and costumed, by four o'clock the next day – two hours before the performance began. Carol suspected she might have just a few notes for the company.

As Marjorie passed Carol, she whispered, 'They say a bad dress rehearsal means a good first night; we've only got one night, so I hope this disaster means it'll be fantastic.'

Carol didn't comment, but congratulated her father on a job well done, and he actually hugged her and told her – all the way home – how he was enjoying himself more than he'd thought possible, and how excited he was for her mother to see him doing his thing, as he put it, the following evening. When Carol got home, she spent some time with Albert in his room, then with her parents and husband, then finally called Annie…who was in a state.

'What's wrong?' Carol thought it best to ask.

Annie was out of breath. 'Tude's almost had a heart attack doing that thing tonight, Car; said he had no idea how stressful it would be. Told me everyone did almost everything wrong, and no matter how much he shouted at them to do it like it said in the script, they just ignored him. Was it that bad, Car?'

Carol gave her friend her honest assessment, which seemed to calm Annie.

'So it weren't as bad as he's making out? Good. But what was all that when Oswald was having a go at the goose? Tude said he'd never heard anything like it.'

Carol explained, as Annie made noises signifying surprise and astonishment. 'Gordon Bennett, sounds like Tude was right about that, then. But you don't know why Oswald went off on one?'

Carol admitted she was at a loss. 'The goose was...very calm about it all. Though they might well have been shouting back at him and we'd have had no idea from the main hall. And I don't know who was in the costume because I never saw them without their head.'

Annie muttered, 'Weird.' Carol agreed. 'Well, I'll try to get Tude to climb down from the ceiling and have a nice cup of tea in his chair before bed, and maybe I'll get him to do some deep-breathing exercises before he goes back there tomorrow.'

The friends said goodnight, and Carol went to bed, quite sure that the actual performance would be better than the dress rehearsal.

27th DECEMBER

CHAPTER THIRTY-SEVEN

Carol had been woken around six by Albert, so was already in her kitchen when her phone rang before seven; it was Mavis.

'Carol, I knew you'd be up, with the bairn. I need you to gather the troops – get everyone to the Dower House, pronto. I can't leave Althea for long; the poor wee woman's in the most dreadful state.'

Carol felt her tummy clench. 'What's happened?'

'It's that man, Featherington: he's gone. And a good deal of Althea's silver has gone, as well as a coin collection she kept in that little glass cabinet. She's…she's not stopped crying since she found the note he left for her. That horrible man has wounded her deeply…we must take action, which is why I suggest we meet here, as soon as possible. Maybe you could give Annie a lift, and ask Christine to make her own way. I must go now, Carol. I'll see you soon.'

Carol talked to David before she phoned Annie, whose response was one of alarm and bluster, followed by a promise to be ready to leave in a quarter of an hour. Carol also woke Christine, who promised she'd get to the Dower House as quickly as possible.

Ian Cottesloe greeted Annie and Carol when they arrived, and showed them into the morning room, where Mavis was pacing. She looked up, her face drawn and pinched.

'Althea's in her room. She's refusing to do anything, and has asked me – begged me – to take no action against the man. Trust me when I tell you that I have made my case for calling in the police very clear to the woman, but she'll no' budge, and I cannae be any more firm with her, given her condition. She's…she's feeling betrayed, of course, and also – I would say – somewhat foolish for having been taken in by the man. He took such a lot of stuff from here – then off he went in that old, rust-bucket car of his.'

Annie sank into a chair. 'Oh heck…Pauline Thomas said there was a traitor among us when she read those Tarot cards for me. That was Oswald all along. So she got two out of three things right – a postman in uniform saved her, and we were all looking at a person who meant someone harm. But…well, the pregnancy thing was still off. Yeah…it's all nonsense, really. So we've come here for nothing, Mave?'

Carol glared at her friend. 'We've come to offer support, even if we can't actually do anything.'

Annie nodded. 'Yeah, I know that, doll…but I could have been just as supportive after a spot of breakfast, or at least a cup of tea.'

As if he'd heard Annie's words, Paul Baker entered the room with a tray of tea and toast. 'I took the liberty,' he said, placing the tray on a sideboard. 'Help yourself. I'm taking a pot up to Her Grace, too.'

'No need, Paul, I'll join my friends.' Carol was surprised to hear Althea's voice and completely floored by her appearance. She was used to seeing Althea when she was out and about in the world, not in her bedclothes and a dressing gown, with her thin hair plastered to her head, and a face blotchy with anguish. She was suddenly – possibly for the first time – very much aware of Althea's age.

The dowager waved away many pairs of hands, all trying to shepherd her to a spot where she'd be comfortable, and allowed Paul to serve her tea, which she sipped almost immediately. McFli dropped his head on his paws at her feet, and looked up at his mistress with doleful eyes.

Just as Paul was leaving the room, Althea called, 'I know it's not usual for breakfast, but I do rather fancy some cake. Might you have anything on hand, Paul?'

'You can have whatever your heart desires – as long as that's my Swiss roll with raspberry jam, because that's what I was getting ready to take down to the Lamb Tearooms. I'll make another for them – this one's for you, Your Grace. Give me two minutes; I'll be back.'

The WISE women and the dowager were drinking tea and eating Swiss roll within five minutes, and all doing so in silence. Carol knew she didn't want to break the ice, feeling that should be Mavis's responsibility – since she both lived with Althea and had summoned the others. In the end, it was the dowager herself who spoke.

'I've been a stupid old woman – and I don't want anyone to tell me I haven't been. I trusted someone I knew almost sixty years ago to be as I remembered them, and they weren't. The trouble is, what I've had to admit to myself over the past couple of painful hours is that…they were never the person I thought they were even back then. Oswald Featherington was not a fun-loving, well-connected dance partner…he was a grasping, ambitious man, who rarely had a good word to say about anyone…but did possess an ability to craft an amusing insult, that's for sure. I was dazzled by him back then – that's what I understand now. And I've allowed myself to be dazzled by him again…and to let him play on my sympathies and gullibility to get what he wanted, and more. He's taken items that I have purchased with my own funds, not ancestral pieces owned by the Twysts, so I alone am able to say that he's welcome to them; no action is to be taken against him regarding those items. He's taken payment from me for services he has – up to a point – rendered, which is fair. He's taken items of personal value from people who live in the village; they are all in his room, upstairs, and will be returned with a note of personal apology from me. So what are we left with, ladies?'

Carol noticed that Mavis was studying her tea, and it looked as though no one was going to supply Althea with a response, so she herself said, 'What?'

Althea nodded, and smiled. 'We're left with the potential theft of something of great importance, and that is what I want you to act to…save.'

The quartet of detectives exchanged puzzled glances.

Annie said, 'You mean the panto, don't you, Althea.'

Althea nodded. 'That must go ahead – somehow or other. And I don't mean just because I once trod the boards in my sallow youth and cling to the tradition that "The Show Must Go On". No, what I mean is that I will not allow that man to steal that experience from my community. So – I open the floor for ideas.'

Mavis sighed. 'I dinnae know the first thing about the panto. If I'm honest, I've steered clear of it, so I've no idea of the challenges presented by Oswald no longer being here. Do any of you?'

Christine replied, 'Only in the most general sense; Alexander's been telling me what he's been up to, and I know that Oswald was playing the title role…so there's that. But, beyond that, not much.'

Annie offered, 'Tude's been studying that script until he knows it backwards, but I haven't seen a single minute of rehearsals or anything. You went to the dress rehearsal yesterday, Car – what do you think?'

Suddenly, Carol's decision to go with her father to the village hall didn't feel as though it had been among her better ones. She wondered where to begin, then went for it. 'Okay, to be honest, Marjorie Pritchard is the one who's in charge of the production now – and everyone's as ready to perform as they're ever going to be. From that point of view, there's no reason why the panto couldn't go ahead. The main – or possibly the only – stumbling block is that Oswald was due to play the part of Mother Goose, and there's no understudy. Having seen the dress rehearsal, I can't honestly say that anyone I saw on the stage made enough of an impression upon me to make me think they could step into Oswald's shoes. I mean…Mother Goose has got a lot of lines, and the whole production basically revolves around the character. So…is there anyone who could be brought in to do it? They'd have had to have done Oswald's version before, I'd say, so they could just focus on the changes he made; all the little mentions of Anwen-by-Wye, and its history, that sort of thing. Do you know of such a person, Althea?'

Carol's heart sank as the little woman shook her head, looking terribly lost. 'I don't, though that was a good idea, Carol.'

Annie asked, 'Not one person on that stage could do it, Car? Really?'

Carol sighed. 'It's all about Mother Goose, Annie. And the character sort of dominates the entire story, and stage. Oswald had taken what was a big part and made it even more central so he could ham it up and get all the limelight – literally, and figuratively. The whole thing revolves around the character of Mother Goose.'

Annie chuckled wryly. 'Yeah, I know what you mean; Tude kept going on about how it was a miracle that anyone else ever had any lines. Said there were just odd bits and pieces for other people, and how Mother Goose was only ever off stage to get into a new costume,

and how she was always in the middle of the stage, and at the front —
whereas all the other stage directions seemed to shove everyone off to
one side or another.'

Carol felt the idea form, and pushed it to one side, condemning it as
too ridiculous.

Mavis said, 'So should we cancel?'

Christine offered, 'Or should we let it go ahead, and get Tudor to
shout Mother Goose's lines from the wings?'

'Or should we ask Tudor to actually be Mother Goose?' Carol hadn't
meant to say it out loud…but she did.

Annie's laugh came directly from her belly. 'Oh that's a good one,
Car — Tude on stage dressed as a dame? Gordon Bennett…I'd pay a
lot to see that, I would.'

Carol said, 'That's the thing, Annie — a lot of people have already
paid to see the panto; all their money would have to be refunded, as
well as there being the disappointment of missing a good night out.
Why don't you ask him, Annie? Explain the situation. He might even
surprise you and say yes straight away.'

Carol watched as Annie's expression shifted. 'Nah, you're not
serious, Car…are you? None of the rest of you think he could do
it…or would – do you?'

Mavis said, 'I bet he would, if he could. Tudor's that sort of man.'

Christine shrugged. 'Don't hate me if I say he's got just the right sort
of face to play a panto dame, Annie — but he has.'

Althea smiled. 'I think Tudor would make a first-class Mother
Goose. You said he'd memorized the entire script, Annie…so he'd
know the lines, and where to be, and what to do, every minute. If he
can't sing, he'll at least know the lyrics and can just yell them if he
wants — part of the comedy comes from the dame not being able to
sing. Most of them can't. So yes, Annie — ask him…no…don't do that.
I'll ask him myself. I'll call for Ian and he can drive me to the village.'

Mavis said, 'I think you'd better dress, first, Althea…and both Annie
and I will accompany you when you leave.'

Althea surprised everyone by almost leaping out of her chair. 'I'll do
that right now, and ask Ian to bring the Gilbern around. Those Monty

Python boys were right, you know – it really does pay to look on the bright side of life. I think this could be better for the village than Ossie being the dame…we'd have our very own home-grown panto, in every way. You'd better finish up that Swiss roll without me – I shall be ready to leave in half an hour.'

When the four women were alone, Carol whispered, 'I'm glad to see her bounce back like this…I was a bit worried about her when I first saw her. She looked so…utterly defeated…and frail.'

Mavis whispered her agreement. 'Her confidence has taken a beating, that's for sure. As she said herself, she's feeling betrayed, and foolish, and that's no' something with which she's familiar. If you could get Tudor to say yes, Annie, seeing this panto actually happen could be good for her, as well as the whole village.'

Christine urged, 'I think Tudor's made for it, honest I do, Annie. Get him to give it a try, at least.'

Annie hissed, 'I can see why you're saying this, I can, and of course I'll ask him…I'll even beg him. I just can't imagine him agreeing to do it.'

Mavis said quietly, 'If we just wind Althea up and point her at Tudor, he'll agree to do it…she could get a man dying of thirst to give her a glass of water, that one. So would you like me to look after the pub this evening, Annie, while you go and watch Tudor dress up as a woman and wow the locals?'

Annie laughed. 'Oh Mave, the idea of you behind a bar and Tude on stage…what's this world coming to, eh? I can't see that you'll need to – but do you even know how to pull a pint?'

Mavis smiled coyly. 'Someone had to be able to work flexible hours when she had small boys and needed income to supplement her husband's army pay, and where do you think I managed to do that?'

Christine ventured, 'Local pub, Mavis?'

Annie laughed. 'Well, I'll get you to make me a G and T, and we'll see how good you really are. Not that you'll be needed to do anything much, I shouldn't have thought.'

Althea stuck her head around the door. 'Stand down, no need for me to go to the village. I phoned Tudor and he's agreed, though he asked if we would request that Marjorie allow him an hour on the stage before everyone else arrives so he can get the feel of it, and practice getting into and out of his costumes – especially the gown for Mother Goose's son's wedding.'

'Gordon Bennett, Althea…how did you manage that?'

Althea dimpled. 'I just asked nicely.'

CHAPTER THIRTY-EIGHT

Mavis had decided to take the opportunity to put her feet up in her room for an hour or two ahead of what she imagined would be probably quite a boring evening standing behind the bar at the Coach and Horses, serving whomever in the village had seen fit to not attend the panto. She was even wondering if it might be possible for her to read a book while she was there, to pass the time, without it bothering…anyone.

She checked her watch: Althea had disappeared after lunch, saying she wanted to rest before going to the panto herself, so Mavis didn't feel guilty that she wasn't sharing time with her chum, who seemed to be doing rather better than expected, given how their day had begun.

A light knock at her door puzzled Mavis. She opened it to discover Ian Cottesloe, looking a little embarrassed. 'There are some people here for you, Mavis. They said not to disturb Her Grace, which I haven't done. I believe Her Grace is…napping.'

Mavis stuck her head out onto the landing. 'Aye, I can hear her napping from here. Who is it, Ian?'

Ian looked confused. 'One of the gentlemen said to say "The Lavender Mob". I think that's right.'

Mavis felt her spirits rise a little. 'Four of them?' Ian nodded. 'You're quite correct, Ian — that's what they're called. Any chance at all that between you and Paul you might rustle up an early tea? Just a few pots and…whatever Paul might have that's suitable.'

Ian smiled. 'I know he baked some scones this morning — we'll get it sorted. They're waiting in the sitting room; how long shall I tell them you'll be?'

Mavis wondered if she should change her clothes. 'I'll be down in five minutes, Ian. Thanks.'

Ian grinned. 'I'll make sure the tea beats you there.'

Mavis took stock of herself in her dressing table's mirror, and told her reflection, 'Ach…you are who you are, Mavis MacDonald, and anyone who's worth anything should be prepared to accept you as such. But a comb wouldnae go amiss.'

Suitably refreshed, Mavis entered the sitting room with a smile on her face. Sir Malcolm Lee shot up out of his chair, followed by Siggy Welbeck, who took a little longer to achieve a completely upright position. Dennis Moore looked puzzled, and a little pink in the face.

Mavis gave her attention to Uma Chatterjee first, because she was obviously relying upon the use of a walking aid – which wasn't something she'd needed when she and Mavis had first encountered each other.

Mavis walked to the woman and reached down to hug her. 'Ach, Uma – have you gone and injured yourself somehow?' She turned and waved at the men to all take their seats. 'Hello there, Sir Malcolm…Siggy…Dennis. What have you been doing with poor Uma?'

Sir Malcolm boomed, 'Nothing to do with us, Mavis, honestly. Tell her, Uma.'

Uma returned Mavis's hug, her small arms just about reaching high enough to do so. 'He's right, Mavis – it was all my own, stupid fault: I decided to change a light bulb in my room at The Lavender. I know that Mr Conti who owns the place has people who do that sort of thing, but I wanted a new bulb, in working order, right away – I didn't want to wait. Oh…by the way – Mr Conti sends his regards. At least, he sent them to Althea, so if you could pass them on, please? I'm sure he sends them to you too, though you know how his head's always turned by a title. Anyway…I stood on a chair and…well, I ended up on the floor. Landed badly, on my side, and broke a couple of ribs. This thing helps to support me as I walk…but, please, whatever you do, Mavis…don't make me laugh.'

Mavis took a seat and looked at the four people she'd met when she and Althea had become temporary residents at the seaside hotel affectionately known as The Lavender, and realized she'd missed them…all.

Once again Sir Malcolm Lee was on his feet. Mavis noted with a smile that the vivid green sweater he was wearing beneath his tan jacket suggested his manner of presenting himself to the world didn't differ from the autumn – when she'd first met him – to the winter.

He said, 'I got everyone to jump in my trusty old Roller, and here we are. We were coming this way for the panto tonight anyway, and thought we'd like to report in on the case you asked us to work on face to face.' He mugged a salute, and retook his seat.

Mavis replied with a polite, 'It's wonderful to see you all, of course, but I wasnae necessarily expecting you all to come here at all…not even for the panto.'

Siggy Welbeck piped up, 'Althea telephoned us, Mavis – left us in no doubt whatsoever that our attendance at your village hall this evening was expected. Didn't she mention that?'

Mavis couldn't help but chuckle. 'No, she failed to tell me she'd put pressure on you to buy tickets, though I dare say it shouldnae come as a surprise to me. She's a wee scamp.'

Siggy asked, 'How is she, by the way? We gathered from that young chap who answered the door that she wasn't available, but – is she doing well?'

Mavis decided to keep the situation regarding Oswald Featherington a private matter. 'Just taking a nap ahead of what will be a long evening – though I'm sure the panto will be…fun. There's been a bit of a last-minute change of plans about who'll be playing Mother Goose herself, but I'm sure it'll all go swimmingly.' She wasn't at all sure it would, but didn't want to alarm the group.

'These are for you, Mavis,' said Dennis Moore, standing and shoving a slightly straggly bunch of some sort of greenish-purplish flowers into Mavis's hands. 'You should get them into water as soon as you can. I've wrapped the ends in wet kitchen paper to keep them moist, but they'll perk up when they get a good drink. Sorry they aren't too…flash, but there's not a lot to bring from the garden at this time of year.'

Mavis examined the blooms, which were of a type she'd not seen before. 'They're stunning, Dennis – those markings are rather like the ones you see on foxgloves. What are they?'

Mavis noticed the enthusiasm in Dennis's eyes. 'They're often called "Christmas Roses", but they're not roses at all. They're hellebores; this lot were already growing at The Lavender when I took over there as the gardener, so I can't claim any credit for them. Hardy things – and so wonderful to see a bit of color at this time of year. But, like I said, they'll need to get into water as soon as possible. And whoever does that needs to wear gloves…they're quite toxic, especially the sap.'

Mavis looked at the bouquet with fresh eyes. 'Why thank you, Dennis; it's not every day that a woman is given a bunch of poisonous flowers.' She smiled as she spoke, but Dennis sat down again with a bit of a thump, and a flush on his neck, she noticed.

Siggy grinned when he said, 'No killer plants from me, Mavis – but I do come bearing gifts. We all do…though in the manner of a cat laying a mouse at its human's feet, I dare say. Your case? We got her…and we waited with her until some local bobbies came to take her off our hands. Despite her injuries, Uma was spectacularly helpful, of course, and Sir Malcolm here was just…spectacular.'

Mavis was intrigued. 'Really? All I asked you to do was find out where exactly a woman lived. We gave you her photograph, and name, and even the name of the street where she lived – how could finding out which house she lived in require anything "spectacular" to be done at all? Have you been making a meal of a simple job, Siggy, just so you can call upon all those fellow "government employees" you used to work with, before you retired?'

Siggy doffed an imaginary cap. 'Not at all, madam. But, please – allow our fearless leader, Miss Chatterjee, to elaborate.'

Mavis raised an eyebrow in Uma's direction. 'You're their leader now? Since when was there even a recognized group to lead? What have you all been up to since Althea and I…left you?'

Uma slightly rearranged herself in her seat. 'If you could just put that cup of tea here beside me, please Malcolm, that would help. Thank you. Well, Mavis, since you and Althea left us, we've all spent a good deal of time together, and you'd be surprised how often little things come up that need…looking into. One of the newer residents at The Lavender happened to mention at tea one day that he suspected that his granddaughter's new boyfriend was a bit shady, and we were able to look into the young man's situation and give the man the facts. There've been a few things like that, so we've…helped people a bit.'

Mavis's eyes darted toward Siggy. 'Using those contacts of yours to do a little questionable background checking? Tut, tut, Siggy.'

Siggy flashed his winning grin toward Mavis. 'Not at all, dear Mavis…I would never…well, you know I would, but only on very special occasions. But, in this instance, Sir Malcolm drove us down to Brighton where, as you know, Uma has some wonderful contacts from her old days at the newspaper, and she was the one winkling information out of people. It turned out the boy in question was doing his best to make the move from being the one who washed some used cars to being the one who sold them, so was walking about telling fibs, making himself out to be a bit…well, I dare say "better" isn't the word, but not quite who he really was. Something and nothing, dear thing. But Uma was our lead on that, and she's by far the best-organized of all of us, so she's now our *de facto* leader, as you are for your WISE women…at least, that's what Althea says.'

Mavis shrugged. 'That's as mebbe. But – please – tell me what's happened regarding our case: you say you managed to track down Hayley Taylor, in Tenby…but what's the exact situation, if you please?'

Uma replied, 'Long story short, Mavis – she's in police custody. We got in touch with your contact in Swansea, DCI Carys James, and we passed word to her when we'd found the Taylor woman. We just…remained on-scene until uniformed officers arrived, and we then left them to it.'

'Always best to let the professionals do their job,' chipped in Dennis, 'though who'd have thought that finding one woman would lead to such chaos.'

Mavis felt her back stiffen. 'Chaos? In what way?'

Siggy waved a hand as if to signify that nothing of any importance had happened; Sir Malcolm appeared to be studying the pattern on the sofa's upholstery in some detail; Dennis was literally chewing his bottom lip…which left Uma staring daggers at the man.

Mavis added, 'Uma…out with it. What happened?'

Uma sighed, gently. 'You haven't seen Malcolm's Rolls Royce, parked outside, have you?' Mavis shook her head. Uma added, 'It's a bit…damaged.'

Sir Malcolm spoke proudly, 'She's still drivable, of course – built like tanks, those Rollers – but she's looking a bit sad, around her rear end.'

Mavis was on full alert. 'And how, pray tell, did you manage to damage a 1965 Silver Cloud III? One of the most beautiful vehicles ever created, by the way.'

Mavis reckoned that the four members of The Lavender Mob exchanged glances in much the same way a group of naughty schoolchildren might have done, if caught at the back of a classroom with something they shouldn't have. She feared a closing of ranks, and a sanitized version of the truth.

Uma began, 'We headed to the street in question, and we'd all familiarized ourselves with what the woman looked like – as per the photos Carol sent us that she'd gathered from Hayley Taylor's social media accounts.'

Dennis added, 'It's a long road, and a bit hilly, so we took up spots all along it – each of us in contact with the others, of course…to be able to alert the team if, or when, we spotted her.'

Siggy noted, 'An overwatch brief can prove rather tedious, Mavis, as I'm sure you're aware.'

Mavis replied, 'I am that…though am I to understand that it was only Sir Malcolm who was inside a vehicle, while the rest of you were – what – out on the street itself?'

Uma shook her head. 'No, Mavis – I'd already injured myself, so Malcolm insisted that I stayed inside his car, while the three men took up positions along the street itself. Which was why…well, you tell her, Malcolm.'

Sir Malcolm Lee looked…despondent, which Mavis could understand if his beloved Rolls Royce was now in need of repair. 'Totally my fault, to be honest, Mavis. I…overreacted. Or maybe just didn't react quickly enough…hard to say. This is what happened: it was Dennis who spotted our target first.'

Dennis nodded. 'Hayley got off a bus, popped into a newsagent's shop, and then came out, about three minutes later. I wasn't certain that it was her when she went inside, so I got the team on the comms – that's what we call our chat-group, when we're out in the field. They were all on standby, and I confirmed that it was Hayley when she finally came out of the shop. I told Sir Malcolm that Hayley was coming in his direction – she was already well past where Siggy was stationed – and described what she was wearing.'

Siggy waggled a hand. 'As you might appreciate, Mavis…I began to hot-foot it in the right direction, not wanting to miss out on the action, but keeping a weather eye about me, in case – for some reason – the Taylor woman managed to somehow double-back on herself. We had no idea how slippery a customer she might be, at that time.'

Mavis thought that Siggy – and the others – were making rather a meal of the whole thing, but nodded politely.

Uma said, 'I saw Malcolm running along the street toward me – away from the direction in which I knew Hayley was walking, which I have to admit puzzled me somewhat. But he threw himself into the car, started her up, and explained that he didn't want me to miss out on anything…so he planned to drive us both toward where Hayley was likely to be, by then.'

Sir Malcom said, 'I was excited, Mavis – that's what happened. Pulled out without taking in my surroundings properly…and got a nasty bump up the backside from – of all things – one of those blessed electric cars. They weigh a great deal, so they can do a lot of damage, even at relatively low speeds…though the vehicle in question was doing just about the speed limit, so the crunch was rather nasty.'

Mavis jumped in. 'Ach, that must have been very painful for you, Uma – with broken ribs already.'

Uma rolled her eyes. 'You're not kidding. I let out quite a scream, truth be told, which frightened poor Malcolm…and his foot hit the accelerator, and off we went…into traffic.'

Dennis said, 'I could see all of this happening, because I'd run across the road, and was following Hayley Taylor…and we'd crested the hill by that time. It was…well, it was chaos, like I said: horns hooting, traffic all stopped this way and that on the street, and people jumping out of their cars to see what was going on. It was obvious that quite a few people must have been phoning the police, and then I saw Hayley starting to hurry…and there were people coming out of houses and shops to see what was going on, and it got so busy that I thought I might lose her…and I told everyone that was my fear.'

Uma added, 'Which was why Malcolm left the car, ran toward Hayley Taylor, grabbed her, and pushed her into a shop…where he slammed the doors and told the shopkeeper to phone the police. Apparently, there was a lot of…screaming.'

Mavis could feel her eyes growing round. 'You physically removed Hayley Taylor from the street and held her against her will? In a shop? Oh dear.'

All four heads hung in shame.

Mavis said, 'And when the police came…how did you explain yourself, Sir Malcolm?'

The well-known, retired garden center entrepreneur spoke quietly. 'By then Siggy had arrived. He was…able to smooth things over.' He looked up. 'Thanks, Siggy. Again.'

'No trouble at all, old boy. All part of the service. Besides, it was rather fun. Except for the damage to your poor car, of course. Though the good news is, Mavis, that Sir Malcolm is well-insured. The repairs are scheduled for next week, by the way, so we were fortunate to have the car to be able to come here today.'

Mavis sighed. 'You're all fortunate you're no' in police custody yourselves, I should think. I've told you before that being private investigators is a profession, not a hobby. Ach, I blame myself; I should never have asked you to do what I did. It was highly unprofessional of me. Had it no' been for this blessed panto that's taking up so much of everyone's time, and causing its own sort of chaos in these parts, Carol could have done it…or I should have done it myself, in the first place. I'm so terribly sorry that I put you in this position. I'd no' have endangered any of you for the world.'

Althea's tinkling laugh drew everyone's attention toward the door, where the dowager was standing…dressed in a cerise tracksuit which Mavis could only imagine had been designed for a much younger person.

The octogenarian moved nimbly to the center of the room. 'Look at you all! How wonderful to see the entire Lavender Mob here, in my home at last. It's lovely of you all to come…you're here for the panto, of course. Oh…and you have scones. Excellent.'

Everyone looked at Mavis, who replied, 'They're here because they gave us a bit of a hand with…something in the Tenby area, dear.'

Siggy added, 'Something that's resulted in a suspect being delivered into police custody, Althea, you'll be pleased to know.'

Althea dimpled. 'But you were talking about chaos when I came in…which sounds so much more interesting than just boringly handing someone over to the police, doesn't it Mavis?'

Mavis decided to nip things in the bud. 'No, it does not. Police custody is an excellent outcome, thank you all. So let's turn our attention to something else – the panto. I dare say you'll all enjoy it…though I'll no' be attending myself.'

Dennis snapped, 'What do you mean, Mavis? I've come all this way to see a panto, but you won't be sitting with us?'

Siggy added, 'Don't you mean that *we've* come all this way to see a panto, Dennis? Thanks to Sir Malcolm driving us.' Dennis nodded vigorously. 'But he's right, Mavis – we had all rather assumed we'd be in the company of yourself…and the lovely Althea, of course.'

Althea wafted the tangerine chiffon scarf she'd pulled from her hair, and said airily, 'Don't count on seeing much of me – I have…responsibilities connected with the production.'

Mavis added, 'And I've volunteered to be behind the bar at the Coach and Horses pub for the evening. The landlord will be on stage, and his partner and her family should certainly be there to see that – so I've said I'll pull the odd pint, and open a mixer or two, as necessary.'

Siggy grinned. 'I can quite picture you behind a bar, Mavis…you'd draw a good crowd to a pub, I dare say.'

Mavis shrugged. 'I've done a bit of bar work in the past; things cannae have changed that much.'

Uma said, 'I tell you what, Mavis…to be honest, I've been thinking that I might not do very well at the panto. I've no idea what your village hall is like, nor how comfy the seats are, but that's almost immaterial because – as I dare say you've noticed – I do tend to keep wriggling all the time. I know it seems to make no sense, but I find that just shifting myself about a bit means I ache less than if I stay still. I wonder, Malcolm, if you and I could look after the pub instead of Mavis, so she could enjoy the panto with…well, with both Dennis and Siggy, if not Althea.'

Sir Malcolm Lee beamed, and puffed out his chest. 'Me behind a bar? I should say so. I love the idea. If you know what's what, Uma, I can take instructions…how about that?'

Mavis said, 'I'm not so sure…' Siggy and Dennis were both staring at her, making her neck tingle. 'I'll talk to Annie and Tudor about it.'

Althea added, 'Best you phone Tudor now, Mavis, because I think he's going to have his hands full this evening.'

CHAPTER THIRTY-NINE

Christine Wilson-Smythe lay, uncomfortably, in bed beside her betrothed – the father of her soon-to-be-born child. He wasn't making a sound, and that was music to Christine's ears…because every time she managed to find a comfy spot, he'd start to snore, so she'd hardy slept at all, and it was almost midnight. Not so late for the Christine she'd used to be, just a year earlier, but now? Now she was lucky if she managed to stay awake until ten o'clock. Of course, tonight had been different, because her wonderful Alexander had been a part of one of the most extraordinary events the village of Anwen-by-Wye had ever witnessed, and she'd been there to revel in it, and in the company of her parents, no less.

The potential disaster that she and her colleagues had feared when the day had begun had been transformed into something that would most certainly be talked about in every household in the village – and many beyond it – for years: it had been discovered by all that Tudor Evans was a born pantomime dame…who was somehow managing to make a living as a pub landlord.

Everyone had meant the standing ovation he'd received after belting out the last notes of 'My Way' – which was exactly what he'd done when it came to portraying Mother Goose; he'd done it his way, not Oswald's way, nor the way any other dame had done it before him.

Within two minutes of the curtain going up, Christine had completely forgotten that Tudor was on the stage at all – he was such a complete dame that was all that she, and the rest of the audience, saw. His delivery of saucy one-liners, terrible puns, and dreadful jokes was impeccable; he allowed others to shine when it was their turn to speak; it turned out that he had a delightful singing voice…and Christine had to admit he even had quite a graceful way with him when he danced – especially considering he was wearing heels.

The entire performance had gone well – though some of the song choices had surprised her, and she'd had to explain rapping to her mother who'd thought it a dreadful noise. The atmosphere at the end had been truly joyous, with everyone leaving the stage to happily greet family members in the audience. And then there was the biggest surprise of the night – a surprise even to everyone on the stage, it seemed – when Priscilla the goose removed her head to reveal…Althea Twyst herself.

That had received another ovation, and then Althea had spoken to the audience, and the Anwen Players themselves, and had said nothing about Oswald's precipitous departure, but had told them, instead, that he'd been called away to a family emergency…covering for her old friend to the end.

Alexander turned over. 'You still awake? Am I snoring?'

Christine stroked his head. 'Yes, and no. I can't stop thinking about tonight. It was…grand, so it was.'

'It was indeed, my love. And what's even better is that we'll be talking about it for years, in our new cottage, with our child being told all about it. At least now we know we can move in early in January.'

'I'm glad about that – the stairs there are so much easier to navigate than the ones here.'

'Not long now before we have all our new beginnings, Christine.'

'Not long at all.'

Carol and David Hill were giggling in the dark. They'd hardly stopped since they'd returned from the pub, which they'd visited after they'd left the village hall…where Carol's mother had smothered her father with kisses in a most embarrassing way once he'd come down from the stage to greet his family.

'I've never seen them be so affectionate with each other,' whispered Carol.

'I thought it was sweet,' replied her husband.

'It was horrible…and lovely.'

Her husband agreed. 'Will we be like that, when we're their age, do you think?'

'I hope so. At least they've got some time ahead of them now without having to tend to the sheep and the farm every hour of the day, and quite a few at night around lambing time, too. I'm glad about that. They deserve it.'

'Any chance of your workload lessening a bit, Carol? I know you're able to do what you need to do more freely with your parents here – but you've been so busy these past few weeks that you and I have had hardly any time together.'

Carol hesitated, then said what she knew she had to. 'To be honest, with Christine due to have the baby soon, I think it's going to get busier, not quieter. She's said she only wants to take a few weeks off, then she'll start to work from home, in London, where she's having the baby, but I know how it feels to say that…then have to do it. It's not easy; and it's not even as though she needs the money. So…I don't know. Mavis won't talk about it, but maybe we'll have to take on less work, or all do a bit more…or recruit someone else to cover while Christine's getting used to motherhood.'

'Who on earth would do that? They'd have to be local, after all.'

Carol snuggled into her pillow. 'No idea, and I don't think I can wrap my brain around that at this moment; I need to sleep. It's been a long, and challenging month, and week, and day…though I have to say that hearing that Hayley Taylor is in custody in Tenby – thanks to that help we got from The Lavender Mob, was good. I feel as though a great big weight has been lifted from my shoulders.'

David grabbed Carol's hand and gave it a squeeze. 'The look on your face while you were listening to that Siggy and that Dennis going on was…quite something, love. I'm glad that Annie and Christine were there too. Well done you; that all happened because of you. I'm so proud of what you do, and how well you do it. You know that, right?'

Carol squeezed back. 'Thanks, *cariad*, that means a lot. As does the fact that we were able to help solve a murder we weren't even really supposed to be working on. With a bit of help from some of Mavis's friends, of course. When I managed that quick phone call with Carys James she sounded…well, quite impressed that we even knew Siggy Welbeck, and I dare say she got to look good in the eyes of her colleagues down in Tenby and even in London, when she literally handed them a killer on a plate. I do feel terribly sorry for all those victims that horrible Larry Merton fleeced: he absolutely caused poor Sylvia Jenkins to take her own life, and that poor Hayley Taylor's entire future has gone now…though, of course, she really shouldn't have taken the law into her own hands by shoving him off that Underground platform. Carys told me that the officers who went to talk to Hayley said she confessed to it on the spot…said she'd been following Merton for days, and that she'd planned to confront him in public, but – when she saw him so close to the edge of the Underground platform – that she…well, she said she "couldn't help herself", apparently…though we all know she made a decision to act. Awful, really – for him of course, because, even though he was a slimeball, no one deserves that. But so awful for her, too. Carys said that Hayley's glad that she'll have a chance to tell everyone about Merton in court, and that she hopes the case will get a lot of media coverage…to help warn other women about this sort of thing.'

David sounded a little sleepy when he said, 'No – you can't go around doing that, you're right. But…yes, if you choose to victimize someone, you can't ever be certain of how they'll react, I suppose. Anyway – well done you…because you're the one who found her.'

Carol smiled, in the darkness. 'Ah well…let's get some rest before His Highness, our very own Prince Albert, wakes us while it's still dark and demands that we give him everything he desires.'

Annie hadn't stopped grinning since she, her mother and father, and the dogs, had watched as Tudor had removed his make-up at the kitchen table, and had even sat there as he pulled off his tights, and wriggled his toes to make sure they could still move.

Tudor had hardly reacted to the tremendous praise that had been heaped upon him since his performance, deflecting plaudits with a small smile and a nod. But Annie? She was glowing. As she lay in bed beside the man she loved, she knew she'd never see him the same way again; how could she after that performance? And it wasn't because of the costumes, or the wigs, or the make-up…it was because she'd seen him become another person. That wasn't something she was used to. And that was niggling at Annie a little; did she have another person hiding inside herself, too?

'Penny for them – I know you're awake, Annie.'

'You were brilliant.'

'Thanks.'

'But you were. And all those people who came to the pub afterwards? They were delighted to see you pulling pints in your costume…I bet word gets out about that. I wonder if people will expect you to do that all the time, now? Mind you – the place looked…well, quite something, didn't it? Everyone all still with their make-up and costumes on in there…all buzzing, and happy. And Carol's dad – what about him? Wales might find itself with a new rap star, or whatever they call it. He was brilliant. But not as brilliant as you, of course.'

'Thank you. I'm glad you enjoyed it.'

'How come you're taking this all in your stride, Tude? You seem so…blasé about it all.'

'Fame is fleeting.'

Annie sat up. 'Are you having me on, or are you trying to be profound, Tudor Evans?'

Tudor also sat up. 'I'm not having you on; it's true. I should know.'

Annie rubbed Tudor's back. 'What, because tomorrow you'll have to get up and change the barrels and clean the lines, like usual?'

'Yes, that – which I don't mind at all, by the way. But, think about it, Annie – all that work, all that effort, and you get a great reaction at the end of it…but if you want to keep getting that reaction you have to do it over and over again. Some people choose to earn their livelihood that way. Me? Never again. Trust me. We thought we had it made when we got our recording contract, and we made a few bob, then it was back to normal life again for all of us.'

Annie thought she'd misheard. 'What do you mean, you had a contract? To make records?'

'Not just me, there was four of us. I played the bass. Did a bit of backing vocals. We only ever made two singles, not even an album. Did *Top of the Pops* once, though. But fame is fleeting. Like I said.'

Annie nibbled her lip. It was late…should she do this now? Yes. 'Tudor flaming Evans…how can we be living together, and this is the first I'm hearing about this? What are you hiding from me? A debauched history as a rock star?'

Tudor was laughing silently – Annie could tell by the way his shoulders were heaving, and the bed was bouncing…and Gertie was whimpering. 'No debauchery at all; we were only seventeen or so. Innocent as lambs we were, which was why we signed a stupid contract and saw almost no money from our record sales; not then, not ever. We gave it a year, then all went back to real life, like I said. Now, go to sleep; remember that we've promised to take Eustelle and Rodney up to Chellingworth Hall for dinner tomorrow night, so best bib and tucker and all that. Your mother's already said she'll want to start getting herself ready around three in the afternoon, which is just when I'd like to be putting my feet up after what I hope will be a bumper bit of lunchtime business. I love you, goodnight.'

Annie kissed Tudor's cheek. 'I love you too. Though I'm not sure who you are any more.'

'I'm the same Tudor Evans that I was this morning.'

Annie wasn't convinced. 'I tell you what, Tude, not even Pauline Thomas could have seen all this coming…you a dame, and a pop star. If there was any truth in all that stuff that she does, then she'd have spotted all that. And she never said a dickie bird about it.'

'I thought you said she'd told you about someone in uniform saving her, and about there being a traitor in your midst – she got those things right. Maybe you weren't thinking about me when you shuffled those cards she had you pick out.'

Annie snuggled down a bit. 'Maybe you're right – I was focusing on the case when I did it, I suppose. But then why did she say that someone was preggers? Other than Chrissy. That was way off, weren't it? Mentioning a non-existent pregnancy as opposed to you in a frock, and being on *Top of the Pops*? Nah…it's all rubbish, Tude, like I said.'

'Well, let's get some sleep, Annie, then you'll have the energy to cope with whatever tomorrow brings, which is bound to include your mother fussing about…which is lovely, in its own way, but a bit, you know…'

'Draining?'

'Hmm.'

Mavis and Althea were still in the sitting room, staring at each other in the lamplight.

Mavis said, 'You should go to bed, dear – you must be exhausted.'

Althea shook her head. 'I'm sure I won't sleep. I'm still quite wide awake. But you go up.'

'We'll go up together, dear.'

Althea dimpled. 'Don't trust doddery old me to get up those stairs on my own, Mavis? I'll manage. I always have.'

'But no' every day's been like today. You've had a big shock…but, there again, so have I. I'm so glad that Uma and Sir Malcolm offered to keep the Coach and Horses open this evening, so that I could see the panto…but you could have knocked me down with a feather when you took the head off that costume and there you were. I still cannae believe it was you on that stage all that time dressed as that goose. You did a wonderful job, dear, but it must have been exhausting.'

Althea shrugged her tiny shoulders. 'I didn't have to do much rehearsing, though I did have the mornings to work with…Ossie. Oswald. I knew that all I had to do was stay close to Mother Goose, so tonight I stuck close to Tudor. He was a wonder, wasn't he? If it were in him to do it, he could make a living being a dame. He was…perfect. But he's just as good at running a pub, and I think he rather enjoys that.'

'We all have a spot in life, don't we, dear? And I think I'm in the right one for me at the moment. I'm sorry I didn't support you more in tackling the problem with Oswald, though, and I quite understand you'd be upset with me. You're no' stuck with me, you know, Althea; if you ever want me to go, I'll go.'

Althea tutted. 'You know when I said earlier today that I realized I'd been a stupid old woman?'

'Aye.'

'Well not even I'm that stupid, Mavis. We're both exactly where we are for a reason; you've helped a good number of people this past week or so, Mavis MacDonald – you've cracked a murder, and helped a woman escape a miscarriage of justice. That's not nothing…and you've helped me, which – to me – is everything. Thank you.'

'Ach, you'll have me crying before bedtime.'

'Then my work here is done. Other than to mention…it was rather wonderful of The Lavender Mob to all come to the Dower House this afternoon, wasn't it? I very much enjoyed seeing them all again. I have to say that I thought Siggy was looking rather grand, with that new haircut of his. Such a clever chap. Well, all of them are, in their own way. I told you when we met them that they'd be a useful group to help you with your investigations…and they are, aren't they? And what about Dennis Moore? Flowers for you, no less. I'd say he's a little sweet on you, Mavis. We should pop down to The Lavender for tea sometime soon, as they suggested.'

'Aye, we'll see, Althea. Now, come along – if you don't come up with me, you'll be tired in the morning, and that's no way to start the day.'

'You're right – I'm not as young as I once was, Mavis, and I'm only too well aware of that, sometimes. Though I have to say that seeing both my children wallowing in their achievements this evening lifted my spirits tremendously. I've rarely seen them like that – happily accepting compliments, together, both with smiles on their faces.'

'Aye, well, let's hope it lasts. We're up at the Hall for dinner tomorrow, with Annie's lot, as well as Stephanie's parents, and Carol's…and it was nice of Stephanie to insist that Christine's parents stayed on, too, so it could be a significant gathering.'

'It's been a long time since so many have dined together at the Hall, and it should be a truly delightful experience. It's such a shame that none of us ever have the chance to get to know your family, though, Mavis. Do you think they might come down at any point, to visit?'

'They all have busy lives, in Scotland, dear. No time for me…which I dinnae mind. It's as it should be, and what I always wanted for my boys – to build their own lives, and to enjoy living them.'

'Which is what everyone deserves, dear.'

'That it is.'

Henry lay in bed, feeling warm and cozy, and hoping Stephanie didn't let in too much cold air when she returned from feeding Hugo.

She did.

As she settled herself, he ventured, 'What an extraordinary evening, my dear. I thought it all went rather well. I never imagined for one moment that it was Mother in that goose costume. Could you believe it?'

Stephanie tutted. 'Who else could it have been, Henry? She'd been front and center in terms of the entire panto thing, then nowhere to be seen on the night itself. It had to be her. Besides, the goose walked exactly as your mother does.'

Henry didn't care to admit that he'd not put two and two together in the way his wife had done. 'I received some extremely kind compliments about the scenery. I'm pleased that Edward was there to share the praise – his expertise was most useful in the matter. Even Clemmie looked happy tonight, don't you think? That has to be good, doesn't it? I've so rarely seen her actually smiling, and laughing.'

'I'd say she was very happy, and that's very good, Henry. It was a delight to see how she and her husband were able to share the joy – once they'd got him down from his perch up in the roof of the hall. I didn't realize he was actually up in that big rig thing he'd built, manipulating the lighting that way. The effects were quite marvelous. I hope that she and Julian talk about this desire of hers to bear a child in a thorough and meaningful way. Having a child is not to be taken lightly.'

'Indeed.'

'As we both know.'

'Indeed.'

'By the way, Henry, I'm pregnant.'

Henry thought he'd misheard his wife. 'I beg your pardon?'

'I'm in the process of creating another child.'

Henry sat up, turned on his bedside lamp, and looked down at his wife. 'Good heavens, Stephanie, how did that happen? No…I don't mean that…I mean…good grief…that's wonderful.' He leaned over and kissed his wife gently on her forehead. 'Well done, Stephanie. Well done. I don't think we should mention this to Clemmie, do you?'

'Indeed not, Henry. In fact, I'd prefer it if we didn't mention it to anyone, for a little while. The doctor told me a few days ago, and I hope you'll forgive me for not telling you until now, but didn't want it to become the sole topic of conversation throughout our Christmas celebrations. That wouldn't have done at all, especially given Clementine's…circumstances. So – if you can manage to not stare at me all the time, or act as though I'm made of glass for just a few more days, my dear – let's get the new year underway before we tell anyone? Agreed?'

Henry turned off the lamp, and pulled the covers under his chin again, a myriad concerns immediately swirling in his head. 'I dare say you're right, dear. You usually are.'

'Indeed, Henry.'

ACKNOWLEDGEMENTS

I've dedicated this book to my mother, knowing this is the first book I've written that she won't read: she died while it was being edited. I won't eulogize her here, because my sister and I did that at her funeral, in Wales, so I'll just say this: Mum was a great reader, and a huge fan of whodunits. It was her copies of Agatha Christie's works that I read from the age of about ten onwards, so it's because of her that I began a lifelong love of all things murderous…fictionally speaking. If I hadn't become a crime fiction reader, I'd never have become a crime fiction writer, so…thanks, Mum, for everything. Literally.

My husband, who's always my support, has been critical in helping me work through this difficult time. My loving thanks to him, as always. And a BIG thank you, and lots of love, to my sister, too.

My editor, Anna Harrisson, has coped with shifting timelines, and has helped me make this a better book, especially given my rather scattered mind during this time. My copy editor, Sue Vincent, has helped to polish it. Thank you both, so very much.

Please believe me when I tell you that we've all tried to make this the best version of this story that it can be, but we're all only human (no dastardly AI stuff here, folks) and I've been told that to err is, in fact, a human quality: please forgive us if anything has slipped past us, pulling you out of the story. (You can let me know about any problems you spot – my email address is at my website.)

I'm also grateful for every blogger, reviewer, librarian, bookseller, friend on social media and *anyone* who's supported my work and helped to get the word out – it's a big world and there are lots of books, so it makes a huge difference when a lone author's voice is amplified.

Finally, thanks to you for choosing this book, and to anyone who helped you find it. I really hope you enjoy/ed spending time with my chums in Anwen-by-Wye as much as I do.

Cathy Ace
March 2025

ABOUT THE AUTHOR

CATHY ACE was born and raised in Swansea, Wales, and migrated to British Columbia, Canada aged forty. She is the author of The WISE Enquiries Agency Mysteries, The Cait Morgan Mysteries, the standalone novel of psychological suspense, *The Wrong Boy*, and collections of short stories and novellas. As well as being passionate about writing crime fiction, she's also a keen gardener.

You can find out more about Cathy and all her works at her website: www.cathyace.com

* 9 7 8 1 9 9 0 5 5 0 3 5 5 *